You ARE
My
DESTINY,

FABIO

ALL AT ONCE, SHE WAS TIRED OF FIGHTING HIM.

She curled her arms around his neck and let herself succumb, if only a little, to the potent feelings White Wolf's nearness aroused. He trailed warm kisses down her jaw, the curve of her neck. Then she felt his hot breath, his wet lips, tickling her . . .

Maggie moaned softly. She had never known such rapture could exist. The intensity of the pleasure racked her with chills. With the devastating intimacy, her resistance faded.

Maggie felt feverish, out of control, her heart hammering, her flesh crying out for her husband's heat. She mused that she must be out of her mind, for she was in the arms of a wild, totally aroused savage determined to have her . . .

Other Avon Books by
Fabio

PIRATE
ROGUE
VIKING

Coming Soon

CHAMPION

COMANCHE

by

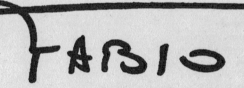

in collaboration with

Eugenia Riley

AVON BOOKS ◆ NEW YORK

COMANCHE is an original publication of Avon Books. This work has never before appeared in book form. This work is a novel. Although some of the names given to Penateka Comanche characters herein are names that may be found in Indian history, the characters who appear under these names are strictly imaginary. Regarding the mention or portrayal of actual historical figures, although certain details and events attributed to these personages are fictitious, whenever possible such depictions have been done within the framework of accepted historical fact.

AVON BOOKS
A division of
The Hearst Corporation
1350 Avenue of the Americas
New York, New York 10019

Copyright © 1995 by Fabio Lanzoni
Photograph courtesy of Fabio
Published by arrangement with the author
Library of Congress Catalog Card Number: 94-96568
ISBN: 0-380-77762-2

First Avon Books Printing: May 1995

AVON TRADEMARK REG. U.S. PAT. OFF. AND IN OTHER COUNTRIES, MARCA REGISTRADA, HECHO EN U.S.A.

Printed in the U.S.A.

RA 10 9 8 7 6 5 4 3 2 1

Fabio gratefully acknowledges
the contribution of Eugenia Riley,
without whom this book would not
have been possible.

ONE

Austin, Texas
Spring 1872

WITH A BOUQUET OF YELLOW ROSES IN HIS HANDS, BRONSON Kane waited impatiently to get a glimpse of his bride.

Outside the Houston and Central Texas Depot, passengers poured off the afternoon Flyer, and acrid black smoke billowed from the engine's stack into the cloudless blue Texas skies. Bronson noted that the people disembarking here at Austin were a hodgepodge: fashionably dressed couples, some with children in tow; colorfully attired immigrants; older spinsters or widows with menservants attending them; and the usual assortment of stray males, from businessmen, peddlers, and cardsharps, to mule skinners and frontiersmen. A number of passengers were being greeted exuberantly by friends or relatives. However, since arriving trains were still a novelty here in the metropolis, many among the crowd had come simply to gawk: Men stood with young children perched on their shoulders, the tots' gazes riveted to the smoking engine; curious young boys waited near the tracks, hoping to chat with the engineer; old-timers strained to get a glimpse of the magnificent wide-gauge locomotive.

Bronson continued to search the ranks of the arrivees for

the young, unattached woman who would soon become Mrs. Kane. Would his bride be everything he had dreamed of, the true prairie star of his vision, the spirit mate he had craved for so long? Unfortunately, he possessed not even a picture of his fiancée. Nonetheless, he smiled ruefully as he recalled his friend Calvin Bryce's telegraph, which even now lay folded inside his breast pocket: "Your bride, Margaret Donovan, will arrive Austin station P.M. March 11, 1872. She's a winner."

Bronson hoped his old friend's words had been sincere, and that Calvin was not playing another practical joke on him, as he had so often during their Harvard days. In truth, Bronson was amazed that his old friend had found him a mail-order bride at all. Even now, he had only a hazy recollection of the night he and Calvin had spent carousing during his last visit to Boston over six months ago. After the two men had visited a notorious bordello near the harbor—in which Bronson had sampled at least three women, all in the same night!—Calvin had declared that Bronson badly needed a wife, and Bronson had laughingly replied that no decent woman in Texas would have him. Calvin, a newspaperman, had announced he would solve this problem by finding Bronson a mail-order bride. When Bronson had half-drunkenly agreed to the pact, he'd never dreamed his old friend would follow through and, half a year later, send him a bride.

At least he'd had the presence of mind on that bacchanalian night to insist Calvin find him a woman who was good-looking, previously unmarried, and no whore. Now, unless this woman possessed three heads and a beard, Bronson supposed he was honor-bound to keep his word and marry her. Despite his sometimes wild behavior, Bronson's sense of integrity ran deep. And he knew his mother would have approved of his turning respectable.

The train had emptied now, except for a few stragglers, and the ranks along the tracks had thinned. Most of the reunions had been completed, the luggage claimed; many of the spectators, having satisfied their curiosity, had headed back toward the center of town.

With the area growing increasingly deserted, Bronson felt a stab of alarm. Would his bride appear at all? Had she changed her mind? Had Calvin indeed pulled the wool over his eyes? Bronson had been carrying around the marriage license in his back pocket for several days, and now pride tempted him to do what he should have done in the first place . . . tear up the damfool thing and walk off. The entire idea of a mail-order marriage was preposterous, anyway.

Then he saw her emerge from the train, and his breath caught in his throat. Yes, it was her—it *had* to be her, for never in Bronson's twenty-eight years had the sight of any woman affected him so. All the sights, sounds, and smells around him seemed to fade away as his hungry gaze drank her in—

She was utterly exquisite, of medium height, with bright red hair that cascaded in luscious curls about her shoulders. She'd be a feisty one with that hair, he mused—the type the People would call a woman of strong spirit. Her features were a portrait of classical beauty: She possessed a strong jawline, a wide mouth, a nicely boned nose, and large eyes he'd swear even at a distance had to be green, settled beneath delicately curving eyebrows and a smooth forehead. She wore a braided emerald green serge traveling suit with lacy jabot, a cinched-in jacket that showed off her rounded bosom and tiny waist to perfection, and a wide skirt that curved over shapely hips and swept down to black, button-topped shoes. A jaunty feather bonnet was perched atop her head and tied beneath her chin with satin ribbons. She carried a carpetbag in one hand, a reticule in the other. She was staring about the area in confusion—looking for *him*, he hoped.

A thrill of pride and anticipation shot through Bronson, and a broad grin lit his sunbrowned face. Yes, his bride was in every way a winner. But more important, she was the mate he had been waiting for for so long. Margaret Donovan, so white and yet so bright, was the true prairie star of his vision.

Now the fingers that only moments ago had itched to tear up the marriage license could not wait to snatch it into hand, and whisk this beauty off to the courthouse ...

As she disembarked from the train, Maggie Donovan's green eyes scanned the boarding area alongside the tracks. She felt exhausted, grimy, and sick to death of endless days spent in uncomfortable train cars or steamboats, of bad food taken quickly at numerous out-of-the-way stations or eateries, and never-ending dust and smoke. She hardly felt in prime shape to be meeting the man she would shortly wed.

"Tall, dark, and handsome"—that was how the newspaperman, Calvin Bryce, had described Maggie's fiancé. During the seemingly interminable journey from Boston, Maggie had endlessly wondered if she was a fool to agree to come west and marry a man she had never even laid eyes on. Her farewell to the spinster aunts with whom she had lived in Boston had been painful and tear-filled. She had also felt apprehensive about traveling to the "Wild West," despite Calvin Bryce's assurances that Texas was civilized now, the hostile Indians largely under control.

But Maggie had realized she really had no choice but to move on and make a fresh start for herself, following what Aunt Lydia and Aunt Prudence tactfully referred to as "The Incident." Though it was in no way her fault, The Incident had caused Maggie's social ruin in Boston and had rendered her future prospects utterly bleak. When she had spotted Calvin Bryce's ad in the *Beacon* for a mail-order bride, the possibility of marrying a wealthy Texas rancher had seemed a godsend to her.

But where was her fiancé? Had he gotten cold feet, and decided not to meet her?

She continued to search the area outside the station house. She *felt* his perusal before she even saw him, as if a beam of light were directed toward the corner of her eye. She turned slightly and beheld him, standing perhaps twenty yards beyond her with a bouquet of roses in his hands . . . Yes, it *had* to be him, for never had the sight of any man affected her so—

He was easily the tallest man standing outside the depot, and why she had not spotted him at once, she was not sure. He appeared striking not only because of his height, which she judged to be over six feet, but also because he was hatless, his long, jet black hair spilling down about his shoulders. His face was sharply, beautifully chiseled, with a broad brow, deep-set eyes, a straight nose, high cheekbones, and a strong jaw. His skin was heavily bronzed, and he was dressed in an impeccable black suit, white ruffled shirt, and black string cravat. He wore beautifully tooled black leather boots.

And he was gazing at her with more intensity than she had ever felt from any human being in her life!

Maggie restrained a shiver at the sight of this man. Even in his elegant clothes and bearing the flowers, he exuded a raw masculinity, a coiled strength that hinted of a wild, undisciplined nature. Being from Boston, Maggie was unaccustomed to men with long hair or darkly tanned skin . . . but perhaps his appearance was normal for a frontiersman, she mused. Aside from being totally exotic and intriguing, he was undoubtedly the most handsome man she had ever seen.

She moved a step toward him and watched him stride toward her, his gait long and assured. Yes, it was him. No doubt of it now.

In front of her, he bowed, then grinned, revealing perfect white teeth and a friendly face. The enticing scent of his bay rum wafted over her, and she found herself staring up into the most vivid blue eyes she had ever seen, shaded by long black eyelashes. Her heart tripped with excitement. Suddenly Maggie wasn't afraid anymore. She felt at home.

"Miss Donovan?" he asked.

"Mr. Kane?" she replied, charmed by the deep resonance of his voice.

"So we've found each other at last," he said. He extended the roses. "For you."

Setting down her carpetbag, Maggie took the flowers and inhaled their sweet perfume. She felt very touched by his thoughtful gesture. "Thank you. This is the prettiest sight I've laid eyes on in many a day."

He winked at her solemnly. "The flowers are not nearly as lovely as the lady holding them."

Maggie felt herself blushing. "Th-thank you," she stammered.

"I trust your journey was not difficult?" he asked.

"It was long and tiring . . . But I'm glad to be here."

"I'm glad you're here, too," he replied, and Maggie felt her blush deepening.

He nodded toward a porter who was still unloading luggage. "You have a trunk?"

"Yes."

"I'll just speak with the man about having it delivered to our hotel," he said. "We'd best hurry if we're going to make it to the courthouse before it closes."

Feeling taken aback, Maggie pressed a hand to her suddenly racing heart. "The courthouse?"

He pulled out a carved gold pocket watch and flipped it open. "They close in less than half an hour, you see, and we'll have to marry today if we're to start out for my ranch tomorrow."

Maggie felt panic encroaching. Things were happening much too fast! "Today! But why do you want to proceed so hastily, Mr. Kane?"

His teasing grin somehow set her at ease. "You don't think I'll give you time to change your mind now that you're finally here? A pretty thing like you?"

Maggie couldn't contain a dry laugh. "You make up your mind rather quickly, don't you?"

His gaze flicked over her with a heart-stopping fervor. "I know what I want when I lay my eyes on it."

For a moment, she was rendered speechless.

"And what of you, Miss Donovan?"

His humor left her feeling caught off guard, but also beguiled; she laughed nervously. "I assure you that, if I weren't of a mind to marry you, Mr. Bronson, I wouldn't have come all the way out here from Boston. Only—"

"Yes?"

"I would prefer a Catholic mass," she said stoutly.

"Ah," he murmured, regarding her quizzically. "You mean with the reading of the banns and all that nonsense?"

"It's not nonsense to Catholics," she admonished.

He slanted her a chiding glance. "Miss Donovan, you of all people should be aware that there's likely not a Catholic priest in all of Texas who would marry us."

Maggie felt the color drain from her face. What did Bronson Kane mean by his odd comment, and why did he assume she would know? Was there something about this man that Calvin Bryce hadn't told her? For a moment she bemoaned her own haste in leaving Boston so impetuously and in agreeing to marry a stranger. She remembered Aunt Prudence ranting, "You know nothing about this man . . . He could be a godless infidel, a rounder, or a drunkard."

"I take it you are not Catholic?" she asked with a frown.

"Among my other shortcomings," came his cryptic reply. "I do hope a civil ceremony will suffice . . . at least for now?"

Maggie almost groaned aloud. Her aunts would have apoplexy when they found out. Even to Maggie, not having a Catholic mass would make her marriage to Bronson Kane tantamount to living in sin.

But Maggie realized the lack of a church wedding was not something she should make an issue out of so early in her relationship with her husband-to-be. In agreeing to this prearranged marriage, she had really given up a lot of her own choices. In a way, she was even glad the legalities would be disposed of quickly; it would mean there would be no turning back for either of them. Surely later on, she could see to it that their union was blessed by the church.

"Miss Donovan?" he prodded.

"Very well," she acquiesced. "A civil ceremony will do for now."

He grinned. "Excuse me for a moment."

Maggie watched him dash off to speak with the porter and give him a tip to convey her trunk to the hotel. As the Negro man turned toward her quizzically, she pointed to her steamer . . .

When Bronson returned to his bride's side, he was feeling gratified that things were going so well. Of course, Miss Donovan had appeared dismayed upon learning that they would not have a Catholic wedding, but she had accepted the prospect of a civil ceremony readily enough. This pleased him, since there was no way he was postponing their nuptials. Hell, if he let her stall their marriage, she might change her mind—and after laying eyes on his captivating bride, this was something Bronson Kane was *not* willing to allow.

He picked up her carpetbag and offered her his arm. "The courthouse is only a few blocks from here. I hope you won't mind walking?"

"Of course not," Maggie assured him, perching her gloved fingers on his forearm. "I'm tired of traveling in cramped quarters. A brisk walk sounds heavenly right now."

Bronson felt a surge of pride as he escorted his bride-to-be down Pine Street. This young woman was obviously of strong stock, not easy to rattle. Most of the young ladies Bronson had met in Rio Concho or Boston would have had histrionics at the thought of being whisked off a train and straight over to the justice of the peace. They would be clinging to their mamas in horror of the wedding night to come. But Miss Donovan seemed to be accepting the breakneck pace of their nuptials with equanimity. She would need that strength of character to cope with his divided world, he mused. But then, she had been aware of the challenges she would face as his bride, or she never would have consented to come west and marry him.

Would she bring that same fire and spunk to their wedding bed? he wondered. He glanced at her, so cool and seemingly self-assured walking beside him. Somehow, he sensed that she would be passionate, that beneath her proper exterior dwelled a hot-blooded Irishwoman, and this realization caused excitement to storm through him as he envisioned the wedding night to come—

"Oh, my," he heard her murmur.

Wrenched from his musings, Bronson caught the astounded look on his bride's face. They had now emerged at the corner of Pine and Congress Avenue, with its long rows of houses and storefronts—mostly elegant structures that seemed incongruous flanking a dirt street teeming with braying longhorn cows, frisky barking dogs, and howling drovers! Bronson delighted in his fiancée's mystified expression as she glanced from the livestock and conveyances clogging the streets to the humanity trooping along the boardwalks. He observed her sniffing at the odors of manure and dust that hung so heavily in the air. At last she braved a smile at him, and he chuckled.

"The Chisolm Trail cuts straight through Austin," he explained. "When the railroad pushes further north, it's likely the long cattle drives will soon become obsolete."

"Long drives?" she questioned.

"Ranchers in Texas still drive their herds to market in Abilene and Dodge City, to connect with the railheads there. That's how you get all those good Texas beefsteaks up in Boston."

"Ah," she murmured. "Actually, my aunts and I don't often eat Texas beef, other than an occasional Sunday pot roast."

"Well, you'll get used to Texas beef down here."

The parade of longhorns finally passed, and Bronson escorted Miss Donovan across the wide, dusty avenue.

Maggie glanced to the north at a huge, sprawling edifice with pillars at the front and a soaring cupola on top. "What's that large building ahead of us in the middle of the street?"

"The state capitol."

"Will we marry there?"

He shook his head. "No—we're heading for the Travis County Court House. It's a few more blocks to the west."

They continued along Pine Street, passing feed stores, hotels, and houses. A couple of old-timers lounging beneath the awning of a harness shop ceased their ruminating and tipped their hats at Maggie as she passed with Bronson. He was getting a real lady for his wife, he mused with delight.

He escorted her to a plain two-story white stone building on the public square, and helped her navigate up the steep front steps. They proceeded inside to a dark, dusty corridor.

Bronson again pulled out his pocket watch. "Whew. Looks like we just made it. Ten minutes to spare."

Maggie braved a smile.

He led her to a door with a frosted glass panel emblazoned with "Justice of the Peace." He opened the door and motioned for her to enter before him.

A thin, balding man with long sideburns and steel-rimmed glasses sat behind a desk poring over a law book. His gartered shirtsleeves were grimy, and a pencil was tucked behind one ear. He peered up at the couple curiously.

"Are you Justice Pierce?" Bronson called.

Standing, the man glanced from Bronson to the young lady. "Yes, sir. What can I do for you?"

Bronson hauled out the license and slammed it down on the desk. "The clerk who sold me this license said you could marry me and the lady, any time."

The man scowled. "Mighty late in the day for a wedding, sonny."

Bronson flashed him an apologetic smile. "I realize this, but my fiancée only now got in on the afternoon Flyer, and we have to start out for my ranch come sunup."

The judge glanced from Bronson to the lady. "A fine-looking bride you have there, mister." He scrutinized Bronson more closely. "But you're a heathen or a half-breed, by the looks of you."

Hearing his fiancée gasp next to him, Bronson struggled to rein in his temper. He started to utter a retort, but his bride spoke up before he could open his mouth.

"You, sir, should be ashamed of yourself!" she snapped.

The man's features darkened with a combination of annoyance and abashment. "Miss, I didn't mean no disrespect toward you—"

"Didn't you?" she countered. "Insulting my future husband in such a reprehensible manner? Why, when I came here from Boston, I never expected folks could be so rude. I'd always heard that people south of the Mason-Dixon line set great store by their hospitality." She sniffed with distaste. "But now it appears I was mistaken."

Squelching a smile, Bronson noted that the judge had the grace to appear abashed, avoiding Miss Donovan's eye and drawing his fingers through his thinning hair. "Er, ma'am, like I said, I meant no disrespect toward you, you being a newcomer to these parts and all. It's just that the hour is late—"

"Is that any excuse for discourtesy?" Maggie asked sharply.

"Er . . . no, ma'am."

"I think you owe my fiancé an apology."

Amazingly, the man was turning to Bronson to do so when he intervened. "That's quite all right, my dear," he drawled to Maggie. "I'm quite capable of securing my own apology . . . assuming I want one."

The judge appeared at a loss.

"Shall we proceed then?" Maggie continued forthrightly. "If, as you say, the hour is late, then it appears to me that you, sir, are wasting time."

While Bronson again fought laughter, the chagrined justice picked up a black book and came to stand before them. "I reckon that's rightly true, ma'am, and we may as well get on with it, you two being so determined and all." Cautiously he glanced at Bronson. "What's your name, sonny?"

"Bronson Kane," came the terse reply.

"Kane," the man repeated with a curious expression. "You wouldn't be kin to *the* Kanes of the Kane Ranch?"

"I own the Kane Ranch," Bronson replied.

Snapping his fingers, the man regarded Bronson with astonishment. "Then you're the one who—"

"Didn't you say time's a-wasting?" Bronson cut in. "Why don't we proceed?"

Self-consciously, the man coughed. "Sure. You two wanna wed, it's your own business, I expect." He turned to Miss Donovan. "Your name, miss?"

"Maggie . . . That is, Margaret Prudence Donovan."

The man smiled shrewdly. "Well, Miss Margaret Prudence Donovan, you sound like a schoolmarm, by the scolding you just gave me."

She nodded archly. "You're correct."

Intrigued by this new tidbit of information concerning his bride, Bronson raised an eyebrow at her, and she winked back. He could have grabbed her and kissed her then, she looked so adorable.

"Maybe you'll teach this heathen some manners, then," the judge muttered under his breath. At Maggie's dismayed gasp, he quickly lowered his gaze to his book. "Oh, I almost forgot. We'll need witnesses. Don't suppose you folks brought any along?"

"Do we look like we brought along witnesses?" Bronson retorted with strained patience.

The judge heaved a sigh and was about to close his book, but he relented at the withering look in Maggie's eye. "If you'll excuse me, maybe I can catch a couple of folks . . ."

The man dashed out of the office, and Bronson and Maggie exchanged a shy smile. "What a rude man," she whispered to him. "Calling you a heathen and a half-breed."

"I've been called worse," he replied dryly. "Although that's quite a dressing down you gave him. I almost felt sorry for him."

She daintily straightened her cuffs. "I've never been one to tolerate boorish behavior."

"I'll keep that in mind," he rejoined.

She stared at him, and he couldn't decide whether she appeared wary or secretly pleased.

Bronson stepped closer and offered her an apologetic

smile. "I'm sorry our wedding has to be . . . well, so rushed and unromantic. I realize this is not what you could have had back in Boston, with you all dressed in white satin, and moving down the aisle of the Church of the Immaculate Conception, with a whole sanctuary full of flowers—not just a bouquet."

She gazed at him in mingled pleasure and astonishment. "As a matter of fact, Mr. Kane, I like these roses just fine. But how did you know about the Church of the Immaculate Conception?"

"Calvin is Catholic," he explained. "While at Harvard, I sometimes attended mass with him and his family."

"Ah, I see. My family attends St. Stephen's."

Reaching out, he smoothed down the edge of her enticingly prim little collar. "So you see, Miss Donovan, I'm not a complete heathen."

"Why, I never said you were one!"

He chuckled, but his tone grew even more intimate as his gaze slid over her. "I just want you to know that you look as beautiful to me standing here in this plain little office as you would all dolled up in Boston's most beautiful cathedral."

As he spoke, Bronson stared into her eyes, and watched as the lovely green seemed to melt; the blush staining her cheeks was equally becoming. Excitement stormed through him. Oh, he was going to enjoy wooing his proper little bride. Indeed, he couldn't wait to get her alone.

She was still staring at him breathlessly when the judge ushered in a middle-aged couple, a man in overalls who looked like a farmer, and a woman in a yellow calico frock and matching slat bonnet. At once, Maggie and Bronson jerked apart and both assumed appropriately sober demeanors.

"These folks was just registering a deed with the county clerk," the judge explained. "Said they'd be right pleased to serve as witnesses to your nuptials."

Maggie smiled at the two. "How kind of you."

"Oh, I purely love weddin's!" the woman declared in a heavy Texas drawl, clapping her callused hands together.

"Jes' make it right quick," her laconic husband added, chewing his tobacco. "I'm all for folks pledging their troth all legal like, but the wife and I need to git on home to the farm afore sundown."

Bronson breathed a sigh of relief as Justice Pierce began intoning the civil ceremony. For a moment after they'd first arrived, he'd been afraid the man would outright refuse to marry them. His bride had told the nosy bastard off but good, he thought with admiration. "Maggie," she'd called herself. He liked the sound of her name; in time, she'd come to accept the other name he already held for her in a sacred place in his heart.

She was a schoolmarm, she'd said. He realized he knew next to nothing about her—and yet he seemed to know everything that mattered. He knew he found her beautiful and exciting; he knew she blushed at his attentions. Already he yearned to feel his bride in bed beneath him, to make them one in body and spirit, to watch the response on her face, in her captivating eyes.

He had a feeling this woman was made for him. He already knew she was his destiny. Especially now as they said the words that bound their souls together forever. Directed by the judge, he clasped her hand and solemnly repeated a vow . . .

Maggie too was immersed in thought as she and Bronson Kane pledged their troth. Everything was happening so fast that she felt like a whirring piece in a kaleidoscope. In mere minutes, she would become Bronson Kane's wife, the bride of a stranger—his until death parted them, his to claim in their marriage bed tonight. The implications filled her with flutters of dread and even more electrifying tingles of excitement. She stared at her husband's broad shoulders and strongly etched face, considered the untamed quality that seemed to lurk beneath his solid exterior, and wondered if he would be a gentle or a wild lover. Remembering how he had wooed her with words while the judge was out of the room, she suspected this man could be either—powerful or tender, reckless or careful, patient or demanding. He exuded an air of unpredictability that was very titillating ... and yet, even though he was in many ways a mystery to her, she somehow instinctively trusted him.

Soon she felt him sliding a cool gold wedding band onto her finger; their eyes met and locked, and the finality of the bond they now shared hit her like a pleasurable fist deep in her belly. She felt so rattled that she stumbled over her final vows ...

As the ceremony concluded, Bronson took note of his bride's pleasurably agitated state, especially when the justice proclaimed, "You may kiss the bride." Bronson stared down into Maggie's wide, expectant eyes, losing himself for an instant in that lovely, vibrant green. Then he leaned over and gently brushed his mouth against hers. He felt her warmth and the slight trembling of her lips beneath his own. Ah, she tasted so soft, so sweet, and he hungered to pull her close and savor her thoroughly—

But not in front of witnesses. There would be plenty of time for all the intimacy he craved later on. He drew back and smiled at her, and she smiled back tremulously. In the background the witnesses added their own endorsements; the farmer's wife sighed ecstatically while her husband expectorated loudly into a spittoon.

The justice clapped his hands together. "Well, folks, that just about does it. I'll just fill in this here license, get all the proper signatures ..."

Within minutes, Bronson had paid Justice Pierce for his troubles and thanked the witnesses, and Maggie had given the farmer's wife one of her roses as a souvenir. Mr. and Mrs. Bronson Kane emerged on the courthouse steps, blinking at the brightness of the setting sun, both feeling slightly dazed.

TWO

"Tell me about yourself, Mrs. Kane," said Bronson.

Thirty minutes later, Maggie and Bronson sat in the dining room of the Cattleman's Hotel, eating their supper. Half of the downstairs of the two-story limestone building was taken up by the dining hall, with its stone floors covered by rag rugs, its homey blue chintz curtains, and matching tablecloths. The guests who had gathered for the evening repast were a diverse group, ranging from smartly attired couples to dusty drovers; several buxom waitresses swept about bearing trays laden with succulent home-style vittles, and the aromas of hot bread, peppery food, and cigar smoke mingled in the air. The serving women were also making big eyes at Bronson, much to Maggie's annoyance.

But her bridegroom seemed oblivious. At their table near the front windows, he was wolfing down fried beefsteak smothered in onions, with grilled potatoes, green beans, and toast. Maggie was nibbling delicately at chicken and dumplings.

She had felt a shiver streak down her spine when her new husband had called her "Mrs. Kane," for his reference made the vows they had just shared seem all the more irrevocable.

16

Watching her husband so enthusiastically consume his dinner, Maggie thought again of how little she knew about him. She knew Bronson Kane was a rancher. She knew he had a deep voice, a breathtaking smile, and warm lips that had shot an incredible thrill through her when he had kissed her for the first time after the wedding ceremony. She knew he was strong and desirable. She knew the touch of his hand was warm and firm, when he had gripped her elbow or clasped her hand. She knew there was a certain mystique about him, a hint of darkness reflected in his jet hair, yet belied by the bright blueness of his eyes. Otherwise, Bronson Kane was a total stranger to her ... a stranger whose bed she would shortly share! This reality spurred the same flutters of anticipation and dread that Maggie had felt during the civil service.

She realized he was staring at her, waiting for her to reply. "What would you like to know, Mr. Kane?" she asked demurely, taking a sip of her tea.

"First of all, since we're married now, why don't you call me Bronson?"

"Very well, Bronson."

"And may I call you Maggie?"

"If you wish."

"So you're a schoolteacher, are you, Maggie?"

"I was," Maggie answered, feeling uncomfortable about the subject matter, as well as unprepared to share with Bronson her painful secret regarding The Incident. "I was educated at Mount Holyoke, and afterward taught grammar in a small private school near King's Chapel. I lived in the vicinity with my spinster aunts, Lydia and Prudence Donovan."

"You're of Irish stock?"

"Yes. My father's family originally immigrated to this country soon after the Revolutionary War, and they settled in Delaware. Then, almost fifty years later, my grandfather struck out for Boston as a young man, seeking his fortune. He became a bootmaker in Burgess Alley."

Bronson whistled. "Burgess Alley. That's quite a hellhole

. . . and quite a leap for your family to make to better parts of town."

She nodded. "I'm most proud of my enterprising forebears. My grandfather turned his small shop into a large, successful boot factory in Waltham—and my father took over the venture upon his death."

"Where are your parents now?"

She sighed. "They died during an influenza epidemic when I was only fifteen. Afterward, I went to live with my aunts."

He flashed her a compassionate look. "I'm sorry, Maggie. Any sisters or brothers?"

Her face grew pinched with remembered pain. "I had one older brother, Patrick, who fought with the Massachusetts Volunteers during the War Between the States. He was killed during a battle with the Confederates on the Rappahannock River at Stafford Heights, Virginia."

Bronson was shaking his head. "My, that's a lot of heartbreak for one young woman. How old are you, anyway? That is, if you don't mind my asking."

"I don't." She delicately wiped her mouth with her napkin. "I'm twenty-four. I realize that must seem like an old maid—"

"Not at all. I'm twenty-eight myself. Besides, you're not an old maid at all, but a married lady now."

"So I am," she murmured, then laughed. "Although I still find it all rather difficult to believe. Everything has happened so quickly."

If you think things have moved fast so far, just wait until I get you upstairs, Mrs. Kane, Bronson replied to himself. To Maggie he said, "That's the way things are here in the West. The pace is quick, but so are the realities of life and death." He stroked his jaw thoughtfully. "I am curious, though."

"Yes?"

His appreciative gaze roved over her. "How come a pretty thing like you got to be twenty-four without a serious beau?"

Maggie felt a blush creeping up her cheeks. "Who says I haven't had a serious suitor?"

He raised an eyebrow. "Ah—so I stand corrected?"

She glanced away self-consciously.

Leaning toward her, he teased, "Don't tell me you're going to keep me in suspense, Maggie? We are husband and wife now."

Heaving a deep breath, she confessed, "I—I was engaged once, at the age of twenty-one. My fiancé . . . also died tragically."

He expression grew incredulous. "Damn, Maggie. So you lost yet another person you cared for. Do you want to tell me about it?"

She shook her head vehemently.

"I'm sorry I brought it up," he added.

"That's all right—you had no way of knowing." Nervously she continued. "And please don't think that everyone close to me meets with an untimely end. Aunt Lydia and Aunt Pru have fared quite famously so far."

"I'm relieved to hear it." He paused, a bemused frown creeping in. "Is the tragedy with your fiancé what prompted you to come to Texas as a mail-order bride?"

Again feeling hellishly uncomfortable, Maggie picked at a dumpling with her fork. "Oh, my life wasn't going quite as I'd hoped in Boston. When I spotted your friend's advertisement in the *Beacon*, it seemed an opportunity for adventure, a new life."

"And perhaps a way to escape painful memories?" he suggested gently.

"Perhaps," she admitted. "You are very perceptive."

He reached across the table and took her hand. "Maggie, like I said, I'm really sorry you lost your fiancé. But I do hope he's not still taking up too much of your heart—for I reckon I'll be a greedy fellow there."

Gazing up into his dazzling eyes, Maggie felt her heart tripping at his words and the heat of his strong fingers on hers. Given the excitement she felt, speaking became a struggle. "You needn't worry on that account, Bronson. There is really much I would love to forget."

"Good," he replied, still appearing a touch perplexed. "I'll try to make forgetting very easy for you, Mrs. Kane."

Feeling even more rattled, Maggie pulled her fingers away from his and tried to collect her runaway thoughts.

A waitress swished by to pick up their plates. She simpered at Bronson and deliberately leaned over close to him, flashing a generous view of her ample bosom, while he appeared hellishly put on the spot.

"You get enough, honey?" she purred.

Maggie bristled. *"My husband* has everything he needs, miss," she informed the woman haughtily.

Watching the chastened woman make a hasty retreat, Bronson glanced at his bride in delight. "Guess you told her, huh?"

Maggie neatly folded her napkin. "I have no patience whatsoever with such shameless creatures. A Boston lady would never behave so disgracefully."

Let's just wait and see how this Boston lady behaves in bed with me tonight, Bronson answered to himself wickedly. With Maggie, he fought laughter and said, "Speaking of Boston, what did you think of my old friend Calvin?"

"Oh, he's a very nice man," she said brightly. "And he certainly presented you to me in a most favorable light."

Bronson remained secretly amused. "Did he now? And do I live up to your expectations?"

"Oh, yes." Feeling a bit uncomfortable, she quickly forged on. "Mr. Bryce said the two of you became close friends while attending Harvard. How did it come about that you, a Texan, decided to attend an eastern university, anyway?"

His features grew taut, his gaze dark, and Maggie feared she had unwittingly ventured into painful territory. Before she could add that he didn't have to answer, he replied, "It was my mother's dying wish."

"Oh, Bronson." Relying on instinct, she reached out to touch his forearm, and she felt the tension in his muscles. "I'm so sorry."

"Don't be," he said tightly. "It appears we have much in common."

She squeezed his arm. "Then I'll say just what you said to me. You don't have to talk about this either, if you don't want to."

"No. If we're to be husband and wife, we must learn to share." He drew a heavy breath. "Ten years ago, when my mother was close to death, my father let her go home to die."

"Home to die?" she echoed confusedly.

"Yes. She was very ill."

Maggie stared at him. Though his pain-filled visage and odd statements prompted many questions in her mind, she sensed she should not try to sidetrack him right now. "Go on."

"Before she passed away, my mother exacted several promises from me . . ." He shook his head ruefully. "I was only eighteen at the time, and I'm rather ashamed to say that I'm only now getting around to honoring some of them."

Maggie was fascinated by the prospect of a son making deathbed promises to his mother; indeed, she found this most endearing. "Such as?"

"That I'd live a clean life, get an education, marry a good woman . . ." He brightened a bit. "Which I've now done."

Maggie felt thrilled by his charming admissions, as well as intrigued by the things he'd left unsaid. "All of that is most commendable, Bronson. But you say you're only now getting around to honoring some of your promises. You've obviously gotten an education—and you've married me." She stared him in the eye. "What haven't you done?"

He laughed. "You don't miss a thing, do you?"

"And you haven't answered my question."

Yet another waitress now sashayed past, refilling Maggie's tea glass. She, too, preened at Bronson until she caught Maggie's frosty glare. As the woman quickly swept on, Bronson offered his bride a sheepish glance. "All right, I'll admit it. I haven't always walked the straight and narrow path. I'm sure I've sown as many wild oats as the next man. But all that will stop now. I take my obligations very seriously—and that will include being your husband."

She lowered her gaze to hide a secret smile. "I'm glad you feel that way."

"Guess it's the lawyer in me."

"Lawyer?"

"Didn't Calvin explain that I studied law at Harvard?"

"No. He mainly talked about your being a rancher. Are you practicing now?"

He shook his head. "I haven't as yet. But I may eventually hang out my shingle." Leaning toward her intimately, he teased, "Forgive me if I'm a bit too distracted right now to be thinking of such matters. For now, I want to concentrate on my bride and my family."

Maggie felt color blooming in her cheeks. "By the way, what made *you* decide to order a bride through the mail?"

"Actually, that was Calvin's idea," he admitted. "The last time I visited Boston, six months ago, I commented to Calvin on the lack of women here in Texas—the respectable kind, that is. He told me of all the advertisements his newspaper runs for men out west seeking brides—"

"And he suggested you do the same?"

"Yes—not only suggested it, but promised he would oversee the whole process and choose me a suitable mate." He broke into a delighted grin. "I must say my old friend did a commendable job."

She nodded shyly, but still doubts lingered. "If you don't mind my asking, Bronson, why did you want a wife? That is, aside from your promise to your mother."

"Why did you want a husband?" he countered devilishly.

She shook a finger at him. "Now, that's not fair! Answering a question with a question. It's a lawyer trick, my aunt Lydia would say."

Amusement danced in his eyes. "I suppose I want a wife for the usual reasons—companionship, children, hopefully love. And you, Maggie?"

"I'm sure I want all those things."

He lifted his mug of beer. "Then let's toast to it. To a long, happy marriage."

"To a happy home," she repeated, clinking her glass against his mug.

"Are your questions answered now?" he teased.

Setting down her tea, she frowned. "Bronson, a moment ago, you mentioned your father . . ."

"Yes," he answered tensely.

"You said he let your mother go home to die," she continued carefully.

"Yes."

"Could you explain that to me?"

Posing her questions, Maggie watched a series of emotions flash over Bronson's face—caution and uncertainty, followed by anguish, and finally a grim stoicism. She wondered if she had somehow offended him. But why should talking about his father affront him? What was he thinking?

Bronson reached across the table and touched his wife's hand. He wasn't sure he could, or should, talk about the painful matter of his heritage so soon. Of course, Maggie had accepted his background, or she wouldn't be here. Still, so often in the past, women had been repelled to hear the details of the double life he led. All his instincts warned that he must proceed with caution.

He squeezed her hand. "Maggie, about my father . . ."

"Yes?"

He gazed earnestly into her face. "I can't make you understand me in one day or even one week. For now, it's enough for me to know that you accept me as your husband, just as I hope it's enough for you to know that I'm delighted to have you as my wife—"

"Oh, yes, of course it is!"

"I want you to understand me, Maggie, but it will take time. And one day soon, I want to take you to meet my father."

"Certainly." Hesitantly she added, "But for now, could you just tell me . . ."

"Yes?"

"Your mother and father's marriage . . . it wasn't happy?"

"No, it wasn't happy." He forced a more cheerful expression. "But ours will be different, won't it?"

"Oh, of course."

"Starting tonight."

Her face went hot again.

Bronson spotted that enticing deep color. He noted that his bride appeared like a timid little bird about ready to take flight. And although the impatient bridegroom in him would have loved to offer her no quarter, the gentleman in him was compelled to respond to her distress.

"Hey, don't look so scared," he chided gently.

"I ... look scared?"

"You look like a skittish rabbit caught in the crosshairs of a hunter's gun."

She actually giggled, easing the tension a bit for them both.

"I don't want to rush you," he continued frankly. "I mean, I want children right away, but if you, that is tonight ..."

She held up her hand and spoke with equal candor. "You're not rushing me, Bronson. We're both mature adults who have consented to this marriage. I want children, too. I'm twenty-four years old now, and I think I've waited long enough."

His grin lit up his entire face. "Well, I'm glad that's settled."

Feeling sudden butterflies in her stomach, Maggie wished she hadn't responded quite so forthrightly. Unfortunately, she had always been one to speak her mind, and now she had sealed her own fate as far as tonight was concerned. She felt nervous, but also strangely exhilarated. At least by morning, her new husband would be *anything* but a stranger.

A waitress brought by a dessert tray, trying her best to tempt Bronson with a swing of her ample hips, as well; Maggie coldly demurred, while Bronson studiously avoided looking at the woman as he made his choice. Afterward, watching her husband devour a huge chunk of devil's food cake, Maggie felt a heightened sense of giddy anticipation as she imagined herself as the next course.

THREE

AFTER DINNER, MAGGIE FELT RELIEVED WHEN BRONSON suggested they go for a stroll before retiring. She knew that soon enough, they would go up to their room, and she would confront the large bed where they would spend their wedding night.

The couple emerged on the stone gallery of the hotel, where several guests sat rocking, visiting, or reading newspapers. Since the hostelry was flanked by the sprawling capitol, Bronson suggested they head away from it, south along Congress Avenue.

They held hands and strolled down the boardwalks in the fading light. The weather was cool and mild, and Maggie could hear birds calling from the trees dotting the avenue. Even this late in the day, hacks and carriages plowed the street, raising dust devils; Maggie spotted a couple of prairie schooners and a Sam Houston Mail Coach plodding along to the south of them.

As they passed Mesquite Street, she glanced to her right at a stately Greek Revival mansion about a block and a half away, situated behind a picket fence.

"Who lives there?" she asked.

"The governor," he replied. "Currently Mr. E. J. Davis."

"You seem to say that with a hint of contempt."

He laughed. "Davis is most unpopular with the general populace here in Texas, due to his radical Republican views and frequent imposition of marshal law, not to mention the fact that he tends to arrest folks who disagree with him. But there's a good chance the Democrats will defeat him next year and kick out all the scalawags."

"Ah," she murmured, "so you're dealing with the final legacies of Reconstruction. Did you fight in the war, Bronson?"

He tensed as a painful memory assailed him; he had *tried* to fight in the war. To Maggie he said simply, "No, I spent those years at Harvard. Uncle Sam felt—"

"Uncle Sam?" she interjected, confused.

He snapped his fingers. "Oh, I forgot to tell you. Uncle Sam is the foreman of my ranch. You'll meet him in a few days."

"I'll look forward to it."

"Sam Kane is a fine person," Bronson continued with pride. "After my mother died, Uncle Sam became like a second father to me. When war broke out, he felt like so many Texas ranchers did . . . we owned no slaves, so it wasn't our fight. He insisted I should go on to college, even though I really wanted to enlist and fight for the Confederacy. Guess I was like a lot of young hotheads then, caught up in the fervor of defending the South."

"But you didn't fight?"

"No," he replied tightly.

"I'm glad you didn't," she said feelingly.

He raised a black brow. "Oh, so I've married a died-in-the-wool Yankee, have I? Don't tell me you're also one of those suffragette types who attends lectures by Susan B. Anthony or Lucy Stone?"

"I heard Susan B. Anthony speak once at the Old Corner Bookstore," she replied stoutly, then glowered as her husband pulled a face.

"Easy, Maggie," he teased back. "After studying law, I'll

agree that females could use a few more rights. For instance, it never seemed particularly fair to me that so often, women aren't allowed to own property—"

"Or to vote, hold office, or serve on a jury," she added passionately.

He whistled. "So I've married a radical *and* a Yankee."

Her expression became turbulent. "My being a Yankee is not the main reason I'm glad you didn't fight in the war, Bronson. It's just hard for me to believe that you might not be here, like so many others . . . like my brother."

At once he grew contrite and squeezed her hand. "You're right. I'm sorry."

They fell into a companionable silence and continued their trek along lower Congress Avenue. They passed a land office, a wagon yard, and the stylish new Raymond House Hotel. Around them, businessmen were closing up shops and families were heading home. Maggie spotted a number of signs of new construction, stacks of lumber and brick arranged around several half-finished edifices.

Bronson watched his bride drink in the sights. He admired Maggie's spunk and intellect, but doubts concerning her still nagged at him. He sensed that she was hiding something from him. Over dinner she'd mentioned having had a fiancé who had died. Was that her secret? Had she given herself to this man, and was she coming to their marriage less than chaste?

Bronson couldn't be certain. Maggie could certainly blush and giggle just like any virginal bride; but he also sensed in her a core of cool reserve that he couldn't quite penetrate. On the surface, she'd had a good life in the East, and had no pressing reasons to move west and marry a stranger. Had she fled Boston to escape some private tragedy?

The possibility that she might not be innocent bothered him, not for moralistic reasons, but for purely emotional ones. For Bronson already felt very possessive of his beautiful, fire-haired bride. Even though he would come to their marriage bed sexually experienced, he selfishly wanted to be Maggie's first lover; he wanted her to be his alone, now and always. If she wasn't pure, he knew he would be disappointed, but he would not judge her; after all, he was hardly in a position to throw stones himself, for he possessed his own flaws, and had his own demons to wrestle. Ultimately he had to respect Margaret Donovan Kane for being willing to marry a man such as himself, when so many women of her station would have rejected him outright.

He smiled as he caught her staring at a saloon across the street from them; the sounds of revelry and tinny piano music spilled out. He caught her wide-eyed expression as she watched a mule skinner stagger out of the seedy establishment with a gaudy dance hall girl in tow.

"I suppose Austin must seem backward compared with the East," he remarked dryly.

"It's not quite as advanced as Boston," she replied tactfully. "In the city, gaslights and heat, along with indoor plumbing, have become commonplace."

"And here, we don't even have streetcars yet."

"Still, for the most part, Austin seems a respectable, nice community. I've spotted a number of church steeples, and we've also passed bookstores and art galleries. With the state capitol here, obviously the city is not totally lacking in the trappings of culture and civilization."

"But it's not Boston. There's no Adelphi Theatre, no Faneuil Hall, no Athenaeum, no festivals on the Common. Will you miss all that?"

She shrugged. "If such pursuits were critical to me, I wouldn't have come here. I want to start a new life, Bronson—to try an existence I've never known before."

"That you will be doing as a rancher's wife."

She smiled. "I can't wait to see your land."

"You will soon. And don't worry, Maggie, I intend for us to travel when my duties at the ranch aren't too pressing. We'll go to San Antonio to the Casino Theater and the museums, perhaps even down to Galveston for the opera." He grinned. "When our children are old enough, I want to take the entire family to Europe."

"That sounds wonderful," she replied dreamily. "To think

of all those places I've only read about before . . . the wonders of Rome, the fabulous galleries of Paris and Dresden. I'd love to see it all firsthand."

"You will," he assured her.

They continued down toward the Colorado River, chatting all the way, Bronson talking about his days at Harvard with Calvin. He spoke of how both men had been members of the Harvard rowing team, and of the pranks they had pulled—gluing together the lecture notes of their most boring professor, adorning a statue in Harvard Yard with a red satin dress. But many of Bronson's recollections of Harvard were more solemn, as he spoke of his respect for the intellect of many of his law professors, and how he had enjoyed hearing the guest lecturers at Harvard, such as Ralph Waldo Emerson, Oliver Wendell Holmes, and Edward Everett Hale.

Maggie listened to her bridegroom with great pride and interest. She was pleased to learn more about this stranger she had married, though a bit perturbed that Bronson had not again mentioned his mysterious father, only the uncle who obviously lived with him at his ranch. Where was his father? From what he'd said earlier, his parents must have separated; if his father lived elsewhere, why hadn't he told her about it?

Nonetheless, she felt thrilled to have married this man. Despite Aunt Pru's fears, Bronson Kane was obviously a decent sort, not a drunkard or a rounder. He was incredibly charming and handsome. All in all, Maggie could not believe her own good fortune.

They paused next to the glittery Colorado, by the pontoon bridge. Bronson gazed out at a couple in a small boat, the man busy rowing while the lady twirled her parasol. They watched a barge loaded with logs drift past.

"I love this country," he said, wrapping an arm about her shoulders. "It's still new and wild and fresh."

Maggie nodded, feeling a thrill at his nearness, and thinking that he, too, was new and wild and fresh.

A chill breeze wafted over them, and Bronson, noting

Maggie shivering, removed his jacket and draped it over her shoulders. "Ready to go back now?"

"Of course," she said with a brave smile.

But Maggie found her knees felt wobbly as they proceeded back toward the hotel. She was painfully conscious of the fact that the handsome, sexy man striding along beside her would soon join his flesh with hers in the most intimate way. Just as his jacket now embraced her with his warmth and scent, soon his entire body would envelop her to make them one. And he was so strong, so virile. Again she found herself wickedly wondering if Bronson Kane would be a controlled or an unbridled lover. Would the night bring her ecstasy or pain? She watched his shirt linen pull at the powerful muscles of his arms and shoulders, and imagined herself being held in those strong, naked arms . . . Ah, this rugged frontiersman prompted thoughts that would definitely be banned in Boston, yet something in Maggie exulted in the aura of excitement and danger he radiated.

They were turning in to the doorway of the hotel when a teenaged lad, dressed in cowboy attire, came rushing outside and almost collided with Maggie. Seemingly oblivious to his own rudeness, the skinny lad was about to go tearing on when Bronson caught him by the sleeve.

"Whoa, sonny!" he ordered, glowering at the kid. "You almost knocked over the lady here."

The freckle-faced kid glanced in embarrassment from Bronson to Maggie. "Sorry, sir."

"Don't say sorry to me," scolded Bronson with a glower. "Apologize to the lady."

While Maggie was fighting secret mirth, the boy turned to her and said sheepishly, "Sorry, ma'am."

"And tip your hat," Bronson added irately. "Where in blazes were you raised, anyway, in a horse trough? Hasn't anyone ever taught you how to act around a lady?"

Gulping, the boy at once tipped his hat to Maggie. "Ma'am, I meant no offense."

Not waiting for additional chastisements from Bronson,

the boy dashed off, and Maggie and Bronson burst into laughter.

"Weren't you a bit hard on him?" she asked.

"After he insulted my wife?" came the indignant reply. "That little wood pussy is lucky I didn't box his ears."

"Are you going to be equally strict with our children?" she couldn't resist teasing him.

He grinned back. "Honey, when it comes to our children, we're going to do *everything* right."

Maggie felt herself blushing over his charming double entendre as he escorted her inside the hotel and up to their suite on the second floor. She felt deeply excited over the possibility that they might conceive one of those children this very night. And remembering Bronson scolding the boy, she felt her fear easing a bit. How could she be afraid to give herself to a man who treated her like his queen?

Just inside the door to their suite, with Bronson standing behind her, Maggie restrained a shiver as she felt her husband slip his jacket from her shoulders. She surveyed the room in which they would spend their wedding night, the expanse softly lit by oil lamps. Just as she had expected, a large brass bed with emerald green velvet coverlet dominated the room, and the sight of it made her heart skip a beat. The other furnishings were of Victorian mahogany, and a fine Persian rug covered the floor. Craning her neck, Maggie caught sight of a small dressing area veering off to the right.

At last she turned and noted her husband's smoldering expression. "It's lovely," she managed breathlessly.

He nodded happily and pocketed the key. "I see your trunk is on the stand next to the dressing table, and the bell-boy put your roses in the vase, just as I asked him to." He gestured toward the dressing room. "If you like, I'll have a bath brought up for you."

Maggie felt relieved by the distraction. "Oh, yes, that sounds wonderful. The train was terribly dusty." She started toward her trunk.

He caught her arm. "Maggie, first . . ."

"Yes?" She turned to him, feeling unnerved by his intimate tone and the fervent way he was staring at her.

He stroked her cheek and smiled. "You know, you're so damn pretty."

Maggie's cheek burned at his touch, and she felt intensely conscious of his nearness and the fact that they were entirely alone. "Thank you."

She tried to start off again, but Bronson only chuckled and caught her about her slim waist, pulling her back against him. Maggie stood before him with eyes downcast and heart hammering.

"Why are you so skittish, Maggie?" he whispered.

"Why do you think?"

He chuckled. "Look at me, sweetheart."

Maggie stared up at him, and felt only partially relieved by the teasing light in his eyes. Bronson reached out, undid the bow on her bonnet, tugged it off, and tossed it on the bed. The intimate gesture left Maggie feeling inundated by uncertainty and longing, as if he had just stripped her naked.

"Your hair is so lovely." He smoothed down an errant curl.

"It's dusty."

"It's gorgeous."

"I . . . I got the color from my mother," she stammered.

"Did you?" He reached out with his index finger to stroke her upper lip. "And where did you get your adorable mouth?"

At his touch, Maggie gasped and her lips trembled, but only for a moment. Bronson hauled her closer and kissed her, smothering her soft, startled cry. The touch of his firm, warm mouth on hers sent hot shivers of desire streaking through her, and the scent and heat of his body further inflamed her floundering senses. Yet his lips were tender rather than demanding, and his gentleness further eased her anxieties.

Seeming to sense that he shouldn't push her too much right away, he ended the kiss with a sigh, tucked her head beneath his chin, and pressed his lips to her hair. Maggie felt delirious, cherished, and very glad her husband's arms supported her. Held as she was, she could hear the strong thud of his heart, and the sound also soothed her.

"I'd like to pull you down onto my lap and undo you right now," he murmured huskily. "You're so tempting, Mrs. Kane, that I'm not sure I can wait for you to bathe. Of course, I could offer to scrub you myself, but maybe you wouldn't appreciate such an intimate gesture just yet."

She gazed up at him, saw the devilment and passion gleaming in his eyes, and felt her stomach knotting pleasurably.

"Oh, I almost forgot . . ." He reached into his breast pocket. "There's something I've been meaning to give you."

As if you aren't enough, she thought. Out loud she said tremulously, "You don't have to give me a wedding present, Bronson."

"This is special." He took her hand and pressed what felt like a necklace against her palm.

Opening her hand, Maggie stared flabbergasted at a long strand of turquoise and silver beads. "What is it?"

"The beads belonged to my mother," he told her solemnly. "Ever since she died, I've been saving the piece for my own bride. I want you to have it now—just as one day soon, I want you to meet my people."

"Your people?" Although perplexed, Maggie braved a smile. "That is very sweet, Bronson, but . . . Isn't this Indian jewelry?"

"Yes," he answered guardedly.

A shiver of apprehension streaked down her spine. "Your mother liked Indian beads?"

He gazed at her in perplexity. "Maggie, as you well know, my mother was married to an Indian."

"What?" she cried, flinching, jerking away from him. "But I know nothing of the kind! You're saying your mother—"

"My mother was taken captive by Comanches, and I was born and raised among them."

Maggie's features went ashen. "You were *what?*"

"Didn't you hear me?" he retorted.

She stared at him in horror. "You can't be serious! You

were born and raised among ... That would mean that
you—"

"I'm half-Indian."

"No!" she cried, and hurled down the necklace.

For a moment, the two stood in electrified silence,
Maggie wearing an expression of abhorrence and pressing
her hand to her heart, Bronson appearing numb as he
watched his mother's necklace slam to the floor, the strand
break, the beads spill in a hundred different directions ...

Bronson glared up at his wife, appalled by her desecra-
tion of a sacred object. "My God, woman, what has gotten
into you? Look what you've just done! How could you?"

"I ..." Gazing at the scattered beads, which seemed to
symbolize their already fragmented marriage, Maggie
started to say she was sorry, but the words became choked
on a sob. In some distant part of her mind, she realized she
must have just hurt him terribly; but right now, she felt too
horrified to care. "I didn't know," she wailed at last.

He shook his head in disbelief. "That isn't possible.
You're actually trying to tell me Calvin didn't inform you
I'm half-Indian?"

"No, he didn't tell me!" she retorted miserably. "If he had
told me, I never would have come here—or married you!"

Bronson stared at his bride, stunned, bewildered, and
hurt, still unable to believe what he was hearing. "But
earlier, when we got married, when the judge called me a
half-breed—"

"I thought he was only trying to insult you! I really didn't
know!"

"You're lying," he accused.

"No! Why would I lie about something so important?"

Bronson began to pace, his mind teeming as he tried to
make some sense of the incredible things his bride was saying. He clenched his fists so tightly that the knuckles turned
white. "I can't believe Calvin didn't tell you!"

"He didn't!"

"But he promised me—"

"I tell you, he didn't, and this changes everything."

"Does it?" he asked sharply, noting the fear and disgust on her face. "You seemed to like me fine until a moment ago—"

"Until I found out you're half-Indian," she interjected bitterly. "Until I found out you married me under false pretenses."

Now he was incensed, and took an aggressive step toward her. "I did nothing of the kind! I had a clear understanding with Calvin that my bride would be fully informed of my heritage—"

She cut his words short with an angry gesture. "You don't listen very well, do you, Mr. Kane? I *wasn't* informed of your heritage, so either you're a liar, or Calvin Bryce is! Besides, if you thought I knew, why didn't you mention your background before now?"

He raked his fingers through his hair. "Because I assumed you understood, and I didn't want to press you about such a sensitive matter right off." His laughter was humorless. "You see, I've learned that my Indian blood is not something I should start talking about willy-nilly. A man doesn't just grab his new bride and say, 'Come on, honey, let's meet my daddy, a Penateka Comanche chief.' "

Maggie's mouth dropped open and she appeared utterly appalled. "Oh, mercy! No wonder you didn't want to talk about him! And you actually thought I would want to meet him, and—and those others? Heaven help me! I've married an Indian!"

He stared at her uncomprehendingly. "Jesus, woman, you talk like it's the end of the world."

She said nothing.

Now Bronson felt sickened, too. "It is for you, isn't it?"

Again she did not respond, though the repelled look on her face was ample answer.

"My God, woman, what is it you have against Indians? I never would have thought that you, a kind, enlightened schoolteacher from Boston, would condemn the People this way."

"Well, think again, Mr. Kane," she retorted, her eyes gleaming with tears and her voice edged with hysteria. "As

far as I'm concerned, you're not just a half-breed and a heathen, you're a charlatan and a fraud. And if you're like the
rest of your kind, I'm sure you're a beast and a murderer,
as well."

Bronson could only shake his head. "How can you say
such horrible things about other human beings? How can
you judge people you've never even met!"

"I—I know I'm speaking the truth!"

"How? How do you know it's true?"

At his aggressive question, Maggie felt herself floundering, fearing she might spill out to this stranger dark secrets
she could never afford to reveal. "Because I—I've heard
things about Indians. Terrible things."

"And I suppose you believed every one of them?" he
snapped.

"I . . ." She began backing away. "Oh, God, I never
dreamed you could be one of them!"

"A savage?" he provided in a sneer.

"Yes!" she cried, succumbing fully to panic. "It's what
you are! Tell me, do you kill, rape, and mutilate like the rest
of your kind?"

A chilling violence gleamed in his eyes. "Why should I
deny it, if you're so determined to believe it?"

Her features blanching with terror, Maggie began backing
away. "I—I have to get out of here."

"Afraid I'll scalp you if you stay?" he asked darkly. "Believe me, at the moment I'm tempted."

Appearing like a scared rabbit, she dashed for the door.

He charged after her, grabbing her arm. "Maggie, like it
or not, we're married now. We both need to calm down and
talk this out rationally. You are my wife—"

"Not anymore! You lied to me and duped me, and I'll see
you in hell before I'll let you try to assert your rights."
Shaking off his grip, she tore his ring off her finger, hurled
it at his feet, and raced from the room.

Bronson was left reeling, staring at the discarded ring,
cast among his mother's scattered beads and his own broken
dreams.

* * *

Maggie raced headlong into the darkened street, tears streaming down her face. What a fool she had been! She should have known Bronson Kane was too good to be true! She'd been so blind—blinded by her own misguided dreams! When the judge had called Bronson a half-breed, she should have listened! Instead, she had believed what she wanted to believe. She had been deceived, lied to, whether by Calvin Bryce or by Bronson, it did not matter. As far as she was concerned, the marriage was fraudulent, meaningless, and Bronson Kane was the cruelest beguiler she'd ever known. She *never* would have willingly consented to becoming an Indian's bride!

At a corner, she paused, breathless, feeling lost, half-afraid Bronson might pursue her, and wondering what she should do. Going back to the hotel was out of the question, even though she sorely needed the belongings she had abandoned there. She hadn't even taken her reticule—although she still had her "emergency money" pinned inside her bodice, as Aunt Lydia had taught her to do. In any event, she could not remain here on the streets, for Bronson might indeed pursue her—

She gazed about her in bewilderment—looking at darkened storefronts and houses. She continued walking, searching for another hotel or rooming house. She passed the Congress Avenue Hotel, but her heart sank when she spotted the 'No Vacancy' sign posted in the window.

At last, as she rounded a corner, a well-lit two story structure seemed to beckon her. She rushed toward the tall, pillared white house. With relief, she noted the small sign near the door—ROOM TO LET.

Maggie's knock was answered by a pleasant-faced, smiling matron. "Yes, miss?"

Maggie spoke urgently. "I need a room—immediately."

By the light of the full moon, Bronson Kane rode out of Austin on his black stallion, his mind racing, his thoughts embittered. Damn Calvin Bryce for not telling Maggie the truth as he had promised. And damn her as well for being an Indian hater.

Bronson's father, Chief Buffalo Thunder, had warned him all his life never to trust the *tahbay-boh*—now he had been betrayed by two White Eyes in the course of a single evening! Being a half-breed raised among the Comanche, Bronson had certainly encountered prejudice all his life. But never had anyone rejected him as cruelly as had his white bride only moments ago. What ailed the woman that she could behave with such callous disregard for his feelings?

What was even harder for Bronson to accept was that his vision of the Prairie Star had been wrong. Ten years ago, while he and his mother still lived with the Comanche, Bronson had gone on his first vision quest. It was then that he had found his sign, his spiritual totem, in his vision of himself as the white wolf, Isa-Rosa. But the white wolf had howled at a single white star looming above him on the prairie; the lone wolf had hungered to join his fierce passion with the distant star's bright beauty. For years Bronson had searched for his spirit mate, his Prairie Star. When he had first seen Maggie today, he had felt certain he had found his mate.

He had been blinded—blinded by what he wanted to believe. How could he have been so wrong about Maggie— assuming she was kind and gentle, noble and accepting of his heritage? In truth, she was no different from the other *tahbay-boh* who had condemned, mistrusted, and hated the red man for so long.

He had made a mistake, but he would not allow this to ruin his life. He would stop by the ranch and explain the situation to Uncle Sam. Then, as he always did during times of great spiritual trial, he would go on to the tribe to seek the wise council of his father.

For, although Bronson was a man of two worlds, a lesson learned most bitterly long ago had been driven home again tonight: Only the Comanche accepted his kind, the half-breed, unreservedly. To the whites, he would always be an embarrassment and an outcast.

FOUR

It was a long, hard ride to Rio Concho, and Bronson's temper didn't improve one bit during the three days it took him to get there. With only his sleek black horse, Blue Wind, for company, he trekked through the Texas hill country, passing farms and ranches and dusty towns. The journey was monotonous, since Bronson trusted Blue Wind to do the navigating; the well-trained Comanche war pony knew this terrain as well as he did, and responded to every turn of landscape, every changing scent on the wind, every subtle movement of his master's body.

Bronson was frequently offered food, water, even shelter, at towns and homesteads he passed. Doubtless the citizens of central Texas thought he was just another cowboy going through, dressed in chaps, shirt, bandanna, and Stetson hat, with his trusty Colt Dragoon holstered at his side, and his Sharps rifle sheathed in his saddle. Bronson often wondered what these good folk would think if they knew he was a half-breed, that he sometimes dressed in Comanche finery and rode with his tribe. He was not ashamed of his heritage, but he was also a practical man; giving away his identity while out on the trail might well mean his death, for the homesteaders and Comanches of Texas had been bitterly at war for many generations.

Gradually he watched the gently rolling, wooded terrain of central Texas give way to cactus, cedar, sagebrush, scrub oak, windswept mesas, and rocky escarpments relieved by cool, cypress-lined creeks and the blooming desert wild-flowers that cropped up in such profusion each spring.

Rio Concho itself was a hellhole, and Bronson rode into town trailed by a tumbleweed and a rusty tin can. On either side of a potholed street, a double line of shacks, saloons, and storefronts sprawled beneath the hot Texas sun, with the Catholic church at one end and the Baptist at the other to beckon the sinful. Rio Concho was one of those western towns that had sprung up around its seedy watering hole and had become increasingly infamous with the coming of the buffalo hunters. It was a town where no respectable person ventured forth alone at night, a town with a corrupt sheriff, a haven for hide hunters, Comancheros, and even Mexican *banditos* willing to pad Lefty McBride's palm at poker. Aside from harboring his disreputable friends, Lefty made a stab at maintaining law and order and protecting citizens who tolerated his shortcomings mainly because no one better had come along to fill his shiftless boots.

The saloon reminded Bronson of his parched throat and how long it had been since he had tasted some of Sally's red-eye. He scowled at the many horses lined up outside the establishment, the mustangs slapping their tails at huge, buzzing horseflies. He felt a stab of anger as he spotted a wagon packed with buffalo hides.

So the hide hunters were in town again, no doubt playing poker with Sheriff Lefty! For years, the sheriff had shielded the hunters as they raped Comanche lands of bison, taking only the hides and leaving the carcasses to rot on the plains. Lefty had even made one of the most despicable of the thieves, Skeet Gallagher, a sort of honorary deputy. The fact that the cravens were in direct violation of the Treaty of Buffalo Lodge, which had ceded specific lands in West Texas to Bronson's tribe, was meaningless to the hunters.

They had simply joined the ranks of legion others—government cavalry, Texas Rangers, Indian agents—who had broken treaties with the Comanche and continued to push the People relentlessly toward the reservations in northern Texas and southern Oklahoma, allowing hunters to plunder Indian territory, and settlers to outright steal Comanche lands for frontier homesteads. Sheriff Lefty was bound by his oath to uphold the law, but such niceties did not concern Bronson's longtime enemy.

Bronson reined in Blue Wind next to the trough, dismounted, and tethered his mount loosely. He strode across the boardwalk and entered the saloon through the double doors, walking through a haze of cigar smoke. As usual, Sally's establishment was noisy and smelly, crowded with drovers, farmers, ranchers, and drifters. Several brightly painted whores were working the customers, to the accompaniment of "Wait for the Wagon," being plunked out on the piano by a black man. José, the bartender, spotted Bronson and waved his towel, and Bronson grinned back. Then he spotted Sheriff Lefty and several bearded hunters playing poker at a scarred table in a corner. Not wanting to provoke the usual confrontation, Bronson headed toward a vacant table on the other side of the saloon.

"Hello, sugar," crooned a familiar voice.

Bronson smiled at Sally, the blond, blue-eyed owner of the saloon. In her early thirties, she was still pretty, full-busted, but beginning to appear frayed about the edges. Heavy rouge coarsened her cheeks, and the lacy neckline of her red satin dress plunged scandalously low. Yet Sally, like the younger whores she managed—Rose, Jessie, and Conchita—knew how to please a man in bed, and Bronson was almost of a mind to be pleased after the mistreatment he had suffered at the hands of his bride.

"Hi, Sal," he replied, tipping his hat. "I've been on the trail awhile and hankering for a taste of your red-eye."

"Go anywhere special, honey?" she asked.

"Nope." No one in Rio Concho—except Uncle Sam—

had known of Bronson's plans to marry, and he intended to keep things that way. "Just to Austin to attend to business."

"Austin—that's three hard days on the trail."

"A long time for a man to be thirsty," Bronson added pointedly.

She raised an eyebrow and whispered, "Sheriff Lefty's here with Skeet, Clyde, and the other hunters."

"I know. You're not trying to run me off so you can play up to them, are you?"

She dimpled. "Never, sugar. I'm just looking out for the hide of my favorite customer."

"This customer can protect his own hide."

She looked him over and licked her lips. "So you can, honey. Have a seat and I'll fetch you some whiskey."

Bronson sat down, propped his feet on the table, took off his hat, and used his bandanna to wipe the gritty sweat from his brow. Another of the girls, Conchita, swished by and smiled at him. He fondly swatted her behind.

"Hello, *querido,*" she purred.

"How's life been treating you, Miss Conchita?"

Her shapely hand stroked his broad shoulder. "Much better since you walked in."

He chuckled.

She ran her fingertips over his muscled arm and leaned over to press her lips close to his ear. He caught the musky scent of her hair, the cheap odor of her perfume.

"Sheriff's here with the hunters," she whispered.

As she straightened, he winked at her solemnly. "I know, Conchita. And don't fret. I'm not some baby still not weaned from his mama's tit."

"Oh, no, *querido,*" she replied huskily, looking him over greedily. "I know all about you and sucking tits."

He howled with laughter. "You're a wicked woman."

"Any time," she murmured, before slinking away.

Bronson grinned as Sally arrived before him, bearing a tray with two glasses and a bottle of whiskey. "Ah, that's better," he said, tossing several coins down on the table.

Sally sat down beside Bronson and poured them both glassfuls. "You on your way to the ranch, honey?"

"Yes." He downed the whiskey neat, grimaced, and poured himself another shot. "Then I'm on to see my father."

Sally took a sip of her liquor. "So how is Buffalo Thunder these days?"

Bronson smiled. Sally and the other girls knew about, and accepted, his heritage. Indeed, the savage part of his nature excited these whores.

Unlike his bride, he thought darkly.

"Honey?" Sally prodded. "You've got one demon of a frown on your face. I do hope your father ain't ailing."

Bronson reached out and clucked her under her chin. "Naw. He's just getting older and more ornery."

"And that sinfully handsome brother of yours? You know, Conchita's been pining away for Black Hawk for years now. She's never forgotten him."

Bronson chuckled. Several years ago, he'd sneaked his full Comanche brother, dressed as a white man, into town— much to the delight of Sally and all her girls, who still craved the strong warrior's body as much as they lusted after Bronson.

"I doubt you'll be seeing my half brother again any time soon," Bronson confided with a frown. "Not with the cavalry and the Indian agent so intent on convincing my father's tribe to move to the reservation."

"You think they'll go, honey?"

"I think it may be inevitable . . . though I'll never convince my father or Black Hawk of that."

Sally was about to comment when another voice snarled, "Well, hello, half-breed."

Bronson glanced up to see his old nemesis, Sheriff Lefty, standing near the table. Lefty was a paunchy, bald, middle-aged runt with a mean, pockmarked, slump-chinned face and a handlebar mustache. Lefty was flanked by two hide hunters—Skeet Gallagher and Clyde Smedley—both obnoxious characters in buckskins, with beards halfway down their chests. Both hunters wore broad-brimmed, feathered hats and sported Colt revolvers, powder horns, and the Green River knives they used to plunder buffalo hides. As always, the hunters exuded a horrendously rank smell, and their clothing was encrusted with proof of their treachery— bison bloodstains and dried bits of flesh and bone.

Wrinkling his nose in distaste, Bronson drawled, "Sheriff Lefty. I wondered when you would get around to saying hello."

Lefty winked at Sally. "Bring the man a squaw."

While Bronson's hand instinctively moved to his Colt, the hunters erupted into laughter.

"Yeah, bring the man a redskin whore," jeered Skeet.

"And a plate of dog meat as a chaser," taunted Clyde.

"Yeah—maybe then this breed'll quit trying to sniff out our women," added Lefty.

As the men continued their scornful laughter, Bronson surged to his feet. But Sally was faster, popping up and placing her ample body between Bronson's and the sheriff's.

"Bronson Kane is welcome to any gal in the house, and you know it, Lefty," she snapped. "Don't you go riling him, or the next thing I know, you folks'll be bustin' up my saloon again."

Lefty sneered at the woman. "We might not git so ornery, woman, if you gals didn't give all your attention to the breed there."

"You want some sugar, Lefty?" Sal asked, slinking up to him. "Why don't you just say so?"

While Lefty looked uncomfortable, the buffalo hunters roared with laughter, and even Bronson had to grin his admiration.

Conchita came up to join the others, winking at the hunters. "Hey, what hombre here wants to buy me a drink?"

"I shore do," volunteered Clyde, leering at the whore.

"Hell, I'll buy you the whole goddamned bottle, honey," added Skeet.

Conchita and Sal quickly maneuvered Lefty and the others back toward their table.

Bronson, not satisfied, called after them, "Hey, Lefty?"

Lefty turned with a scowl, while Sal, next to him, rolled her eyes at Bronson in exasperation. "Yeah, half-breed?"

"There are some illegal hides outside on a wagon—hides stolen from Comanche territory."

"What makes you think they was stole?" called Skeet belligerently.

"Because the only bison left in these parts are on Indian lands."

"Well, maybe we got 'um in Oklahoma," scoffed Clyde.

"And that's a goddamned lie," drawled Bronson.

"You callin' me a liar, breed?" Enraged, Clyde started forward.

Sally again intervened, grabbing the irate hunter by his fringed jacket. "Hey, boys, give it a rest. Go back to your cards, and it'll be free drinks on the house." She shot Bronson a warning glance.

Sally's ploy worked. The hunter glared, then spat on the floor and strode off with Sally and the others.

Bronson sat down and gulped another shot of whiskey. He almost wished the girls had not intervened, for he was itching for a fight. He'd love to rearrange the faces of all three of those bastards. Then maybe he wouldn't feel so angry about everything.

A moment later, he watched his favorite whore, brown-haired, brown-eyed Jessie, rush up. Worry pinched her painted face. Leaning toward him, she confided, "Honey, Sal says you're in a mean mood and to get you outa here right quick."

"Don't worry, I won't bust up Sal's saloon," he grumbled.

"Sugar, please." Wringing her hands, she appeared desperate.

"Sure," he snapped, standing, clapping on his hat, and walking out with her.

Outside on the boardwalk, she caught his hand and smiled. Her longing-filled gaze drank him in thoroughly. "Honey, if you're needing your horns clipped, we can go up

the back stairs and do it right now. You don't even gotta pay
me, or use protection if you don't want to."

Bronson smiled at her. His using "protection" was his
way of honoring one of his deathbed promises to his
mother. He'd vowed to live a clean life, but since respectable women wouldn't have him, he'd bedded a lot of
whores since he'd made the vow. He felt he had fulfilled his
promise by using condoms, which meant he would come to
his wife without disease, and have children only with her—

That wife was supposed to have been Maggie.

Staring down at the pretty, eager girl, Bronson found that
part of him hungered to take her up on her offer; he was
definitely in a mood to make a woman climb the walls right
now. But that wouldn't be fair to Jessie, he quickly realized;
he *was* in a mean mood, and he might end up taking out his
anger on her.

He stroked Jessie's cheek. "Thanks, honey. You know
you're mighty pleasing, but I'd best head on back to the
ranch."

Disappointment sagged her features. "If you change your
mind, Bronson—you know, any time—"

"I know, honey," he said quietly. Kissing her cheek, he
strode off in the wake of her dismayed sigh.

Before heading to his horse, Bronson stopped at Blake's
General Store a few doors down. The familiar scents of tobacco, leather, and spices greeted him as he entered the
homey establishment. He spotted his friend Judy Lynn
Blake behind the counter—a pretty young matron with
shiny chestnut hair, wearing a homespun dress covered by a
large white apron. He and Judy Lynn had a long history together. Ten years ago, on a pain-filled night, they had become lovers. Even though the relationship had not endured,
they had remained friends. Now she was married to another
man and expecting his child.

"Hello, Judy Lynn," he called.

She looked up at him and smiled. "Bronson. Haven't seen
you in a month of Sundays."

He stepped closer. "You got any of that horehound candy

Uncle Sam enjoys so much? I'm trying to break him of smelling up the house with those Cuban cigars he's so fond of."

She laughed. "Yes, I just got some tins of candy in from New York."

Bronson glanced at the shelves. "I'd also like some licorice and a couple of bolts of that pretty calico."

Judy Lynn raised an eyebrow, then leaned toward him conspiratorially. "For your red brothers?"

He nodded. "The children love the candy."

Watching her turn to climb the stepladder and taking note of her expanding stomach, he quickly protested. "Hey, let me—"

"I'll take care of that," a male voice called.

Both of them turned to watch Judy Lynn's husband, George, come in the back door. George was a tall, thin, rather taciturn man in his mid-thirties, with dark hair and hollow, pockmarked cheeks. Bronson suspected that Judy Lynn had confessed to her husband of their past affair; George's attitude toward him was invariably polite, but cool.

"Hello, George," Bronson called. "I was just asking Judy Lynn for some horehound candy for Uncle Sam, and some other supplies. But I don't want her climbing that ladder to get it."

"Of course not. You must be more careful, dear." Throwing his wife a chiding glance, George climbed the ladder and, at his wife's instruction, pulled down the items Bronson had ordered. Placing the goods on the counter and climbing back down, he asked Bronson, "Anything else?"

Bronson drew out his wallet. "No, thank you."

Bronson was pulling out a bill when a voice from behind them drawled, "You letting your wife talk to the breed again, George?"

Judy blanched and George frowned as Skeet Gallagher strode in. He sauntered up to the counter, glancing at Bronson derisively, then ogling Judy Lynn. Observing the man's leer, Bronson was tempted to knock him to the floor.

But that was George's responsibility now, not his; he would not insult the merchant by intervening to defend his wife.

"What can I do for you, Skeet?" George asked tensely.

Skeet expectorated tobacco juice on the floor, then grinned at Judy Lynn, revealing gaped, yellowing, brown-stained teeth. "You got any twenty-gauge shot?" He glanced with scorn at Bronson. "I might just have to kill me a few varmints I seen crawling about town."

Bronson smiled back and drawled, "Careful you don't shoot yourself in the foot, Skeet."

Skeet growled at Bronson. To George he snapped, "And gimme some more of them Green River knife blades."

"Why do you want the blades, Skeet?" Bronson asked softly.

"Why do you think, breed?" Skeet snarled.

"Those bison hides are pure hell to slice off, aren't they?" Bronson continued with contempt.

Watching Skeet move menacingly toward Bronson, George hastily intervened. "Hang on a minute, Skeet. I'll get your supplies."

Skeet sneered at Bronson. "Why you hanging around, breed?"

Shrugging, Bronson handed Judy Lynn a bill. "It's a free country, isn't it? Maybe I'm just waiting for you to leave."

"Well, maybe I don't feel like leaving, breed." Skeet winked at Judy Lynn. "And maybe I don't like your kind sniffing around respectable women like Mrs. Blake."

"Maybe I don't give a hoot in hell what you like or don't like," Bronson replied.

Skeet's face reddened and his gnarled fingers moved to the hilt of his knife. "Why you low-down—"

"Here's your order, Skeet," George interrupted nervously.

The merchant placed two boxes in front of the hunter, effectively cutting short the confrontation. After giving Bronson a last, blistering look, Skeet turned and paid his bill.

Both Judy Lynn and George heaved a sigh of relief when

Skeet at last strode out. "I'm sorry about that, Bronson,"
said Judy Lynn.

"No problem," he said.

"If you ask me," added George, "the good people of Rio
Concho are getting damn tired of his kind, and Sheriff Lefty
protecting them."

Bronson nodded. "Then maybe it's time for the good citizens of Rio Concho to do something about it."

"Oh, honey, that's terrible, just terrible."

At the boardinghouse in Austin, Maggie sat in the homey
kitchen with her landlady, Minnie Walker. Over the past few
days, she had become friends with the kindly widow. This
afternoon Maggie was at last pouring out her heart to
Minnie, trusting her new friend with the shocking, tragic details of her current plight. She was pleased to have the
woman respond with sympathy and not condemnation.

"It was quite a shock to receive on my wedding night,"
Maggie concluded.

"Oh, honey! To think you married a half-breed without
even knowing it! So his mother was the Indian?"

She frowned. "No, I think it was his father. He really told
me very little about the man. But I do know Mr. Kane's father took his mother captive long ago, and he was born and
raised among the Indians. When he was eighteen, his father
let his mother go home to die. I assume that's when he left
the Indians, as well."

"How awful!" declared Minnie. "But I can't say I'm surprised. The Comanche are notorious for taking white
women captive as their squaws. Melinda Lockharte and
Cynthia Ann Parker are two famous ones. With poor Cynthia Ann, they broke her spirit and turned her into an Indian.
Even when the cavalry rescued her, she never could adapt to
civilization. When her half-Indian daughter died, she wasted
away from a broken heart."

Maggie felt sobered. "Any idea why the Comanches take
white captives?"

"I've heard it's because of the low birth rate of their

women. If you ask me, though, it's done out of sheer meanness. And I can't think of anything more cruel than for a man to order a bride and not tell her he's half-redskin."

Maggie frowned. "Mr. Kane claimed that his friend was supposed to have told me."

Minnie waved her off. "If you believe that, honey, then I know of some land in the East Texas swamps that I'm sure you'll be itching to buy."

Maggie laughed, her first genuine moment of pleasure in days. Then a worried expression drifted back in. "What am I going to do, Minnie?"

The woman sadly shook her head. "I'm not sure. You're not worried he'll come after you?"

Maggie's laughter turned bitter. "I think I've pretty much scared him off for good." She shook her head in self-recrimination. "Oh, when I think of the things I said about Indians—such horrible things—"

"And why shouldn't you have?" Minnie interrupted stoutly. "After the low-down way he deceived you?"

"It's just that . . . I really launched on a diatribe that I do regret. Just because he acted dishonorably doesn't mean I had license to be cruel, as well. During our argument, I also broke his mother's necklace, which must have been very precious to him. Actually, I went back to the hotel the next day to get my trunk and see if I couldn't find the beads, perhaps even get them restrung. But by then, all of his things were gone, even the wedding ring that I hurled at his feet in my anger—"

Minnie reached over the table to grasp Maggie's trembling fingers. "Now, honey. Quit torturing yourself. You're not to blame."

Maggie's features were anguished. "That's not entirely true. I behaved disgracefully. I think I reacted as I did because I was so frightened, so utterly panicked—"

"Of course you were."

"You don't understand," Maggie continued passionately. "You see, I had a special reason for acting as I did."

"Yes, honey?" Minnie prodded gently.

Maggie shuddered. "Three years ago, I was engaged to a very fine man back in Boston, James Brewster. We were to be married after he served his stint with the cavalry in Minnesota. But only months after he was stationed out west, he was captured by the Sioux, tortured and killed by them . . ." Maggie's voice trailed off and she fought a sob at the memory.

Minnie squeezed Maggie's hand. "Oh, honey. Bless your heart. No wonder you can't abide Indians. It's just as well you scared Bronson Kane off—because with a half-breed, you never know if he'll turn Indian again and go live with the tribe."

"I know," Maggie said feelingly. "He even mentioned wanting to take me to meet his father, his people—"

Minnie sucked in a horrified breath. "Well, good riddance to the lot of them, then! You're much better off without him. And you need to get on with your own life."

"How?" Maggie implored. "Bronson Kane is still my husband."

"I know." Minnie scowled. "I don't mean to pry, honey, but the marriage . . . well, it wasn't consummated, was it?"

Embarrassed, Maggie shook her head.

Minnie scowled with determination. "My friend Wilma Stodges has a smart lawyer son. We'll see if he can't arrange you a discreet annulment."

"Do you think it can be done?" Maggie asked.

"Sure, why not? I'm no lawyer, but the way this half-breed lassoed you in sure sounds like fraud to me."

Maggie considered the argument. "You're right. Perhaps I should seek legal counsel."

"Then what will you do, dear? Return to the East and live with your aunts, continue your schoolteaching there?"

Maggie hesitated. She'd told Minnie about her life in Boston, but had left out the scandalous circumstances of her departure. Now she quietly confessed, "Minnie, I can't return to Boston. You see, I was a teacher at a prestigious private school near King's Chapel, and a father of one of my students made improper advances toward me during a conference in my classroom. The headmistress walked in on us and assumed the worst. Since the man was from a very prominent family, my side of the story was never given any credence. I was dismissed on the spot. So I'm afraid the chances of my acquiring another post in Boston are all but nil."

Minnie's kindly features twisted with sympathy. "Oh, Maggie. You don't have to explain anything to me. There's many a good, righteous woman who ends up in Texas under similar circumstances. It's a man's world, honey."

"So what will I do?"

Minnie snapped her fingers. "Start over here!"

"Here?"

"Why, yes, we're always needing schoolteachers here," Minnie continued excitedly. "I'm betting one of our boarders, Miss Faulkner, can help you. She teaches over at Austin Collegiate Female Institute. And the new public schools are just starting up, and they'll be hiring lots of teachers, I'm sure. Besides which, this town is filled with eligible men— lawyers and legislators, merchants and bankers. And a pretty girl like you . . ." Minnie winked. "You could do right well for yourself here, dear."

Maggie's eyes gleamed with new hope. "Perhaps I could. But what if Mr. Kane comes after me?"

"Didn't you just say he wouldn't?"

Maggie nodded and bucked up her spine. "You're right— he'll never come, and perhaps I can start over here."

Even as Maggie bravely said the words, she wondered why the realization made her feel even more depressed.

FIVE

Bronson rode onto Kane Ranch territory, galloping through tall buffalo grasses and sagebrush, past cedar brakes and stands of chaparral, navigating around the familiar windmills next to the tank where the brightly mottled long-horns watered, and waving to the drovers busy gathering up spring calves. The scents of the ranch and spring filled his senses—grass, nectar, and dew mingling with the odors of sod and cow chips baking in the sun.

Bronson looked forward to seeing Uncle Sam, but not to conveying the news about the failure of his all-too-brief marriage. Sam had been delighted to hear Bronson had a bride coming in from the East—likely because Sam knew marriage to a white woman would more strongly bind his nephew to the civilized world Sam wanted him to embrace.

Bronson's roots in this life went deep, anyway. Almost three decades ago, Bronson's mother, Agnes, had come to Texas as a bride married to Sam's brother, William, who had bought and established the Kane Ranch. The newly-weds had been happy out here on the new, raw frontier, de-spite occasional troubles with Comanches. But that first year, a double tragedy had occurred—Agnes's first preg-

53

nancy had ended in miscarriage, and shortly thereafter, William had been killed in a wagon accident. William's brother, Sam, had come out from Tennessee to help the widow, and gradually a sense of normalcy had returned to the ranch. Indeed, a romance had been developing between Sam and Agnes when she had been kidnapped by Comanches; Sam had been out riding the range with the drovers when three Comanche warriors, including Bronson's future father, Chief Buffalo Thunder, had boldly snatched the young widow from the yard of the ranch house, leaving behind a feathered lance, driven into the earth, to brag of their feat. Sam had become distraught, summoning the sheriff, the cavalry, even the federal marshal. All attempts to locate the roving band that had kidnaped Agnes ended in failure; like Cynthia Ann Parker before her, Agnes had disappeared to become another faceless squaw and breeder living among the People.

Buffalo Thunder had taken Agnes as his third bride, and Bronson had been born almost exactly a year later. Even as a child, he had realized his mother was a beaten and unhappy creature who was highly resentful of his father's having so many wives. Of course, he had always known his mother was white; he had picked up English as well as Comanche, and revered the name she alone called him, Bronson, as much as he later came to respect his adult Comanche name, Isa-Rosa. Still, he had been largely oblivious of the tragic circumstances that had brought Agnes to the Comanche.

Indeed, he had seen his father beat his mother only once, when Buffalo Thunder had caught Agnes trying to tell her young son the details of how she had been kidnapped from the whites. Buffalo Thunder had charged between them, grabbing Agnes, yelling at her in Comanche, and then . . . The sight of his father abusing his mother had devastated Bronson so much that, afterward, whenever Agnes had tried to broach the subject of her abduction, Bronson had stormed away, refusing to listen, while inwardly fearing his father might again punish his mother.

Throughout his life, Bronson had overheard his mother

pleading with his father to let her and her child "go home"—although Bronson couldn't even be sure what "home" meant to her, since *his* home was always the roving Comanche camp. At last, when Bronson's mother was close to forty years old and very consumptive, Buffalo Thunder had relented and allowed eighteen-year-old Bronson to take his mother back to the Kane Ranch to die. Before they departed, Buffalo Thunder had counseled his son regarding the other side of his heritage. Soon after Bronson had gone on his first vision quest, the two men had sat together beneath the full moon. Bronson would never forget his father's fateful words.

"Isa-Rosa," Buffalo Thunder had said, "you are a man now, and faced with a man's choices. All your life I have tried to shelter you from the evil that lies in the hearts of the *tahbay-boh*. But soon you will learn of the white blood that runs in your veins, along with the blood of the Nerm. Like the white wolf when confronted by a fork in the road, you will be compelled to choose which path you must take—the path of the white man or the trail of the red man—and in which world you will spend your years. Only you can make these choices."

Bronson had learned the full truth of Agnes's circumstances when he brought his mother home to the ranch and met Sam Kane. His mother's death had been slow and painful, stretching out over many weeks; during that time, Bronson and Sam had talked endlessly, Bronson finally learning the truth about his mother's abduction by Comanches. Prior to that, Bronson had never realized that Agnes had been snatched away so cruelly from her life among the whites, or that he was heir to this vast cattle empire near the town of Rio Concho. For the first time, Bronson was made to understand the harsh toll the kidnapping had taken on his mother, and how her own life, her own dreams, had been shattered. It was particularly wrenching for him to watch Sam sob over Agnes's deathbed, to see them looking at each other with the anguish of a love never fulfilled. And

Bronson had felt deeply touched to have Sam regard him as the son he and Agnes should have had together.

Although all his life, Bronson's loyalty had been with the People and against the "white devils," he had finally realized then that there were two sides to every story. The whites had come west seeking their own lands and destinies; the Indians, feeling their territories had been invaded, had retaliated, destroying lives and dashing hopes, as they had done with Sam and Agnes.

As his mother lay dying, Bronson began to consider the hard existence she had endured, and to wonder if she might not have lived a much better, and longer, life among her own people. He began to question his own identity, and to realize that for him, the world was a very complex place.

Before she died, Agnes exacted from her son a promise that he would give the white world a chance: that he would gain a white education; that he would live a clean life, avoiding adulterous behavior and the hallucinogens the Indians sometimes used; that he would never rape or beat a woman, never torture or kill a man if an alternative could be found. Deeply affected by his mother's suffering, Bronson gave his word. As Agnes died, she clutched in her hands the multicolored beaded necklace Bronson's father had given her on the night he first brought her to the village. For Bronson, his mother's hold on the beads was the only proof he had ever had that Agnes felt some affection for his father. After Agnes died, Bronson kept and cherished the necklace, saving it for his own future bride—

The bride who had shattered his dreams in Austin.

Bronson resolutely turned his thoughts away from Maggie and resumed his musings about his past. After his mother was laid to rest on Kane land, Bronson had spent several years learning about the white man's world; while the Civil War raged elsewhere, he had gained an education at Harvard, studying law. Because of his stunning good looks—his mother's bright blue eyes, his father's coal black hair—white women were often attracted to him. Although Bronson could pass as a white man, he always refused to hide his heritage; when women discovered he was a half-breed, some were excited by this savage side to his nature, while most felt repelled.

Following his years at Harvard, Bronson returned to Texas, where, for a time, he helped run the ranch with Uncle Sam. It was then that he began to feel more intensely torn between the white and Indian worlds. He often left Rio Concho to spend weeks or even months with the Comanches, joining his brothers for seasonal activities such as buffalo hunts or feasts, while avoiding the spring raids his brothers made on white homesteads. After each sojourn with the tribe, Bronson would return to his ranch and his friendship with Uncle Sam.

The citizens of nearby Rio Concho began to look on Bronson with suspicion, especially when Comanches stole their cattle or pillaged their fields. In time, he was able to convince his red brothers to leave the town alone, yet the hostile climate lingered, the two sides operating under an armed truce rather than in peaceful coexistence. In more recent years, the tensions had escalated again due to Sheriff Lefty's shielding of the buffalo hunters. Even now, Bronson frowned as he thought of the despicable Skeet Gallagher and his kind, and wondered how much longer outright warfare could be avoided between the hunters and the Indians—and ultimately, how many innocent lives would be lost on both sides.

Just beyond a gentle rise, Bronson spotted the sprawling ranch house in the valley below, a one-and-a-half-story white frame structure nestled near a clear stream and protected by the sheltering arms of giant pecan trees. About the homestead were sprawled the familiar corrals and outbuildings.

Blue Wind headed instinctively down into the gulch and forded the shallow stream. Bronson was cantering his horse toward the swept yard when he spotted his dog, Chico, bounding out from the side of the house, barking gleefully.

Bronson dismounted and let his horse head back to the stream to water. "Chico!" he called, hunkering down.

The small brown and white dog leaped onto Bronson's lap, wagging his tail and licking his master's face.

Bronson laughed and petted his friend. Chico, originally a stray mongrel pup in the Comanche village, had adopted him two years ago. Like Bronson, he lived a double life and was equally adept at playing with Indian children at the Comanche village, or cutting cows with the drovers here on the ranch.

"Hello, boy," Bronson said. "You'd think you hadn't seen me in a month of Sundays."

"Bronson!" called a familiar voice.

Setting down the dog, Bronson looked up to watch Uncle Sam emerge from the ranch house. Handsome and trim for a man pushing fifty, Sam had hazel eyes and light brown hair—hair now liberally streaked with gray. He wore the inevitable checked shirt with bandanna, denim trousers, boots, and a white Stetson hat.

Bronson stood as Sam rushed to his side. "Howdy, Uncle Sam."

Grinning broadly, Sam clapped a hand on Bronson's shoulder. "Good to see you back so soon, boy. I thought you'd still be honeymooning in Austin."

"Yes. Well . . ."

Sam glanced about them in confusion. "Where's the new missus? She the shy type or something?"

Bronson shoved his hands into his pockets. "That's why I'm back so soon. Things didn't work out in Austin—so I've only stopped by here to get Chico and some fresh clothes and supplies. Then I'm off to the tribe to see my father."

Sam's face twisted with disappointment and incredulity. "What happened, boy? Was she a witch or somethin'?"

Bronson laughed humorlessly at the apt characterization. "It's that damn Calvin Bryce. He ruined everything."

"What do you mean? I thought the two of you were *compadres.*"

"*Were.* As you're aware, Calvin promised me he wouldn't send me a woman who wasn't fully aware of my heritage."

"Yes."

"Then he sent Maggie Donovan here believing I was a full white man."

Sam's mouth fell open. "You're pulling my leg."

"I wish I were. When I laid eyes on her at the station house, I . . ." Bronson had to stop as a powerful stab of pain assailed him. "I thought she was right for me, and I whisked her straight off to the courthouse, where we said our vows. It wasn't until that night, when I gave her Mother's necklace, that she learned I was half-Indian."

"Then what happened?"

"What the hell do you think happened?" Bronson countered irritably. "She lit outa there like her goddamned tail was on fire—after calling me and my kind every dirty name in the book."

"Oh, Bronson." Sam groaned and shook his head.

Bronson's shrug belied his inner turmoil. "Like I said, things didn't work out. The woman was a goddamned Indian hater."

"Maybe she was just overreacting. Maybe in time she'll calm down."

Bronson's eyes gleamed with rage and pain. "Damn it, Sam, she broke Mother's necklace."

Sam's face was crestfallen. "Son, I'm deeply sorry."

His jaw tight, Bronson squatted down to pet his dog. "Can you spare me for a few weeks while I'm with the People?"

Sam nodded. "We have spring roundup under control. I just hate to see you leaving like this. Whatever happened in Austin, it can't have been so bad as to send you running off to the Indians—"

"Sam, you know you can't talk me into turning my back on my brothers," Bronson cut in with passion.

"I know, son." Sam heaved a great sigh. "It's just that your mother suffered so much at the hands of Buffalo Thunder and the others. And you should have been my boy, damn it."

Standing, Bronson smiled with the faint pain of under-

standing both sides of the story. "I am your son in many
ways that matter, Sam. I am a son of two worlds."

"So you are," Sam conceded. "And you're right—I
shouldn't try to further divide your loyalties. But why can't
you find your answers here?"

Bronson spoke earnestly. "It's not a reflection on you,
Uncle Sam. You're the best man I've ever known in the
white world. It's just that I've always been able to sort
things out best when I'm with the People." A look of contempt darkened his countenance. "So that's the best place
for me to forget that coldhearted little shrew I married."

Sam appeared amazed. "B-But you and this woman exchanged vows. You can't just pretend it didn't happen."

"Watch me," Bronson snapped back, whistling to summon his horse, so he could unpack his saddlebags.

SIX

A DAY AND A HALF LATER, BRONSON AND CHICO APPROACHED the Penateka band. The People were frequently on the move, but Bronson, Blue Wind, and Chico always found them, seeking them out by a scent on the wind or the snap of a twig. Somehow, the whereabouts of the tribe was imprinted on the consciousness of man, horse, and dog. Comanche bands instinctively knew how to locate other Penateka tribes—just as they also knew how to find their friends, the Kiowas, Cheyennes, and Arapahos, and to avoid their enemies, the Lipan Apaches, the Tonkawas, and the White Eyes. During his years roving with the tribe, Bronson had befriended Quanah Parker of the Quahadi, White Shield of the Cheyenne, and Lone Wolf of the Kiowas. His brother Black Hawk often hunted with Stone Arrow, chief of another Penateka band that roamed the area. Bronson particularly enjoyed the joint counsels held by all the friendly tribes in the region during winter months.

Bronson crested a rise and spotted the camp beneath him, two dozen tepees sprawled next to a cypress-lined stream. Everywhere was activity: women scraping hides, washing clothes, or tending babies; children racing about, screaming gleefully; men grooming horses, smoking or talking, gambling or pounding arrowheads.

The sight of the tribe filled Bronson's heart with joy. Here was home, for the roots of the Penateka were anchored deep in his soul. As he always did when he rejoined his Comanche brothers, he left his white identity behind and became the white wolf, wild and free again. Now, bellowing an exuberant Comanche yell, he cantered his mount into the valley. A group of laughing children in breechclouts raced forward to meet him, some of them his sisters, brothers, or cousins, all frolicking with Chico and calling out his Comanche name, Isa-Rosa. He dismounted near the center of camp, where several adults also greeted him affectionately, the men pounding his shoulders, the women acknowledging him with shy smiles.

Happy chaos erupted as White Wolf dispensed his gifts. The children tore into the tins of licorice; the squaws exuberantly carried off the bolts of calico. White Wolf observed his Comanche brothers and sisters with pride; to him, they were a handsome and simple people. The squaws were dressed in pretty beaded deerskin dresses and moccasins; the men wore breechclouts, fringed buckskin leggings, and were bare-chested, with bear-claw necklaces and eagle feathers in their hair. White Wolf couldn't wait to doff his own white man's clothing and roam freely wearing no more than a breechclout and moccasins.

The People chatted in rapid Comanche, telling White Wolf of events that had occurred since his last visit: Autumn Quail had born Antelope a son; Gray Eagle had taken a third bride; Black Hawk and a group of warriors were away hunting with another Penateka band. As usual, no one scolded White Wolf for his absence, for the Comanches had always accepted his comings and goings with complete tolerance.

Among those greeting him was the medicine man, Spirit Talker, a gaunt elderly man clothed in a breechclout and copper armbands; his many charms and rattles dangled from his leathery neck. He waved a bear-claw charm over White

Wolf and said in Comanche, "Isa-Rosa, I bless your home-coming. May your medicine be strong."

White Wolf bowed solemnly to the *puhakut* and replied, "Thank you, Mook-war-ruh."

"Welcome home, Isa-Rosa," called another familiar voice.

White Wolf turned to watch as his younger brother, Silver Knife, came forward with his pretty half-white bride, Creek Flower. White Wolf had always felt a special affinity with Creek Flower, who, like himself, had been born of a white captive mother and raised among the People. Unlike himself, however, Creek Flower had never left the tribe, had never seen the white world. The girl's ignorance might well be a blessing, he mused darkly. The two did make an appealing couple, Silver Knife tall, slender, and handsome, Creek Flower petite and beautiful, with her green eyes and long chestnut brown hair.

White Wolf smiled to Silver Knife. "Hello, my brother."

"You have been gone for too many moons," the young man replied.

"Yes, I have missed you, and seeing the sunny face of your lovely squaw," White Wolf said. "I trust you have both been well, and that the Great Spirit will soon bless you with your first son."

Silver Knife beamed at his brother's words, while a blushing Creek Flower stepped forward and offered Bronson a cup of water flavored with mint; he thanked the girl and drank deeply.

An older brother, tall, barrel-chested Big Bow, joined the circle with his wife, Fast Fox. "Isa-Rosa, you are home at last," he greeted his brother jovially. "Tonight we celebrate."

"Yes, I am happy to be among the People again," White Wolf answered.

"You must stay this time, and ride with us to capture wild mustangs," Big Bow continued. "The Comancheros gave us many fine Sharps rifles for our herd gathered last spring."

White Wolf nodded, though he was saddened by the reality that his brothers were using the fruits of their labors to buy weapons to better kill the *tahbay-boh*. "I will try to stay for a time."

Big Bow jerked his elbow toward Fast Fox. "I give you my bride this night to warm your homecoming."

As several other braves cheered, White Wolf glanced at the pretty young woman, who was blushing and giggling. Fast Fox was one of several squaws in the Comanche village who had previously shamelessly pursued him, no doubt hoping for a marriage proposal from Buffalo Thunder's half-white son; he suspected his brother's offer might well have been spurred by the squaw herself. White Wolf did not feel completely comfortable with the Comanche tradition of wife-sharing among brothers—perhaps it was the white man in him. But he realized that to refuse such a generous gift would require tact.

Bowing to his older brother, White Wolf said earnestly, "Thank you, Big Bow, for the great honor you have bestowed on me. The favors of your beautiful squaw would compliment any brave, but I have come to seek the counsel of my father, and thus I must keep my mind free from all earthly temptations in order to receive his wisdom."

Big Bow grinned as if he understood, and White Wolf figured he might even feel grateful not to have to share his bride's favors.

A hush fell over the group as Buffalo Thunder came forward, an utterly noble presence with his flowing silver hair, his buffalo robe, his deeply lined face with prominent hawk nose and deep-set black eyes. White Wolf could clearly see part of himself in his father's visage—in the high cheekbones, the spare lips, the strong jaw. But he noted with dismay that his father's beloved face had gained many additional grooves since he had last visited the tribe, and even as the old man joined the others, he hacked out a wrenching cough that gave stark evidence that his days among the People would be numbered.

According to tradition, White Wolf waited for his father to speak first.

"Welcome home, my son," Buffalo Thunder said in Comanche.

"I am pleased to be among our people again, Father," White Wolf replied. "I have thought much of you and my brothers in the many moons we have been apart."

"Since your last visit, the grass blades grow long and flowers bloom on the prairie," Buffalo Thunder continued thoughtfully.

"I have been away too long," White Wolf concurred.

"You come here for a reason," added Buffalo Thunder wisely.

"Yes," White Wolf admitted. "To seek your counsel, my father."

Buffalo Thunder snapped his fingers to one of his elderly wives, Fair Moon. "Prepare the meal. My son and I will eat and have council by the fire."

As White Wolf knew, Comanche braves made council in tepees in inclement weather, and out by the fire on mild occasions such as tonight. For a father and son to hold council alone was unusual, since normally all braves of the village were welcome to attend. Tonight, however, the other warriors seemed to respect that Buffalo Thunder and White Wolf needed time alone.

With Chico lounging nearby awaiting scraps, the two men first ate. Fair Moon served them the rich buffalo stew she had prepared in a hide pouch suspended from a tripod. Buffalo Thunder cut off a small slice of his meat and buried it to honor the gods, and White Wolf, following a lifelong tradition, did the same. Once both men had eaten their fill and tossed the remnants of their meal to the dog, Buffalo Thunder smoked his pipe and contemplated, while White Wolf sat in respectful silence.

The night enfolding them was clear and beautiful, a thousand stars gleaming in the black heavens overhead. Beyond them on a ridge, Spirit Talker was singing softly and beating his drum, his squatted form awash in a beam of moonlight; closer to camp, a group of warriors laughed over their game of dice. Squaws moved about quietly, doing their chores, many of the females bearing sleeping babies on cradle-boards. The aromas of woodsmoke, dew, and honeysuckle filled the air. White Wolf mused wistfully that the scene was utterly idyllic and peaceful.

At last Buffalo Thunder spoke. "Your brother Black Hawk has been gone for five days now. With Stone Arrow and his warriors, he hunts for food. Yet the buffalo spirit is displeased, and the bison grow scarce since the *tahbay-boh* hunters have come to fill the prairies with the wail of the beasts and the rotting carcasses of the dead."

White Wolf nodded.

Buffalo Thunder paused to hack out several coughs before he continued. "My heart bleeds. Without our friend the buffalo, soon our women will weep, our children will go na-ked and cry out from hunger. Your brother Black Hawk wishes to raid Rio Concho and kill the White Eyes sheriff for shielding the hunters. I have counseled against this—for when the White Eyes are killed, many more come to take their place. The *tahbay-boh* are like ghost spirits that rise up from their own ashes . . . very bad medicine. But I may not be able to deter your brother much longer. It is spring, and for our fiercest warriors, blood is on the wind, and the trail of vengeance beckons. Only three moons past, the white In-dian agent came out again from Fort Defiance, imploring me to move all our people to Oklahoma." Buffalo Thunder's gaze darkened with sadness. "But there are no bison there, my son . . . the hunters have slaughtered them all. The prai-ries are lined with bones, and there our people will find no succor. Black Hawk says our people will die by his hand before he allows them to be herded to the reservation like so many sheep." Buffalo Thunder sighed deeply. "Why will the White Eyes not let us live in peace?"

White Wolf listened in sorrow. He mused ironically that, to an outsider, it might seem odd that Buffalo Thunder would discuss with his half-white son the problems the tribe was having with the *tahbay-boh*, but the People did not make such blood distinctions. They accepted White Wolf as a full Comanche brother—it was only the whites who regarded him with fear and prejudice.

White Wolf had no solution to offer his father. What was happening between the Comanches and the whites was an inevitable clash of cultures that could bring only tragedy, he feared. Ultimately the People would become outnumbered by sheer brute force, and defeated by the decimation of their food supply. He reflected sadly that the days of his wild, free, Indian brothers would soon come to an end, when their noble spirits were trapped and destroyed on the reservations, as had happened to so many red men before them. The whites were unable to recognize the essential differences between the two cultures, and if they were not educated regarding the red man's ways, disaster was certain.

Only when his father was finished speaking did White Wolf comment. "What you say is true, my father. I have seen the hunters you speak of in Rio Concho. Their wagons are piled high with hides pillaged from our plains. Sheriff McBride knows of the treason of his White Eyes brothers, but he refuses to uphold the law."

Buffalo Thunder nodded grimly. "No white law is enforced to the benefit of the red man."

White Wolf made a gesture of resignation. "Perhaps I can help our People in the white world, through my knowledge of white man's laws."

Buffalo Thunder considered this with a scowl. "You are needed here, my son."

"You may speak the truth," White Wolf conceded. "But who will make the white man honor his word, his treaties, if not someone like me, who has lived in both worlds?"

Neither had an answer, and both fell silent. Around them, Spirit Talker had ceased his singing, and many of the warriors were heading for bed. With amusement, White Wolf watched the entry flaps of two adjacent tepees flutter as a leather rope attached between the two was tugged. A moment later, Running Deer, second wife of Straw Horse, trudged out of one of the tepees and went to join her husband inside the other one. A dark frown drifted in as White

Wolf considered the absurd prospect of his fire-haired *tahbay-boh* bride ever behaving so obediently.

His father seemed to sense his thoughts. "We will speak of other matters now. The White Wolf has come to his people with a heavy heart."

Surprisingly, White Wolf found it easy to spill out his pain to his father. Never before had he mentioned to Buffalo Thunder his arranged marriage, but tonight he held back nothing. He told his father the full truth about his white bride: of his own certainty, upon meeting her, that Maggie Donovan was the Prairie Star of his vision; of the wonder of the brief hours they had shared, getting married and becoming acquainted; of the horror of her rejection. He spoke of how he now wanted nothing further to do with the heartless shrew he had so foolishly wed. She was bad medicine, this woman, an Indian hater; he would be blessed never again to lay eyes on her.

Throughout White Wolf's discourse, Buffalo Thunder listened patiently. Only when his son fell silent did he comment, and both his words and his visage were grave. "My son, you have exchanged vows with this woman, even if they were white man's vows. The two of you have taken a path that cannot be altered."

White Wolf glowered. "Now you are sounding like my uncle in the white world."

Buffalo Thunder smoked his pipe, and White Wolf thought he detected the faint glimmer of a smile on the old chief's lips. "No Comanche brave with strong medicine would allow his wife to reject him and make a fool of him in this manner."

"Then what are you suggesting?" asked White Wolf.

"You must make this woman live up to the vows between you. As I did with your mother many moons ago, you must kidnap the white squaw and bring her to live among the People, there to teach her to become a proper Indian bride to you."

White Wolf was incredulous. "Yes, I'll teach her to live

with me in hatred and rancor, as you did with my mother for almost two decades."

Wisely overlooking his son's show of temper, Buffalo Thunder replied, "Better that, my son, than to see you dishonored by a woman—and a White Eyes."

White Wolf grimly considered the advice. His father was saying he should kidnap Maggie, bring her to the tribe, and force her to honor their marriage vows? A vindictive smile curved his lips. From the standpoint of gaining pure, meanspirited revenge, the prospect was appealing, he had to admit. Maggie had abused his pride terribly, and he perversely delighted in the prospect of torturing her a bit.

Then he laughed aloud at the sheer absurdity of the idea. "My white bride is likely halfway back to Boston by now."

Buffalo Thunder was not deterred. "Then you must find her, my son, and force her to honor the vows between you, even if you must first journey far into the white man's world. Not to do so will bring great dishonor on the sacred covenants between a warrior and his squaw."

Was his father right? White Wolf wondered. Were the vows between him and Maggie sacred, even if unconsummated? In dismissing his marriage through pride and anger, had he also spurned a deeper obligation to make the union work?

"How can I be certain the course you suggest is right?" he asked.

Buffalo Thunder gazed solemnly at the heavens. "Meditate on the matter, my son. Ultimately I can only advise you. Every warrior must decide for himself which path to choose . . . just as I alone must decide who will lead the People after me, you or your brother Black Hawk."

With these words, Buffalo Thunder fell into a new fit of coughing; a moment later, he signed a good-night to White Wolf and struggled to his feet. Watching his father walk toward his tepee with the painful gait of old age, White Wolf reflected sadly that the day when Buffalo Thunder was compelled to choose his own successor might not be long in coming. White Wolf felt terribly torn; could he abandon the tribe to the violent path of his brother Black Hawk, when he might be able to lead the People to a more peaceful future through mediating with the whites? Could he help his people more in the Indian or in the white world?

He shook his head at the irony of his dilemma. How could he consider pursuing his bride when he wasn't certain where his own future lay? No matter how cruelly Maggie had treated him, was it fair to capture this woman and drag her off, when he wasn't certain whether he wanted her as a squaw or a wife?

Yet some elemental part of White Wolf's being cried out that he wanted both. He wanted this proud shrew to be humbled; he wanted her to accept and embrace both sides of his nature, to be willing to lie naked with her warrior husband beneath a Comanche moon, or in a big featherbed at his ranch house. He wanted to claim her, shame her, tame her . . . to make her rue the day she had dealt with him so heartlessly. But most of all, he simply *wanted* her. Those brief hours they had shared had imprinted her on his spirit and memory, and he couldn't forget her now . . . He suspected he never would.

He clearly desired the impossible, and yet he could not ignore the wisdom of his father's counsel. The central question remained: Should he pursue Maggie, or let her go? Perhaps, as his father had wisely suggested, the Great Spirit would guide him.

White Wolf closed his eyes and sang softly in the darkness, hypnotizing himself with the haunting Indian chant his father had taught him long ago. He meditated long by the fire, until he received his answer from the heavens . . .

At the boardinghouse in Austin, Maggie was drifting off to her best night of sleep in over a week. Several days ago, she had seen a lawyer who thought she could proceed with an annulment on grounds of fraud and desertion. She had made inroads into securing a post with the newly formed Austin Public Schools. Her small nest egg of money was holding out, and the kindly Minnie Walker had insisted

Maggie could help with chores around the boardinghouse in exchange for room and board if there was any delay in her gaining employment. She had made friends with several other boarders—including a Mr. Tippitt, a very nice gentleman who owned a local haberdashery and seemed interested in Maggie romantically. As for the man she had married . . . when forbidden thoughts, tormenting guilts, and secret stirrings for the half-breed sprang to mind, she simply would not allow herself the luxury of such treacherous cravings. She would make a new life, she vowed, and forget Bronson Kane had ever existed.

This was Maggie's final, firm thought as she succumbed to slumber. It may have been minutes or hours later that she began to thrash in the throes of a nightmare, to find the blackened face of an Indian warrior looming over her in her dream. Her scream became stifled in her throat as a cloth gag descended over her mouth. She was roughly shoved over onto her belly, a hard knee braced at the small of her back as the rag was tied tightly at the back of her head. Her struggles proved meaningless. She was rolled up into a blanket and hoisted, squirming helplessly, into the unyielding arms of the savage; then she was borne out of the room and into the hallway in the wake of his soundless footsteps.

It wasn't until the night air hit her on the street, blowing the male scent of him across her, it wasn't until she was hoisted astride a pony, her wrists roughly bound to the saddle pommel, that Maggie realized her nightmare was *very* real!

SEVEN

Maggie felt terrified as she and her Indian abductor galloped away, riding relentlessly out of Austin and onto the moonlit prairie. She remained gagged, her hands tied to the pommel, her pinto pony tethered to the Indian's black horse. Maggie was no horsewoman, and they were proceeding at a breakneck pace that both petrified her and ensured that her most tender parts were pounded against the saddle. Her nightgown was also scandalously hiked, her legs spread and bared. Never had she felt more vulnerable or threatened.

Who was this demon who had stolen her away into the night? In the velvety darkness, all she could see was his broad bare back, his black hair tangling in the wind. Surely this couldn't be her husband! She shuddered at a memory of the blackened face that had loomed over her only moments earlier. True, Bronson Kane was half-Indian, but he hadn't seemed a complete animal; and why would he have left Austin over a week ago unless he, like she, had no desire to proceed with their marriage?

Then a new fear set her heart to thumping. What if he had come after her to seek revenge for the cruel things she had said to him? That possibility was too harrowing to contemplate.

If her captor wasn't Bronson, then this savage who had claimed her could be anyone—a barbarian intent on taking her off, raping, torturing, and murdering her. Desperation choked her as she recalled the grisly details of how her fiancé had been remorselessly tortured day after day by the Sioux—specifics she was sure his old friend had never intended to spill out to her that day he had come calling to offer her consolation. Would her fate be similar—a slow, ghastly, excruciating death? How would she bear it?

Oh, she never should have come to Austin in the first place, and she never should have stayed after learning the truth about Bronson Kane. She had never imagined Austin to be a place where civilized folk could be snatched from their beds and carried off by savages in the middle of the night!

At least when daybreak came, she might look her captor in the eye and demand that he release her—much as she suspected such hopes were futile . . .

Riding ahead of Maggie, the Comanche White Wolf had no intention of releasing his bride. Four nights ago, before he had left his father's camp, he had received his answer from the Great Spirit: In a new vision, he had seen the white wolf pursuing the elusive prairie star, leaping up into the heavens to close the distance between them and make them one. He knew now that his destiny was with Maggie, his Prairie Star, even though his bride had not yet recognized him as her true spirit mate. Nonetheless, he had realized his father had spoken the truth; just as Buffalo Thunder had done with his mother so long ago, he must bring his mate to live among the People. There he would teach her to become a proper Indian bride. He knew now that there would be no hope for them in either the Indian or white world unless she first became a part of the Comanche culture. He would not force her to live up to her vows, but he would master her. And never would he allow his white bride to see

how badly she had wounded him through her cruel words
and uncaring actions on their wedding night . . .

At last, just as a crimson dawn was breaking across a
landscape filled with cedar brakes, cacti, and wildflowers,
Maggie's captor pulled both horses to a halt in a stand of
scrub oak sprawled next to a narrow stream, beneath a sheltering limestone bluff. Maggie felt cold and miserable—her
bottom sore, her wrists raw from her bindings, her mouth
dry from the gag, her eyes stinging from the dust of the
trail.

Her distress only increased as she watched her captor
calmly dismount and stride toward her. The sight of the savage by the light of day made her heart pound in her ears. He
was huge, bronzed, utterly fearsome. His muscled chest,
massive shoulders, and sinewy arms were bare, save for a
bear-claw necklace strung around his neck and a copper
armband circling one arm. An orange and black braided
headband bound his long black hair. Otherwise, he wore
only a breechclout, buckskin leggings, and moccasins. The
muscles of his hard thighs rippled as he moved.

Never had Maggie seen such a scantily clad man—and
certainly not an Indian! She was utterly horrified.

Next to her horse, he paused to scrutinize her, and she felt
sickened by fear. His unhurried gaze roved up her bare legs,
and she could have died of humiliation. He inched his stare
higher, over the curves of her hips, at last pausing on her
heaving bosom, the tight nipples straining against the thin
cloth. She shuddered as she glimpsed the black paint that
still obscured his warrior face. Then, as he stared boldly up
at her, she found herself gazing down into brilliant, merci-
less blue eyes—joltingly familiar eyes that gleamed with
anger and fierce determination—and at last she recognized
her captor—

Her husband, Bronson Kane! A sound of strangled rage
rose in her throat.

The savage untied the bindings on her wrists, and Maggie
at once snatched the gag from her mouth. As her husband

hauled her off the horse, she reacted in an explosion of righteous anger.

"You!" she screamed, pummeling his hard chest with her fists.

He easily grabbed her wrists and glowered down at her. "You were expecting someone else?"

She yanked free and resumed pounding him. "How dare you do this to me! You beast! You bastard! You scared the living daylights out of me!"

He seized her wrists again, his fingers so tight on her chafed flesh that she winced. Bravely she continued struggling, and managed to kick his shin. He cursed vividly, grabbing both her wrists in one of his large hands and using his free hand to soundly swat her bottom. She shrieked her outrage, then froze at the look of fury in his eyes as he yanked her up against his hard body.

"Attack me again, Maggie, and I'll thrash you but good," he warned. "Don't think I won't do it." He stared at her skimpy nightdress. "Right now, it would be damn easy— and damn tempting—to skin off that gown and turn you over my knee."

Maggie's mouth dropped open, and for an instant, she was too blinded by anger to respond. This man had terrified her, abducted her, abused her, and now he dared to scold her for retaliating against his own violence?

At last, she whispered incredulously, *"Why,* in the name of God, why have you done this to me, Bronson Kane?"

He shoved her away and crossed his muscled arms over his broad chest. He spoke with consummate sarcasm. "We're married now. Or have you forgotten?"

"Have I forgotten?" she all but screamed back at him. "Forgotten that you deceived me, and duped me into marrying you? Forgotten that I traveled halfway across this country for nothing, thanks to you? And now you think you have the right to dress up like a savage and steal me off in the middle of the night?"

His smile was frightening. "Yes, I have that right. I am your husband, Maggie. And I *am* a savage."

"Believe me, I haven't forgotten that either," she snapped, "or that you enticed me into this sham marriage under fraudulent circumstances—which means you have *no right* whatsoever to treat me in this despicable manner!"

He raised an eyebrow at her. " 'Fraudulent circumstances.' That sounds like lawyer talk to me. Have you learned so much in the brief week we've been apart, Maggie?"

She balled her hands on her hips and faced him down. "I have, indeed! I've learned that this union is purely laughable—and will be duly annulled. And if you don't want to get yourself into even deeper trouble than you're already in, Bronson Kane, you'll take me back to Austin this very instant!"

"Sorry, but I can't do that," he drawled. He strode off to his horse and flipped open a saddlebag. "Particularly not if you're planning to have our marriage dissolved." He glanced at her over his shoulder, giving her a searing look that made her stomach churn. "I'll just have to keep you with me until annulment is no longer a legal possibility, won't I?"

Her mouth fell open. "You intend to take me off and force yourself on me?"

"No." His hard gaze flicked over her again. "I didn't say that."

For a moment she was speechless. "Then exactly what are your intentions toward me, Mr. Kane?"

He rifled through the saddlebag. "My intentions are to make you honor the vows between us."

"What?" she cried.

"You heard me."

"Why, for heaven's sake?"

He came toward her and hurled a bundle into her arms. She caught the items, not even bothering to look at them.

He loomed over her, every ounce of him the menacing warrior. "Because we are man and wife now, and my people, the Comanche, hold such obligations sacred, even if our marriage may mean no more to *your kind* than the paper it is written on. I am taking you to live with me at my father's tribe, there to teach you to become a proper Indian bride."

Maggie was appalled. She dropped the clothes and glared at him. "You are out of your mind."

"No, Maggie, I've never been more serious."

"You really think you can just steal me off like this, and expect me to spend the rest of my life with—with Indians?"

"Not your entire life. Only as long as it takes for you to accept my world and honor our marriage vows."

She almost stamped her foot at him. "Then you're talking about much more than my entire life—for I'll see you in hell before I become your squaw, Bronson Kane."

Something dangerous flickered in his eyes. He seized her by the shoulders and spoke vehemently. "Whatever it takes, Maggie. How much you suffer because of your stubbornness is entirely up to you. But you are my wife now, and you will live up to the vows you have made. Hear this and hear it well: I will not walk in your world until you understand mine."

Studying her husband's implacable visage, Maggie struggled to rein in her roiling emotions, and tried to reason with him. "Mr. Kane, surely you can't mean to do this despicable deed, knowing I have no desire to be your wife. Surely you can't expect me, a civilized white woman, to live among Comanches!"

"I expect you not only to live among my people, but to accept the entire way of life you have scorned. Sorry, Maggie, but you can't walk away from this—or from what I am."

"You walked away in Austin."

"Can you blame me? You ran away first."

"Can you blame me?"

A muscle jerked in his cheek. "I have come to my senses now. I have realized we both gave up our right to walk away when we said our vows."

"Fraudulent vows do not count!"

He caught her face in his large hands and glowered down at her. "They count to me—and as far as I'm concerned, they weren't fraudulent. Our marriage is legal and binding in every way."

Maggie felt as if she were trying to reason with a post. She felt burned by his rough hands, the heat of his gaze smoldering down into hers.

Abruptly he released her, retrieved the items she had dropped, and shoved them back into her hands. "Now, put on these garments. I grabbed them from your room before I took you away. We'll attract too much attention riding through the Hill Country, me dressed as an Indian and you in your nightgown."

"Yes—that might alert people to the foul deed that has actually been perpetrated here."

"Stop arguing and change your clothes."

She glanced at the items again, spotting her yellow muslin dress and sturdy brown shoes. "These are white women's clothes, and yet you say you are taking me off to become your squaw."

He sneered. "I'm not a fool, Maggie. We're heading through white man's territory and I'm changing to my civilized clothing, as well."

"Ashamed of your heritage, are you?" she baited.

"No. Just not wanting to get us both killed."

She looked him over in amazement. "Then why did you dress like a savage in the first place, and smear that horrible warpaint on your face?"

"Why, to live up to every terrible cliché you already believe about me," he mocked.

She could have strangled him. "You frightened the wits out of me!"

"Good," he replied ruthlessly. "I hope I scared some sense into you. I want you to worry about what I'll do to you if you disobey me." He stepped closer and smiled that unnerving smile again. "Who knows, Maggie? Maybe everything you've heard about Indians is true."

She gasped, speechless and terrified.

His voice took on a hard edge. "Now, strip off that nightgown and put on your clothes, before I do it for you. Frankly, at the moment, it would be my pleasure."

"You wouldn't!"

"I will." He took an aggressive step toward her. "One more defiant remark and I'll be delighted to demonstrate. Now, get moving or else!"

She blushed crimson. "You expect me to dress in front of you?"

He shrugged. "You can hide behind a tree if you want to. But try to run off, and I'll beat you, Maggie."

That last calm threat proved too much for her. She was exhausted, hungry, and at her wits' end. "You savage!" she hissed, hurling down the garments. "Is this how you fulfill your vows to your mother on her deathbed? By abducting a white woman and forcing her to become your squaw?"

Maggie was stunned when her husband seized her by the shoulders and shook her until her teeth rattled. The violence in his voice jarred her even more. "Don't you dare ever again mention her in that tone of voice! You have no idea what her life was like or what she endured."

"But I'm about to find out, aren't I?" she scoffed.

He almost struck her. She watched him struggle as he drew back a fist and heaved in huge, infuriated breaths.

At last he grabbed her shoulder again and spoke in murderous tones. "You're not going to taunt me into doing something I'll regret, Maggie. You can try, but you won't succeed." Then, without taking his eyes off her, he began pulling off his moccasins and leggings.

She was appalled. "What are you doing?"

"Didn't I tell you I'll be changing, too?" he asked, tossing the leggings at her feet.

She gaped at his bare legs. "You would . . . unclothe yourself . . . in front of me?"

He smiled nastily. "You don't have to look, and I sure as hell don't have to hide—not from my own wife."

"Oh, you are insufferable!"

He began untying his breechclout.

Mortified, Maggie snatched up her clothing and dashed

behind a tree. She stood there for a moment, breathing rapidly and trembling with rage. The nerve of this man, stealing her off, telling her he would keep her his captive among savage Indians until she learned to become his submissive squaw! She would rot in hell before she did so—and see that he did, too.

But even as shocked and enraged as she was, she was also perversely fascinated by this man who had taken her away in the night. She found herself irresistibly turning to peek at him around the tree. Her eyes grew enormous. Her husband stood with his back to her. He was naked, all magnificent savage—hard, brown, and unashamed, his long legs and buttocks splendidly formed, the lines of his back, shoulders, and arms like satiny bronze. She watched in awe and horror as he strode to some grasses, then stood there brazenly relieving himself, his beautiful, jet black hair whipping about his shoulders in the breeze. She watched him go to the stream, hunker down, and splash water on his face— she presumed to wash away the war paint.

Then he turned and stood, and she saw the front of him, the noble face and broad chest, the trim waist, the thick manhood nestled among black curls. Her face was scalding hot, yet she felt rooted to the spot, unable to take her eyes off him. He was so big, magnificent, and untamed.

Mercy, what was she doing? She was behaving scandalously, indulging in iniquitous behavior no proper lady would *ever* allow. She should turn away in shame, and yet she was mesmerized by her husband's stark, wild beauty.

It was only then that she realized he was staring back at her, grinning arrogantly. He *knew* she was watching him! Humiliated to her Puritan soul, she jerked away, to the sound of his low laughter. Trembling badly, she doffed her nightgown and donned the undergarments, the yellow muslin dress, the stockings, shoes, and bonnet he had given her . . .

On the other side of the tree, Bronson smiled at Maggie's low gasp, feeling eminently pleased by his bride's curiosity. They were man and wife now, whether she was willing to acknowledge it or not, and he felt no shame that she had seen him unclothed. In time, she too would come to him naked and without modesty, as the Great Spirit had intended for them both. He had already feasted his eyes on her smooth, creamy legs, had watched her rounded breasts strain against that provocative, thin nightgown. In time, he would delight in every inch of her.

She was a feisty one, a woman of great fire and spirit. The Comanches appreciated such soul in a woman. She was determined and proud, but then, so was he. Now that he knew he was taking the right path with his bride, he would not be stayed. He would bring her around through sheer force of will if necessary. He would overcome Maggie's prejudice, teach her to respect and understand his people, make her realize what a sacrilege she had committed when she had broken his mother's necklace . . . and then he would make her his. In time, Maggie would make him a fine wife and bear him many sons, even if he had to tame her first.

EIGHT

AFTER BOTH OF THEM CHANGED THEIR CLOTHES, BRONSON OFfered Maggie a breakfast of boiled coffee and ground pemmican, which was his trail staple, an Indian meal composed of jerky mixed with dried berries. He watched her eat the food and sip her coffee, all the while contemptuously ignoring him. He fought a grin at her cool defiance. She looked very prim sitting on the sun-dappled earth, wearing her dainty bonnet, with her yellow skirts spread about her. But Bronson was not fooled by his bride's innocent facade, or her silence—he knew that soon enough, she would rail out at her fate again, attack him verbally or even physically, and probably try to escape. She would fail in all respects, of course. She would fail in *every* respect until she embraced her own destiny, chose to obey him, and became his bride . . .

As she ate, Maggie was painfully conscious of her husband's scrutiny. Ever since she had glimpsed Bronson in the glorious altogether, she had struggled against the forbidden urge to feast her eyes on him again. One glance at him in his buckskins had confirmed for her that she was treading on very shaky ground. The leather outfit hugged his muscled body like a second skin, and was very provocative, especially where the jacket jutted open from his corded neck almost to his trim waist. She didn't even have to look at him to know how devastatingly gorgeous he was, for that unsettling image was already emblazoned across her mind.

She was beset by so many conflicting emotions. Part of her simply couldn't believe she was in the company of the same man she had married a short week ago. Bronson Kane could be a sweet-talking gentleman or an implacable savage, a blunt-spoken Texan or an educated lawyer, a cold stranger or a raw sensualist. He was complex and dangerous, and she had clearly underestimated him on every level. Never would she have dreamed that the civilized man she had met and married in Austin would kidnap her and carry her off to live among Indians!

What made matters worse was the traitorous attraction she felt for him, despite everything. The knowledge of his savage nature somehow titillated her as much as it frightened her. To her horror, she was more intrigued by her husband now that she knew he was half-Indian than she had been when she had assumed he was a staid rancher and a proper gentleman. And she was deeply shocked to realize that she, a proper lady, could be lured at all by the uncivilized.

Such feelings were perilous, she knew, for they could ultimately threaten her very identity and defeat her. Just sitting with Bronson now, painfully conscious of the fact that he was watching her intently, produced a tension so excruciating, she was practically jumping out of her skin. She was almost grateful when he tossed the dregs of his coffee into the fire and brusquely ordered her to mount up. When she tried to protest, he merely grabbed her, plopped her none too gently on the pinto, and grabbed the pony's tether . . .

They rode at a brisk pace for the rest of the day. Unused to being on horseback, Maggie was soon squirming in the saddle, but was not about to complain to her husband, since she knew exactly how much sympathy she would get.

They passed several homesteads. Bronson exchanged friendly words with a couple of farmers, but politely declined offers of food or drink. Maggie wanted to call out for help, but fully aware of her husband's ruthless nature, she feared endangering the lives of the farmers or their families. She was very conscious of the fact that Bronson carried both a Colt pistol and a large repeating rifle.

At last, near sunset, they paused next to a cypress-lined stream. As Bronson prepared a trail supper of beans, bacon, and coffee, Maggie washed up at the stream. By the time she returned, he was serving their meal on tin plates.

She sat down on the bumpy ground and grimaced, muttering a grudging thank you as he handed her a plate and cup.

"You're wiggling a lot, Maggie," he teased. "Saddle-sore?"

"You are crude!"

He chuckled. "I imagine Boston schoolmarms don't spend a lot of time riding."

Taking a bite of the surprisingly good beans, she retorted sarcastically, "On the contrary, I canter my horse around the Common at least twice daily."

"Not likely, the way you're squirming now." He winked at her. "Maybe I can think of a way to help soothe you."

Glancing at his cynically amused, sinfully handsome face, she just managed not to hurl her food at him.

"Why don't you smooth down those ruffled feathers a little," he went on. "It's two more days to my father's village—a long time for you to stay mad at me."

"I'll be angry at you, sir, until you release me or hell freezes over!"

Ignoring her outburst, he set down his dishes and stretched out lazily, propping his weight on an elbow. "Like I've already told you, that's not going to happen, Maggie, so you may as well get such foolish notions out of your head."

Grinding her teeth at his words, Maggie tried not to stare at the way his buckskin leggings pulled at his powerful thighs. "Are you saying you don't mind being a kidnapper, then?"

He howled with laughter. "Maggie, you never should have come west with such foolish notions in your head. Texans tend to look at their wives as property. There's not a court in this state that would charge me with kidnapping for taking my wife for a little obedience training—"

"Obedience training!" She bristled. "You talk about me as if I am a horse!"

Ignoring her burst of temper, he finished, "—even if I am a half-breed."

Those words gave Maggie pause and stirred her guilt. She struggled within herself for a long moment, then eyed him guardedly. "How exactly did that happen?"

He scowled. "How exactly did what happen?"

"How did you come to be born half-Indian? I remember you mentioned a few details on the night we met—"

"On our *wedding* night," he corrected heatedly.

She felt color rising in her face, but forged on. "I seem to recall that you said your mother was carried off."

"Yes, my mother was a new widow, and heir to the Kane Ranch, when the Comanches kidnapped her. My father, Chief Buffalo Thunder, made my mother his third bride. I was born a year later in the Comanche village."

Maggie set down her dishes and twisted a bit of her skirt in her fingers. "Were there . . . Did your father have any other children with your mother?"

"After me, there were a couple of miscarriages, but no other living children. My mother and I stayed with the Comanche until I was eighteen, and I took her home to die."

"Home to your ranch?"

"Yes. My uncle Sam had cared for my property all the years we were away. Sam came to Texas shortly after his brother, my mother's first husband, was killed in an accident." Bronson sighed. "Sam also fell in love with my mother, right before she was carried off."

Maggie was incredulous to hear all these specifics. "Didn't you hate your father for what he did to her?"

He stared at her with utter sincerity. "No. There's no part of my heritage that I despise, Maggie."

She laughed bitterly. "Then I suppose I needn't hope you'll hate yourself for what you're doing to me now."

He did not comment, though his expression hardened.

"Don't you see what is happening here?" she went on passionately. "A lot of this isn't your fault, Bronson. In many ways you are a victim—"

"I don't consider myself a victim at all," he interjected.

"But you're willing to make me one. You're making the same mistakes with me that your father made with your mother."

His response was a stony scowl.

Realizing she had hit a nerve, Maggie quickly drove home her point. "She can't have been happy with the Comanches, or she never would have asked to go home to die."

He was silent for a long moment. Watching his jaw grow tighter, Maggie sensed a looming explosion.

"*She* never said vows first," he said at last.

"And *I* never gave you permission to come take me!"

His smile was pitiless. "So you didn't. But you made the commitment and you're mine, anyway. Don't think for a minute I'll let you go."

Maggie struggled to hold on to her patience, especially in the face of the treacherous excitement her husband's possessive words stirred. Yet she well knew that behind that possessiveness loomed fierce anger, wounded pride, and a vengeful determination to punish her. In many ways, she understood her husband's volatile feelings—for she had certainly contributed to them. Yet awareness made his motivations no easier to swallow.

Still hoping to reason with him, she forced a contrite smile. "Look, Mr. Kane, I'll admit I overreacted on our wedding night. I was shocked and angered and I said things I never should have said, things I deeply regret. I'm sorry, all right?"

He regarded her coolly.

"But don't compound our initial mistake by following through with this lunacy of forcing me to live among Indians," she pleaded.

He continued to listen implacably.

"Take me to your ranch instead," she suggested desperately. "If you do, I promise I'll try to give this marriage a fair chance."

He laughed. "If I do, you'll hightail it at the first chance you get."

"I won't. I'll try to work things out with you." She leaned toward him beseechingly. "After all, you are civilized, Bronson . . . aren't you? When you presented yourself to me in Austin as a prosperous rancher, that wasn't a masquerade, was it?"

"Of course not," he snapped. "Did you think I was hiding a tomahawk under my jacket?"

"Then why take me to the tribe, when you already have a home set up for us in the white world?" she reasoned.

"I have a home for us in *both* worlds," he uttered. "During the past ten years, when I wasn't at Harvard, I spent much of my time at the ranch with Uncle Sam. But I never forgot my roots, and I still spend several months out of each year with my tribe."

She gulped. "What of your plans to practice law, all the dreams you had for our future that you told me about in Austin?"

"*Have,* Maggie," he corrected firmly. "I still have those dreams, and hope we'll realize them one day. There's a part of me that's a white man. But there's also a part of me that's a red man. You're going to come to understand that part first."

In her exasperation, she beat a fist on the ground. "While you try to decide in which world you belong, in which world you want us to live? Is that fair? No one ever told me this!"

"Damn it, you were supposed to have been told."

"Well, I wasn't!" She took a deep, bracing breath. "Take me to your ranch. I—I give you my word I'll try."

He sat up quickly, his expression dark and resolute. "You

gave me your word already. I'm your husband, you're my wife, and it's a little late for you to start dictating terms to me."

Maggie's frustrations burst. "Then you're taking me off to live with savages out of pure revenge!"

Anger flared in his eyes. "If you think that, then you know nothing about me or my people. But you're going to learn, Maggie. You're going to learn. After the Comanche world becomes *your* world, then maybe you and I can renegotiate."

The steely determination in his voice chilled her deeply, and she felt too frustrated to continue their argument.

They exchanged hardly a word for the balance of the evening. Maggie felt desperation encroaching at her failure to dissuade her husband from his dastardly plans. She felt angered and confused by his insistence that she must come to accept the Comanche culture. Why couldn't he understand that such a way of life was anathema to her, totally alien to the civilized existence she had always known?

She remembered Minnie Walker's sobering account of the experiences of Comanche captives such as Cynthia Ann Parker. Although Bronson had hinted he would not keep her his prisoner indefinitely, his tactics bespoke otherwise, since they were certainly consistent with what Comanches often tried to do—to obliterate the white person's identity, to reshape their captives into Indians. And if she did acquiesce and "become Indian" for Bronson, what incentive would he have to "renegotiate"? The very idea made her shudder.

Eager for any distraction, she offered to tidy up from supper. As she returned to their camp with the clean dishes and utensils wrapped in a cloth, she noted to her dismay that the sun was sinking low, a chill settling over the landscape.

Putting down her bundle, she observed Bronson underneath a tree, laying out two bedrolls side by side. She seethed. Her husband had removed his jacket and boots, and the sight of him bare-chested and barefoot, his jet black hair spilling over his powerful shoulders, was most unnerving, leaving her not just enraged but also shockingly titillated.

Nonetheless, she rushed over to confront him. "If you think I'm going to sleep beside you, Bronson Kane, you've got another think coming."

Smoothing down one of the beds, he glanced up at her. "Then you won't mind being tied up all night—and possibly defenseless if a coyote or bear should enter our camp?"

She flinched. "Must I choose between bondage and sleeping with you?"

He laughed. "You'll only be sleeping next to me. I'm not going to rape you. You see, if you're nearby, I won't have to tie you up. I'll also know instantly if you try to escape— and I'll blister your butt."

"Like the savage you are!"

"Any man will discipline a disobedient wife."

"You mean any brute in Texas. A Boston gentleman never would."

Glancing up at his irate bride, he sighed. "Look, Maggie, I'm tired. We've got a hard day's ride ahead of us tomorrow. Quit arguing and come to bed."

"No."

Maggie sucked in an outraged breath as Bronson hauled her down onto her knees beside him. She was stunned even more as he tumbled her beneath him, his strong hands pinning her shoulders, his lower body pressing into hers. The shock of his male hardness against her pelvis sent an obscene thrill coursing through her. Maggie wanted to fight him—to thwart his show of brute strength, to resist the appalling desire he excited in her—yet something in his eyes warned her that this was not the moment to cross him.

"Don't say no to me, Maggie," he whispered.

She said nothing, speechless with shock.

For a moment, neither spoke, and for Maggie, the burgeoning night sounds—crickets, frogs, owls—seemed to scream out all around them. They just stared at each other, his heavy, rigid body crushing hers, his naked chest hovering above her heaving breasts. The tension was so agonizing that Maggie felt as if her heart might burst inside her.

Then Bronson's tormenting fingertip stroked the curve of

her jaw. Electrified by the contact, she writhed and cried out.

"Don't you dare touch me!"

With a look of unflinching determination, he continued the deliberate caress. "Oh, honey, I'm going to touch you—and a lot more before you and I are finished."

She gasped.

"Want to get undressed for bed?" he asked softly.

She shook her head.

"Sure?"

"I—I'll sleep in my clothes."

"In your shoes, too?"

"I—I'll remove them."

"You don't need help?" he pressed ruthlessly.

"I am in no need of your assistance, sir!"

He chuckled. "You sure do like to order me around, don't you, woman? Is that what you proper ladies do with your men in Boston?"

"I—I have no idea."

His voice was still low, but also frightening. "Maybe you wish you had married some Boston milksop, a mealy-mouthed coward you could have controlled and manipulated. But you married me, honey, and you're not going to keep me under rein. I can't be controlled, Maggie. In fact, I can be downright wild."

"A wild Indian?" she sneered, but with a telltale quiver.

He arched against her, prompting a scandalized gasp. "I could take you right now if I wanted to. You're under my control and I'm calling the shots. You got that, Maggie?"

She glared at him.

"You'd best remember it, woman. You can't reason your way out of this—you can't wheedle or cajole me into letting you go. Tempt me too much, and I'll demonstrate exactly how determined I can be."

She made a sound of helpless anger. "You are a beast! I wish I'd never come here! I wish I'd never laid eyes on you."

Abruptly he rolled off her. "Then you made a big mistake, didn't you, honey?"

Maggie, who almost never cursed, snapped back, "Damn right!" and turned her back to Bronson. She yanked off her shoes and crawled into her bedroll. She fumed in the darkness, wishing with all her might that she could escape this despicable brute. He'd promised to beat her if she tried to make a run for it, but it still might be worth the risk. Otherwise, he would force her to live among savages, and how could she bear that?

If she gave in to the shocking cravings this scoundrel aroused, her humiliation and defeat would be worse. Even now, she trembled not just with anger, but with frustrated desire. She longed to escape these devastating feelings as much as she burned to escape him.

She remained tensely awake until she heard his deep, regular breathing. Gathering all her nerve, she stirred slightly, and sat up—

At once his forearm was clamped down hard on her waist, and she was hurled back down on the pallet.

Her husband's angry visage loomed over her. "What the devil do you think you're doing?"

"I—I have to go to the woods!" she protested miserably.

He laughed. "Like hell you do."

"I do."

He jerked his head to the south of them. "Head straight over to that stand of chaparral, and come right back. Go anywhere near the horses, and I'll make you sorry. *Very* sorry."

Shoving him away furiously, Maggie followed her husband's orders to the letter. She returned to the pallet, flounced down, and positioned her body as far away from his as possible. But slumber proved elusive for a long, long time as she smelled her husband's intoxicating scent and heard his regular breathing beside her.

Bronson, too, felt restless. He knew Maggie was desperate to escape him, and he would have to watch her like a hawk to ensure that she didn't succeed. But being this close to her was also torture. He'd almost lost all control when he'd tumbled her to the ground and felt her lush curves trembling against him. She was so enticing, and yet she was forbidden. His senses were still filled with the sweet womanly scent of her skin, the rosewater aroma of her hair. How he longed to reach out and touch that rigid back of hers, to caress that rounded bottom, to pull her into his arms and soothe her gently, seduce her with his kisses . . .

Yet she considered him her enemy, and an enemy could offer no succor. Right now if he touched her, she would react like a wildcat. He wouldn't force her, even though his bride's beauty and pride were making his own desires very difficult to contain.

NINE

IN THE MIDDLE OF THE NIGHT, MAGGIE FELT SOMETHING BRIStly brushing against her arm. She recoiled, too terrified to call out. A split second later, Bronson's arms came around her tightly and he pressed a forefinger to her lips.

"Shhh!" he admonished.

"Something touched me," she whispered frantically, while her heartbeat pounded at his nearness.

He smiled and nodded toward the creek. "I know. You're in no danger. Don't scare them away."

Maggie twisted about in his arms to see what he was talking about, and spotted an entire raccoon family—mother, father, and two babies—hunched over the stream washing their food.

"Raccoons," she murmured. "They could be rabid."

He chuckled. "Maybe where you come from, but here in Texas, rabid raccoons are not as common. It's skunks, and an occasional mad dog or cat, that are worrisome."

"Not to mention bobcats, snakes, and bears," she put in importantly.

His eyes glinted with amusement. "A rabid snake—that's a new one."

She glowered at him. "I meant that snakes are a nuisance—*not* that they're rabid."

"I realize you're not used to the frontier, Maggie—but you'll adapt."

"As if you've given me a choice." She turned her head to look at the little family, trying to make out details in the wan light. "I do hope they're not eating our food."

He pointed overhead at a tree branch. "That's why I hung the saddlebags high, so I'd hear any critters trying to raid our pantry."

"Oh." She glanced above them to see the bags suspended from a tether attached to a high branch. "You must have done that while I was washing the dishes at the creek."

"Yeah. I know."

"You watched me?"

"I watch everything you do, Maggie," came the husky reply. "You know what they say about Indians having eyes in the backs of their heads."

"You are contemptible!"

She wiggled out of his embrace and continued observing the animals. She could make out the raccoons dipping berries into the water with their tiny paws, then munching warily, their little eyes glowing. "They're really kind of sweet."

She felt his arms slip around her waist again, then he nestled her back against his chest. "So are you."

Maggie froze, feeling Bronson's lips against her hair, his breath tickling the nape of her neck, and becoming very conscious of the heat of his naked chest seeping into her back, the potent male scent of him. The beast hadn't given her a corset, so only two thin layers of cloth—her dress and chemise—separated her from his hot, muscled body. One large hand was braced firmly at her middle, the fingers caressing upward, indecently close to her breasts.

"Release me!" she insisted in a trembling voice.

"After I've comforted you so tenderly?" he teased back. "I think you should at least reward me with a kiss. I'm your husband, after all."

"Only on a piece of paper," she argued breathlessly.

"No, Maggie," came his obdurate reply. "We're man and wife . . . whether you accept that or not."

"I'll never accept it. And let me go."

In response, he tugged her about until she faced him. Eyeing him mutinously, she could tell by the slight smile tugging at his mouth that he was up to mischief.

"I'll release you only after you reward your husband for comforting you. Indians are great bargainers, you know."

"Oh?" she replied flippantly. "I'd always heard they are accomplished thieves."

"A man can't steal his own wife. She's already his."

"This man just did."

To her increasing chagrin, he ignored her protests and snuggled her closer to him, until her breasts were crushed against his firm chest. Even as she squirmed, he whispered, "And I may just steal a kiss, too, if you don't offer me my just reward."

Maggie floundered. Given her husband's tormenting closeness and sensual teasing, she was actually tempted to offer a kiss and much more, though she would never admit it to him. She struggled to keep her breathing under control, so as not to betray her growing excitement.

She suspected he was not fooled. His teasing fingertip slid across her lips again, wrenching a gasp from her, and his tone grew more intense and solemn. "It feels like forever since we sealed our vows, Maggie. I've been yearning to taste your lips again ever since."

"Well, you can yearn until you turn into a pillar of salt!" she shot back.

He chuckled. "Do you really think I kidnapped you just because you are my wife, Maggie? I also did it because I *want* you. I've wanted you from the instant I laid eyes on you at the train station in Austin."

She was speechless, for the truth was hard to deny. She had wanted him, too—just as much.

His strong, rough hand cupped her chin, raising her rebellious face to his. The intensity of his gleaming eyes seemed to probe into her soul. A split second later, his demanding

lips claimed hers, and Maggie felt both outraged and secretly thrilled. Potent yearnings streamed through her at the
raw heat of his mouth, the overwhelming closeness of his
powerful body. She fought him nonetheless, thrashing
against him and pummeling his chest, while incoherent protests rose in her throat. He was heedless, his lips remaining
tight on hers until at last she ceased her struggles and gave
in to the passion she felt.

The moment she quit fighting, his tongue penetrated between her lips, plundering her mouth roughly and intimately. Maggie struggled anew, inundated by indignation,
lust, and wonder. Spasms of shock built into even more potent stirrings of desire. Never had she known that a man
could kiss a woman in such a scandalous manner; James
Brewster's kisses definitely paled in comparison! Mortified,
she considered biting him, then thought better of the rash instinct, fearing Bronson's temper, his potent virility. Again,
he did not force her, but simply let her exhaust her struggles
against him. She realized in ire and grudging admiration
that he intended to hold her captive in his arms until she
gave him the kiss he felt he deserved. After a while, it became easier, and yes, much more pleasurable, not to fight.
Maggie felt her traitorous arms stealing up to curl around
his corded neck. At once his kiss intensified, and he sank
his fingers into her hair to hold her face tightly to his. The
groan rising in his throat aroused an answering ache deep
inside her womanhood.

Abruptly he rolled onto his back with her still in his
arms, bringing her atop his massive body. She stared down
at him breathlessly, and almost winced aloud at the look of
implacable yearning in his eyes. She felt weak and helpless
against that predatory look, and even more enervated by
longing. She could feel her nipples instinctively tightening
and tingling against the pressure of his chest, and those
same darts of desire radiated low to settle in scandalous
parts of her. She felt totally unnerved, out of control.

"Kiss me," he demanded. "Kiss me now."

Shamelessly she complied, pressing her trembling lips to

his. Bronson crushed her so hard against him, she feared her spine might snap, while he possessed her mouth so intimately and thoroughly that she felt stripped of all defenses, totally vulnerable to him. His hands roved up and down her spine, caressing the curves of her bottom, her upper thighs, making her shiver and burn at once, as if those bold, tormenting fingers were actually penetrating inside her. Feeling him swell up hard against her pelvis, she moved against him instinctively.

He flipped her off him as if she had just struck him. They regarded each other with explosive tension in the night, both breathing hard. His eyes glowed like burning coals.

"Woman," he said with husky urgency, "you had best not wiggle against me again like *that,* unless you want me to give you something to wiggle about."

Maggie was too appalled to respond as Bronson turned his broad back on her. She pulled up the covers and shivered in shame and frustrated longing. She could not believe how easily she had lost control, lost all her convictions, and had almost given herself to her husband. The magical, potent desires he had stirred had swept her away on a powerful tidal wave.

On the other hand, she couldn't believe he had stopped. She had all but invited his advances, yet he had held back. What hidden motivation was driving him? How could he kiss her with desperate passion, hold her with bruising strength, and yet still gather the will to shove her away? His behavior made him seem all the more complex, enigmatic—and yes, desirable!

Next to Maggie, Bronson found himself fighting these same frustrated passions. His bride's sensual wiggle had just about been his undoing, and had spurred new doubts about just how chaste she might really be. Although he felt heartened by the evidence that his wife desired him, that she felt the same strong urges he felt, there were still too many unresolved issues looming between them for him to make love to her just yet. If he overwhelmed her before she was truly ready, she might later claim coercion, and anger, bitterness, and recriminations could easily poison their relationship. For these reasons he had rolled away from her, although doing so had nearly killed him.

Knowing he had made the right decision made it no easier for him to rest, with his bride so temptingly near, and memories of her uninhibited kiss torturing him throughout the night . . .

TEN

T<small>HEY STARTED OUT AGAIN SOON AFTER DAWN.</small> B<small>RONSON</small> led off on Blue Wind, with Maggie following on the pinto, tethered behind him. Remembering last night—Maggie's sudden fear, her stirring kiss, and how wonderful she had felt in his arms—Bronson smiled. He had wrestled with his thoughts—and desires—all night afterward, wondering why she had kissed him back, and whether or not she truly was a virgin or a soiled dove. Whatever her actual status, she had responded to him, and he gloried in that, more hopeful than ever about ultimately making her his spirit bride . . .

Hearing a groan, he glanced behind him and watched her bounce in the saddle. He grinned ruefully. She must already be sore as blazes after yesterday's ride—and he sure didn't want to see her tenderest parts ruined, especially not before he got a chance to enjoy them.

With a gentle pressure of his thighs, he halted Blue Wind, and pulled Maggie's pinto to a halt beside him. He dismounted and untethered her horse, eyeing her in the saddle; she sat astride but was perched stiffly, her skirts bunched between her thighs.

"Can't you manage to sit in the saddle any better than that, Maggie?" he asked irritably.

She rolled her eyes at him. "My, my. How could I have so quickly forgotten my equestrian skills?"

He chuckled. "Obviously you need some riding lessons."

"Obviously," she sneered. "But you didn't exactly think about that when you plucked me from my bed, did you, Mr. Kane? As a matter of fact, an immediate detour back to Austin would be even more greatly appreciated."

He stroked his jaw and considered her posture again. "You look about as comfortable as a tenderfoot sitting on a prickly pear."

"I *am* a tenderfoot, Mr. Kane."

"Are you?" He grinned wickedly and she blushed. "Well, Maggie, whether you're a true novice or not, at this rate, you're going to become blown before you ever become my bride."

"I beg your pardon?" she demanded shrilly, her face crimson.

"You've never heard of a blown horse?" he asked mildly.

"Of course not! It sounds depraved!"

"It's only a horse that has lost its wind," he teased devilishly.

"Ah. And I take this obscure allusion to mean that you would prefer to have a wife who has not lost *her* wind?"

He rocked on his bootheels. "Come to think of it, there's little chance of that ever happening with you."

She glared.

He reached up and grabbed her behind.

Shocked and horrified by his audacious move, Maggie squirmed, screamed protests, and flailed out at him. But he deftly dodged her flying fists while keeping his hand firmly rooted on her writhing rear end.

"What in hell do you think you're doing?" she shrieked, still struggling. "Take your disgusting hand off me at once!"

"No. Hold still, damn it." Bronson pinched her, further inciting her wrath, then grabbed the pinto's reins with his free hand. "I intend to teach you how to properly sit in the saddle, woman. So my *disgusting hand* will remain exactly where it is—"

"It will not!"

"—right on your tight little butt. Relax it, Maggie."

Her face burned. "Relax what?"

"Your squirming rear. You'll suffer a lot less if you just sit back and enjoy the ride."

With an outraged cry, Maggie eyed his cynical face to see if he had meant what she suspected he meant. From his grin, her assumption was correct, and he was positively vile. She gritted her teeth and churned in indignation.

"Relax, Maggie," he repeated.

"No."

He pinched her again, and when she bucked and screeched, he only grabbed a bigger handful of her posterior.

"You finished?" he asked.

Burning with frustration and feeling as if an octopus had dug its tentacles into her, Maggie realized that there was no reasoning with this beast, that she would have to endure his obscene grip until she complied with his orders. Hating him to the depths of her being, she relaxed against the saddle. Fighting a grin at her capitulation, Bronson wrapped the reins about his free hand, clucked softly, and the horse trotted forward, while he followed along with his other hand still maddeningly in place. Even with the horse walking slowly, Maggie began to bounce, to chafe her tenderest parts against her husband's hand—and to wince again.

"No." Grabbing a handful of her skirts, Bronson eased her bottom down against the saddle. "Ride *with* the horse, not on it."

She shot him a murderous look.

"Let's try again."

Ignoring her protests, Bronson continued the "lesson," pulling the pinto around in a circle while pressing his wife's rear into the saddle. For Maggie it was exquisite torture, though the torment came not from her saddle sores, but from her husband's shocking touch.

At last she gasped, "I think I understand."

He halted the horse and glanced up at her skeptically. "We'll see."

Releasing her at last and retethering the pinto, Bronson mounted his own horse and they galloped off. At once Maggie resumed bouncing, stifling her own gasps of discomfort so Bronson wouldn't be impelled to teach her any further "lessons."

But he turned and caught her grimacing. With a muttered curse, he again halted both horses.

"Damn it, woman," he said in disgust, dismounting and loosening the cinch on his saddle. "For a teacher, you're a slow study."

Watching him pull the saddle off his mount, Maggie wondered what devilment he was up to now. "Well, maybe you're teaching lessons I have no desire to learn."

He dropped the saddle and started toward her, hauling her down off the pinto. Tugging her back toward his own horse, he said, "You'll be riding with me, on Blue Wind, until you learn how to sit. I've taken off the saddle so you can feel the rhythm of the horse."

And him! "No!" she cried, digging in her heels, utterly appalled.

But he merely grabbed her about the waist and hoisted her astride his blanketed pony. Then he turned, throwing the extra saddle across the pinto's back. For a moment, Maggie considered trying to escape on Blue Wind, only to quickly remember that she had already observed Bronson summoning the pony with a whistle or even a gesture. If she tried to make a run for it, she'd be recaptured immediately, and from her husband's previous warnings, this time the touch of his hand on her bottom would be anything but gentle.

Her opportunity ended as Bronson strode back to her side. Anchoring the pinto's tether to his reins, he mounted in front of her. Mortified to have his body positioned so close to hers, she tried to scoot away.

His voice was unyielding. "Squeeze up closer to me, Maggie, so you can feel my body move with the horse."

"No!" The protest came out choked.

"Would you prefer to sit in front of me?"

In his lap, more likely! she thought frantically. "You—you wouldn't force me to—"

"Try me. Now, snuggle up tighter, or I'll help you."

Hating him to the depths of her being, she wiggled forward tentatively, groaning as her pelvis slid into his hard buttocks.

"Closer," he demanded.

Maggie was floundering. "Bronson, please—"

"Damn it, Maggie, quit acting like a blushing virgin and follow my instructions. We've got a lot of ground to cover, and at this rate, you'll never make it. Put your arms around my waist and mold your thighs to mine. Then I'll teach you how to really ride."

Oh, heavens! Maggie thought, fully aware of what the proposed "ride" would do to her. She hesitated, trembling, close to panic.

"Do it, Maggie."

Breathless, she complied, scooting even closer and curling her arms about his waist. She stifled a groan at his tormenting nearness.

"Press your knees against the backs of my thighs."

Maggie was close to the breaking point. "I can't."

He reached back with both arms, caught her beneath the knees, yanked her forward, and locked her thighs against his. "That's better."

It might have been better for him, she mused, but for her it was sheer torture. She was dying a hundred slow deaths to have her body locked so intimately with her husband's. She could feel Bronson's heat, his raw strength, his hardness, the subtle language of his body. She could hear his breathing, and could smell the enticing maleness of him. They were locked as tightly as two lovers; she couldn't even tell where she ended and he began.

Then the horse cantered forward, and the real agony began. The two of them, and the horse, moved as one being. With each powerful forward thrust of the horse, Maggie and Bronson's bodies glided tightly together, then contracted, as if they were engaged in the most scandalous act. Maggie's heart thumped wildly and her entire body went hot and flushed; she felt half-dizzy, her breath coming in shallow pants. She clung to her husband's waist not just for support, but also for her own emotional equilibrium.

"See?" he murmured in front of her. "You're not so hard to teach, after all."

Thinking of all the other lessons he intended to teach her, Maggie very much feared she would soon become his eager pupil.

Bronson, too, delighted to having Maggie's supple body molded to his as they glided over the prairie. Soon, they would truly be one, he vowed fiercely, when their bodies moved together in an even more intimate joining.

For Maggie, the "lesson" mercifully ended at noon, when they paused for lunch on a gentle rise carpeted with blue-bonnets. They ate in silence, broken only when Maggie's curiosity got the better of her toward the end of the meal.

"How soon before we get to the Indian village?" she asked.

Bronson glanced at Maggie. She was squatted on the ground across from him, her skirts a splash of pale yellow amid the vibrant blue flowers. She was sipping water and watching him warily with her pretty green eyes. He well knew what was on her mind. She was wondering how much of a reprieve she had left, and when she might escape him—

After feeling her lush body so close to him all morning, she didn't have a chance in hell!

He took a sip of coffee and replied, "With luck, late tomorrow."

Her chin rose a notch. "And I cannot talk you out of this?"

He tossed the dregs of his coffee into the grass and stood. "No." Stretching the kinks from his body, he asked, "Think you can manage to sit properly in your own saddle this afternoon?"

"Yes!" she spat back.

Although Maggie's expression was mutinous, she refrained from further conversation as they broke up camp. That afternoon they rode separately and talked little, moving over rolling hills and across wildflower-strewn prairies.

Staring at her husband's broad back as he rode before her, Maggie seethed at how relentless and stubborn he was. But she had to admit that her ride was a lot less painful now that she had learned to move in harmony with her horse.

As the day lengthened, her thoughts remained focused on escape. Time was running out. Tomorrow they might well reach the Indian village, and who knew what would happen to her then?

Toward sundown, they passed through a very large Hill Country ranch, and Maggie spotted a number of drovers out on the ranges rounding up calves. Maggie and Bronson waved to the ranch hands, and they waved back. She took especial note of the fact that most of the men were heavily armed with pistols or rifles.

She and Bronson stopped to make camp just beyond the ranch's last line shack. Again Bronson chose a site near water, with a bluff and a long stand of sheltering willow trees. Studying the wooded area, Maggie recalled that the tree line and the creek had extended back well onto the ranch, and she at once recognized this corridor as an excellent escape route. If only she could manage to evade Bronson for a moment or two! If she ran really fast, she might reach the ranch half a mile behind them, before her husband even noticed she was gone. Surely if she reached the armed drovers and told them her story, they would defend her. And if Bronson was foolish enough to pursue her, then he would get exactly what he deserved.

Convinced she had to give her rash plan a try, Maggie felt as nervous as a cat as she and Bronson set up camp. At the first convenient moment, she asked to be excused to see to her needs. She was relieved when Bronson merely nodded and led off the horses to water at the creek.

As soon as he was out of earshot, Maggie tore off into the trees, wincing as she was clawed by branches and brambles. Using the stand for cover, she rushed back in the direction of the ranch. Her breathing grew tortured and her mind raced. How much time would she have? Had Bronson already noticed she was gone?

She soon had her answer. She was rushing through a small clearing when she heard the sickening thud of hoofbeats. She turned and froze in horror—

A split second later, she was snatched off her feet so violently that the wind was knocked from her lungs. She groaned as she was hurled facedown across Bronson's lap on his horse. To her intense frustration, she realized he had retrieved her as easily as if she were a lost hat! They galloped off, Maggie feeling hellishly uncomfortable with her belly jabbed by the saddle horn, her posterior perched in the air, her skirts flying, her mortified face pressed close to her husband's strong thigh.

Seconds later, they were back at camp, and she was dumped unceremoniously. She landed hard on her bottom, disheveled and humiliated. In a flash, Bronson was down beside her, hauling her roughly to her feet, every inch of him radiating fury.

"I figured you'd try to make a break for it here," he said disgustedly.

"Yes, you would have—you bastard!"

He shook a finger at her. "Maggie, if I were you, I wouldn't be provoking me right now. If your bottom hadn't already taken such a pounding, I'd smack it good."

"My bottom is none of your damned affair!" she shrieked. "When will you get it through your thick head that I hate you? When will you take me back to Austin?"

"When you become a true wife to me," came the unflinching reply.

"Never in a million years!"

He ignored that. "Maybe afterward, if you're still unhappy, I'll think about letting you go. But you can't just walk away from this, Maggie. You can't escape me. I won't let you. You are going to give our marriage a chance."

She stamped her foot at him. "Oh, you are despicable! How dare you insist I fulfill my wifely duties when you know I want nothing to do with you! If we proceed as you are demanding, any number of things could happen . . . There could be a child—"

He gripped her shoulders, and his blue eyes smoldered into hers. "You'd hate that, wouldn't you, Maggie? My Indian seed growing inside you."

Maggie felt convulsed with sudden shame. "I . . . didn't mean that. I could never hate any child." She bucked up her spine and gave full vent to her wrath. "It's you I despise."

"Because I'm half-Indian."

"No!" she screamed back. "Because you deceived me and carried me off against my will! Even an Indian should have honor—and you, sir, have none!"

"Oh, and you're some kind of high and mighty saint, aren't you?" he sneered back. "Rejecting me because of my blood?"

"I . . ." Again Maggie felt her conscience needling her, and she was beginning to despair of ever being able to reason with this obdurate man. She clenched her fists and pleaded, "Bronson, this will never work. Just take me back. Please."

"No," he snapped, then seized her face in his hands. "And let me give you a piece of advice, Maggie. You'd best not try escaping once we get to my father's camp, because I *will* recapture you, and I will abide by the traditions of my people in disciplining you. Any brave faced with a defiant wife will beat her before witnesses. Not to do so would mean a terrible loss of face with the other warriors."

Her mouth fell open. "You really mean to follow through with this insanity!"

"You've been warned, Maggie," was all he answered as he strode off to gather firewood.

Maggie reeled with anger and incredulity. Once again,

she felt staggered by the complex nature of the man she had married. She had met Bronson the gentleman, Bronson the lawyer, Bronson the Texan—

More and more he was becoming Bronson the Comanche.

ELEVEN

"We'll be at the village soon," said Bronson.

Maggie glanced at her husband sharply and did not comment. Ever since her disastrous escape attempt yesterday, and her argument with him afterward, the two of them had hardly exchanged a word, and she had burned in rage and helpless frustration. The fact that they were now approaching the Comanche village only heightened her fear and exasperation. It meant that escape would become all but impossible. Her husband was obviously a skilled tracker, in tune with her every movement, possibly even guessing her thoughts and motives. She felt trapped, depressed, and more angry with him than ever. Who knew what horrors lay ahead for her? She was sure to be scorned by his people, at the very least.

It was clear to her now that she had married a man with a conflicted nature, that her husband was torn between the Indian and white cultures. And even though he had told her he might eventually return her to civilization, she didn't trust him. After all, he was all but insisting she "become" Comanche. What if he decided they should remain with the

Indians permanently? She would be stranded with him and his people in the savage wilderness!

She had noted the landscape changing in the last day. They had left the Hill Country behind and were entering an area of vast, grassy prairies which she had heard Bronson refer to as the easternmost edge of the Great Plains. Even now she spotted a small herd of bison grazing to the south. The terrain stretching before them was of low, flat stretches broken by stark mesas, of grass and cacti and wildflowers, clear skies occasionally circled by a red-tailed hawk or a bald eagle.

Although they were not in the true desert, they had moved past the civilized parts of Texas to the frontier, where the climate was more arid and much greater distances loomed between the cypress-lined streams. Here, even a successful escape might well culminate in her own death through exposure—if other hostile Indians did not threaten her. Her friend Minnie Walker had mentioned that, even though the federal government was trying its best to secure the Texas Indians on the reservations, hostile Kiowas, Arapahos, and Comanches still raided settlements all along the frontier.

"Did you hear me, Maggie?" Bronson asked.

She hurled him a glare. "I heard you. And if we are close to the tribe, then this is your final chance to behave with honor and take me back to Austin."

"You already know what my answer is there."

"Then why are you rubbing salt in my wounds?"

He regarded her grimly. "Because you have to understand that once we are in the village, things must be . . . different."

"Different," she scoffed. "Are you afraid I'll offend your Indian brothers with my White Eyes ways?"

"You might," he conceded tightly.

"And you think I care?"

"You should. Because, by tradition, there is only so much I'll be able to tolerate from you."

"You're just itching to thrash your disobedient squaw, aren't you?" she sneered.

"I'll do whatever is necessary to keep you in your place," he drawled back.

"And damn you for putting me in this position—and having the gall to take delight in your own treachery."

He responded with strained patience. "I'm really not enjoying this, Maggie. I'd be much happier if you accepted who I am—and that you're my wife."

"I accept who you are, all right—a low-down liar and a kidnapper! I simply want nothing to do with you."

A muscle jerked in his jaw. "You can bait me all you want, but it won't do any good. Before we reach the village, you'd damn well better listen to what I have to say—that is, unless you enjoy pain."

Fury flared in her eyes. "By all means, proceed. As you're aware, I'm your captive audience, Mr. Kane."

He was silent for a long, tense moment, making Maggie wonder if he would resume his lecture, or do some violence to her. She mused that her Irish temper would likely be the death of her before this was over.

"When we're with the tribe I won't be Bronson," he began at last. "I'll be White Wolf—Isa-Rosa. And you won't be Maggie—you'll be Prairie Star, Stella-Sanna."

Maggie bristled anew at this announcement. "How dare you give me an Indian name without my permission!"

He shot her a dark look. "You'd best remember it, because after we reach the tribe, I won't be using your white name any longer."

"And I won't be answering to anything else."

"You'll be answering to me—if you know what's good for you," he said with low menace. "As a squaw, you'll be expected to serve your husband—"

"I will never become your squaw and I will never serve you!"

"You'll also be expected to learn Comanche."

She went speechless with anger.

"I'll give you a few weeks to pick up the dialect," he

continued sternly. "After that, all communication between us will be in Comanche, or through signing."

"Hah! It will be a pleasure not to have to communicate with you at all."

"Oh—aren't you smart enough to learn another language?" he taunted.

"I'm plenty smart. I simply have no desire to!"

"I learned Latin at a white university," he stated. "You can learn my people's tongue."

"I will not."

"You will."

"Why, Bronson?" she demanded with an infuriated gesture. "Why must you insist on following through with this crazy, doomed venture?"

"I've already told you. I won't walk in your world until you understand mine. So how long you have to remain among my people is strictly up to you."

"Right. I kidnapped myself, didn't I?"

"You married me."

Through clenched teeth, she snapped, "Is there anything else?"

"Yes. You'll be sleeping in my lodge as my bride should."

"Never!"

"Never?" He grinned nastily. "You may not want to be so hasty. You see, if you're outside, exposed to the rest of the braves ... it is a tradition among Comanche brothers to share wives. And I have *many* brothers, Maggie."

She was mortified. "You—you would let them—"

"No. But if you sleep away from my tepee, it will be much more difficult for me to protect you, and harder to convince my brothers that I can't spare you on any given night."

"What a heartwarming custom!" she declared. "Tell me, do you partake of it?"

"Do you care?"

"No! That is, not unless you force me to contract some pox you caught from one of your brothers' squaws!"

Throughout their tense conversation, Bronson had tried to maintain his patience, but now his control snapped. He reigned in both horses, reached across and grabbed her by the hair. As she cried out and cringed in horror, he spoke with raw fury. "Maggie, more Indians have died from venereal disease and other maladies contracted from white devils than have ever been killed in battle. The greatest calamity ever befalling the People was the cholera epidemic of the early fifties, brought to the Plains by white settlers. Nearly half the Comanche died in the outbreak, all due to the gold fever of the *tahbay-boh,* who spread their pestilence across our territories. So if you want to taunt me, you had damn well better learn your facts first. Otherwise, be warned you can only push me so far."

As he released her, she glared at him and rubbed her scalp. Bronson galloped on, tugging the pinto into motion behind him. He mouthed curses under his breath, too angry to even look back at her. Sometimes he wondered if the Great Spirit was playing a cruel joke on him. For this quarrelsome woman often seemed more trouble than she was worth. She seemed determined to push him until he killed her—and at the moment, he was not far from obliging her.

Only moments later, as they crested a mesa, Maggie caught her first glimpse of the Indian village sprawled in the valley beneath them. Approximately two dozen buffalo-hide lodges, many sporting paintings of various animals, were sprawled near a stream lined with huge cypress trees. Maggie spotted a number of Indians roaming the camp, both children and adults, many of them half-naked. Horses grazed in the distance, the many-colored mustangs contained inside a makeshift corral composed of stacks of logs and brush curving outward along the tree line. Smoke curled through the camp, and dogs cavorted everywhere.

The sight of the village was totally alien and frightful to her. She felt nauseous with fear, her heart galloping and sweat breaking out on her hands and face. Realizing that in a matter of seconds, she would be thrust among savages, she for once abandoned her pride and turned to Bronson with desperation in her eyes.

"Please, it's still not too late," she beseeched.

Bronson whistled low under his breath, stunned by the look of panic on her face, by how genuinely frightened Maggie was of Indians. What had made her that way? Overheard horror stories? Or some more personal trauma?

Realizing she would not share her feelings with him even if he asked, he replied firmly, "Don't look so terrified, Maggie. Just what do you think my people are going to do to you—stake you out on an ant bed? You are my bride—and you had best remember that *being* my wife is your biggest protection here."

She didn't reply, but blinked rapidly in betrayal of her anger and fear.

He tugged on the tether, and they navigated down the embankment into the valley. At once hordes of Indian children rushed forward, barking dogs at their heels, as they exuberantly greeted Bronson with cries of "Isa-Rosa!"

Maggie studied the children while clinging tensely to the saddle horn. Many of the younger ones were adorable, with hard, brown, half-naked bodies, long black hair, rounded faces, and dark, bright eyes. They laughed and chatted with Bronson, while regarding Maggie warily.

Bronson led them toward the center of the encampment, where they were joined by adult Indians, who ranged from squaws in buckskin dresses with braided hair, to half-clothed braves and old men in buffalo robes. Maggie noted that many of the adults sported face or body paint, and wore gaudy jewelry ranging from silver earrings to strands of beads and copper armbands. Even from a distance, she could smell the rank odor of their bodies and the buffalo grease that they so liberally applied to their flesh and hair.

Obviously Bronson's arrival in the camp with a new woman was quite an event, Maggie mused, for it appeared as if every Indian in the tribe had now gathered about them. Like the children, the adults greeted Bronson in a friendly, familiar manner; they eyed Maggie with a curiosity mingled with distrust that left her feeling most uneasy.

Bronson dismounted and pulled Maggie down beside him. A small mongrel dog appeared, yapping insistently at Bronson's heels, and he hunkered down to pet the animal. "This is my dog, Chico," he told her.

Intensely conscious of the many dark eyes regarding her, Maggie did not respond.

Bronson stood and waited in silence as a man with flowing silvery hair, and wearing a buffalo robe, came forward. Judging by the old man's slight resemblance to Bronson, Maggie guessed he was her husband's father.

The man spoke briefly to Bronson in Comanche, and the only word Maggie understood was her husband's name, "Isa-Rosa."

Bronson answered briefly, gesturing toward Maggie, then the old man said something directly to her. She, of course, couldn't understand his words, but his tone seemed sincere.

Bronson turned to her. "My father, Chief Buffalo Thunder, welcomes you to our tribe, Prairie Star."

Chafing at Bronson's use of her Indian name, Maggie nonetheless acknowledged the folly of alienating the village chief, especially when the old man's words to her had been kind, even generous under the circumstances. Not knowing whether it was appropriate to look at or address Bronson's father, she whispered to him, "Please thank your father for me."

At her words, Bronson broke into a grin that maddened Maggie. He turned to relay her message to his father, and a moment later, Maggie detected a half smile on the old chief's face.

Suddenly a half-clothed warrior burst into the small circle. He was shorter than Bronson, with a lean, hard body, a proud hawk nose, and savage, coal black eyes. His hair was shoulder-length and black, like White Wolf's, and he wore a slender braided lock by either ear. The sight of the brave, his features so fierce and eyes so dark and feral, sent a shiver down Maggie's spine. He ogled her greedily, then turned to Bronson, his stance and tone very arrogant as he said something to her husband in Comanche and jerked his thumb toward Maggie.

As she stood helplessly on the sidelines, a long argument followed between the warrior and her husband. The brave kept pointing at her aggressively, and Bronson kept shaking his head. Remembering what her husband had told her about brothers sharing wives, Maggie wondered with horror if this man could be one of Bronson's brothers, and was demanding the right to bed her. The very possibility put Maggie in a near panic, especially as she recalled her flippant exchange with Bronson on the subject of wife-sharing. Would he give her to this half-clothed beast just to teach her a lesson?

Finally her husband grabbed her arm and pulled her away from the others. Maggie breathed a huge sigh of relief as they proceeded through the rows of lodges. "What was that about?" she demanded in a whisper.

He grinned, then confirmed her suspicions. "My half brother Black Hawk finds my white squaw most beautiful—with hair of fire and eyes of green ice. He demanded the right to bed you tonight."

Maggie gulped.

"Don't worry, I said no." Solemnly Bronson winked at her. "Now, don't make me sorry I've defended you."

"Oh!"

"Black Hawk will survive," Bronson added. "He already has several wives."

She jerked to a halt as a horrible possibility dawned on her. "Do you have other wives?"

"Not *yet,*" he answered meaningfully. "Does the prospect make you jealous?"

"Don't overestimate your charms," she snapped. "What about your father?"

"What about him?"

"How many wives does he have?"

His expression grew taut. "At one time, he had four. Only two remain living."

In her own emotional distress, Maggie didn't pause to wonder whether her careless words might have hurt him.

"And what did your mother think of your father's having so many squaws?"

"Not much," came the clipped reply.

He had just tugged her onward when a group of older women overcame them, several of the squaws bearing quirts in hand. Maggie blanched at the many hostile looks being cast her way. The leader of the group, a stout, rawboned creature whose leathery face bore a belligerent expression, stalked forward to confront Bronson, speaking to him in angry tones and jerking her head contemptuously toward Maggie.

Another long argument followed in Comanche between Bronson and the woman, then at last the group of squaws marched off.

Maggie stood with a palm pressed to her thumping heart. "What was the meaning of *that?*"

Bronson stared grimly after the group. "The women feel I violated tradition in not handing you over to them as soon as we arrived."

"What?" she cried.

"White female captives are usually turned over to the older squaws immediately, to be soundly thrashed and thus quickly adjusted to the demands of forced labor."

She gasped.

"Don't tempt me," he drawled, and tugged her inside a tepee.

Blinking at the dimness, Maggie stared at the surprisingly spacious, buffalo-hide-lined interior of the lodge. Two animal-skin pallets flanked a cold fire pit at the center. Along the eaves were stacked firewood, a bow and beaded quiver, and large parfleches which Maggie assumed held clothing and other personal items.

She raised an eyebrow to Bronson. "And what is this, Mr. Kane?"

"This is our lodge, Prairie Star," he replied. "And if you want me to answer you in the future, you will call me either White Wolf or Isa-Rosa."

She stared murder at him.

He began pulling at his shirt buttons.

Her eyes went wide. "What are you doing?"

He doffed his shirt and tossed it down. "Putting on the customary clothing I wear when I'm with the tribe." He leaned over to retrieve a parfleche, pulling out and handing her a white deerskin dress and beaded moccasins. "You will put these on."

Though the dress was soft, the moccasins lovely, Maggie was not about to follow her husband's dictates. "I will not!"

"Then shall I go fetch the women?" he asked mildly, proceeding to scandalize her by untying his buckskin trousers. "They'll be a lot less gentle with you than I'll be, if I'm forced to wrestle you down and strip you."

"I won't undress in front of you!" she said through gritted teeth.

"Fine. I'm changing my clothes, and then I'm waiting for you outside. I'll give you exactly one minute—"

"One minute?" she mocked. "So you keep a pocket watch out here in the wilderness?"

"I don't have to. Here I know time. And I repeat that you'll have one minute to change and hand me your *tahbayboh* garments, or I'm fetching Battle Ax and the others."

"Battle Ax?"

He broke into a self-deprecating grin. "My pet name for the old dragoness I was just arguing with. And she's not quite smart enough to realize the name is an insult."

"Perhaps someone should tell her," Maggie put in sweetly.

"Rather difficult to do when you don't know the language," he countered. "But let me assure you that Battle Ax and the others are strong enough to set a spitfire like you in her place, if that's what it takes."

Maggie did not reply. She watched Bronson begin shucking his trousers, and knew he was deliberately trying to shock her. Refusing to be baited, she stood her ground and stared at him defiantly, though the sight of his glorious nakedness made her hard-pressed not to shiver. If anything, the beast only seemed pleased by her perusal, damn his eyes! He donned a breechclout, knee-high, fringed mocca-

sins, and a bear-claw necklace, grinning at her the whole
time!

"One minute, Prairie Star," he warned, and ducked outside.

Muttering curses that would have put Aunt Prudence in
her grave, Maggie tore off her dress and shoes and donned
the Indian clothing. She hurled her frock and shoes out
through the tepee opening.

But her husband was not fooled, and she soon heard his
low, adamant voice. *"Everything,* Prairie Star. You will not
be allowed to keep any white clothing here."

"No!" Maggie protested, near panic. "I refuse to give up
my chemise or my ... bloomers. There are no undergarments included with this Indian regalia."

Her husband's voice came laced with a wickedness that
made her burn as she imagined the devilish look on his
face. "You won't need undergarments here, Prairie Star. Especially not with me."

"You are a heathen!" she screamed.

"Comanches believe in convenience," she heard him
drawl. "Now, throw me your underclothes."

"No!"

"Shall I come help you? Or shall I call Battle Ax?"

In less than a minute, the undergarments were hurled
through the opening. Maggie was livid as she emerged from
the lodge in the Indian dress and moccasins. Beneath the
dress, she was stark naked, and never had she felt more vulnerable.

She spotted her husband hunkered down, starting a fire,
Chico perched nearby. The small dog wagged his tail at
Maggie's approach; Bronson glanced up at her with an ap-
preciative gleam in his eyes.

"You look lovely, Prairie Star."

Clenching her jaw in fury, Maggie looked down to see
her civilized garments going up in smoke. She could have
eagerly clawed her husband's eyes out.

TWELVE

Staring at his wife, White Wolf had to struggle not to smile. Prairie Star did indeed look lovely in the fringed deerskin dress that hugged her shapely body like a glove; the cream color created a lovely contrast to the curly red hair that spilled down upon her shoulders. But every inch of his curvaceous white squaw radiated defiance, and her green eyes blazed at him.

He knew Prairie Star was furious at him for forcing her to don the Indian dress, then burning her white clothing. But as far as he was concerned, there could be no turning back for them. If they were to have any future at all, Prairie Star must join herself with him and his world, as in his vision. They would never become true spirit mates unless she first embraced the Indian way of life both intellectually and emotionally. White Wolf knew this transition would not come easily, for Prairie Star was determined to defy their destiny to the depths of her being. But luckily, here with the tribe, the traditions of the People would shape and mold her in a way that would save him from having to be unduly harsh with her: If she did not work, she would not eat; if she did not accept his people, they would shun her equally and undermine her in a dozen subtle ways. She was stubborn to her soul; but the People, bound up in their own culture and taboos, would be equally unyielding in their response to her obstinacy.

"You just *had* to destroy my clothing, didn't you?" she snapped at him.

He stood, dusting off his hands. "You won't need them here—and keeping your *tahbay-boh* garments might encourage you to escape."

"Meaning you plan never to allow me to leave?"

"That's not what I said."

"If you think my attitude toward you or these other savages is going to change one bit, just because you've forced me to don this ridiculous attire, then you are out of your mind."

He sighed wearily. "I've no more time to argue with you now. I must join my brothers for council. As for you . . ." His gaze flicked over her meaningfully. "I suggest you go find the other women and help them prepare supper."

She blinked at him incredulously. "It'll be a cold day in hell before I cook anything for you or those other heathens."

He crossed his arms over his muscled chest. "Then I presume you aren't hungry. Squaws who don't pull their weight around here aren't fed."

"For the last time, I'm *not* your damned squaw!"

He shrugged and started off, snapping his fingers to signal the dog to follow him. "Suit yourself."

She rushed forward and grabbed his arm, her face pale and her eyes large. "You're—you're just leaving me?"

He grinned. "Why, Prairie Star, do you crave my company more than I would have thought?"

She released his arm as if burned. "Don't delude yourself! That's not what I meant at all! Only a savage like you would leave me at the mercy of wild Indians."

"Right," he muttered, and started off again.

"Aren't you afraid I'll try to run off?" she called recklessly.

He swung about again. "No. There's no water around for fifty miles in any direction."

"I could make fifty miles on a horse," she asserted with a rebellious flip of her curls.

His eyes glittered dangerously. "Don't try it. The pinto you rode here is not your property, and my brothers abhor horse thievery. If you stole one of the ponies, there's not a brave in this tribe who would not skin you alive—and I wouldn't be able to stop them."

She gulped. "But Comanches steal horses from whites all the time."

"To their way of thinking, such are legitimate spoils of battle. But for a member of the tribe to steal from another would never be tolerated."

"So I'm a member of the tribe now?"

He stalked back to her and caught her shoulders. "Let me make something clear to you. The average white captive female brought to live among the Comanche is stripped, beaten, raped, and tortured. Yes, I'd say you're about as close as any white woman can get to being accepted as a member of this tribe."

Her eyes gleamed with fear and indignation. "How can you live with people who would do such despicable deeds?"

"Whose land was it first, Maggie? You tell me that! Who broke the treaties, stole our mustangs, squatted on our hunting grounds, and killed our bison?"

White Wolf stormed off, trailed by Chico, and it took Maggie a moment to realize that, in his agitation, her husband had slipped and called her by her white name. She stood in place a moment, twisting her fingers together nervously, wondering what to do. As much as she despised Bronson Kane and what he'd done to her, now that he'd abandoned her to fend for herself among hostile Indians, she felt utterly forsaken. Would he come to her aid if the others tried to harm her? Though it galled her to admit it, she'd given him very little reason to stand up for her. She'd reveled in defying him—but her defiance had exacted a price.

She watched him stride toward the center of camp, then

pause to speak with a pretty young squaw. Unaccountably, jealousy surged within her. She became further confused when he pointed toward her, then strode off.

The young squaw approached Maggie, and she was astonished to note that, although the girl had Indian features, her skin was fairer than that of the others, and her eyes were blue. She was really quite beautiful, short but slender, with long, chestnut brown hair in thick braids. She greeted Maggie with a shy smile. "You're white!" Maggie exclaimed.

"I Creek Flower," the girl replied solemnly. "I help you."

"Help me?" repeated Maggie. "But how?"

The girl hesitated, obviously struggling for the right English words. At last she said, "White Wolf ask I help. Teach duties. Teach Comanche."

"Oh, the beast!" cried Maggie. Watching the girl blanch, Maggie touched her arm in reassurance. "I'm sorry. Please don't let me scare you off. I'm angry at White Wolf, not you. It's really generous of you to offer to help me. And besides, this is not your fault, since you're a white captive too, aren't you?"

"White captive?" the girl repeated confusedly.

Maggie struggled to remember the word Bronson had so often used. *"Tahbay-boh?"*

"Ah," the girl murmured. "Creek Flower not *tahbay-boh*. Mother white, like White Wolf mother. Creek Flower mother taken squaw of Fire Lance. Creek Flower half-breed, like White Wolf. Creek Flower learn English from mother, like White Wolf."

"I see," said Maggie, feeling encouraged that there could be another full white woman living among the tribe. "Where is your mother now?"

"Happy Hunting Ground," the girl muttered, hanging her head.

"I'm sorry," said Maggie sincerely.

Creek Flower nodded, then continued earnestly. "I teach Prairie Star be good Comanche bride. I know—I be squaw of Silver Knife since autumn."

"Oh, congratulations," Maggie muttered, unsure what she should say. With grim determination she added, "And it's kind of you to offer lessons, Creek Flower, but I'm afraid they'll be wasted on me. You see, I want a divorce from White Wolf."

The girl was mulling this over with a perplexed frown when a group of squaws trooped past them, all eyeing Maggie with contempt and muttering behind their hands. The group included the harridan Maggie recognized as Battle Ax. The huge squaw wore a fearsome scowl as she stared at Maggie, and she spat at the girl's feet as she passed.

Maggie jerked back with an outraged cry. "Oh! The nerve!"

"Battle Ax think you lazy White Eyes," confided Creek Flower. "I hear her talk with other squaw. Think you unworthy bride for White Wolf. Want daughter, Brown Thrush, marry with White Wolf. Many maidens want marry with White Wolf."

"Wonderful," Maggie replied, musing that she had doubtless raised the hackles of most every female in the village.

Suddenly Creek Flower giggled. "Battle Ax proud to have name given by White Wolf. Think great honor. Not know name is insult to *tahbay-boh.*"

Remembering her argument with Bronson on this same subject, Maggie replied sarcastically, "It would be a shame not to educate her, don't you think?"

Creek Flower frowned in puzzlement and took Maggie's hand. "We help other squaw now," she said, pointing toward the creek, where many women had gathered. "Men at council. We prepare food. We feed warriors."

"You mean *you* feed," Maggie replied irately. "I refuse to become a slave to the beast who calls himself my husband."

Creek flower hesitated, obviously not fully comprehending Maggie's remark, but grasping the overall meaning well enough. "Squaw not work, not eat," she warned.

"Fine," declared Maggie.

Nevertheless, she grudgingly followed Creek Flower toward a section of stream not far from the center of camp, where she spotted women squatting at their labors beneath the sheltering branches of huge cypress trees. Maggie had to admit the setting was lovely—a cool breeze rustled the tree leaves, and the waters of the creek flowed sweetly over a small natural dam.

At creekside, every squaw in the village seemed to be present, as well as all of the older girls. Some of the women were nursing babies, others scraping hides stretched out on pegs, a few weaving and sewing, the balance stirring pots of buffalo meat, chopping roots or washing berries, or grinding pemmican. Maggie spotted her nemesis, Battle Ax, working on a tepee liner with sewing awl laced with sinew. Several younger women, who were gathered near the old shrew, eyed Maggie with resentment. Studying a heavy squaw who appeared to be a younger version of Battle Ax, Maggie wondered if this was Brown Thrush, the daughter Battle Ax had yearned to marry off to White Wolf. The girl's belligerent face and rawboned frame certainly matched the features of the older squaw.

About twenty yards to the east of the women, at the center of camp, were gathered the men, including Bronson, with Chico by his side. All of the braves were seated in a circle surrounding a large fire, and all were ignoring the women. The fierce warrior Maggie recognized as Black Hawk stood addressing the group in angry tones, making signs for emphasis and stalking about arrogantly. Maggie wondered if the brave was again demanding the right to bed her—from the grim expression on her husband's face, this might well be true. In any event, it galled her that all the males were lazing about this way while the females labored.

Maggie was following Creek Flower through the group of women when she suddenly tripped over an outstretched foot. With a startled cry, she crashed to her hands and knees.

Jolted by the painful fall, Maggie sprang up to the laughter and jeers of the other squaws. She at once spotted the culprit—the young squaw who so resembled Battle Ax. The girl was sneering at Maggie triumphantly, while Battle Ax grinned nearby.

Heedless of her own safety, Maggie grabbed a handful of dirt and flung it in the young squaw's face. "You did that deliberately, you big bitch!"

A chorus of gasps rippled through the ranks of the women. With a cry of rage, the squaw who had tumbled Maggie was up and charging her. Maggie managed to step aside in the nick of time, using her own ankle to trip her attacker. The large girl fell with a giant crash and a shriek of anger.

In a rush, four other squaws, including Battle Ax, charged up to attack Maggie, tearing at her hair and pummeling her with their fists. Although Maggie had never considered herself to be a scrapper, she fought for her life, ruthlessly hitting and kicking her assailants. Creek Flower bravely entered the fray, helping Maggie fend off the others while screaming at them in rapid Comanche. At last, after Maggie heard Creek Flower yell her husband's Comanche name several times, the women backed off, though they heaved in rage and glared at Maggie. After a tense moment, Battle Ax stalked off to pull the fallen squaw to her feet, and the group lumbered away, still hurling malicious looks at Maggie over their shoulders.

Maggie rubbed a bruised arm and waited until the women had proceeded a comfortable distance away from her and Creek Flower. She glanced at the circle of men, noting to her chagrin that her husband and the others appeared to have taken no note of her altercation with the bellicose squaws. Burning with indignation at her husband's callous disregard of her own safety, she turned to Creek Flower.

"Whew! I almost got scalped there. Thanks for helping me."

Creek Flower tugged at Maggie's sleeve and beseeched her with frantic eyes. "We go now. Not safe. You help Creek Flower pick berries."

"Wait a minute!" protested Maggie. "I want to know what's going on here. Who was the squaw who attacked me? Was that Brown Thrush?"

The girl nodded. "Yes, Brown Thrush. And Fast Fox, Meadow Lark, Morning Sun. All attack Prairie Star. All want marry White Wolf."

"Oh, splendid," Maggie groaned.

"Come, we leave," repeated Creek Flower urgently. "Pick berries."

"I'll come," conceded Maggie, adding defiantly, "but I won't pick."

Creek Flower tugged her off. "Come."

Maggie followed Creek Flower farther down the stream. Leaning against a tree trunk and trying to regain her equilibrium, she watched the girl pick dewberries near the rushing waters, gathering the fruit in her skirt. But the pastoral scene hardly soothed Maggie, since she remained furious at Bronson for not coming to her aid earlier.

"Not help, not eat," Creek Flower called plaintively.

"Don't presume I care," snapped Maggie.

Spotting Creek Flower's crestfallen expression, Maggie at once hated herself for the mean-spirited remark. Creek Flower had been the soul of kindness to her. The girl was also a victim just as Maggie was, a victim who had risked her own safety by coming to a white woman's aid. Still Maggie's pride forbade that she give in and perform "squaw work," for to do so would be indirectly giving in to Bronson. Although he claimed he only wanted her to understand and accept the Indian part of his heritage, she still didn't trust him, and suspected his real purpose was to make her his squaw forever. If she steadfastly refused to become his Indian bride, surely in time he would tire of her defiance and take her back to the white world.

Maggie simply could not believe all that had happened to her. Scant weeks ago, she had been a refined Boston lady; now she was parading about in a squaw uniform, scandalously minus her undergarments; she was engaging in fistfights with the most disagreeable creatures, and curs-

ing like a fishwife. She was in grave danger of losing her
white identity and spending the rest of her life in the
wilderness—

It was all Bronson Kane's fault.

THIRTEEN

WHITE WOLF SAT BY THE FIRE WITH HIS COMANCHE BROTH-
ers. He had just watched the other squaws attack Prairie
Star, and it had taken all his restraint to keep from charging
up and rescuing her. It was beneath the dignity of any brave
to intervene in a dispute among women; still, had Prairie
Star proven to be in true peril, he doubtless would have
gone to her aid, and risked the loss of face. All in all, he
had to admit she had done a good job of defending herself,
and he silently blessed Creek Flower for standing up for her.

He returned his attention to the council meeting. His half
brother Black Hawk was addressing the gathering in angry
tones. "My brothers," he said, "my spirit is greatly troubled.
The black hawk soars high in the heavens to protect his
people, but when darkness falls, the evil cannibal owl stalks
his loved ones in the night.

"My fellow warriors and I have been gone for many
days. With our brother Stone Arrow and his band, we rode
after the buffalo, but found the plains lined with the rotting
carcasses left by white hunters. Still we rode on, until our
horses stumbled and our bellies hurt. At last the buffalo
spirit blessed us, guiding us to a small band of bison. We

129

howled with the joy of the hunt, and our lances met their
mark. We brought back meat to our people—our children
are happy, our women smile, and our bellies are full.

"But soon more White Eyes will come with their fire-
shooting rifles. They will turn the plains white with bones,
and our people will starve. We cannot live on water and the
berries that grow near the rushing creeks. I beg you, my
brothers, to join me on the warpath against the white devils,
to save our people from being driven from their lands and
forced into extinction, as were our brothers the Cherokee
before us."

At his brother's reference to the Texas government's cruel
removal of the peaceful Cherokees from East Texas in 1839,
White Wolf noted several braves grunting in agreement.
Soon other warriors spoke up. Straw Horse endorsed the
call to battle, calling the white hunters treaty breakers without honor or soul. Rock Coyote suggested the tribe move on
to new territory. Black Hawk took the floor again, insisting
that if the tribe went on the move, the White Eyes would
sense their weakness; they would give chase and would not
rest until the People were herded to the reservations to be
locked behind fences forever, just as the Quaker Indian
agent wanted. The People must make a stand here, Black
Hawk argued. As he sat down, his words were met with
cheers from the other braves.

A silence settled over the gathering, with only the snapping of the fire and the puffing of pipes to fill the void.
White Wolf looked to see if Buffalo Thunder would speak.
But the old man merely nodded to his half-white son, signaling to him to take up the oratory.

"My brothers," White Wolf began in Comanche, "I urge
you not to act in haste. If we kill the White Eyes, the white
rangers and cavalry will hunt us. Many more warriors,
women, and children will die. Our band will be forced to
stay on the move. What will we have accomplished?"

"We will have defended our honor and our hunting
grounds!" argued Black Hawk, waving a fist. "We will have

taught the white devils they cannot steal our food and horses."

At the conflicting views between brothers, loud dissension broke out among the ranks. Several of the more bellicose warriors endorsed Black Hawk's aggressive statement, while others supported White Wolf's plea for caution.

At last, when all others had exhausted their arguments, Buffalo Thunder spoke his mind, his argument succinct and powerful. "A man may always kill an intruder on his own land. To mount a raid in retaliation is also acceptable, but the risk is much greater. When warriors venture into unknown territory, many Nerm lives can be lost."

White Wolf noted to his relief that most of the warriors nodded, evidently mollified by the wisdom of their chief, and willing to accept the more moderate course of action he proposed. Black Hawk, however, appeared far from appeased; although he honored etiquette and did not directly contradict his father, his black eyes smoldered with repressed violence.

Soon the women came forward to feed the warriors plates of buffalo meat, edible roots, and berries. White Wolf was angered to note that Prairie Star did not appear with the other squaws; instead, the lovely young Fast Fox, wife of Big Bow, brought him his tin plate and cup. Taking the food, he scanned the immediate area for Prairie Star, and spotted his bride standing in the distance, leaning against a cypress tree beside the creek. She was staring straight at him, a picture of defiance, her arms crossed over her bosom and her chin tilted at a proud angle—White Wolf could have cheerfully throttled her.

His brothers had also taken note of the insult his bride had dealt him, judging from the way they kept whispering to one another and laughing at him behind their hands.

Black Hawk was the first to address the matter before the group. With an angry gesture toward Prairie Star, he declared, "The white squaw of my brother dishonors him by not serving him. White Wolf must thrash her before witnesses or suffer loss of face."

White Wolf was glaring at his half brother when Buffalo Thunder spoke up. "Every warrior must decide how he disciplines his own squaw. It is not the place of a man to interfere in the lodge of his brother."

Black Hawk grudgingly backed down, but the snickering among the braves continued, and White Wolf's fury toward his bride only intensified. Prairie Star was obviously determined to defy him to the bitter end, while giving no thought to the risks she was taking.

Fast Fox brought him another slab of meat, and White Wolf deliberately smiled at the pretty squaw. The girl blushed and giggled before moving on.

He glanced again at his bride, and found that the proud set of her jaw had turned hard and angry. Good, he thought with perverse pleasure. Let Prairie Star see that, if she would not serve him, others would eagerly perform the task.

Maggie was indeed feeling jealous as she watched a lovely young squaw, with waist-length black hair, dimpled cheeks, and large, dark eyes, serving her husband. She was sure the girl was one of the squaws who had attacked her before dinner. Her temper boiled as she watched White Wolf smile at the girl.

Then she caught her husband staring at her, and she glowered back. Had he deliberately played up to the girl to taunt her, after she had refused to become his squaw and serve him his meal?

Did she care?

Unfortunately, Maggie found she *did* care. Even though she had vowed never to perform such menial duties, it irked her badly to watch another woman serve her husband and flirt with him. It maddened her to realize this man had such a hold over her.

It was also obvious that the warriors were taunting her husband regarding her defiance, and this made her feel guilty, as well as fearful of White Wolf's response. On top of these woes, Maggie was very hungry, and she would likely go to bed even more ravenous. She was feeling pretty wretched.

She chided herself for allowing such weaknesses to chip away at her resolve. Why did she feel torn and upset, when she knew she had charted the only acceptable course for herself? She had to resist White Wolf, or she would be lost . . .

Maggie was relieved to watch Creek Flower approach. "Who is the squaw serving my husband?" she asked the girl.

Creek Flower glanced back at the circle. "Fast Fox, squaw of Big Bow."

"She's one of the ones who attacked me today," Maggie related grimly. "Didn't you say she once wanted to marry White Wolf?"

"Many maiden want," replied Creek Flower. Slanting Maggie a chiding glance, she added, "Maybe White Wolf want second bride now. White bride not serve." She lowered her gaze. "Dishonor teacher."

Maggie sighed, feeling like a shrew. "Look, Creek Flower, I'm really sorry I didn't help you, especially after you risked your own safety to rescue me before dinner. And I realize Bronson—that is, White Wolf—is going to be furious at me—"

"White Wolf lose face."

"I know. I'm just sorry if you've had to suffer for it in any way."

The girl mulled this over for a moment, then tugged on Maggie's sleeve. "You come Creek Flower now?"

Intrigued, Maggie replied, "Of course."

She followed the girl through the trees. Once they were a safe distance away from the others, Creek Flower pulled Maggie to a halt. Glancing toward camp to make sure no one had followed them, Creek Flower untied a small pouch from her belt and handed it to Maggie. "Eat now."

Maggie was amazed and touched. "What is this?"

"Pemmican. Eat now, or go hungry."

Maggie opened the pouch and gratefully gobbled down

the mixture of jerky and dried fruit. "Thank you, Creek Flower," she said between bites. "You've been a true friend. And in the future, I'll try to figure out how to help you without giving in to my husband."

The girl nodded, although Maggie suspected she hadn't understood much of what she had just heard. After Maggie finished her repast, the two women were moving out of the thicket when one of Maggie's long locks caught on a yaupon branch. She cried out at the painful yanking.

Creek Flower reached out to free the curl. "Need braid hair."

"No!" cried Maggie.

Creek Flower lowered her gaze.

Maggie again felt terrible for rebuking the girl's kindness. "I'm sorry. You're right, I need to braid my hair for practicality's sake. Would you be so kind as to teach me?"

Creek Flower beamed. "Beautiful hair," she said, touching another of Maggie's locks. "Hair of fire. I braid."

The two women chose a quiet spot by the creek and sat down together. As Creek Flower gently tugged the tangles from Maggie's hair with a comb made of bone, Maggie enjoyed the brief, idyllic moments away from her troubles. She felt the cool breeze caressing her skin, watched the gilded light of the setting sun ripple over the waters, and actually laughed at the antics of a beaver building a dam downstream from them.

Once Maggie's thick locks had been smoothed out, Creek Flower carefully plaited Maggie's hair, tying the two thick braids with thin strips of rawhide. Creek Flower was all smiles over her handiwork, and Maggie felt thrilled to have pleased her new friend through this small acquiescence.

Dusk was falling by the time the women moved back toward camp. Maggie gasped and clutched her heart as suddenly Black Hawk loomed in their path. Magnificent, wild, half-clothed, the warrior stood tautly before them, his eyes dark with lust as he glanced first at Creek Flower, then at Maggie. A shiver streaked down Maggie's spine at the frightening intent in his gaze.

Then he jerked his head toward Creek Flower and stalked on. Without even glancing at Maggie, Creek Flower dutifully followed the brave behind a nearby tree. Maggie considered protesting, then bit her lip. She watched Creek Flower docilely lie down on her back, and in a flash, Black Hawk was on top of her—

What occurred next left Maggie rooted to the spot, fascinated and appalled. Although the tree trunk shielded the middle of the couple's bodies, it was obvious that the two were copulating—she could see Black Hawk's strong naked thighs thrashing, and could hear Creek Flower's low moans. Never in her life had Maggie seen two people engaged in the sexual act, and the sight of it excited her in a primal way that left her horrified—

Why on earth was this happening? Creek Flower had said she was the squaw of Silver Knife. Why was she allowing Black Hawk to abuse her this way? Unless Silver Knife was a brother of Black Hawk, she thought quickly; that would explain everything—but left Maggie feeling no less shocked and unnerved. Indeed, she had a feeling the virile warrior had staged this little demonstration partly for her own benefit—to shock her, and God only knew what else.

It was over in one intense, violent minute. Black Hawk stood, straightened his breechclout, and stalked past Maggie, giving her a lascivious look that made her blood run cold.

A moment later, a disheveled Creek Flower rejoined Maggie. Maggie noted to her relief that the girl did not appear frightened or abused. Creek Flower exuded an earthy, sensual aroma that scandalized Maggie. She reached out and gently plucked several twigs from the girl's hair, then brushed leaves from her dress.

"Are you all right?" she asked with concern.

Creek Flower nodded. "Comanche brother share wives."

"I've heard of the custom, but—"

"Black Hawk brother Silver Knife."

"Ah, I see. But doesn't it make you feel violated?" At the

girl's confused look, she explained, "Like you've been raped?"

Creek Flower continued to appear bewildered. "Black Hawk great warrior. Honor Creek Flower by bedding her. Maybe give great warrior son."

Maggie could only shake her head.

"Black Hawk bed all wives of brothers," Creek Flower added.

"*All* wives?" Maggie repeated shrilly.

"Bed Fast Fox and Spring Lark." More ominously, she continued, "Want Prairie Star now. I hear Black Hawk ask White Wolf for Prairie Star over meal."

Maggie gritted her teeth.

Creek Flower touched her arm and regarded her worriedly. "Prairie Star be warned. I hear talk in council. No more dishonor White Wolf. Black Hawk want punish Prairie Star for brother. Want bed, too. White Wolf lose face . . . maybe give Prairie Star to brother to punish. No good."

"Thanks for the warning," said Maggie humorlessly.

The girl nodded. "We go back. Almost dark."

With Maggie leading off, the two moved through the woods toward camp. They hadn't gone fifty yards when Maggie collided with a hard male body. She jumped back, terrified that they had again encountered Black Hawk, and found herself gazing into the smoldering blue eyes of her husband.

FOURTEEN

IN THE DEEPENING DUSK, WHITE WOLF'S FINGERS CLOSED over Maggie's wrist, and he tugged her off toward their tepee. She could tell from his forceful movements, and the fact that he hadn't even greeted Creek Flower, that he was furious at her.

He pulled her inside the lodge, where the embers of the banked fire still glowed. They faced each other warily in the dim light.

Eyeing his bride's braids, White Wolf couldn't resist flashing her an arrogant smile. "I approve of your hair. At least you're beginning to *look* like an Indian bride."

She harrumphed. "Well, I don't care what you do or do not approve of, sir! And don't get any ideas that I'll now become your subservient squaw. Creek Flower braided my hair, strictly for convenience sake, after I snagged a lock on a tree branch."

Maddened anew by her defiance, he grabbed her arm and hauled her hard against him. "I'd like to snag you on me," he muttered nastily, and felt pleased when fear and uncertainty flared in her lovely green eyes.

Then he watched his feisty, self-righteous bride seize control again. "Have you any additional crude remarks to offer, Mr. Kane?" she snapped. "I assume your purpose in dragging me off here is to behave as disgustingly as possible."

Dropping her arm, White Wolf ignored her barbed comments and her use of his white name. "I brought you here because it is time for us to sleep. Tomorrow our day will begin before dawn."

"What will we be doing then—pounding arrowheads?" she sneered. "Or perhaps roasting live captives?"

"Maybe I'll be roasting *your* backside if you don't learn some respect for your husband."

"Husband! How dare you presume to call yourself that."

"That's what I am, Prairie Star, and I'm tired of arguing with you. Get ready for bed."

She glanced warily at the two pelt pallets. "I can't believe you still expect me to sleep in this tepee with you!"

He smiled nastily. "You're welcome to sleep outside, but I must warn you that I won't be held responsible if one of my brothers takes you to warm his bed. Black Hawk lusts after you terribly, in case you haven't noticed."

"He lusts after everything in a dress!" she retorted with a furious wave of her hand. "Including poor little Creek Flower, whom he ravished right in front of my eyes."

White Wolf went pale. "He raped her?"

"Creek Flower seems too naive to realize she was being used."

White Wolf sighed. "I'm sorry my brother chose to assert his rights in such a blatant manner," he told her sincerely. "Our culture may be different from yours, Prairie Star, but we do not rape our women. I would fight my brother if he violated any woman in this village."

"Do you expect a medal?" she shot back. "All your high-minded ideals do not keep you from forcing me into virtual slavery!"

"Obedience of a squaw toward her husband is another matter altogether," he went on sternly. "As a matter of fact, Black Hawk thinks you deserve a sound thrashing for your contemptuous attitude toward me during supper, and he is eager to perform the task in my stead." Pausing, he jerked his head toward the tepee opening. "So by all means, sleep outside if you will, Prairie Star. It's your choice."

"I've had no choices ever since you abducted me, and you damn well know it!" she blazed.

He sat down on his pallet and began untying his moccasins. "And maybe you had best start accepting the realities of the situation."

"Such as?"

"I'd advise you to start acting more reasonable around me . . . and toward the rest of the tribe."

"Is that a threat, Bronson?"

He didn't answer.

"Are you threatening me, White Wolf?" she all but screamed.

"I'm warning you."

Her gaze beseeched the heavens. "Ah, a warning. I should be so grateful. So I'm to roll over and die when she-wolves like that obnoxious Brown Thrush trip me?"

"Were you hurt?"

"You didn't care!"

His voice rose a notch. "I said were you hurt?"

"*She* was."

He actually chuckled, and watched her bristle in response. "You'll have to earn the respect of the other squaws, Prairie Star. There's little I can do to help you there."

"There's little you *will* do."

"And if you know what's good for you, you *will* begin demonstrating a more befitting attitude around me and the other braves."

"On my back with my skirts hiked?"

He fought a grin at her unremitting feistiness. "That might be a good beginning—but only with your husband. For your own protection, you had best start serving me."

"Serving you?" she repeated sarcastically.

His gaze flicked over her meaningfully. "Yes . . . in more ways than one."

"Just as Fast Fox was so eager to serve you *in more ways than one* during dinner tonight?"

He grinned.

She waved a fist at him. "You brute! These tepees will turn to Boston brownstones before I ever serve you in *any* way."

He began removing his breechclout, enjoying the way she flinched and struggled to avert her curious gaze. "You've never wanted children, Prairie Star?"

She gulped. "I didn't say that."

"You don't want half-breeds?"

"I don't want *you.*"

"Don't be so hasty, Prairie Star. If my brothers don't observe you breeding soon, they may assume I'm not equal to the task."

"You're not!"

Something snapped in White Wolf then, and he lunged to his feet.

Maggie instantly regretted her diatribe, and fully expected White Wolf to kill her. Her husband loomed over her in a black rage, stark naked, an immense, hard-muscled brown savage, his chest heaving, his fists clenched and eyes blazing, his manhood *very* aroused. Maggie felt horrified and fascinated, going weak at the overwhelming power of the man confronting her, and especially at the size of his thick erection straining against his belly. Oh, God, she had erred terribly, affronting him past redemption. Now he would rape and kill her . . .

He continued to face her in his fury, and she was stunned when he did not hit her, strangle her, or throw her down to ravish her. Instead, after a charged moment, he bent over, picked up her pallet, and flung it on top of his.

"Wait a minute!" she cried. "Now where will *I* sleep?"

"I don't give a damn!" he roared back as, with quick, economical movements, he lay down, pulled a bearskin pelt up over his body, and turned his broad back to her.

Maggie seethed in helpless frustration as White Wolf continued to ignore her. The fire was almost gone now, and the

tepee was growing dark and cold. At last she gave up and
lay down on the thin buffalo-hide tepee liner, all that separated her from the hard, bumpy ground.

Almost at once, she began to shiver. Not since White
Wolf had kidnapped her had she felt a chill like this . . . but
then, every night she had slept beneath thick blankets or
heavy pelts. If White Wolf wanted to punish her for her
reckless tongue, then he was doing a masterful job.

At last, miserable and shaking, she abandoned her pride.
"Bronson, please, I'm cold."

He ignored her.

"White Wolf, I'm cold."

He still did not respond, though she heard him thrashing
about in the darkness. She struggled within herself, her conscience nagging her and her teeth chattering. The truth was,
she *had* gone too far, insulting her husband horribly. But
what if she apologized? Would White Wolf assume she was
willing to sleep with him? After seeing him in the glorious
altogether, she trusted her own instincts no more than she
trusted him . . .

White Wolf, too, was struggling within himself in the
darkness. Prairie Star had defied him terribly, but it would
be cruel of him to let her continue to shiver. He'd stolen her
pallet in the hope that she would become compelled to seek
his comfort, his warmth . . . and all the passion his hard
warrior body yearned to give her. Her defiance had only further fueled his desires, making him long to tame her in the
most elemental way. Even now, it took all his control to
keep from grabbing her and somehow persuading her to let
him have his way.

He was about ready to give in and toss her a pelt when
he heard her moving about, crawling toward him. He turned
slightly and could just make out her form in the shaft of
moonlight slanting in from the smoke opening above them.

"White Wolf?" Her voice shuddered with cold.

He grunted.

"Look, I'm sorry I insulted you so. I went too far, all
right? I'll admit it."

He said nothing.

Her voice lowered an octave, becoming almost seductive, though still trembling slightly. "I—I think you've shown me what you're capable of doing."

Realizing her intentional double entendre, White Wolf almost laughed.

"I didn't mean to insult your manhood. And I'm freezing cold. *Please,* will you give me—"

Turning and catching her nape in his large hand, he asked huskily, "What do you want me to give you, Prairie Star?"

He felt the trembling of her flesh, and heard the quiver in her voice. "A blanket!"

"No," he teased back. "I think my bride wants much more, and the white wolf is most eager to please her."

White Wolf hauled his woman down beside him on the pallet. Predictably, Prairie Star balked. For a few seconds they struggled wildly, but White Wolf's superior strength easily subdued her, and soon he held her pinned beneath his naked, aroused body.

"No! No! Let me go!" she protested, sounding almost hysterical.

He grasped her face in his hands. "Prairie Star, look at me. *Look* at me."

At last she ceased her resistance, though she was still gasping for breath as she met his eyes warily in the pale light.

"I'm not going to hurt you—or force you," he said solemnly. "But I *am* going to kiss you . . ."

He lowered his face slowly toward hers, and Maggie felt powerless, riveted to the spot. To her horror and amazement, she found she understood her husband's feelings entirely. She felt the same urgent, potent need. It was as if the entire day, all the bickering between them, had built toward this explosive moment.

When White Wolf's hard, warm lips captured hers, the contact was electrifying, intensely exciting. He felt marvelous on top of her—so hard, so muscled, his body hot against her chilled flesh. His turgid manhood burned its imprint into her pelvis. Only her deerskin dress separated her from his tempting nakedness. He could so easily raise her skirt and take her virginity. And yet, instead of inspiring terror as it should, this knowledge made her ache with desire for him, until she throbbed.

All at once, Maggie was tired of fighting him ... especially when giving in felt so good. She curled her arms around his neck and let herself succumb, if only a little, to the potent feelings his nearness aroused. He responded with a groan and plunged his rough tongue into her mouth, and she shuddered with pleasure and stroked him with her own tongue. The taste of him was warm and drugging, the scent of him a potent aphrodisiac. He began undoing the ties on her bodice, and when she squirmed in renewed fear, he stilled her struggles with more thorough kisses. His deft fingers moved quickly at her breasts, his passionate lips more slowly. He trailed warm kisses down her jaw, the curve of her neck ... Then she felt his hot breath, his wet lips, tickling her bare nipple. She bucked in renewed panic, but he held her fast, taking his time, teasing the ripe peak with his skilled, tormenting lips. Maggie cried out and arched ecstatically. The sensation was exquisite, shattering. Her nipple tightened in a painful response that left her writhing. He murmured soothing words, only to prompt her renewed struggles when he boldly sucked the tender bud into his mouth.

Maggie screamed softly. She had never known such rapture could exist. When White Wolf drew hard on her breast, engulfing her flesh with his mouth, the intensity of the pleasure racked her with chills. With the devastating intimacy, her resistance faded ... She found herself wantonly thrusting her nipple against his wet, flicking tongue, digging her fingers into his broad, satiny back, and quivering against him.

Suddenly his hands were everywhere, slipping up her dress, caressing her legs and thighs, cupping and kneading her bare bottom, kindling the ache between her thighs into a blazing need. Maggie tossed her head and sobbed under her breath. Wolf White sought her lips, skillfully smothering the frantic sounds. Maggie felt feverish, out of control, her heart hammering, her flesh crying out for her husband's heat. She mused that she must be out of her mind, for she was in the arms of a wild, totally aroused savage who was determined to have her—

And having her would also mean she would become White Wolf's squaw forever! This jolting knowledge at last brought full-fledged panic crashing in on her, and hurled Maggie to her senses. Somehow, she managed to wrench her lips from his.

"Bronson, no! No!"

In her incoherent state, she did not realize what name she spoke. He intensified her panic by hiking her skirt to her waist, making her state of mind, and her desires, equally frenzied. She felt his shocking hardness probing between her thighs, and a reckless, forbidden thrill shook her. He found the feminine center of her with an ease that took her breath away, and began to burrow there, the large tip of him hurting her slightly. Maggie gasped and squirmed, her mind careening.

"White Wolf, no!" she cried.

This time she reached him. He pulled back, breathing hard and staring at her in the darkness. Although he stopped short of impaling her, he did not withdraw from her flesh.

"Please, no," she repeated.

"Calm yourself, Prairie Star," he whispered, slipping a hand beneath her to keep her from squirming away from him.

She shuddered. "How can I be calm with you—with that—"

He pressed a finger to her mouth. "I told you I won't force you. Just feel me now."

He pushed against her a little, prompting a low wince as she felt the power of him against her own tightness. She could not trust herself to speak over the thundering of her heart.

He reached down and stroked her cheek. "You are a virgin, aren't you?"

She nodded in mute misery.

"I will be your first man," he said proudly. "Your only mate—ever."

Again words failed her.

"This is how it should be," he went on tenderly. "I want to be so close to you, Prairie Star. I want to penetrate inside you until our souls are joined. Your defiance will fade once we are one mind, one body, one heart. Let me make you my bride, my spirit mate."

His ardent words made her want the intimacy, too—want it with all her heart—and made her body go moist with longing. The involuntary response shamed her on one level, and yet she gloried in it, too.

He spoke her thoughts for her, while rubbing against her provocatively. "You want this, too—you grow wet to receive me even as I speak our hearts. Take me deeply inside yourself where I belong."

"White Wolf, please, I can't," she whispered miserably.

He heaved a pained breath. "You are sure?"

She nodded, while wondering what terrified her the most—the prospect that he would heed her demands, or that he wouldn't.

He withdrew from her, and Maggie wasn't sure whether to feel relief or disappointment.

"You are not ready yet," he murmured patiently, kissing her cheek. "But soon you will be—for it is the destiny of the White Wolf and the Prairie Star to be joined."

He rolled away from her. Afraid of what she might do if she remained on the pallet next to his magnificent body, she crawled off into her corner, only to curl up in a ball, agonized with need. The humiliation, fear, or rage she should have felt were totally absent—she felt only the fiercest longing, the keenest regret that her world and White Wolf's were so far apart, and that she could not give herself to this captivating, untamed man. She wanted him now with a vehemence that left her deeply shaken.

Even more unsettling, Maggie was now very much afraid that her husband had spoken the truth—that something very spiritual and elemental drew them to one another. As they had kissed, she had felt the intensity of that bonding in her heart and soul, though her intellect sadly recognized that joining herself with this man of another culture could bring her only disaster, removing her not just physically but also emotionally and intellectually from the civilized world she so badly needed in order to sustain her own sense of identity.

Oh, what was she to do? If she stayed here much longer, and continued to share his tepee, she was certain to succumb to him!

She shivered with cold, and the painful awareness flooding her. A moment later, she felt a buffalo pelt slip over her shoulders, and heard White Wolf's whispered words, "Sleep now, Stella-Sanna."

But the blanket offered a warmth her desire-starved body could no longer feel . . .

As he returned to his own pallet, White Wolf also missed Prairie Star's warmth, even as his warrior body burned with sexual frustration.

Nevertheless, he was glad he had not forced her, for he knew he would never be satisfied with anything less than her complete surrender. He exulted in the intimacy they had shared, and especially in his own discovery that she was a virgin—*his* virgin. Now he would no longer have to worry that the memory of some previous lover might intrude in her thoughts as she lay in his arms. She would be his alone, his to awaken to the sensual, his to taste and savor . . . and tonight the taste of her had been so sweet, leaving him ravenous for more!

Yet new doubts tormented him. He was convinced Prairie Star was hiding something, that she had fled some dark secret in Boston. He still could not fathom her intense fear and hatred of Indians, her diatribe and destructiveness on their wedding night. Why was she so determined to reject his kind, when, as far as he knew, she'd never before had any contact with people of his heritage? Why couldn't she understand that the two of them had to become one in the Comanche world before they could consider a return to civilization?

He vowed that in time, he would unlock all her secrets. He would teach her the folly of her own destructive pride, even if the lesson brought her pain in the teaching. She was his bride, and he would not settle for having less than all of her, body, heart, and soul. No part of her would be safe from him . . . and especially not that tight, wet part of her he was so hungry to plunder.

FIFTEEN

WHEN MAGGIE AWAKENED THE NEXT MORNING, WHITE WOLF was already gone. She was relieved not to have to face him following her own scandalous lapse last night. Never would she have dreamed she could feel such fierce yearnings for a man who was half-Comanche; but her lust for White Wolf was now as real and powerful as her resentments and anger.

After carefully separating their pallets, she ventured outside. The morning was cool; the scents of woodsmoke, dew, and nectar laced the air. A cardinal sang in the nearby brush, and blue jays and mourning doves flitted about in the light-dappled trees. Maggie had to admit that the pastoral scene was appealing, the tranquillity a marked contrast to the city noise she was accustomed to in Boston. She could understand how White Wolf would find this life, and the lure of the savage tribe, irresistible. So irresistible that he might never want to leave this untamed country . . . and she had best not come to appreciate it too much herself!

The wilderness also spawned the inevitable inconveniences, she thought ruefully, ducking into a wooded area to relieve herself. She emerged and headed back toward the center of the village, passing women cooking, men grooming horses, children playing. But still she did not see White Wolf.

"Good morning, Prairie Star," called a feminine voice behind her.

Maggie turned to see Creek Flower approaching. "Good morning to you. Have you seen White Wolf?"

"Your husband ride with Silver Knife," Creek Flower explained. "He ask I watch you. Soon he return."

"Ah—so that's where he is."

Creek Flower took Maggie's hand, and asked conspiratorially, "You hungry?"

"Yes."

Creek Flower led Maggie to a small clearing that fronted her own tepee; the two women squatted by the open fire and ate corn mush in gourd bowls, using crude wooden spoons.

"You have baby soon with White Wolf?" Creek Flower asked.

Maggie half choked on her mush. "I don't think so."

Creek Flower frowned, appearing confused. "White Wolf make pretty baby with Prairie Star—red hair, blue eyes. Very pretty."

Uncomfortable with the subject matter, Maggie asked, "What about you? Do you and Silver Knife want children?"

The girl's expression turned wistful. "Yes—but not have yet. Comanche bride no breed good like white captive. Even when Comanche squaw breed, many miscarry, many papoose die young."

"Maybe you should give it some time," Maggie said gently, while inwardly she sobered at the thought of any woman trying to raise a child here, beyond civilization.

"Maybe Black Hawk help Creek Flower make husband happy," the girl replied.

Maggie was astounded by Creek Flower's nonchalant assumption that she would please her own husband with another man's child! The customs of these people were incredible! Maggie also felt sorry for Creek Flower, because she could readily see that the Comanche's nomadic way of life doubtless did diminish the fertility of many of the squaws. Although Maggie had only been with the tribe for a day, she was already appalled by the Comanche diet, which was so dependent on buffalo meat and so lacking in dairy products, fruits, and vegetables. The absence of sanitation in everything from food preparation to personal hygiene was also troublesome to her. Awareness of the poor quality of life here only increased Maggie's determination to leave, especially before she risked becoming pregnant herself!

Once the two women finished eating, Creek Flower set aside their dishes and pulled Maggie to her feet. "You come now. I teach good today, please White Wolf."

Maggie groaned at this evidence that her husband had left behind instructions that she was to be given additional "squaw lessons." But she liked Creek Flower and needed her friendship too much to risk alienating her by refusing the overture. She dutifully followed the girl through the village, watching and listening as Creek Flower pointed out various tasks being performed by the Indian women.

Although Maggie remained determined to resist indoctrination into the Indian way of life, the teacher in her watched in awe as an elderly squaw intricately beaded the covering for a cradleboard. She observed another squaw weaving a basket in such an airtight manner that, as Creek Flower explained, the vessel could actually hold water without leaking. She watched wood being gathered, hides being stretched, pegged, and scraped, buckskin clothing being sewn, corn being ground, and buffalo meat being roasted. Outside one tepee, she was fascinated to observe a teenage girl fashioning a doll for her little sister by shaping and tying cattails, and to watch the girl's mother prepare colorful clothing dyes by simmering chopped-up plants and roots.

All of the squaws went about their labors with an amazing energy, devotion, and contentment. Although Maggie was not greeted warmly, she noted to her relief that at least there was none of yesterday's hostility. For the most part, she was politely tolerated; even Battle Ax and Brown Thrush seemed restrained, ignoring Creek Flower and Prairie Star when they paused to watch mother and daughter make hickory brooms by painstakingly slicing many layers of strips into straight lengths of wood. Maggie had to chuckle at the sight of the brooms—for never in her life had she encountered two likelier witches!

What fascinated Maggie most were the youngest children. Although the older youths were reserved around her, the tots on their blankets, with their dolls and rattles, seemed fascinated by her, with her fair skin and red hair. Several of them cooed or gurgled at her as she passed, and she smiled back, careful not to venture too close to the little ones when their mothers regarded her with open hostility.

Nonetheless, she paused when she felt a tug on her dress, and looked down to see a small boy, who appeared no more than two and a half, grinning up at her and extending a bouquet of wildflowers. Maggie was enchanted.

"Little Bear Claw like you," announced Fast Fox.

Maggie squatted to get a better glimpse of the Indian cherub, who stared back at her with equal fascination. Dimples adorned his precious, rounded face; dark eyes flashed with mischief; thick black hair hung about his chubby shoulders. His cute little belly curved outward, and he was totally nude, except for a bear-claw necklace and a breechclout. His shy smile stole her heart away.

"So you're Little Bear Claw," Maggie said, pointing toward the flowers in his fingers, then toward herself. "Are those for me?"

He shoved the bouquet in her face and crowed loudly.

Laughing, Maggie took the flowers, deeply touched by the sweet, innocent gesture. "Thank you most kindly, sir."

Suddenly Maggie heard a woman shrieking in rage, and the next thing she knew, she was hurled backward and lay sprawled in the dirt, the flowers having flown off in all directions. Grimacing from the jolting fall, she sat up to see an irate squaw looming over her, clutching the baby possessively. Little Bear Claw appeared on the verge of tears, his face pinched with fright as the woman holding him shouted at Maggie in rapid Comanche.

A moment later, the squaw turned on her heel and stalked off with the child, and Creek Flower rushed forward to help Maggie to her feet.

"What was the meaning of that?" Maggie demanded, brushing herself off.

Creek Flower sadly shook her head. "Meadow Lark, mother of Little Bear Claw, not trust Prairie Star. Think you harm baby. Not understand."

Maggie was outraged. "Oh, of all the . . . How could she possibly think I would harm an innocent, precious child?"

Creek Flower grimly lowered her gaze. "*Tahbay-boh* kill children at Council House fight, women at Plum Creek. Little Bear Claw son Black Hawk. Maybe one day be great chief. Mother must protect."

Maggie mulled this over with a frown. "You mean that harpy who attacked me was Black Hawk's wife?"

"Yes, was Meadow Lark. One of six squaw of Black Hawk."

"*Six?*" Maggie repeated in horror. "You can't mean he has six squaws and he still lusts after the brides of all his brothers?"

Creek Flower's gaze darted toward Meadow Lark, who stood at some distance, glaring at them. The girl nervously tugged at Maggie's sleeve. "We go now. You no mean harm. Soon Meadow Lark forget angry."

Trudging off after Creek Flower, Maggie could hardly share her friend's optimism. The two women retreated to their spot outside Creek Flower's tepee, and the half-Indian girl spent the balance of the morning teaching Maggie Indian words and signs. Maggie learned that *Nermernuh* meant "People"; *puha* meant "medicine"; and *tejano,* a Spanish word invariably spoken with contempt, was the name used for the hated Texans. She learned that the name of this particular Comanche band, *Pehnahterkuh,* meant "honey-eaters." Then, at Creek Flower's insistence, she mastered the rolling, snakelike motion of the fingers that meant "Comanche," the horns-on-the-head sign that meant "buffalo," and the various open palms to crossed hands and circled fingers gestures that signified her own Comanche name, "Prairie Star."

Maggie tried to be a good pupil, but her heart was not in her lessons following the frightful encounter with Meadow Lark, the blatant evidence that she was *not* wanted here.

The morning that had started out so lovely had been ruined for her. Why had White Wolf brought her here? She would always be an outsider, as feared and distrusted by these people as she feared and distrusted them. The prospect of spending the rest of her life here, always feeling separate from the others, watching herself and her children endure hardships she couldn't even imagine, was daunting indeed.

SIXTEEN

WHITE WOLF RODE THE PLAINS WITH HIS YOUNGER BROTHER Silver Knife. He loved moments such as these, when he could commune with the natural world. Astride his fleet black pony, he felt alive, wild, and free, the wind in his hair as he galloped through the waving grasses and succulent wildflowers. A screech of flying quail created a dramatic backdrop to the thundering of horses' hooves.

His thoughts remained very much focused on Prairie Star and how close they had come to consummating their feelings last night. How he dreamed of the day when they were truly one, when they could ride this vibrant prairie together.

He knew he could have completed her seduction last night; a little more patient wooing would have defeated her panic. But he had stopped because he had to have all of her. And he would not allow even a hint of force on his part to threaten their future relationship.

Would she continue to resist him, resist learning about his world? He hoped not, and this was one reason he had ridden off this morning, leaving her to be taught by Creek Flower. Perhaps with him absent, she might give in to what he was sure was a natural curiosity about the tribe, without losing face.

But in leaving her, he had also taken a risk, for what if she foolishly chose to try to escape? The frontier held many dangers, and if Prairie Star did try to run away again, the greatest threat to her would likely come from other sources and not his people . . .

Abruptly White Wolf's thoughts scattered at the sound of a rifle discharging in the distance. Sensing danger on the air, he reined in his horse, and signaled to his brother to do the same. The two warriors paused their mounts beneath the branches of a scrub oak. The spirited war ponies snorted and stamped the ground as the brothers communicated briefly through signs. White Wolf asked Silver Knife if any braves from the tribe were out hunting with rifles today; Silver Knife shook his head, and White Wolf signaled that they would investigate.

They cantered their horses on, following the sounds of the rifles, advancing warily to the crest of a nearby mesa. Both stared in disgust at the scene unfolding beneath them. In a sea of tall buffalo grass, a gang of at least a dozen hide hunters were pursuing a small herd of bison. White Wolf was certain he recognized Skeet Gallagher among the buckskin-clad scoundrels who were felling the buffalo right and left with blazing Sharps or Hawken rifles. A haze of smoke hung over the prairie as the beasts collapsed in their tracks with bellows of pain.

In the distance waited the hide wagon, two buffalo skinners ready to advance when the slaughter was completed. Soon the hunters and skinners would wield their sharp knives and cut off the coveted hides, leaving the meat to rot, and thus stealing food from the Nerm. It was just another travesty on Comanche lands, White Wolf mused grimly, a theft sanctioned and even encouraged by the white authorities.

But today the villainy of the *tahbay-boh* would not be tolerated!

White Wolf turned angrily to his brother. The two again

communicated through rapid signs, debating whether they should stay and try to take on the hunters alone, or go for help. They quickly decided upon the second course, and galloped off.

Maggie was alarmed to watch White Wolf and Silver Knife gallop into the village, both men gesturing angrily, and shouting words in Comanche. At once, the other Indians converged on them, and an angry roar of fomenting bloodlust filled the air.

Maggie grabbed Creek Flower's arm. "What is happening?"

Creek Flower's features were fraught with apprehension. "White Hunters intrude on our lands again—kill many bison. Warriors will make council, decide what must be done."

Just as Creek Flower had predicted, the braves of the camp quickly gathered in a circle and began passing the pipe and making council. Maggie stood in the background with the women; she could see White Wolf, but could not catch his eye ...

Sitting with legs crossed beneath him, White Wolf listened as one warrior after another endorsed a call to battle. Fists were raised and voices surged in anger at the reported treachery of the *tahbay-boh*. Although White Wolf abhorred violence, he realized that this time his brothers were right. Their food supply was threatened, and they must act.

When his turn came, White Wolf stood and spoke quietly, while reinforcing his words with dramatic signs. "My brothers," he began, "you all know of the white wolf's hatred of bloodshed. You know my heart bleeds when our warriors must fight, when they must die for our people and their squaws weep, their children go hungry. But this time the *tahbay-boh* hunters have given us no choice. They have invaded our hunting grounds. They have stolen food from the mouths of our children, and they must be driven from our lands. If the council issues a call to battle, the white wolf will ride with his brothers."

White Wolf picked up his lance and drove it into the ground, to the cheers of the others. Even Black Hawk stood and yelled triumphantly, "The white wolf has found his medicine at last!"

More hooting followed, then a hush fell over the warriors as all waited for the chief to add his wisdom. Nodding soberly, Buffalo Thunder said, "My sons have spoken the truth. You must drive the thieving White Eyes from our lands. Otherwise, our women and children will starve."

A mighty whoop went up from the braves. With his brothers, White Wolf drew out his paint bag and smeared his face with black for battle. Soon several of his brothers were howling a war dance around the fire, waving lances or tomahawks, stomping the ground to the slow beat of the war drums. Spirit Talker joined the others, singing his incantations, waving his bear-claw charm, and beseeching the wolf spirit to give the warriors savage strength this day. A few of the warriors approached the medicine man to have purification rites performed on their war shields.

While the dancing and battle cries of his brothers continued, White Wolf sought out Prairie Star. He found her standing apart from the others, looking anxious, and watched her grow even more pale as she spotted his blackened face. He realized they were facing each other like two strangers, as if the intimacies they had shared last night had never occurred. And he knew that seeing him thus frightened and revolted her. Hurt and regret seared him at the barriers still looming between them. Would she ever accept him as he was?

"What are you doing?" she demanded.

"Silver Knife and I spotted hunters slaughtering bison on our land. I'm going with my brothers to chase them off."

"But . . . that's dangerous. Why don't you just leave the hunters alone?"

"Because it's our land, Prairie Star, and because the hunters are threatening our food supply."

He watched her gulp. "You will kill them?"

He glanced toward the dancing braves. "Believe it or not, Prairie Star, I take no joy in slaughtering others."

"And your brothers?"

"I'll try to persuade them just to scare off the hunters—but it won't be easy."

"You could be killed," she muttered.

He glanced at her sharply. "Would it matter to you?"

She was silent for a long moment, and he could see the struggle on her face. "Yes, it would matter," she said at last. "You would leave me stranded here with the others."

"Have you thought that the others may be all that's protecting you from the hunters?" he countered ironically.

"Protecting me?" she repeated bitterly. "One of the squaws knocked me down this morning, just because her child had given me some flowers!"

He touched her arm. "Are you all right?"

She moved away, turning her back to him. "Why don't you just go?" she asked hoarsely.

White Wolf could hear the confusion in her voice, and he felt torn. "We're leaving my father and several other older braves behind in case the hunters should head this way. You'd be advised not to leave the village, Prairie Star. If you should run into the hunters—they're not known to respect white women."

She was silent.

He started off, only to hear her calling him. He turned. "Yes?"

Grudgingly she said, "Please be careful."

They stared at each other for one stark, unguarded moment, and then he left.

White Wolf rode off with the others, he and Black Hawk leading the company of fourteen of their fiercest warriors. He glanced about at his brothers. With their battle regalia, their black-smeared faces and buffalo-horned helmets, the war party appeared utterly fearsome.

Several of the braves, including White Wolf, had brought along the Sharps rifles the tribe had acquired from Comancheros. All the braves carried battle whistles, lances, bows, and arrows. White Wolf held his sacred war shield that Spirit Talker had just purified; on the night of his first vision so many moons ago he had emblazoned his shield with the image of a star.

That very star had become a thorn in his side! he mused. Yet Prairie Star's obvious turmoil as he had left her had tugged at his heart.

The group soon crested the mesa and spotted the hunters busy skinning half a dozen dead bison on the prairie beneath them. White Wolf glanced at Black Hawk, and the latter nodded grimly. His face contorted in fury, Black Hawk let out a blood-chilling war whoop and led the charge, his lance shooting through the air, his pinto war pony flying down the embankment toward the enemy. Whistles trilled, rifles cracked, and arrows flew as the other warriors followed fast on Black Hawk's flanks.

Discharging his rifle in the hope of scaring away the hunters, White Wolf glanced ahead to observe the reaction of the White Eyes. For a moment, the group of hunters seemed frozen in panic at the Comanche advance. Blood-smeared knives paused in midair and frightened eyes became riveted on the approaching terror. Fortunately for the hunters, White Wolf noted, they had the advantage of being able to spot the charge from a considerable distance. After a split-second hesitation, the White Eyes abandoned the bison and their wagon, and made wild dives for their guns and horses.

The war party thundered into the valley. Arriving first, Big Bow and Antelope were both able to drive home shafts, wounding one hunter in the arm, another in the hip. The men's cries of agony rent the air, but both wounded men were able to hobble onto their horses and escape, leaving neither brave able to count coup. Several other hunters returned fire as the group galloped off. By the time the entire Comanche war party arrived in the valley, the hunters were retreating over the next rise.

White Wolf blew his whistle, signaling to the others to halt.

Black Hawk reined in his mount and faced his brother in anger, waving his arms while his pony snorted and pranced. "Cowards! They run like women! Let us pursue them and kill all the white devils!"

"No," White Wolf replied, gesturing toward the buffalo carcasses. "The hunters left behind great bounty for our tribe, much freshly killed meat. Let us take home our spoils and celebrate our victory."

"No," protested Black Hawk, "we will pursue them."

"And leave a feast for the vultures?" reasoned White Wolf, gesturing overhead toward several black birds that were already circling the skies. "Let us ask our brothers what they think."

The group debated the matter briefly, but ultimately the majority of the warriors displayed their innate Comanche practicality by siding with White Wolf. The group dispatched two braves to go back to the village to fetch the women and the pack animals, while the rest of the warriors remained behind to guard the meat.

A great cheer rose from the women when two braves galloped into the village, whooping victory cries. After conversing with one of the men, Creek Flower happily informed Maggie that the buffalo hunters had been driven off, and the meat belonged to the Comanche. Maggie, noting that White Wolf was not among the returning warriors, fretted for his safety, while the other women burst into activity, gathering knives and squares of buffalo hide, and rounding up pack animals. When a confused Maggie asked Creek Flower what was going on, the girl explained that it was the duty of the women to go out to the plains and butcher the bison, and pack up and bear home the meat. Only the oldest squaws would be allowed to remain behind to watch the children.

Still anxious about White Wolf, Maggie followed the other women on their long trek as they led the pack animals

out to where the men awaited them. A distant gathering of
vultures in the skies unsettled her, but she soon realized the
birds must be craving buffalo carrion. She heard several rifles discharging and fretted anew, until she watched the vultures fly off and concluded that the men were only trying to
scare them away.

When the group at last descended the mesa and Maggie
spotted White Wolf unharmed, sitting on the ground and
eating raw buffalo liver with his brothers, she breathed a
sigh of relief.

At least White Wolf was safe. Maggie wished she had
been able to communicate more concern toward him before
he had left. Indeed, the sight of him as a half-naked, black-
faced savage had aroused shivers of an emotion far more intense and shocking than apprehension. That was why she
had turned away. Whenever she felt herself responding to
the savage in him, she feared losing that civilized part of
herself, feared he would guess her treacherous desire for
him.

Standing apart from the others, Maggie observed the rest
of the scene. Several dead bison littered the landscape,
most of them not yet skinned. The overpowering scent of
the just-killed beasts was heavy in the air. At the edge of the
area stood an unmanned wagon hitched to a team of mules.
Maggie assumed the hunters must have abandoned their
conveyance.

Maggie was amazed to watch the Indian women move in
with their knives, quickly skinning and butchering the bison,
dividing the meat into large chunks, wrapping the sections
in buffalo hide, and tying the bundles onto the pack animals.
The atmosphere was exuberant, the woman chattering happily as they labored. Battle Ax and Brown Thrush comman-
deered the abandoned wagon, piling it high with meat and
hides. Maggie had to chuckle when she watched Battle Ax
charge after a vulture that was trying to carry off a chunk of
meat.

As the squaws joyfully and precisely performed all the
heavy labor, the men, including Maggie's husband, arro-

gantly ignored the females and remained in their circle, passing the pipe, laughing, and obviously bragging of their feats. Maggie could only shake her head. If *she* were one of those squaws, she would grab the men's pipe and pound a few stubborn male heads!

Maggie gasped as Creek Flower came forward, her dress blotched with blood, a dripping knife in her hand. But the girl's expression could not have been more cheerful.

"Big feast tonight!" she announced. "No one go hungry . . ." She paused to smirk at Maggie. "Not even lazy White Eyes squaw."

Watching Creek Flower dash off to help another squaw, Maggie laughed at this apt description of herself. Although she hated to admit it, there was something admirable in the primitive vitality, enthusiasm, and practicality of these people. She'd seen the love and devotion in the work the women had performed this morning, and now she viewed their ingenious efforts here. Her conscience nagged her for refusing to help the squaws, and the resulting guilt made her feelings of moral superiority toward the indolent men slip a notch.

Soon the group started back toward the village, the men on their proudly strutting ponies, the women again on foot, leading the pack animals. Trudging along with the other females, Maggie was surprised and touched when White Wolf rode up beside her, leaned over, and scooped her up before him on his horse. Her husband's arms were slick with sweat as they held her, and he smelled of the hunt. To her astonishment, she found she felt not the least bit repelled by the scents of man and beast. To the contrary, the raw savagery of him again excited her deeply—and frightened her just as much!

"Are you all right?" she asked tremulously.

She couldn't control a shiver as she felt his lips against her hair. "Yes. No warrior from our village was hurt—this time. The hunters were routed, but my brother Black Hawk still wants more blood."

Maggie frowned, lost in thought.

"Why did you come out here, Prairie Star?" she heard him ask softly. "Were you afraid for me?"

Maggie floundered at the direct question. "I ... I'm not sure. Curiosity, I suppose."

She felt her husband's arms tighten about her, and his next words came very huskily. "The white wolf welcomes your curiosity, Prairie Star. He is eager to satisfy it completely, any time."

His words were laced with hot sexual innuendo, and left Maggie feeling breathless and flushed, and all too eager to have him satisfy her. She was staggered by the level of sexual excitement she felt, and found herself understanding one element of Indian culture ... primitive desire, how lust for blood could turn into lust for the flesh. She felt that lust right now, with an intensity as fierce as the savage who held her. It was frightful to think that she, Margaret Donovan Kane, a prim Boston lady, might be capable of abandoning *all* her civilized convictions.

Heaven help her ... she could lose herself here.

SEVENTEEN

BACK AT THE VILLAGE, MAGGIE WATCHED THE PEOPLE prepare for the victory feast. Women filled pots with buffalo steaks; warriors passed peyote buttons and performed wild victory dances around the fire. Children raced about joyously, shrieking chants. The sounds of drumbeats and triumphant howling filled the air.

Maggie hung back from the others near the tepee she shared with White Wolf. As usual, she did not offer to help the women with the meal. She realized she felt increasingly at loose ends. Except for Creek Flower's friendship, she was a loner here, shunned by the women, while most of the warriors regarded her with contempt or lust. She had little to occupy her hours. She found herself resenting all the time White Wolf spent with his brothers—while obviously expecting her to fit right in and take up her duties as his squaw. She would have loved to play with some of the small children, perhaps even to watch them as their mothers labored; but following her daunting chastisement at the hands of Meadow Lark, she dared not go anywhere near the tots.

She was touched when Creek Flower brought her a tin

plate filled with buffalo steak, nuts, and berries. "Thank you," she murmured, taking the food. "So you really meant it . . . even lazy White Eyes squaws get to eat their fill tonight?"

Creek Flower beamed with happiness. "Feast. No one go hungry."

As Creek Flower dashed off to serve Silver Knife, Maggie sat down outside the tepee and ate her meal. When Chico bounded up, wagging his tail, she welcomed his sunny company and fed him several scraps of meat.

She stared at White Wolf, seated in the distance by the fire with his brothers. She watched Fast Fox take him his food and preen over him. Before the girl moved on, she hurled a triumphant glance in Maggie's direction. Maggie gritted her teeth and almost abandoned her pride, so strong was her urge to set Fast Fox in her place by serving White Wolf herself. Yet she could not take this symbolic step that would announce to White Wolf and the entire village that she had yielded and accepted her place as his squaw. She could not afford to give in, for she remained convinced that White Wolf intended to convert her to the Indian way of life permanently, just as his people had previously done with white captives such as Cynthia Ann Parker.

She studied her strong, virile husband, remembering the heat and the exciting scent of him as he had held her earlier on his horse. She recalled how he had felt last night in their tepee, the sensual shock, the hardness of his aroused manhood pressing into her womanhood. He was so virile, so charged with raw male instinct. How much longer, she wondered, before he sought his ease with Fast Fox or another squaw? She wanted him, too, honesty forced her to admit; she craved him with an intensity that made her weak each time she thought about it. Still, she feared the consequences if she gave in. She remained unsettled by the emotions he had stirred today after the hunt, the sweetly savage feelings that had overwhelmed her, the urge to leave her civilized self behind. When White Wolf was so tormentingly close,

memories of herself as a proper Boston lady began to fade,
and this disturbed her greatly . . .

White Wolf could feel his bride's perusal as he ate his
dinner. It troubled him that Prairie Star remained aloof from
both him and the tribe. Even the celebratory mood had
failed to entice her into participating. The other braves were
being brought food and drink by their squaws, and the fact
that his bride had again refused to serve him had been duly
noted by the others. White Wolf feared he was beginning to
look weak in the eyes of his brothers for not disciplining his
bride. Certainly he did not wish to humiliate Prairie Star totally, to break her spirit; but if she was to understand him
and his heritage, she would have to accept her obligations as
his wife. They must fulfill his vision before they could decide in which world they truly belonged. Yet he was beginning to wonder if she ever would relent, or if maybe the
differences between them were too great to overcome.

The sound of a raucous cheer interrupted White Wolf's
thoughts. He glanced across the fire and listened as Black
Hawk addressed the assembled warriors with a vengeful
voice and angry gestures. His brother's ravings were certainly nothing new: The evil buffalo hunters had insulted the
People long enough; they must be hunted down and exterminated, just as they were trying to annihilate the red man's
food supply; they must be tortured and killed slowly, to pro-
vide the proper example to the other cowardly, thieving
White Eyes.

White Wolf glanced at his father, and the two exchanged
a sober look. White Wolf had no taste for this kind of blood
vindictiveness; unfortunately, he knew Black Hawk would
continue his harangue well into the night, until he incited
the other braves to a peyote-induced frenzy.

The fact that many of the warriors had turned to hallucinogens in the past few years also troubled White Wolf
greatly. Only desperation in their conflict with the White
Eyes had compelled the braves to seek the euphoria offered
by the narcotic. Tonight the peyote would bring the warriors
false courage and false hope; at Black Hawk's insistence,

another war party would doubtless embark before the night ended, a raid launched in pure retaliation. White Wolf knew he would be powerless to stop his brothers, and again he reflected on the grave danger to the tribe if Black Hawk, with his bellicose ways, should succeed Buffalo Thunder as chief. He sensed that, if he expressed a strong interest, his father would choose him as the new chief; but would that be fair to his bride, for him to decide to spend the rest of his days with the People? Again he felt torn between his obligation to her and his duties toward the tribe.

These thoughts of Prairie Star spurred him to leave the others and join her. He strode over to where she sat outside their tepee. She looked lovely in her deerskin dress, with her bright, braided hair, and he was pleased to note her petting Chico, who was crouched beside her. But her features grew wary as she spotted him approaching.

He nodded toward her empty dishes. "You have eaten your fill?"

She raised her chin a notch. "Creek Flower informed me no one is allowed to go hungry during a feast—not even lazy White Eyes such as myself."

A rueful smile tugged at his lips. "Then perhaps you could use some exercise. Go with me for a walk, Prairie Star?"

She feigned amazement. "What, and desert your brothers pontificating by the fire? Aren't you afraid you'll miss something terribly important?"

He gathered his patience. "The evening is lovely—the sun won't go down for a while, and I thought you might enjoy seeing the wildflowers."

She shrugged. "Yes, I'd like to escape the war drums for a while."

He leaned over, took her hand, and pulled her to her feet. "Those are victory drums, Prairie Star."

She harrumphed. "I sincerely hope I won't be staying here long enough to learn the difference."

Her pointed comment left a tense atmosphere in its wake, and they fell into silence, not touching as they walked out onto the prairie, trailed by Chico. They strolled through a field where bluebonnets, Indian paintbrushes, and sunflowers bloomed. Bees and monarch butterflies flitted among the flowers, and the cool evening breeze was scented heavily of nectar; the sweet calls of a mourning dove mingled with the chanting of the warriors in the distance.

Noting Prairie Star's abstracted expression, White Wolf wondered how his bride could seem so unaffected by the lovely setting. He leaned over, plucked a few wildflowers, and stuck them among her braids. She offered him a bemused glance, but did not resist or comment.

"It's a beautiful evening," he murmured.

"So it is."

He cleared his throat and glanced at her awkwardly. "I wish our life could be more like this . . . just you and me."

She raised an eyebrow at him. "That does not keep you from spending most of your time with your brothers."

He grinned. "Jealous?"

She did not answer directly, and he was pleased to note the beginnings of a guilty blush on her cheeks. "What do all of you do anyway, spending so many hours gathered by the fire?" she asked.

He watched Chico chase after a jackrabbit. "Oh, we tell war stories, plan future strategies . . . the usual important male undertakings."

She rolled her eyes at him.

"Do you wish I would spend more of that time with you?" he pursued.

"That might encourage you to think we can have a future together," she answered frankly.

"And you are still convinced we don't?"

"We can't ignore the realities of our situation, and our different worlds."

He glanced at her sharply. "It's funny—as I sat by the fire, I was just thinking the very same thing."

"Then why won't you take me back to my world, Bronson?"

He stared at her and didn't reply.

"*Why,* White Wolf?"

"Because I won't give up on our marriage—even if you already have," he replied with quiet determination.

She did not respond but walked on, her features tight.

He followed after her. "Why won't you make any effort to adjust to life with my tribe?"

She laughed incredulously. "Do you actually think I could ever be happy living among a band of roving Indians?"

"You could give it a chance . . . which is a helluva lot more than the rest of your kind have done."

Maggie felt a stab of Anglo-Saxon guilt. Even in Boston, she had read editorials about the mistreatment of the red man. And she had understood the angry feelings of the warriors today, when they had gone after the hunters who had intruded on their lands and destroyed their bison.

Eager to draw the conversation away from herself, she asked, "Today, were any of the buffalo hunters killed?"

He shook his head. "A couple were wounded, but otherwise, we just scared them off. But my brother Black Hawk wants to launch another raid in retaliation. And he wants to massacre the entire town of Rio Concho for shielding the hunters."

She whistled at this sobering revelation. "Will you go on the next campaign?"

"No. Today I helped my brothers protect their food supply. But as I told you earlier, I abhor violence. I won't join in a raid launched out of pure revenge."

She regarded him thoughtfully. "You must feel very torn joining your Comanche brothers at all when they battle the whites—you being half-white and all."

White Wolf felt pleased by his bride's insightful statement. "I do see both sides, and it can be painful."

"You're caught between the worlds, aren't you?"

"I suppose I am."

"Yet you won't see yourself as a victim in this?"

"No—because to do so would denigrate my Comanche heritage, which I'm very proud of . . . even if you aren't."

Maggie felt another twinge of guilt at his last, pointed comment. "Tell me why the Comanche so hate white men."

He took her arm and pulled her to a halt. "Tell me why *you* so hate the Comanche."

Jolting by the direct, unexpected question, she glanced away, her face hot. "I . . . that's not fair. I asked first." She bucked up her courage and met his gaze bravely. "And I would like to understand your people."

White Wolf stared into her earnest face, feeling shocked and rather touched by her curiosity. Yet, on another level, he wasn't sure just how much he could trust her seeming change of heart.

"Why the sudden interest in the Nerm, Prairie Star?" he asked ironically.

She appeared disconcerted again, avoiding his eye, and he took a measure of perverse delight in unsettling her. "There aren't many Indians dancing around Boston Common," she muttered.

"True. I remember."

"But I have heard—read—of horrible things, atrocities committed by Indians . . ."

"And not by whites?"

"I was getting to that!" she retorted. "I'm sure there are wrongs perpetrated on both sides."

He nodded sadly. "The basic conflict between Anglos and the Comanche has not changed for hundreds of years. Essentially, the whites have refused to acknowledge the Indian ownership rights to their hunting grounds."

"The Indians own no lands?" Maggie asked in consternation. "But I thought we were in Comanche territory now."

"Territory, yes. My father's tribe was given rights to this land in the Treaty of Medicine Lodge, which was signed by the Comanche and the federal authorities in 1867. But treaty accessions do not constitute true ownership—and the whites have violated the treaties repeatedly by intruding on Comanche territory."

"And that is the central problem?"

"Yes, it's a major one. But there's also a vast difference

between the Indian and white cultures. The two peoples simply think differently. Comanches are born nomads, hunters, and raiders. That's why efforts to civilize the tribes, to make the Indians over into white men, have failed so badly. In the past, several Comanche tribes have been gathered onto the reservations at Fort Sill, given white man's clothing, and educated in farming. Again and again, these efforts have failed."

"Why?"

"I'll give you an example. A few years ago, the Quaker Indian agent Laurie Tatum was assigned to Fort Sill. One of his duties was to issue cattle to the Comanches living around the reservation. But the Indians had no concept of raising cattle, and knew only how to hunt. So, whenever the braves were given steers, they freed the animals and pursued them on horseback with their bows and arrows. Once the animals were killed, the women butchered the meat—"

"Just like today!" Maggie put in.

"Exactly. My point is, old traditions die hard, Prairie Star. An entire culture can neither be obliterated nor ignored. But the whites do not learn these lessons—they expect proud warriors to dress in white man's clothing and take up plows. Thus, every time the People have been rounded up on the reservations, they have eventually fled to hunt and raid."

"And kill the people they feel have intruded on their lands?"

"Yes—and do battle with the government officials who have broken the treaties and cheated them out of their rightful tribute."

"Tribute?" She frowned confusedly. "You mean the Indians have been cheated in ways other than the breaking of the treaties?"

"Indeed. The Indians are usually offered commodities—bribes, actually—to stop harassing the whites. The gifts often amount to worthless baubles and inferior goods. For many years the Indian agents pilfered the supplies outright, cheating the Comanche out of promised rations and clothing. Now the Comanche have been turned over to Quaker agents who are more honest, but seek to convert the People to their way of religion—forgetting that the Comanche have their own gods and taboos."

"I see," she murmured.

He continued in a resigned tone. "According to my father, the Quaker Indian agent recently assigned to this territory has twice visited our village. I haven't met him yet, but I understand he's a gentle man, totally without violence. He brings his presents, which my brothers accept while laughing at him behind his back. I don't think he realizes that the People can never embrace his civilized Christianity, that they will never become the pacifists he wants them to be."

"Could the problem be solved if the Indians were given their own permanent hunting grounds?"

"Yes, that might help. But the government will never do that—or if they do grant the People lands, they'll break their word and steal them back. Twenty years ago, Congress gave the Black Hills to the Dakotas, and huge chunks of Colorado and Kansas to the Arapahos and the Cheyennes. Of course, those agreements have now been broken, the territories stolen back from the tribes. As for the Comanche, they have never been granted ownership of any land in Texas, despite numerous promises in treaties that their hunting grounds would remain inviolate."

"It's not a very comforting picture."

He nodded grimly. "Essentially, the entire white-Indian policy has been a disaster, due to inconsistency as much as anything else. During the Republic of Texas period, Houston sought to pacify the Indians, then Lamar tried to annihilate them. By the time Houston returned to power and again tried reconciliation, the damage was done and the Comanche would never trust *tejanos* again. In the intervening years, the Comanche were beaten back several times by the cavalry or the rangers, then allowed to raid freely during the Civil War. Now they are being prodded toward the reservations through a combination of harassment by the cavalry and attempted pacification by the Quakers. The army leaders—Sherman and Sheridan—seem to be moving toward the conclusion that destroying the Comanche is their only viable alternative, and President Grant tacitly endorses the policy of his favorite generals."

Maggie glanced back at the celebration, which seemed a tragic irony in light of what she'd just learned. "Then the future for your people appears bleak."

He followed her gaze and drew a heavy breath. "Now the government has made things even worse by unofficially sanctioning the activities of the buffalo hunters. I guess the logic is that if the bison are completely exterminated, the People will have no choice but to go to the reservations with broken spirits, and beg for the generosity of the whites."

"You sound very bitter."

"Look what the whites have done already, annihilating the Cherokees, purging Texas of the Creeks, Kickapoos, and Delawares. Settlers and buffalo hunters keep moving west, penetrating the hunting grounds of my brothers. I'm not hopeful that the situation will result in anything but tragedy."

"And yet you bring me into the middle of this," she argued passionately. "You say that Indian and white cultures are basically incompatible, but you expect me to capitulate and become your squaw. What makes you think I can understand the Indian world any better than the Indians can understand the whites?"

He spoke adamantly. "*I* understand both worlds, Prairie Star."

"You are from both worlds—I am not!"

He caught her by the shoulders. "That may be true, but you could try. I believe it is our destiny to become one, to bring our worlds together."

"You may think it is *your* destiny, White Wolf, but becoming an Indian is certainly not mine," she replied vehemently.

He drew a heavy breath. "You still haven't explained why you so hate and fear my people. I've spoken my heart . . . Why won't you?"

She glanced away in discomfort. "I can't."

"You could if you wanted to."

She didn't answer, but stood with eyes downcast and jaw clenched.

He continued more gently. "I am not saying that this will be easy, nor am I saying our sojourn with the tribe will last forever. I am saying I know we're meant to be together. Don't you remember what I told you right after I kidnapped you? There will be no hope for us unless you first accept the red man inside of me."

She glanced up at him, bitter tears burning in her eyes. "There never was any hope for us, White Wolf—not from the moment you brought me here against my will. You toy with me, hinting that if only I'll become an Indian for you, you'll take me back to civilization. Well, I don't believe you, and your people's history with white captives suggests otherwise. I can never trust you again, not after what you did. To me, that's the saddest part of all."

His hands dropped to his sides and he stared at her sadly. "You are saying I had no right to make you live up to our vows?"

"Not by force. This will never work unless I come to you willingly."

"And didn't you almost do so last night?"

He knew he had gotten to her then, for she stood trembling with emotion, her eyes bright. "You—you know you overwhelmed me last night!"

"Did I?" he countered, pinning her with his heated gaze. "I know you overwhelmed *me.*"

She started to reply, then clamped her mouth shut, turned on her heel, and walked away. White Wolf stared after her, again feeling jarred by her confusion. More and more, he was beginning to fear that bringing Prairie Star here had been a mistake. This woman had fought him and his culture; now she had not only denied the magic between them, but had also made clear that she would never trust him or his motives.

His conscience nagged at him to let her go. But he wasn't sure he could.

Late that night, after a small war party had departed, White Wolf joined his father by the fire. The two men sat alone amid the snapping flames, the sawing crickets, and the distant howls of coyotes. White Wolf watched Buffalo Thunder draw on his pipe, then cough violently. The sound alarmed him—he feared his father, like his mother, was growing consumptive.

"You should give up your pipe, my father," he admonished. "It aggravates your cough."

"It gives me solace in my waning days," came the hoarse reply. Buffalo Thunder set down his pipe and regarded his son curiously. "Why are you not seeking the comfort of your bride?"

White Wolf shrugged. "Prairie Star still does not welcome me. And I am beginning to feel doubt . . ."

"In what manner, my son?"

White Wolf's unhappy gaze met his father's. "I watch our battle with the whites escalate, and I feel torn between my bride and my desire to help our people."

Buffalo Thunder nodded. "Just as you are confronted by troubling choices, so are our people. Should we stay and do more battle with the White Eyes? Or should we flee, and try to find some lost cranny of wilderness where they will not find us?" The old chief sighed. "Soon I must leave these grave matters to you or your brother. Black Hawk would slay the *tahbay-boh*—you would try to pacify them. I fear neither course will bring true prosperity to our people."

White Wolf did not answer, for he knew of no solution, and the choices facing his people would indeed only further complicate his own dilemma with Prairie Star. The father and son sat in contemplative silence, staring out at the vast prairie, the black, star-dotted heavens, the world that belonged to the Nerm . . . if only for now.

EIGHTEEN

THE RAIDING PARTY RETURNED IN THE MORNING, TIRED, GRIM-faced, and bearing no scalps. Watching a furious Black Hawk hurl a tomahawk into the ground, White Wolf felt relieved that at least no lives had been lost on either side.

Another skirmish with the hunters occurred two days later; although White Wolf wasn't along at the time, he soon learned the details from other braves. Antelope, Big Bow, and several other warriors were out rounding up mustangs when they encountered four hunters tracking bison several miles west of the village. The band of braves pursued the hunters, and the whites again panicked and fled. That night at council, Big Bow and Antelope bragged of their feat for hours.

Given the increasing menace from the *tahbay-boh*, the warriors of the village spent much time debating about the best way to deal with the threat. Black Hawk still wanted to launch a retaliatory raid against the town of Rio Concho. White Wolf argued that perhaps the tribe should simply move farther west. Silver Knife sided with Black Hawk, pointing out that every time the People moved farther north or west, the evil White Eyes followed to steal more land and bison from the red man; thus, the People must hold their ground and fight here. The medicine man, Spirit Talker, warned that the White Eyes had spirits of the evil crow and were never to be trusted; it was best the People avoided them altogether. Buffalo Thunder cautioned that if white lives were taken by the People, the white cavalry was certain to come and kill many warriors in retaliation.

On and on the argument went. The dissension among his brothers weighed heavily on White Wolf's mind, as did his continuing troubles with Prairie Star. Black Hawk in particular goaded him about his inability to control his bride.

All of these tensions only increased the day some unexpected visitors dropped in on the People. White Wolf knew something was amiss as soon as he spotted three of the village scouts galloping into camp, yelling out the alarm. He and the other warriors converged on the returning braves, and White Wolf heard one of the scouts, Straw Horse, yell, "The Quaker is coming! We have spotted him down the creek, with his four Tonkawa guides!"

All around White Wolf, voices were raised in anger and disgust. Several warriors jeered the word *"Tonkaweya,"* and spat on the ground. As White Wolf well knew, Indian agents were distrusted by the People; but the Tonkawas, who often did make excellent scouts for the whites, were detested by all other Indian peoples because they were cannibals.

Black Hawk let out a horrific battle yell. "Let us slaughter them all!" he screamed in Comanche, waving his lance. "Let us rip out their cannibal spirits and leave them forever as ghosts to howl at the moon!"

At Black Hawk's words, a great roar of bloodlust went up from the other braves, and White Wolf felt sickened, afraid he could not contain his brothers' thirst for vengeance. Nonetheless, he thrust himself into the center of the group.

"Listen to me, my brothers!" he yelled in Comanche. "We must not kill the Quaker agent. He is a gentle man who has done us no harm."

While most of the braves eyed White Wolf in resentment, Black Hawk yelled back, "He is a White Eyes. All White

Eyes are evil. He brings cannibals among us. He makes good talk, then his Tonk guides will attack us in the night like cannibal owls. We must kill them all."

"No!" cried White Wolf. "Not all White Eyes are evil. I am half-*tejano*. I am not evil. I will reason with the White Eyes, and persuade him to keep the *tahbay-boh* hunters away from Comanche territory."

Now all the warriors appeared indecisive, mumbling to one another, save for Black Hawk, who still openly defied his brother. "Talk is foolish. White Eyes speak with forked tongue." He waved his weapon. "Comanche speak with lance!"

Amid new clamor from the other braves, Buffalo Thunder slowly stepped forward. A respectful silence gripped the ranks as the old chief held up a hand. "Let us make council with the White Eyes first, before we decide what is to be done. Perhaps the agent brings tribute for the People—or new treaty."

"Treaty worthless!" retorted Black Hawk, breaking his lance over his knee and stalking off.

White Wolf was frowning at the sight when Prairie Star rushed up, appearing anxious. "What is going on?"

He turned to her. "The Quaker Indian agent is on his way here with four Tonkawa scouts."

She lifted her chin with pride. "I want to leave with them."

"You'll be doing nothing of the kind," he retorted.

She balled her hands on her hips. "And just how are you planning to stop me?"

"You will stop yourself."

"You are demented."

"I'm not, Prairie Star. Comanches protect their possessions to the death—"

"Oh, so I am your possession now?" she asked furiously. "And you will kill a gentle Quaker just to keep me?"

"No, I won't kill anyone. But my brothers will slay the agent before they will allow him to take off the squaw of their future chief."

Her jaw dropped. "You actually intend to become chief of these people?"

His expression was grim. "My father must soon choose between me and Black Hawk as his successor, and I fear my brother will take the People down the wrong path."

"All the more reason for you to allow me to leave now."

His patience wearing thin, he grabbed her arm. "Didn't you hear me, Prairie Star? If you try to leave with the agent, it will mean his death, and the deaths of his scouts. My people despise the Tonkawas, and will doubtless torture them for many days before they die. Is that what you really want?"

Revulsion filled her features and her voice. "You could stop it!"

"Perhaps. But I won't. The choice is yours, Prairie Star."

"What choice?" she half screamed at him, shaking off his touch. "*You* are the only one who has had any choice in this marriage! And you have made your decisions with no concern whatsoever for me!"

"That is not true!"

"Yes, it is!" She waved a hand in exasperation. "You just told me you may become chief of these people—"

"*May.*"

"Don't you realize one day you *will* have to make a choice between the Indian and white worlds? You can't spend your life riding the fence, White Wolf—or Bronson, or whoever you are. It won't work. And the choice you make will affect me and the rest of my life!"

He held on to his patience with an effort. "We cannot argue about this now—there's no time. I'd advise you to get out of sight immediately, and to wait in our tepee. If the Quaker sees you, he'll feel honor-bound to intervene—and you can be assured that my brothers will resist violently."

She stormed off. He sighed, sobered by the words she had spoken, words that were all too true. With his father's days numbered and tensions between the Indians and whites escalating, he *would* soon become compelled to make a choice, and that painful decision would affect her. He already knew in his heart that if he did become chief of his band, he could never force Prairie Star to remain with him permanently.

Hearing a shout from one of his brothers, he turned to watch the Quaker appear over the rise with his scouts; the Tonks led several pack horses laden with what White Wolf assumed were the customary gifts. The Quaker was dressed in traditional black and wore a sedate hat with a flat, round brim; the scouts wore garish calico shirts and dark trousers; their hair was braided and they wore huge, high-crowned black hats adorned with eagle feathers and many gaudy trinkets and bells.

White Wolf had not met this particular agent before, although Uncle Sam had recently mentioned that a special Indian agent had been assigned to nearby Fort Defiance, the stockade that had been named in honor of the famous Fort Defiance of Texas revolutionary days. Uncle Sam had said the agent was entrusted with the task of helping persuade the Comanche to move to the Oklahoma reservations.

White Wolf did not envy the man his duties. He was a fool to venture among the People without a cavalry escort; but then, the Quaker Indian agents White Wolf had heard of previously were a naive lot who believed in the essential goodness of all men and often acted with no regard for their own safety. Given the current hostility between whites and Indians, this Quaker's trust was misplaced.

The strangers entered the village slowly, amid the curious, suspicious glances of the Indians. The Quaker smiled at one and all, ludicrously tipping his hat to Indian squaws who merely regarded him with contempt or spat at his horse. At the center of the camp, the five newcomers dismounted and waited to be greeted.

With the other warriors hanging back, Buffalo Thunder stepped forward and stood proudly regarding his guests. The Quaker spoke to one of the scouts in English, and the Tonkawa approached Buffalo Thunder and began signing. Ignoring the scout, Buffalo Thunder gestured to White Wolf to come forward.

White Wolf joined his father. The Quaker, who had a square, florid face with a prominent, bulbous nose, smiled at him eagerly.

White Wolf addressed the man in English. "I am White Wolf, son of Chief Buffalo Thunder. I welcome you to our village. Your translator will not be needed, as you may speak to my father through me."

The Quaker peered at White Wolf in astonishment. "You are a white man."

"I am half-Comanche," answered White Wolf.

"Well, this is most fortuitous, my son," said the Quaker with a broad grin, extending his hand. "I am Jedediah Kemperer, and I am most pleased to make your acquaintance."

White Wolf shook the Quaker's hand, then turned to his father and translated what the Indian agent had just said.

Buffalo Thunder listened to his son, then asked in Comanche, "Why has he come to see the People?"

White Wolf turned to the Quaker and asked in English, "What is your business with my father's band?"

"I wish to make council," replied the Quaker. "But first"—he paused to gesture at the nearby pack animals—"I bring gifts for all."

White Wolf relayed these messages to Buffalo Thunder, and he nodded. White Wolf invited the Quaker to join the braves at council, and the Indian agent instructed his scouts to bring forth the gifts. White Wolf, Buffalo Thunder, and the Quaker sat down together near the central fire. The other braves of the village, including Black Hawk, warily followed suit, gathering to complete the circle.

The scouts came forward, piling the Indian agent's bounty before the old chief: bolts of cloth; tins of beans and stew; bags of grain, sugar, coffee, and flour. Buffalo Thunder signaled to the women to come take the gifts; after the squaws greedily grabbed the supplies, Buffalo Thunder thanked his guests by presenting the Indian agent with a pair of knee-high moccasins that were heavily beaded and fringed. Kemperer took the moccasins and thanked Buffalo

Thunder effusively through White Wolf. Meat and drink were brought; when White Wolf spotted Fast Fox about to give the Quaker a cupful of the firewater the braves had captured in one of their recent raids, he solemnly shook his head. A moment later, the girl brought the agent a cup of water.

Only then did the powwow begin. The agent spoke to Buffalo Thunder through White Wolf. His oratory was predictable.

"Why does this small band of the Penateka exist so far away from their Comanche brothers?" he asked. "If the People remain here, they will face tragedy and destruction. The buffalo are growing scarce, and the white settlers keep pushing westward, making conflict with your people inevitable. The Great Father is willing to take care of all of you, to offer you free land and rations on the Oklahoma reservation. Why will you not go there now and join your brothers?"

After the agent finished his discourse, Buffalo Thunder was thoughtfully silent for a long moment. When he spoke through White Wolf, his response was also predictable.

"I know the White Eyes speaks with sincere heart," he replied. "But my people are warriors and hunters, not farmers. The reservations will steal our pride and rape our spirit. And dangers also lie there. Each spring, the White Eyes blame innocent reservation Indians for raids on white homesteads. In the past, vengeful White Eyes have even attacked the reservations and slaughtered many of the People who lived there and were blameless. This Penateka band will live where they can be free to roam and hunt the buffalo, and it is the responsibility of the Great Father not to round up the People like sheep, but to enforce his own treaties and keep the white hunters and settlers off Comanche lands."

Having said his peace through White Wolf, Buffalo Thunder fell silent, and even Black Hawk, who had intently listened to the exchange, seemed to approve, nodding to his father and then glaring at the Quaker. Appearing disappointed by the chief's negative response, Jedediah Kemper-

er restated his argument through White Wolf, and following
another potent pause, the old chief again responded in kind.
Spotting the deeply dismayed expression on Kemperer's
face, White Wolf felt sorry for the well-meaning man. Most
significantly, his father did not offer Kemperer the peace
pipe, which White Wolf knew both signaled to the agent
that his visit was a failure, and also notified him that he had
worn out his welcome.

In due course, the Quaker thanked Buffalo Thunder for
his hospitality, then trudged off toward his horse with his
scouts. White Wolf followed and took the Quaker aside.

"You would be advised not to return here," he warned.
"The People are stirred up because the hunters keep intruding on their lands, and the white government will do nothing about it."

The man nodded morosely. "I'm aware of this."

"The only way you can really help my father's people is
to keep the whites out of their territory."

"You must know, my son, that this is impossible,"
Kemperer replied heavily. "Were it up to me, I would give
your people all the lands of the West that are rightfully
theirs. But the truth is, these lands have already been stolen
by the whites, and I find myself hopelessly caught between
the two factions. The Texans hate the red man, and even the
federal government has become much less benevolent following activities by your people during the War Between
the States. Now the cavalry is launching raids against your
people. Indeed, Colonel Morgan at Fort Defiance has received orders to remove your people to the reservations before midsummer, by force if necessary. He distrusts your
people and implored me to come here today under cavalry
escort. I refused, hoping I could reason with your father, and
now I must return and confess that I have failed. Can you
not convince your father that the only way to save his people is to take them to the reservation?"

White Wolf spoke with all the passion of his own torn
feelings. "Have you thought that taking these people to the
reservation may be a surefire way to bring them to ruin? If

the spirit of these people is broken, they are defeated utterly. Perhaps the greatest tragedy of the government Indian policy lies in the fallacy of thinking the wild bands can be civilized—or converted to your white way of religion."

"But if this does not occur, the tribes will be destroyed."

"Yes," White Wolf concurred sadly. "I fear my people will be crushed in any event. Only the specifics of their annihilation remain undecided."

The man eyed White Wolf curiously. "You said before that you are half-white. How do you fit into all of this? You speak as if you are an educated man."

"I am. My mother was a white captive. I have lived in both worlds, and have gained a white education."

The man touched White Wolf's arm. "Then perhaps the greatest cruelty of all is laid on your shoulders, my son."

"And how is that?"

"Understanding both worlds, but being caught between them, and able to do little, if anything, to effect true change."

White Wolf nodded as he recalled Prairie Star's words to the same effect, that he could not successfully ride the fence between the two worlds. He flashed a smile at the kindly man. "You must go now. There are those among my brothers who will kill you all if you remain for long."

Jedediah Kemperer drew himself up with pride. "A man who fears God need not fear death."

"I respect your convictions," said White Wolf, "but do not be a fool. Leave at once."

Nodding, the Quaker mounted his horse and stared anxiously down at White Wolf. "Please try to persuade your father to move the tribe. If he doesn't, sooner or later, the calvary will come do it for you—or the rangers."

"I'll see what I can do," White Wolf muttered, shaking his head as the Quaker and his scouts rode off.

White Wolf was striding off to his tepee to check on Prairie Star when Black Hawk loomed in his path. The brave's black eyes glittered with defiance and anger.

"Why do you side with our enemies?" he demanded.

"The Quaker agent is not our enemy," replied Bronson patiently. "He wants to help us—"

"By breaking our spirits and making farmers of us?"

"The man's heart is sincere, even if his suggestions may be wrong for us."

"He is a White Eyes!" Black Hawk raved. "As for you, my brother, if you ever hope to lead our people, you must give up your loyalty to those of white blood."

"It's not that simple," White Wolf argued.

"You are a coward to think otherwise! You let the White Eyes Quaker make a fool of you, just as your *tahbay-boh* squaw has already made a fool of you. You are powerless in your own home, and as a chief you will also be powerless."

"Perhaps you and I define power in different ways."

"Your way is the weak path of the *tahbay-boh.*" Stepping closer, Black Hawk said fiercely, "You and I both know that soon our father will die. We have watched him go frail, watched the spirit leave him. If you wish to save our people from disaster, you must tell our father you have no interest in becoming chief. Instead, we must have a leader whom women will fear and men respect."

"A leader like you?" White Wolf sneered.

"Yes!" Black Hawk replied proudly, pointing toward his chest. "I am the true warrior, the true Comanche!"

Black Hawk strode off, and White Wolf stood grimly watching him. His brother strutted arrogantly past a group of squaws, and jerked a thumb toward Fast Fox. She hopped up, eagerly following him to his nearby tepee. He rolled back the entry flap and motioned for her to precede him inside. As she scrambled into the lodge, Black Hawk turned to grin triumphantly at White Wolf, as if to say, *I can bed the squaw of any of my brothers . . . You cannot even tame your own bride.*

The truth of Black Hawk's point sank home with a vengeance as White Wolf stalked off to his own tepee and ducked inside. He spotted Prairie Star sitting near the far wall with an angry, rebellious expression. Again Black

Hawk's message rose to taunt him, and he retained his patience with an effort.

"You can leave the tepee now. The agent is gone."

"Oh, so the coast is clear?" she replied sarcastically.

"Prairie Star, it was a very tense, and potentially dangerous, situation. It's just as well you were out of sight."

Radiating defiance, she struggled to her feet. "What did the man want?"

"To try to persuade my father to move his people to the reservation."

"And he wasn't successful?"

"No. I imagine, though, that the tribe will soon change locations. The cavalry at Fort Defiance will shortly be informed of our whereabouts, and the agent warned me that the soldiers may try to remove our band to Oklahoma by force."

"If the tribe moves, that will make my rescue even less likely, won't it?"

"Yes."

She bristled at him, and he considered her continuing mutiny and the increasing threat from the government. He realized that if he kept Prairie Star with the tribe for too long, she could be in danger—something he had never intended. So far, her attitude toward him had not softened one bit. Perhaps Black Hawk had spoken some truth; perhaps it would take a firmer hand to force her to understand his culture, especially with time possibly running out for them. If that meant he had to be a stern husband and disciplinarian, then so be it.

He pinned her with a forbidding look. "Prairie Star, I think I have been patient with your stubbornness long enough."

She was silent, her eyes eloquent with defiance.

"You are making no attempt to live with me as my Indian bride. If you never serve my needs as my squaw, you will never understand that part of me that is Comanche, and our marriage will be doomed."

Even as her expression appeared torn, she heaved a

breath of frustration. "Don't you think it's about time you accepted that it is?"

He shook a fist at her. "No. I accept nothing. You are the one who is going to give in."

"Meaning what?"

"Meaning tonight you will serve me my dinner in front of my brothers."

"I will not!"

"You will."

"Or?" she challenged.

"Or you will rue the consequences."

NINETEEN

Maggie fumed over her husband's ultimatum. What did he intend to do—beat her, starve her now if she would not play the squaw?

She also remained furious that White Wolf had not allowed her to leave with the Indian agent, after he had claimed on several occasions that he would not force her to remain with his tribe indefinitely. His actions today were simply more evidence that he could not be trusted, that he had never intended to allow her to leave the tribe. Despite all his pontification about destiny and the two of them joining their worlds, he was really determined to break and dominate her, to keep her here forever. As far as she was concerned, the distance looming between them could never be bridged, and especially not by forcing her to assume a subservient identity that was alien to her own background and beliefs.

She wandered down toward the creek, where the Indian women were happily washing the grain the agent had brought, while others were busy fashioning garments from the bolts of calico and broadcloth. The late afternoon setting was lovely, the light dancing over the creek and through the trees, a slight breeze, heavily perfumed with the smells of flowers and greenery, wafting over the landscape. A dozen or more small children frolicked about.

Maggie sat apart from the others on top of a small rise overlooking the water. As always, she felt like an interloper. Halfway down the bank, between her and the women, was Little Bear Claw, Black Hawk's son. The two-year-old boy was playing in the grass, happily pounding his rattle, and Maggie instinctively kept a protective eye on him. How she wished she could go down and frolic with him, lift him high over her head and hear his laughter; but to do so would surely provoke another round of fierce retaliation from Meadow Lark.

Creek Flower stopped by, sitting down next to Maggie. "You are all right?" she asked in half sign, half Comanche.

Maggie nodded. Although she would never admit it to White Wolf, in the scant days she had been here, she had already learned a number of Indian words and signs from Creek Flower. She had rationalized that her capitulation on this issue was the only way to relieve her boredom. Besides, Creek Flower often slipped into Comanche dialect or sign when she conversed with Maggie, so it was near impossible not to pick up some of the Indian style of communication. Creek Flower had also been a true friend to Maggie, often sneaking her food, and Maggie was not about to alienate this special young woman in any way.

It was even harder for Maggie to admit to herself that she had become fascinated with Comanche culture, especially as she had begun to realize that, even though she was an outsider viewed with fear, the Comanche were essentially a content people who treated one another with respect and kindness. She had observed the women working together harmoniously, as they were doing now; she had watched the men treat each other with humor and camaraderie. The Comanches seemed to have a good world here . . . although it could never really become *her* world, especially not with the People's entire way of life increasingly threatened by the whites.

Creek Flower now asked Maggie a question in rapid Comanche, while her fingers danced through the air making signs. Maggie heard the word "Quaker," but could make out little else. Laughing, she held up a hand. "Please explain in English. I can't quite follow you."

Creek Flower smiled. "Quaker bring many gifts."

"Yes, I suppose the People are pleased."

The smile faded. "Always price for gifts. Quaker want People move to reservation."

"I know."

Creek Flower studied Maggie thoughtfully. "You angry White Wolf? Prairie Star want leave with Quaker?"

Maggie nodded. "My husband told me I had to hide during the Indian agent's visit, or I might cause the man's death."

"Now you angry?"

"Yes. I wanted to leave." She hesitated a moment, then confided, "White Wolf has become more stubborn than ever regarding my role as his wife. He has warned me I must serve him his dinner tonight, or suffer the consequences."

The girl appeared confused. *"Conse—"*

"I'll be punished," Maggie clarified.

"Ah." The girl nodded. "Thrashed. Squaw no serve warrior, big loss of face."

Maggie angrily snapped a twig in her hand. "I realize this. But if I displease White Wolf as his squaw, why won't he simply let me go?"

Creek Flower's lovely features twisted in perplexity. "Among the People, marriage sacred. Is not so among White Eyes?"

"A marriage that has not been consummated can be annulled," Maggie said.

"I no understand."

"If a man and his wife have not yet been joined in body, the marriage vows can be voided ... broken." She snapped another twig to demonstrate.

Creek Flower gasped. "You and White Wolf not joined?"

"Not yet."

"Among the People, squaw belong to husband forever," Creek Flower related solemnly. "Warrior never give up squaw, unless maybe give to brother. Vows never broken."

Maggie sighed. White Wolf had already more or less communicated this same stance to her. She had feared that among the Comanche, the lack of a physical consummation of their marriage had no particular validity, and that she was indeed considered White Wolf's "property." No wonder he was so obdurate about keeping her here and not releasing her from her vows.

Creek Flower touched her hand. "I help other squaws. You come?"

Maggie shook her head, and the girl trudged off. She watched her friend pat the head of Little Bear Claw before she proceeded down the bank to join the other females.

Maggie felt torn about her isolation from the others. She glanced at the pastoral scene beneath her—the women happily working and laughing, Little Bear Claw crawling around in the grass, a group of small girls playing with dolls, a throng of boys with play bows and arrows chasing one of their number who crawled about wearing a buffalo pelt with horns. The Indian children were so adorable that Maggie was often hard-pressed not to grab them and cuddle them, despite certain retribution from their mothers.

Would these people accept her if she allowed them to? Maggie considered the novel idea. Increasingly she sensed that mistrust, rather than true hatred, separated her from the others. After all, the People had accepted White Wolf and Creek Flower—although, of course, both of them had Comanche blood, and she did not. Still, she sensed that her ostracism here was mostly of her own making. Certainly it made no sense for her to establish roots in the tribal community, when she was still determined to escape White Wolf and somehow annul their marriage. Yet, even though she was determined never to "become" Comanche, she yearned to at least alleviate some of her feelings of tension and isolation.

A child's scream snatched Maggie violently from her reverie, and she glanced down the embankment to see that Little Bear Claw had crawled onto an anthill. Instantly wild with terror for him, Maggie bolted up and raced toward him, only to shout in agony as she stumbled into a prairie dog hole, violently twisting her ankle and crashing to the ground.

Every inch of Maggie ached at her violent jolting, but Little Bear Claw's petrified shrieks proved far more compelling. Although the pain in her sprained ankle was excruciating, sheer willpower forced her to her feet. The joint balked badly at supporting her weight as she frantically hobbled down to the panicked baby. She scooped him up, only to discover he was covered with ants—

Her instincts taking over, she limped desperately to the creek and jumped into the waist-deep water with the child, immersing him, then quickly bringing him up for air—

He screeched with fear from the dunking, but Maggie noted that the ants were gone, thank God. Hugging the drenched boy and cooing to comfort him, Maggie was carrying him back onto the bank when he was suddenly snatched from her arms. Her entire body exploded with pain as half a dozen squaws, frenzied with rage, attacked her, screaming deprecations.

"Ants!" Maggie yelled helplessly, raising her forearms to shield herself from the rain of blows. "Please, it was ants!"

Then she heard Creek Flower shrieking in Comanche. A split-second later, her friend jumped between Maggie and the other females, while continuing to yell at the squaws loudly until they backed off.

Maggie and the group of squaws regarded each other warily, all of the women breathing hard. Maggie was relieved to note that at least Little Bear Claw was calming in Meadow Lark's arms. Then one of the older boys came forward with Little Bear Claw's rattle. He extended the toy toward Creek Flower, then cried out in pain as one of the ants crawled off the rattle and bit him.

Heedless of her own safety, Maggie grabbed the boy, hurled down the rattle, and frantically brushed the remain-

ing ants off his skin. When a couple of other squaws started
to intervene, Creek Flower angrily rebuked them.

Maggie and the child turned to face the group. The
squaws watched in charged silence as the boy gratefully
slipped his arms around Maggie's waist and hugged her protectively. Deeply touched by the unexpected gesture,
Maggie patted his head and blinked at tears.

The bemused squaws moved off together in a huddle,
consulting among one another while glancing at Maggie
covertly. The little boy smiled up at Maggie winsomely,
then darted off to play with his friends.

Creek Flower stepped closer and touched Maggie's arm.
"You are safe?" she asked anxiously.

Maggie nodded toward the squaws. "Yes, unless they still
decide to burn me at the stake."

Maggie feared her grim prophecy might prove true as
suddenly the women turned, let out a mighty whoop, and
made a dive for her. At first she was terrified, until she
heard the squaws' exuberant laughter and felt herself being
hoisted high over their heads. They carried her up the embankment and back toward the village, while many of the
children joined in the procession, cheering . . .

White Wolf was at his tepee, picking burrs off Chico,
when he heard the commotion near the creek. Alarmed, he
raced in that direction and encountered a group of shrieking
women approaching the center of camp. He spotted Prairie
Star sopping wet and being carried on their shoulders, a
stunned expression on her face. At once he felt frantic for
her safety. He burst between the women and grabbed her,
holding her protectively in his arms. She was wet and trembling and appeared slightly dazed.

"Are you all right?"

She nodded.

Still holding her, he turned to Creek Flower and demanded in Comanche, "What has happened? Why is my
wife wet? Has she been harmed?"

Creek Flower answered brightly, "Prairie Star save Little Bear Claw from ants."

Meadow Lark stepped forward with Little Bear Claw in her arms and added her own proud endorsement in Comanche. "White Wolf squaw rescue nephew."

White Wolf smiled at the tot, noting that he seemed to have only a few scattered ant bites on his face and body. Then he glanced downward to note a bruise already forming on Prairie Star's cheek. He scowled formidably at the women. "If she saved the child, why is my bride hurt?"

"Prairie Star jump with baby into creek, wash off ants," explained Creek Flower. "Other squaws not understand, think Prairie Star hurt baby. Attack Prairie Star until Creek Flower explain."

White Wolf stared grimly at the women. "I'll take care of my wife," he muttered to Creek Flower, stalking off with Prairie Star and leaving the other squaws to stare after them in confusion.

White Wolf carried Prairie Star inside their tepee and gently laid her down. "Where else are you hurt?" he demanded, running his hands over her body, then stopping when she screamed as he touched her ankle. "What is wrong?"

"My . . . ankle," she replied, shuddering with pain. "When I heard the baby scream and spotted him covered with ants, I raced toward him and stepped into a prairie dog hole, twisting my ankle."

"Prairie dogs," White Wolf muttered with disgust. "I once had to shoot a good horse following a similar mishap."

Her eyes went wide.

He chuckled and brushed a strand of wet hair from her brow. "Don't worry, Prairie Star, I'm not going to shoot you. I'm amazed you managed to rescue the child after having hurt yourself so badly."

"I couldn't allow an innocent child to suffer." She bit her lower lip. "Do you think my ankle is broken?"

He gazed at her tenderly. "I'll have to feel the bones carefully—and it will hurt."

She grimaced. "All right."

He examined the ankle, and she again cried out. "Easy," he murmured. A moment later, he glanced up at her face, now white and drawn with pain. "I don't feel anything broken, but the swelling is already bad. I'll wrap it, and you'll need to stay off that foot for a few days."

She nodded, sucking in her breath between clenched teeth.

Using some strips of deerskin, White Wolf tightly bound Prairie Star's ankle. She moaned more than once, but found the pain was alleviated somewhat once the ankle was wrapped.

He glanced at her hands and wrists, grimacing at the sight of the nasty welts forming. "I'll see if Spirit Talker has a poultice to help with those ant bites. In the meantime, we need to get you out of your wet clothes."

"I—I can see to that," she murmured back in embarrassment.

He was grinning at her when the sounds of women giggling outside caused him to stand and leave the tepee. A minute later, he stepped back inside, his eyes dancing with devilment.

"What is going on?" she demanded.

"It's now news all over the camp that you saved Little Bear Claw," he explained. "Meadow Lark has insisted you be honored, and she and several other squaws wish to help you dress for the feast."

Maggie was astounded. "They . . . what? A feast just because I drowned a few ants?"

"Prairie Star, last year Running Deer's baby died after a similar mishap."

"Oh." In a mortified whisper, she asked, "But must I allow the squaws to dress me?"

"You must, or your refusal will be considered an insult."

She breathed a sigh of capitulation. "Very well."

He left, and three squaws, including Meadow Lark, burst in, giggling and bearing a deerskin dress, matching moccasins, and jewelry. Maggie was amazed to find herself quickly stripped by the squaws, and dressed in a soft, white garment that was heavily decorated with beading of silver, turquoise, amber, and pearl. Then, taking care for Maggie's hurt ankle, Meadow Lark helped her pull on a pair of heavily fringed knee-high moccasins that were equally exquisite. The squaws combed out and replaited Maggie's hair, lacing ribbons and baubles through her braids, and afterward hung length after length of beads about her neck. Only then did they leave, and her husband swept back in. He regarded her with amazement.

She glared up at him. "Look at me! All these baubles . . . not to mention, bells in my hair. I'm sure I look ridiculous."

He chuckled and leaned over, scooping her up in his arms. "You look pretty fetching to me."

White Wolf carried Prairie Star out to the center of camp and placed her down beside him in the circle the braves normally used for council. Other couples and families had also gathered for the feast; bowls of buffalo stew and berries were being circulated. Several warriors danced with tambourines or rattles by the fire, to the accompaniment of drum and flute.

Maggie felt very moved as members of the tribe came forward to present her with gifts, which White Wolf explained were to thank her for saving the child: Buffalo Thunder gave her a beautifully crafted wooden saddle, fringed and covered with buckskin; Autumn Quail presented her with an intricately braided, silver-studded headband; Spring Lark placed before her a lidded basket with leather quillwork lining. Maggie thanked each person in turn.

Next, Black Hawk came forward and spoke to Maggie soberly in Comanche. When he had finished and stood waiting with arms akimbo and head held high, she turned anxiously to White Wolf. "What did your brother say?"

"My brother says he will hunt for you the finest mustang to thank you for saving the life of his son."

Maggie beamed at Black Hawk; he grinned back.

"And he offers to bed you tonight to honor your great service to our tribe," White Wolf added tensely.

Maggie gasped, her smile fading. Black Hawk scowled and glanced at his brother. White Wolf solemnly shook his head, and Black Hawk made a sound of frustration and proudly strode off. Maggie breathed a sigh of relief, and did not protest when she felt White Wolf's arm slip possessively around her waist.

After everyone had eaten and drunk their fill, Spirit Talker came forward to stand over Maggie. The old man removed a tiny pouch from his medicine bag and waved it over Maggie's head as he sang an incantation. The other Indians watched and listened as if mesmerized.

"He is summoning good spirits to guard you," White Wolf whispered, and Maggie smiled.

When he finished his song, Spirit Talker presented Maggie with the small bag. She solemnly accepted his gift, thanked him, and whispered to White Wolf, "What is it?"

He took the tiny pouch, opened it, and sniffed the pungent contents. "Yarrow balm," he murmured, and rubbed a little of the salve on her wrists. "It will soothe your ant bites."

Indeed, Maggie found the balm soon alleviated the itching and stinging of her bites. Meanwhile, Spirit Talker was dancing and singing again, and waving his rattle. Afterward, he turned and addressed the entire tribe. Maggie grew bemused to watch the women of the tribe approach her with children in their arms, and set the young ones down beside her and White Wolf. Meadow Lark even came forward and placed Little Bear Claw in Maggie's arms. The boy gurgled up at Maggie happily, and a great cheer went up from the People.

Maggie turned to White Wolf to see him smiling at her with deep tenderness. "What does all this mean? Why have all the children been brought to me?"

"You have been made guardian spirit of the children, Prairie Star," he replied proudly. "It is a great honor. Never before in the history of the People has such great homage been given to a White Eyes."

The gesture, so moving and unexpected, was devastating to Maggie. She looked at the precious children surrounding her with their sunny smiles, at the People regarding her with new reverence and trust, at her husband staring at her with a devotion that could only be called love. And she burst into tears.

TWENTY

WHITE WOLF STOOD. HE GENTLY TOOK LITTLE BEAR CLAW
from Prairie Star's arms, and walked over to give the boy
back to his mother. Returning to his bride, he scooped her
up into his arms. She ceased her sobs and stared up at him
in uncertainty. After smiling at her tenderly, he turned to regard the bewildered faces of the People.

"Prairie Star is very moved by the honor you have bestowed upon her," he told the others in Comanche. "Her
heart is warmed and her eyes are filled with tears of joy."

A collective sigh of appreciation rose from the group, and
looks of mystification were replaced by happy smiles.

"But Prairie Star is very tired now," White Wolf continued soberly. "She injured her ankle badly today while rescuing Black Hawk's son, and she must rest."

Amid nods and murmurs of agreement from the People,
White Wolf carried his bride off to their tepee. A near-
painful joy welled in him as Prairie Star nestled her head
beneath his chin and did not resist him in any way. He felt
very touched by the emotion she had just displayed, by the
way she trembled in his arms. He felt such fierce pride,
such love for her.

Could she at last be responding to him and his People? Would she accept her proper place as his bride and the mother of his children? He pressed his lips to her hair and heard another soft sob escape her. He clutched her tightly to his heart.

Stooping down, he entered their tepee. He laid her down on her pallet and knelt above her. For a moment the two stared at each other starkly, their eyes expressing all the anguish of the barriers still separating them. He watched a tear roll down her cheek, and then she held out her arms to him—

White Wolf could have wept with happiness. He carefully lowered his body on top of hers, and pressed his lips to her sweet, quivering mouth. He tasted her tears, heard her low gasp, and then her arms were wound tightly around his neck and she was kissing him back with a passion that unleashed a wild flame of desire inside him. The mating of their mouths grew hot and unbridled, their tongues plunging deeply, exploring and melding. Fearing his weight might hurt her, White Wolf rolled onto his side and brought Prairie Star's supple curves against him, coiling his arms around her and kissing her ravenously several more times. He could tell from the way she shivered, from the tightening of her nipples through her deerskin dress, that she was as aroused as he was.

After a moment, both pulled back just to breathe. White Wolf stared down into his bride's tear-streaked face, her lovely visage outlined by the hazy light spilling in from the smoke hole opening above them.

"Don't cry, Prairie Star," he soothed. "I'm here. I'll comfort you."

"Perhaps that is what I'm afraid of," she whispered back convulsively.

"Why do you cry?" he asked. "Is it because you were moved by the ritual?"

She nodded. "It was a great honor. But I cry because . . ."

"Yes?"

"I cry because this is impossible."

"Why? Now you are a part of me—a part of my people."

"No," she denied hoarsely. "I can never be a part of this, and that is why I weep. I can't become emotionally caught up in the struggles of your tribe, especially not when the People's very existence is in jeopardy. I can't ..." Again her voice caught on a sob, and she shoved her fists against his shoulders in a gesture of futility. "I can't love these children."

"Or me?" he asked in torment.

She didn't reply, but her eyes were luminous with sorrow. "Why, Prairie Star?"

"Because sooner or later this must end!" she cried. "You have kept me here against my will, convinced that sooner or later I will accept you and the others. But you have sadly deluded yourself. I can't abandon the entire civilized way of life that I built for myself before coming to Texas. And perhaps the most tragic part of all is that you seem incapable of accepting my feelings—or even deciding in which world you're meant to live."

She began to weep again, and White Wolf held and comforted her, while the truth of her words tortured his soul, and his heart ached with an unbearable grief that was surely equal to her own. She had told him she was moved by him and his People, but she would never accept this life, or his half-Indian blood. Unless she understood and embraced the Comanche part of him in her soul, the love he felt for her was doomed. And he did love her, he realized, for never had any woman's suffering affected him so. How much longer could he let her be tortured, when he was responsible, when, indeed, he was the only person who could release her from this purgatory?

When she fell asleep against him, he kissed her smooth brow and covered her, then moved away to his own pallet, not trusting himself if he lingered too long beside her sweet, tempting body. He lay awake for many hours, looking up through the smoke hole at a single white star looming far above him.

A tear burned his eye. Was he living a fool's dream?

Were the two of them doomed never to share the love of his vision, never to become as one mind, one body, one spirit, as the prophecy had promised? After Prairie Star had spoken her heart, even as he had held her, he had felt so lonely. Now he feared the distance between them might never be bridged.

But he would still try. Until the day he took her back to her own world, he would still try to win her love . . .

Maggie awakened in the middle of the night in terrible pain. Her ankle was throbbing horribly. She reached down to touch the bindings and gasped in torment.

Instantly White Wolf was beside her, hovering over her, his breath warm on her cheek. "What is wrong?"

"My ankle hurts," she panted.

"Perhaps the bindings are too tight," he replied. "I'll loosen them."

Fear of additional pain made her panic. "Please, no—"

"Don't you trust me, Prairie Star?"

"This has nothing to do with trust. It's just that—even touching it is agony."

"I'll be gentle . . . and I'll make it better."

Although she stiffened with anticipated discomfort, his deep voice soothed her, and his touch was careful as he unwrapped her bindings and then ran his fingers over the throbbing joint. Even though he took great care, she bit her lip and fought tears.

"It's very swollen," he murmured with concern.

"I know."

"One time after I hurt my knee in a riding accident, I found it really helped to soak the injury in the creek. I'll take you there. We'll soak the ankle and also wet the bandages with the cool water."

Before she could protest, she felt herself being lifted into his arms and carried out of the tepee. He bore her quietly through the camp and toward the creek. The velvety night embraced them, with its moist, nectar-scented breeze, its sounds of cicadas and owls. But Maggie found the splendor of midnight paled in comparison with the mesmerizing power of the man who held her, his arms so strong beneath her back and knees, his chest hard and hot against her side, his scent filling her with potent, primal urges.

What was happening to her? She remembered holding her arms out to him earlier, something she *never* would have done mere days ago. Of course, she had been at the emotional breaking point then. Never had she expected such kindness and warmth from his people; never had she expected to be accepted by them so unreservedly. Still, in her heart she knew that her reaching out to White Wolf had gone far beyond the mere need to be comforted. The physical and spiritual bond between her and her husband was growing strong, frighteningly so, threatening to swallow up the civilized Maggie she knew.

She tensed as they approached the moonlit embankment. "Careful," she murmured. "You might trip in the same prairie dog hole."

He chuckled. "Concern for me, Prairie Star? I'm touched."

She fought the building excitement she felt. "I don't want to take another spill! Especially not if *you* should fall on top of me!"

"Do you fear my weight will crush you? I didn't hear any such complaints earlier."

Maggie fell silent, all too charmed by the sensual teasing. White Wolf's weight had felt wonderful earlier. Still, she hoped he would not expect her to grant additional favors now, for if he did, she feared she would be lost! Maybe he had no such designs in mind, she hoped desperately. Hadn't she explained things to him earlier, outlining logically why there could never be a future for them?

Yet logic seemed to have little effect when they were close like this, when memories of his wonderful kisses inundated her, making her feel starved for more!

He continued steadily down the embankment, taking her to a small shelf of packed, smooth earth fronting the rushing stream. He set her down carefully and plopped himself beside her. She gulped as she viewed him sitting next to her, outlined in the moonlight. He wore nothing save a breechclout, and his glorious, near-naked body was mere inches away from her own, breathtaking in the quicksilver light. She felt sorely tempted to reach out and caress one of those magnificent, hard-muscled thighs covered with coarse black hair.

"Put your ankle in the stream," he directed.

Grateful for the distraction, Maggie immersed her foot in the cool, rushing water. "Oh, that feels good."

"We'll stay here until the swelling goes down," he replied.

Sensing sexual innuendo in his tone, Maggie studied his face. Spotting a glint of mischief in his eyes, she dared a glance downward and spotted a hard bulge straining against his breechclout. Her mouth went dry. She heard his low chuckle, and hastily averted her gaze.

For several moments they sat quietly together amid the sounds and scents surrounding them, the perfume of honeysuckle and night sage mingling with the rushing sound of the creek and the distant howls of coyotes. In the seductive ambience of the night, Maggie felt as if she and White Wolf were alone in the entire, vast world. If only there could be just the two of them, she mused sadly. If only they did not come from such diverse worlds which might never become reconciled. Otherwise, she could love this man, she thought—she could give her heart to this tender warrior who ministered to her despite her refusal to serve him.

She felt his hand on her shoulder, and stiffened slightly. But when he began carefully kneading her tight muscles, she relaxed and even moaned in contentment.

"Better?" he murmured after a moment.

She nodded. "With the coolness of the water, I don't feel the pain in my ankle as much—although I doubt I'll be able to sleep tonight."

Maggie instantly regretted her words, for they were a blatant invitation to White Wolf to fill her restless hours. Judging from the slow grin spreading across his face and revealing his perfect white teeth, this meaning was hardly lost on him.

He reached out and gently stroked her cheek. She shuddered with combined fear and excitement at the intense passion burning in his eyes.

"No," she whispered.

"No?" he teased back. "And you don't even know what I want yet."

Her heart was pounding in her ears. "I know what you want."

"Do you?"

He surprised her then. With a gentle, fluid motion, his large hands gripped her beneath both knees. He eased her onto her back and pulled her up toward him, kneeling between her spread calves.

Maggie pressed her thighs together and gazed up at him, wide-eyed. "No," she whispered again, with less conviction.

"No?" He smiled. "I just want to massage your ankle, Prairie Star."

"My ankle and what else?" The reckless words tumbled from her mouth, without thought.

"That sounds perilously close to an invitation, woman."

"It—it isn't."

"We'll see."

He caught her swollen ankle in his hand and lifted her leg, hiking her skirt in the process and leaving her to squirm and frantically tuck the deerskin between her thighs, so he would not be afforded a generous view of her forbidden recesses. She nearly died when he raised the ankle to his mouth and tenderly kissed the bruised joint.

"No—you shouldn't . . ."

His tormenting lips moved over the aching flesh, soothing her in a manner she found quite shocking. "I should not kiss your ankle? Do you think there is any part of you I would not kiss, Prairie Star? I would be most pleased to demonstrate, you know."

Maggie sucked in huge breaths and did not trust herself

to reply. White Wolf propped her heel on his bare thigh, and she cried out as he began massaging the sprain.

"Relax," he whispered. "You're making the pain worse by fighting it. Trust me."

She breathed a convulsive sigh and tried to relax. He continued to knead the swelling with his thumbs, and after a moment, she found the massage did feel very good. Then, when his titillating fingers grew bolder, tracing a trail of fire from her ankle to the sensitive back of her knee, she found herself fighting an altogether new kind of tension. She knew she should tell him to stop, but somehow she couldn't.

He stared deeply into her eyes. "You know, sometimes pleasure can make a person forget about pain."

Maggie was already eminently aware of that fact.

"It happened to me one time."

She studied his face carefully and was intrigued and touched by the taut emotion reflected there. "Tell me."

He sighed, a faraway look drifting into his eyes. "After I took my mother home to die, I stayed on at the ranch for a time, trying to plan what I should do next, while Uncle Sam made inquiries about my education."

"That was when you were eighteen?"

"Yes. And I met a girl."

Maggie stiffened. "Who was she?"

"Judy Lynn Tucker, the daughter of the rancher who owned the spread next to ours. Judy Lynn and I used to go riding together, but in secret. She was fascinated by the Indian in me. We spent many hours talking about my years with the tribe."

"What happened?"

White Wolf's titillating fingers stroked the back of Maggie's knee, then moved higher. Her thighs clenched more tightly, but he took no notice.

"Everything was fine until the world intruded," he related with some bitterness. "The first time I went into town . . . There were some mule skinners at the saloon who'd heard I was a half-breed. They started to taunt me about not wanting to share the bar with trash like me. When I refused to leave, all six of them dragged me outside and beat me half to death."

Maggie gasped at this image of a young, proud, vulnerable boy being battered by a gang of sadistic miscreants. "Oh, White Wolf. I'm so sorry—"

Bitterness shone in his eyes. "Sheriff Lefty saw the entire incident, but refused to intervene. Those bastards left me to die like a dog on the street. Judy Lynn was going through town in the buckboard, and that's when she spotted me."

White Wolf's hand was now halfway up Maggie's leg, his fingers trying to entice her into spreading her thighs for him. She tensed even tighter, and he increased the subtle pressure.

"Did she help you?"

"She took me to one of her father's line shacks, and nursed me there." Abruptly his knee slid powerfully between her thighs, prying them apart.

Feeling the hair-roughened skin of his knee next to her most intimate recesses, Maggie gasped, horrified and scandalously aroused. Her attempts to close against him only resulted in deeper, more shocking contact. "White Wolf, please . . ."

His knee retreated, but was promptly replaced by his fingers, which stroked her inner thighs. "And even though I was half-dead, she gave me her virginity that night."

For a split second, Maggie froze. His words left her so shocked, and so irrationally, intensely jealous, that she abruptly stopped fighting him. He sensed her surrender at once and moved his fingers into her feminine cleft, stroking her gently, tormentingly. Pleasure swamped her in devastating waves that had her drawing in fevered breaths between her clenched teeth.

"So you see, Prairie Star," he went on, "that's how I learned that a little pleasure can obliterate a lot of pain."

Maggie was beyond answering.

"Let me take away your pain," he whispered, and pushed a finger inside her.

Maggie's body welcomed the brazen invasion. White Wolf's words and touch had left her reeling in a combination of feverish ecstasy and wild jealousy. But even as transported as she felt, she had to know how his story ended. "What happened . . . with you and this woman?"

"I wanted to marry her, but when her father found out, he forbade the marriage, and she refused to disobey him and run off with me. Since there was no child, there was nothing else I could do."

"Were you hurt?"

He stroked deeper. "I think I loved her."

She clenched a fist and struggled not to move against his electrifying touch. "Do you still?"

He shrugged. "She's somebody else's wife now. I wouldn't have married you, Prairie Star, if my heart were not free."

"And if there had been a child with this woman?"

"I would have forced her hand, carried her off. I never would have allowed any woman to steal my child."

"You carried me off, and there was no child."

His rough thumb found her tiny nub and caressed it expertly; she cried out, arching away from the powerful pleasure, and his other hand slipped beneath her to hold her still.

"That is because we are one, whether my seed is in your belly or not."

Maggie tossed her head in desperation. "White Wolf, please . . . You must stop."

"Stop?" His mesmerizing thumb moved in a slow circle, and her raw sob only emboldened him. "But you do not want me to. Your thighs are spread widely now and you are slick with wanting me. You are still fighting the instinct to move with all the passion you feel, holding back due to pride and fear. But soon all your doubt will vanish, your pride and your resistance will crumble."

Could this man read her mind? The prospect was devastating to Maggie, and made her feel totally vulnerable to her tender, skilled lover. "We can't . . . we mustn't risk having a child." Her gaze beseeched him. "Please. Not now."

"Not yet?" he added meaningfully.

She nodded.

He stared down at her intently for a moment, then murmured, "You are right. We will make a baby together only when you give yourself to me in total love. And you will soon. For now, I wish only to take away your pain."

He continued stroking and probing, and Maggie cried out in torment and shattering pleasure. After his sharing, she felt so close to him, and felt a deep yearning to help heal *his* hurts. Tears welled in her eyes as she again imagined him as a proud young warrior, spurned by society, a battered outcast who had sought comfort in a young woman's arms, only to feel the cruelty of a second rejection by her and the community that feared him.

"Move with me, Maggie," her husband urged huskily. "Let yourself feel the pleasure."

Ultimately it was her new emotional awareness of White Wolf that broke Maggie's control. Uttering a ragged moan, she let her inhibitions slip away and writhed against his wonderful hand. Soon pleasure engulfed her with a force that was frightening. White Wolf's mouth settled gently over hers, soothing her as the pressure built relentlessly, hurling her toward a riotous ecstasy she had never known before. As she whimpered with the force of her climax, he drowned her with a violent, rapacious kiss that in every way matched the savage power of her own rapture.

His fingers left her and she gazed up at him, panting, feeling almost bereft.

"Give me your breast," he whispered.

Shamelessly Maggie ripped open the ties to her bodice. For a moment her husband stared down at the ripe globes with their tight peaks. Then he leaned over, tugged on a hypersensitive nipple with his teeth, and she moaned in abandonment. She heard him dipping his hand into the water, and wondered why he was doing this. Surely he wasn't going to—

He was. A moment later, two cool, slick fingers pushed inside her, stretching and penetrating until they rested, hard and frigid, deep inside her smoldering heat. Maggie cried out at the incredible splitting pressure, the shocking tactile sensation. She felt hot and cold all over, consumed by shivers. Her muscles went into spasms around the unyielding probe, and she arched her back as a second dazzling climax began to seize her. White Wolf sucked deeply on her breast and used his fingers to drive her past the devastating pinnacle. Maggie sobbed with frustration, uncertainty, and finally, incredible ecstasy.

When at last his fingers left her and he knelt above her, she lost all control and reached out to stroke him through his breechclout, finding the splendid hardness of him. At his agonized groan, she was certain he was going to take her, but instead, he folded back his breechclout and rubbed himself against her crevice, stroking and probing, teasing and retreating, driving her mad. Wantonly she caressed his satiny, hard shaft with her fingers, increasing her strokes to a frenzied pace, encouraged by his moans. Soon she was trying to impale herself on his rigid length, but she could not effect penetration without his assistance. She yearned to crush his splendid body to hers, to feel his hard naked chest against her bare breasts. But even as she held out her arms to him, he hung back, his gaze tortured as he continued to rub himself rapidly against her.

Maggie watched a mighty shudder roll through his massive body, and then his warm seed spewed over her. She felt no shame; indeed, bittersweet tears filled her eyes. She realized that, although it must have killed him, he had kept his word not to give her his child.

She was only distantly aware of him cleansing her between her thighs with a wet rag, then washing the strips in the cool water and rewrapping her ankle. She clung to him as he carried her back to the tepee. She felt replete, yet strangely hungry for more.

"Why didn't you let me hold you?" she whispered in a small, tortured voice. "I wanted to so much."

Another powerful shiver rippled over him, and he spoke hoarsely, his lips against her hair. "You know why, Prairie Star. If you had clutched me to your heart, your womb would now be holding my child."

Maggie realized her husband made perfect sense, but her chest ached with emotion, nevertheless.

TWENTY-ONE

Maggie was not certain how to react to White Wolf the following morning. From the moment they awakened, sensual awareness was thick in the air between them.

She opened her eyes to see him sitting on his pallet across from her, his forearms folded on his knees. He was dressed in breechclout and long leggings, and was watching her solemnly.

"How is the ankle?" he asked.

She braved a smile. "It's . . . better, I think."

He left his bed and moved to her side, removing her bandages and running his fingers over the bruised joint, then rewrapping the sprain. "The swelling is down," he commented with approval, "but it's still too early for you to try walking on it."

"Then how will I, er . . . ?" She blushed, all of a sudden painfully aware that she needed to relieve herself. "How will I do anything?"

"I'll help you," he replied.

She raised an eyebrow.

He laughed, scooping her up in his arms and carrying her outside and into some nearby trees.

Maggie hobbled behind a broad-trunked cypress to see to her needs. She mulled over her magical moments with White Wolf last night. She recalled how the painful memories he had shared had left her feeling so very touched, so close to him. She remembered her own wanton surrender. Her husband had moved her both physically and spiritually, bringing her to a dazzling ecstasy she had never dreamed was possible. Even when he had spilled his seed on her intimate parts, she had felt no fear or distaste, only an intense desire to take his vibrant essence inside herself, to become one with him completely. When she had awakened just now to find him staring at her, she had felt giddy in his presence, craving a repetition of last night's fevered passion with an intensity she knew could only defeat her.

Oh, what was she going to do, as bewitched as she was by him? She was going to lose herself, leave Maggie behind and become Prairie Star, the squaw. At the moment, she wasn't sure she even cared, so caught up was she in the potent, addictive feelings White Wolf aroused.

She limped back around the tree and he was there in a flash, sweeping her up into his magnificent arms, cradling her against his hard, muscled chest. The sound of his deep laughter filled her heart with joy. She stared up at his handsome, noble face, his untamed hair. Her beautiful savage. It occurred to her that he belonged in this primitive, wild setting.

Did she? The very thought unnerved her as much as it excited her.

"Thank you," she whispered breathlessly.

"Thank me with a kiss," he demanded huskily.

At once shameless again, she curled her arms around his neck and kissed him ardently, as around them bees buzzed and birds sang. Their lips parted slightly and their gazes locked, hungry and searching. Then White Wolf crushed her lips again, kissing her back.

After a languorous moment, he winked at her. "That was some kiss. In your present state, you tempt a man to take advantage."

"And you didn't last night?"

"Did I?"

"No," she whispered, and White Wolf's mouth descended on hers again, his kiss sweeter and fiercer than before.

The next days passed happily for Maggie. White Wolf saw to her every need, carrying her around the village and bringing her food and water. Maggie felt more and more shame and uncertainty regarding her refusal to become a true wife to him, especially since no task seemed beneath his dignity as he cared for her. He was behaving so endearingly that she very much feared she was falling in love with him, even as she knew that for her, loving a half-Indian would always be impossible.

When Maggie was not with White Wolf, she was now surrounded by children. Ever since she had been appointed "guardian spirit of the children," she had assumed a new place, and new respect, among the tribe. No longer did the squaws snatch their young ones out of Maggie's path when White Wolf proudly carried her past. Now the tots were left with her while their mothers attended to their chores. Since it was still nearly impossible for Maggie to walk, she soon found herself directing the children in rapid half Comanche, half sign, and beseeching the older girls to retrieve the younger babies when they wandered off. She enthralled all the children with stories and games, teaching them how to jump rope and play hide-and-seek, and telling them fairy tales such as "Puss 'n Boots" and "The Three Bears." Little Bear Claw in particular became Maggie's almost constant companion. He would sit in her lap and play with her braids or beads, demand she teach him how to count with his fingers, or doze against her shoulder with his thumb in his mouth.

The first time Little Bear Claw threw his arms around Maggie's neck and kissed her cheek, she had to fight back tears. White Wolf, passing by with Chico, glimpsed her cuddled with the child, and winked at her. Watching her husband stride away, Maggie found herself wanting his Indian baby with an intensity that threatened all her convictions and left her trembling. At times such as this, she again found it difficult to remember her civilized life back in Boston.

Further battering Maggie's resolve was the fact that the People now constantly showered her with gifts, bringing her food or flowers or clothing. True to his promise, Black Hawk presented her with a beautiful white pony he had captured and trained himself, to thank her for saving his son. This total change in the People's attitude toward Maggie hit her very hard. She still felt wary of Indians and the tribe; and yet they accepted her without qualm as one of their own. After spending so much time with the People, she did find she was beginning to understand both the pride and the tragedy of the Comanche experience: They were a brave people, born hunters, who had seen their food supply, the buffalo, slaughtered for hides, while the white man broke treaties, stole their lands, and drove them inexorably toward a civilized life on the reservation that they could never truly embrace, short of violating their noble, wild spirits.

Yet for Maggie, all these verities were coupled with the demoralizing, unchanging knowledge that she could not truly be happy here. She could never become White Wolf's obedient squaw-bride, devoting her life to menial tasks, watching her children grow up among a roving band having to scrape for its every bite, and at war with the *tahbay-boh*. For if what White Wolf had told her was true, the days of his people roaming and living free were numbered.

But knowing the truth didn't make it any easier for her to face reality when, emotionally, she was becoming more caught up in her marriage and the Comanche world. She was certain her husband must have noticed her softening attitude, but he did not comment directly, nor did he try to push her physically to consummate their relationship. He did treat her as if she was his now, touching her with a possessive intimacy that kept her constantly rattled and often breathless. Sometimes she felt as if he were deliberately toying with her, when his hand cupped her bottom intimately while he carried her about, when his strong fingers lingered on her thigh as he laid her down, when he leaned over to steal the day's third kiss, and left her in a state of terrible agitation and desire . . . Increasingly she sensed that he would never have to force her to surrender to him completely, for the strength of her own passions would soon compel her utter capitulation.

White Wolf was pleased by the change in his bride's attitude. He liked having Prairie Star depend on him, and having her appreciate all the little things he did for her. He was careful, however, not to push her too far; her reservations were starting to melt away, and if he only took care, she would soon be his. When he caught sight of her holding and loving one of the babies, he ached for the day when she would welcome his seed inside her. Would she ever accept him, and the Indian part of him, so fully?

He felt disappointed on the fourth day after her mishap, when one of the village elders, Rock Coyote, presented her with a makeshift crutch he had whittled for her from an oak branch. Prairie Star took delight in the gift, and was soon hobbling around on her own. White Wolf felt rather hurt to watch her reassert her independence, and he feared she did not need him anymore. He missed touching her, holding her in his arms . . .

Maggie sorely missed depending on White Wolf and having him carry her around. Her body ached to feel him close again. Nonetheless, it was nice to be able to make her rounds on her own, and she enjoyed watching the activities of the other squaws, and even taking part, chopping roots with Creek Flower, weaving baskets with Battle Ax and Brown Thrush.

On that bright morning when she joined the mother and daughter at their labors near the creek, Maggie detected no lingering contempt as the two squaws instructed her on weaving dried grasses together to make a grain-storage basket. The women tutored Maggie patiently, and all three laughed over her initial clumsiness. Before the morning ended, Maggie found she couldn't resist having a bit of fun. Communicating partly in Comanche, partly in sign, she patiently explained to Battle Ax that the "pet name" White Wolf had given her was an insult. At first the older woman seemed confused, scowling and demanding additional explanations. Then as she finally understood, an expression of outrage gripped her fleshy face . . .

White Wolf had observed the women with their heads together near the creek, and he wondered what was going on. He was very pleased to see his bride joining in on some of the activities of the other squaws, but from the giggling he had overhead, he also suspected Prairie Star might be up to some mischief.

A few minutes later, Battle Ax walked past while he was playing dice with his brothers, and calmly dumped a container full of dirty wash water over his head. White Wolf's brothers howled with laughter, watching him cough, sputter, and wipe globs of hair from his face. The large squaw merely lumbered off proudly, leaving White Wolf to stare after her in consternation.

Next, at the midday meal, a smiling Battle Ax brought White Wolf a bowl of buffalo stew. He accepted her gift with a wary scowl, then glanced downward to see several live worms swimming around in the gravy! With a muttered curse, he tossed the bowl aside, much to his brothers' further amusement.

Finally, late that afternoon, White Wolf was bathing downstream in the creek when he watched the harridan steal out of some bushes, grab his clothing, then dash off, ignoring his angry shouts. Unable to face the prospect of parading through the village stark naked, White Wolf was forced to remain in the frigid water until one of his brothers happened along and could go fetch him a breechclout.

White Wolf had endured these assaults with forbearance; but when he retrieved the rest of his clothing in the brush and discovered that the old witch had filled his moccasins with mud, his patience snapped and he grimly sought out

Prairie Star. Still barefoot and dripping wet, he found his bride sitting on the embankment, telling a story to a group of fascinated children. All fell silent at his approach, and observed him with amazed expressions.

White Wolf waved the muddy moccasins at his bride. "What is the meaning of this? Why is Battle Ax tormenting me?"

She smiled guiltily. "Why, I have no idea."

"Not true," he retorted as several children held hands over their mouths to stifle giggles. "I can tell you are in on this up to your eyeballs."

The eyes White Wolf had just referred to gleamed with mischief as Prairie Star looked her husband over in his breechclout, her gaze lingering on his wet, gleaming flesh. "Well . . . didn't I tell you someone should inform Battle Ax that the name you gave her is an insult?"

Amid the snickers of the children, White Wolf shook a finger at her, although he too was now fighting laughter. "You'll be punished for this, woman."

Turning and striding away, White Wolf meant his words. The instant he was able to get Prairie Star alone, he pinned her against a tree and chastised her thoroughly with passionate kisses . . .

That evening, Maggie helped the other squaws prepare the meal. Creek Flower handed Maggie a plate of buffalo steak and asked in Comanche, "You take to White Wolf?"

It was a moment of truth for Maggie. Noticing that all the squaws were intently waiting for her response, she died a little inside. She never would have dreamed that such an innocent question would bring so much pain. After all, her husband had served her for days now; he had also melted her heart with his kindnesses and kisses. It was only just that she serve him now.

Yet Maggie couldn't bring herself to perform even this simple duty; for she well knew that serving White Wolf now would signal her capitulation, would tell him that she was prepared to become his Comanche bride, to share his bed and bear his children. This she could not do.

She knew she had already become far too fascinated with the Comanche culture; at times, when she spoke in the Indian tongue or in sign, when she participated in traditional activities with the other women, she felt almost totally disconnected from her old civilized self. She was intensely grateful to White Wolf; she was moved by him, proud of him, possibly even in love with him. But she could not become his squaw and risk spending the rest of her life roaming with the tribe, her white identity swallowed up, as had happened to Cynthia Ann Parker before her. For days, she had tried to avoid this sobering, central truth, but she could no longer.

Fighting tears, she shook her head to Creek Flower. "I'm sorry. I just can't."

Sitting with the other braves, White Wolf watched their women bring food. Then he spotted Prairie Star standing apart from the others; she did not come to serve him.

Outrage welled in him. After all that he had done for her, could she not extend him this one, small courtesy?

The terrible insult was duly noted by the other braves. "Your bride makes a fool of you, White Wolf," remarked Black Hawk with a disapproving frown. "For a week, you have been her slave, and now she ignores your needs."

White Wolf received this admonishment in sober silence.

"The woman has too much pride," commented Big Bow. "She needs to be humbled, to be taught her place."

Even Buffalo Thunder seemed of a similar mind. "Sometimes a warrior must be very stern with his squaw," the old man said. "The refusal to honor the obligations of marriage is a most grave matter."

White Wolf had had enough. He got up and stalked off to confront his bride. "Why do you not bring me my food like the other women do for their husbands?" he demanded.

Prairie Star hesitated, her eyes bright and her lower lip

quivering. She appeared on the verge of tears, but he felt neither satisfied nor appeased.

"Why?" he pressed. "I have served your needs for days, Prairie Star. Is it beneath your dignity to bring me my meal?"

She breathed a deep sigh. "White Wolf, I am grateful for all you have done for me. But to serve you . . . That would be saying I'm your squaw. And I can't become an Indian for you."

"If you will not even try to understand my culture, then you will never understand me," he reiterated vehemently.

In her torment, she clenched her fists. "Isn't that merely your excuse to keep me here, forcing me to embrace a doomed way of life, possibly compelling our children to do the same?" Choking back tears, she forged on. "Do you think this has been easy for me? Do you think sometimes I don't yearn to give in? I'm fighting for who I *am* here. Why can't you understand that?"

He regarded her with pride and anguish. "I think you are still fighting who *I* am. From the moment I tried to give you my mother's necklace, you have rejected my Indian heritage. Before we can address the question of our future together, we must fulfill our destiny to live together as a Comanche warrior and his squaw."

"Our destiny," she repeated hoarsely. "That has a very final ring to it. Tell me, do you ever intend to let me leave here?"

He was silent for a moment, blinking rapidly. "I have made my feelings clear, and you have responded once again with defiance. Do not think for a moment that I won't treat you as any other brave treats a disobedient squaw."

"I'm not afraid of you!" she asserted with bravado.

"Then you are a fool," he snapped back, stalking off to rejoin his brothers.

TWENTY-TWO

SADNESS AND CONFUSION ASSAILED MAGGIE FOLLOWING HER confrontation with White Wolf. It was clear to her now that her husband was telling her that they had to give the Comanche way of life a chance in order for their marriage to survive. In a sense, she could understand his thinking, and his turmoil seemed genuine. It was true that she hadn't fully accepted White Wolf's Indian blood. Part of her wanted to yield and give his way a chance, but she felt uncertain of the consequences if she did. For if she became White Wolf's squaw, wouldn't she be robbing him of all incentive to take her back to civilization? And wouldn't she possibly be depriving herself of her one remaining chance to leave the tribal community? Logic still argued that if she gave in, White Wolf would expect her to remain among his people forever—whereas if she continued to resist, sooner or later he would have to admit defeat and return her to her own kind.

Yet despite her doubts, Maggie felt agonized by the distance between herself and her husband, especially when she still wanted him desperately, and yearned to make him happy. She didn't know what to do.

* * *

Even as Maggie wrestled with her dilemma, White Wolf battled within himself. The resurgence of feelings of alienation between himself and his bride was painful to bear, especially after the closeness they had known following her injury. He felt at war between his wounded pride, his determination to make her give in, and his desire to do the right thing, the nagging voice of his conscience, which argued that he should take her back to live among her own kind. Increasingly it became apparent that she would not become a true Indian bride to him short of his resorting to physical force, a possibility his own values denounced. They seemed at an impossible impasse.

Then sudden tragedy struck the People. White Wolf was grooming his horse one afternoon when he watched Silver Knife and Straw Horse ride into the village, their faces grim as they led two horses on which bodies had been draped. White Wolf joined his brothers at the center of camp. Pandemonium erupted as the People observed the dead, mutilated corpses of Spotted Deer and Antelope; both men had been scalped, their eyes gouged out, noses sliced off, and flesh scored. At the hideous sight, the warriors howled a lament and the women shrieked and tore their hair.

"What happened?" White Wolf asked Silver Knife.

The brave slid to the ground, his features taut. "Buffalo hunters. Antelope and Spotted Deer were out rounding up mustangs when the white hunters murdered them and disfigured their corpses. Straw Horse and I came upon the scene just as the hunters were riding away."

These awful details rippled through the ranks of the People like a venomous curse. Battle cries and demands for vengeance spewed forth from the warriors; fists were waved in anger, and rifles and bows were grabbed. White Wolf noted that the wives of the slain warriors had thrown themselves near the corpses and were wailing piteously; two of the women were already slashing their own hands or faces with knives, and their blood flowed freely.

Buffalo Thunder took in the scene with a tragic face. Af-

ter exchanging an anguished look with White Wolf, he knelt
by the fallen warriors and began rocking and singing a lament. Spirit Talker started toward the spectacle, then
stopped in his tracks with a look of horror; White Wolf
guessed he was momentarily too overwhelmed by this evidence of bad medicine to even approach the corpses.

White Wolf watched an ashen-faced Prairie Star rush up
and take in the grisly sight of the disfigured corpses and the
squaws slashing themselves.

"What has happened?" she demanded of her husband.

He pulled her away from the others. "Stay back, Prairie
Star. You must not interfere."

"But why are the warriors dead, and why are the women
cutting themselves?"

"Spotted Deer and Antelope were killed by buffalo hunters. Now their widows immolate themselves to show their
grief."

"But they could be badly hurt—or even die!" she protested. "We must stop them."

She started off, but White Wolf grabbed her arm and
yanked her back. She tried to jerk free, and he shook her
slightly.

"No, Prairie Star," he said sternly. "This is Comanche tradition. You must not interfere."

Her mouth fell open. "These women are mutilating themselves, and you say we must just allow them to do so?"

"It is a part of our culture you may never understand, but
you cannot change it. The widows' grief will be all the
more intense because their mates have lost their souls . . ."

"What do you mean, lost their souls?"

"They have been scalped," he replied bluntly. "According
to Comanche belief, scalping destroys the soul, and thus the
spirit may never go on to the Happy Hunting Ground."

"This is why Indians scalp whites?"

He nodded grimly.

She shook her head in bewilderment. "And you believe
this cruel hogwash?"

"It's not hogwash to the Comanche," he retorted. "I'd ad-

vise you to heed your tongue, since you are obviously incapable of understanding my people or their traditions. There
will be a council over this—"

"And a retaliatory raid?" she pressed.

"Yes."

"You will ride with the others?"

"Spotted Deer was my cousin—and Antelope was one of
my uncles."

Her features softened. "I'm very sorry."

"If you know what is best for you, you will heed my
words and stay away," he warned, and walked off to speak
with his father.

Maggie stood with her eyes riveted to the ghastly demonstration beyond her, feeling more nauseated by the immolation rite than she had felt on spotting the corpses. It was bad
enough that the bodies of Antelope and Spotted Deer had
been so horribly maimed; but now the blood of their griev-
ing squaws poured over them, and this, to Maggie, seemed
nothing short of obscene. Why wouldn't White Wolf do
something to stop it? He might be half-Indian, but he was
also half-white. Didn't he realize that these women might
bleed to death, or die of infection from their wounds?

In the space of only a few moments, Maggie's sense of
affinity with the People had been shattered. Although there
were elements of the Comanche culture that she could understand and appreciate, here was a custom totally alien and
incomprehensible to her. What she was witnessing now re-
inforced in her mind as never before the sobering reality
that there was no meeting ground between hers and the Comanche world.

Feeling a tug on her skirts, she looked down to see Little
Bear Claw standing beside her, his face drawn with fright
and confusion. Compassion welling in her, she scooped him
up into her arms and comforted him, taking him far away
from the shrieking and the immolation.

The mood of the council that day was angry and vengeful. White Wolf sat with the others, solemnly hearing Black

Hawk's long oratory: All white hunters were bad medicine, bad magic, he argued; they must be hunted down like mad dogs and destroyed, as must the whites in Rio Concho who sheltered them.

For once, White Wolf felt hard-pressed to mitigate his brother's demands for blood, since he too was sickened and enraged by the needless deaths. When his turn came to speak, he agreed that those responsible for the murders must be held accountable, but he insisted that innocent lives must not be taken. White Wolf made his statement with a heavy heart: In truth, he was sickened by the possibility of violence; but he knew some action was called for against the hunters, or the white devils would feel free to slaughter the People, and steal their bison, with impunity.

Several other warriors took the floor, supporting Black Hawk or White Wolf, or suggesting that the tribe pick up and move as far away from the evil *tahbay-boh* as possible. As usual, Buffalo Thunder became the mediating force. Today he sided with White Wolf, agreeing that the true culprits must be made to pay, but pointing out that if an all-out war were launched against the *tahbay-boh,* the white calvary and rangers would become stirred up like hornets knocked from their nests, and would hunt and kill the Nerm until they were extinct.

Ultimately Buffalo Thunder's wisdom prevailed. It was decided that tomorrow, following the funeral of Spotted Deer and Antelope, a raid would be launched against the buffalo hunters. As a precaution, the camp would also be moved.

Once the council ended and most of the braves had dispersed, White Wolf lingered by the fire with Buffalo Thunder. "Do you think we have chosen the right path, my father?"

Buffalo Thunder nodded. "The code of our forebears demands that we avenge our slain brothers. We must also drive the hunters from our lands, or else we will all starve." Buffalo Thunder gazed solemnly at White Wolf. "Like you, my son, I take no joy in the necessity to kill on our own

lands. But we will do our duty to the tribe. And I have decided I will lead the expedition this time."

White Wolf grew alarmed. "No, my father. Your health
will not withstand the rigors of the journey. I have seen you
coughing up blood of late, and you must not go."

But Buffalo Thunder only shook his head, while both
sadness and great dignity shone in his dark eyes. "Every
warrior must fight his last battle, and every chief must lead
his braves for the final time." He touched White Wolf's arm
and spoke soulfully. "This is my time, my son, and we both
know it. Do not try to dissuade me from being a man and
commanding our brothers to avenge the blood of our own."

Staring into his father's noble, time-ravaged face, White
Wolf nodded sadly. He understood and honored his father's
wishes, though the truth that he would soon lose his father
wounded him like a knife in the heart.

The next day, only hours after the bodies of Spotted Deer
and Antelope were borne back to the village, Antelope's
widow, Autumn Quail, collapsed and died from blood loss,
her baby screaming on the cradleboard still attached to her
back. Another nursing mother, Running Deer, at once rescued and adopted the baby, but the loss of Autumn Quail
caused great lamentation among her older children and the
rest of the tribe.

By that night, the ominous cadence of war drums began,
and most of the braves danced by the fire, shaking rattles
and tomahawks, their faces blackened, their voices raised in
battle songs and yells. Maggie was both horrified and
amazed to watch her husband join the others, wearing only
his breechclout, moccasins, and war paint. She stared at
White Wolf through the smoke, utterly mesmerized. There
was no hint of a white man left in the Comanche who now
danced about the fire, his black hair hanging about his
shoulders, the muscles of his near-naked body gleaming and
rippling in the flickering light of the flames. White Wolf
seemed caught up in some primordial vengeance rite that
went deeper than blood and was totally beyond Maggie's

comprehension. Yet as she watched her magnificent savage move to the beat of the drums, his body performing rhythms older than time, she felt desire stir in her at his raw virility. The intense response left her breathless and aquiver; she felt both repelled and fascinated by her primitive response, her treacherous longing to lose herself in him and in the Comanche culture, whatever the ultimate price she must pay. When she thought of how he might be killed in the raid, her anguish was unbearable, and it took all her strength to finally turn away.

She could not sleep that night, for on went the dance, the drums, the battle yells. She heard some of the warriors galloping off, screaming cries of fury in the night, and she prayed White Wolf was not among them.

After some of the younger, more impatient warriors rode off to launch an impromptu raid in the night, White Wolf sat with Buffalo Thunder by the fire. The two men discussed tomorrow's planned campaign, then Buffalo Thunder dozed against a stack of firewood, snoring loudly until Fair Moon came to nudge her husband gently to his feet and lead him off to bed. White Wolf lingered outside, concerned by his father's plan to lead the expedition. But mainly he was lost in thoughts of Prairie Star, awash in the painful knowledge that tomorrow they would be separated.

Yet had they ever truly been one? He had seen his wife watching him as he danced the war dance with his brothers, and he knew she was moved. Desire had ignited him as well at the sight of his beautiful bride standing beyond the smoke, the wind rippling her deerskin dress against her curves as she stared at him as if hypnotized.

He was tempted to go to her now and unleash the savage in himself. If he was killed in tomorrow's raid, this might be their last chance to be truly joined.

Yet he held back. Prairie Star was still not ready to give herself to him completely. And what if he gave her his child this night, and then tomorrow he was killed? To leave her a widow and pregnant would burden her terribly. Although he had seen proof over past days that she would love a part-Indian child, the sad truth was that Prairie Star still had not accepted him as her husband, nor had she completely embraced his culture. If he died after giving her his seed, she would not be happy until she left the Comanche and raised the child far from the People and everything Indian. The thought of this part of his heritage being annihilated forever was unbearable to him. Although he had always intended eventually to return Prairie Star to her own culture, he had also hoped that throughout their lives, they would maintain at least some contact with the People.

He stared up into the vast heavens until he found her, his white, bright star. He burned for her, but she was still far away and unreachable. Perhaps their destiny would never be fulfilled. Perhaps he should have recognized the bad omen back on their wedding night, when she had cruelly shattered his mother's necklace.

This was White Wolf's last, anguished thought as he lay down by the fire and drifted off to sleep.

Before dawn, White Wolf was awakened by sounds of the hunting party returning. The young warriors galloped into the village, empty-handed and obviously frustrated. One of the braves broke his bow in disgust and tossed the pieces into the embers of the fire that still glowed near White Wolf.

Watching the braves stalk off, White Wolf smiled ruefully. Only the younger, more hot-blooded braves had ventured forth again last night; the more experienced warriors knew it would be far easier to track the hunters by the light of day.

White Wolf went to check on Prairie Star. He stood just inside the tepee staring down at her. She looked very sexy sprawled on her pallet; she had undone her braids, and her flame red hair spilled about her lovely face. One knee was raised, hiking her skirt and giving him a tempting view of creamy calves and thighs, as well as displaying the enticing curves of her bottom.

It was a lovely way to remember her, he thought, and felt his chest tightening with poignant emotion. How he wished he could awaken her with a kiss—but to do so might well defeat the far more sobering purpose gripping his heart this morning.

As if she sensed his presence, she jerked awake, flipped over, and stared up at him. "What is wrong?" she whispered groggily, rubbing her eyes.

"The funeral of Antelope, Spotted Deer, and Autumn Quail will be held shortly," he informed her. "I thought you would want to be there."

"Thank you, I'll get ready," she replied, sitting up.

He offered her his hand and pulled her to her feet. "After the ceremony, the raiding expedition will depart. We could be gone for many days, until we find the white hunters responsible for the deaths of our brothers."

"It could be very dangerous," she murmured.

"Yes. While we are away, you and the other women will move the village to a safer spot further west."

"But how will you find us?"

He shrugged. "We will know. Most likely, you'll set up camp in a more secluded spot along the creek."

He was turning to leave when she called, "White Wolf?"

"Yes?"

She bit her lower lip. "Where were you last night?"

He raised an eyebrow in astonishment. "You really want to know?"

She glanced away awkwardly. "I heard warriors leaving in the night. Were you among them?"

"No. I slept by the fire."

She gazed at him boldly. "Why?"

He stared back at her with equal intensity. "Why do you think, Prairie Star? I'm no longer sure I can sleep in this tepee and keep my hands off you. And I didn't think it would be fair to go off to raid with my brothers, risking my life, and possibly leave you pregnant."

Obviously rattled, she stammered, "But you *are* leaving

me—and you just expect me to move on with the other women?"

"Yes."

Twisting the fringe on her dress, she said, "Isn't this postponing the inevitable—taking me even further away from civilization, when you know what my feelings are about this marriage?"

"I know you have closed your mind against this ever working," he rejoined bitterly, "or ever accepting who I am."

She stood with eyes downcast. Finally, she asked, "Be careful, will you?"

He stared at her for an anguished moment, then crossed the distance between them, crushing her in his arms and kissing her as if he might never kiss her again. "I'll take care, Stella-Sanna."

He left quickly, not trusting himself to remain.

Maggie was both amazed and moved by the funeral ceremony. The two warriors and the woman were dressed in the finest deerskin and draped with beads and baubles. Their faces had been painted yellow, black, and orange, and feathers were stuck in their hair. They were placed near trees, facing the rising sun.

As the medicine man approached the corpses, dancing and intoning his incantations, the People brought forth gifts and belongings for the dead, laying next to them everything from bottles of water, sacks of grain, and pouches of pemmican, to bows and arrows, saddles and tomahawks.

Standing near Creek Flower, Maggie whispered, "Why all the supplies for the dead?"

"For journey to Happy Hunting Ground," replied the girl.

Maggie was bemused. "Will Spotted Deer and Antelope ever get there, after being so horribly mutilated?"

The girl shook her head. "The People fear they haunt the earth as ghosts. That is why tribe must move. Ghost magic very powerful, very bad."

After the ritual, the men prepared to depart, the women helping them load their horses with provisions. Maggie cautiously approached White Wolf, feeling vulnerable and uncertain following their wrenching moments in the tepee.

He stood with his back to her as he checked the girth on his Spanish-style saddle, and for once he was dressed from neck to toe in fringed buckskins. Attached to his saddle were parfleches with his rations, his war shield, bow and arrow, and a rifle in its sheath. A shiver of premonition shot up her spine at the sight of the gun. Oh, God, was she going to lose him now, when there was still so much unsettled between them? Her pride and her fear seemed to matter little now.

As if feeling her presence, he turned to regard her tensely, and it occurred to her that they were as wary as two strangers.

"You are taking rifles?" she asked.

He nodded. "We'll have to have guns to successfully take on the buffalo hunters. In the past, many Comanche bands have been annihilated by Colt repeating pistols carried by Texas Rangers. I have a Sharps rifle and a Colt Dragoon, and several of my brothers are similarly armed."

"Just don't let one of those flying bullets catch you," she scolded. "I may not agree with everything you have done to me, White Wolf, but I wish you no ill."

He nodded, appearing to accept her sincerity. "Silver Knife will be staying behind to help move the village and to guard the women. I've gotten his promise that if I'm killed, you will be returned to your people."

Maggie was deeply touched by his gesture, and again jarred by the possibility that she might never see him again. Staring at his beautiful, noble face, the vivid blue eyes that could burn so brightly with passion or dance with laughter, she hungered to touch him one last time, to try to close the vast gulf between them. She yearned to beg his forgiveness, even though her intellect argued that he was the one who should seek atonement.

Even as she struggled within herself, battling powerful impulses, White Wolf proudly mounted his pony and rode off with his brothers.

TWENTY-THREE

MAGGIE WAS ASTOUNDED BY THE MOBILITY OF THE VILLAGE. Twenty minutes after the men departed, the women had taken down all the tepees, rolled the stakes up in the lodge covers, and attached the long bundles to travois. The Indians' other belongings, clothing, pots, tools, and weapons, were quickly lashed together or stuffed into parfleches, and tied to pack animals. Maggie helped out where she could, but felt inept around the skilled women.

Then the long trek began, the search for a new base camp. The group of more than three dozen women and children trudged across the wildflower-strewn prairie. In the next five days, they hiked over fifty miles. Although the weather was mild, with light afternoon showers relieving the noonday heat, Maggie soon felt exhausted, especially because, like the other women, she carried a child in her arms the entire time. Her charge was Little Bear Claw, and even though her arms soon ached from bearing his weight, she was grateful for his sunny company, and glad that she had freed his mother, Meadow Lark, to carry his older sister in her arms, his baby brother in the cradleboard on her back. Maggie had to admire the stamina and courage of the Indian women, who never once complained during the grueling journey.

However, the arduous trek took its toll, especially on the children of the village. The infant girl whom Running Deer had adopted following Autumn Quail's death failed to thrive, and the tiny papoose was buried along the way. Another small boy succumbed to an infection only days after stepping on a large, sharp bramble. Watching the dead boy's mother wail over him, Maggie was once again daunted by the prospect of ever having a child herself amid such harsh and uncertain conditions.

At last the group set up camp in a distant canyon sheltered by mesquite and scrub oak. A fork of the creek provided an accessible water supply.

Maggie was relieved to be off the trail, but worried about White Wolf. During the entire trek, there had been no word from the hunting party.

Midnight found White Wolf and his brothers perched on the edge of a rise, the Comanche war party utterly still and silent, save for the soft sounds of their ponies snorting in the night.

To White Wolf's left was Black Hawk, to his right Buffalo Thunder. His father had endured the difficult journey with exceptional stoicism, although he often coughed until he was doubled over in pain, and White Wolf had noted that Buffalo Thunder had definitely lost weight during the hard five-day ride. He often mused sadly that the old chief kept going through the strength of his will alone.

Now, at last, their expedition had found its target. Beneath them in the valley were sheltered at least a dozen buffalo hunters who had made camp surrounded by their wagons and horses. The White Eyes, blissfully unaware of the threat from the Indians, were drinking and gambling around bonfires. They were also taking turns raping a white woman they had staked, spread-eagled, to the ground. The sound of the woman's screams echoed hideously through the night, filling White Wolf with disgust. He wondered

how she had come to be among the *tahbay-boh* hunters;
most likely, she was a whore or a dance hall girl they had
either taken by force, or enticed into joining them as a camp
follower.

White Wolf glanced in turn at Buffalo Thunder and Black
Hawk, and received a sober nod back from each man. The
time was ripe to launch their attack. He signaled to the other
braves, and the mounted group moved stealthily over the
rise, proceeding downhill until they were within striking
range. Black Hawk let out a war whoop, and the party
charged, braves shrieking and ponies prancing, for the kill.

The Comanches advanced like a black cloud of death and
vengeance. The ground shook with their hoofbeats; the
night rang with their ferocious screams. The braves rapidly
encircled their prey, coiling about the enemy like a spitting
serpent, creating a moving circle of dancing horses, flying
arrows, howling lances, and blazing bullets.

The hunters were taken completely by surprise. Several
of them fell dead even as they scrambled for their weapons
or horses. White Wolf watched as one of the scoundrels he
remembered from Rio Concho took a lance through his
chest and collapsed with a roar of agony onto a fire.

A number of the hunters did manage to grab rifles or pistols, and returned fire; White Wolf groaned as he heard Big
Bow's yelp of pain and watched him tumble from his horse.
White Wolf drew out his Colt and quickly shot the bastard
who had just possibly killed his brother; grim satisfaction
surged through him as the scoundrel emitted a harrowing
yell and tumbled to the earth. Then White Wolf cursed as he
spotted two hunters who strongly resembled Skeet
Gallagher and Clyde Smedley mounting their horses and
riding off, hell-bent for leather, into the night.

He considered pursuing them, then changed his mind,
wheeling his horse as he glanced about the scene. For his
brothers, the battle had already ended in victory. Almost a
dozen white corpses littered the ground, and except for the
two men who had escaped, all of the hunters were casual-
ties. White Wolf's brothers had already slipped off their po-

nies and were exuberantly bellowing their victory yells, taking scalps and counting coup, while Buffalo Thunder knelt singing a lament over Big Bow, who lay ominously still in the shadows.

White Wolf spotted one bearded hunter jerking in agony on the ground; he dismounted and strode over to discover that the man had a gaping belly wound.

"Please," the man whispered convulsively, blood oozing from his mouth as he clawed at White Wolf's moccasin. "Please help me."

"I'm afraid there is no help for you, my friend," White Wolf replied, and heard the man's gasp of astonishment at the English words.

As the wounded man fell into new, piteous moans, White Wolf realized there was no chance the man would survive his wound, though he might linger in agony for some days. If he did not expire at once, the other braves would likely take him back to camp, to be horrendously tortured by the women. This possibility White Wolf could not bear; nor could he abide the prospect of Prairie Star having to witness such frightful suffering.

He raised his Colt, gritted his teeth at the man's look of horror, and quickly killed him with a shot through the forehead.

Then a high-pitched feminine scream had him whirling. About twenty yards away, Black Hawk was about to scalp the white woman who was spread-eagled on the ground.

"No!" White Wolf yelled, racing toward his brother.

Black Hawk paused, his brutal, black-painted features outlined by the shimmering flames of a nearby bonfire. One hand cruelly gripped the woman's blond hair, while the other wielded his knife. "Good scalp—I take!"

"No!" Arriving at the scene, White Wolf grabbed his brother's wrist to restrain him. "The woman is blameless. She is not an ally of the hunters, but a captive they were brutally abusing. Let us take her back to camp."

Black Hawk hesitated, his face gripped by a mighty scowl. "Make slave?"

"Or squaw."

Black Hawk appeared far from appeased. "Give me your *tahbay-boh* squaw for her," he demanded arrogantly.

White Wolf promptly removed his pistol from its holster and extended it toward his brother, grip-first. "I'll give you my Colt for her."

Black Hawk scrutinized the handsome weapon, obviously wavering. After a moment, he glanced at the terrified woman, then shoved her away, grabbed the pistol, and stalked off. The woman fell back with a piteous moan.

Heaving a breath of relief, White Wolf knelt beside her, quickly cutting her bonds and pulling down her skirts. She cringed from him. He noted that her face and body were badly bruised, her clothing in shreds.

"Do not be afraid," he said gently. "It is all right."

Still trembling violently, she sat up and regarded him with dread and amazement. "Y-You speak English, mister?" she asked in hoarse frontier accents.

He nodded. Despite the girl's battered appearance, she was clearly very young and pretty, with pale blond hair and even paler blue eyes. "Yes, I am half-white. What are you doing here?"

Her lower lip trembled and she appeared ready to burst out sobbing.

He touched her arm. "Please—no one will harm you now, I promise. Now, tell me what happened."

She blinked at a tear, then nodded convulsively. "Two days ago, I—I was serving drinks at a cathouse not far from Fort Defiance. These characters come in and commenced flirtin' with me. They asked me to come along with 'um on the trail, and I said no way in hell. Musta riled 'um good, I reckon. Anyhow, when I left the saloon that night, they coldcocked me and carried me off."

White Wolf grimaced. "That sounds like a stunt Skeet Gallagher and Clyde Smedley would pull."

She gasped. "You mean you know the bastards that took me off?"

White Wolf's tone was bleak. "I've encountered them before, and I'm sure sorry they escaped tonight."

"Well, I'm plum thankful you folks come along when you did, even if you are Injuns," the girl replied earnestly.

White Wolf smiled at the young woman's gratitude, considering all she had endured. "You are safe now, though you may end up living with the Comanche for a time."

"No!" Possessively touching her hair, she hissed, "That black-eyed fella was fixin' to scalp me, mister, and I don't trust him for a minute."

"Do not worry," White Wolf reassured her. "Black Hawk is my brother, and I have convinced him not to harm you."

Her eyes went wide. "You bought me from him, didn't you?"

White Wolf chuckled. "No, I simply ensured that my brother would not lose face. You will be secure with our people now. My wife is white and she will also help you. Perhaps later on we can get you back to your own kind, but for now, I'd advise you not to complain."

The girl nodded soberly, only to cry out with fear as White Wolf's youngest brother, Bobcat, strode up to them. White Wolf was aware that the tall, handsome young man had recently completed his rites of manhood. Now he was staring at the white woman in fascination. Her look of panic quickly faded when he solemnly handed her a water bottle. Accepting the vessel, she flashed him a tentative smile. Bobcat grinned back before striding off; the white woman drank deeply.

White Wolf left her. He foraged around in one of the hide hunters' wagons until he found a hat and some buckskins for the woman to wear, since her own garments were a shambles. Then he coaxed to his side one of the abandoned mustangs of the buffalo hunters, and decided the small mare would make a fitting mount for her.

Leading the pony toward her, he paused and grabbed a Walker Colt that lay discarded beside one of the corpses. Holding the weapon up toward the moonlight, he noted that it appeared in poor condition compared with his Dragoon, but back at camp he could carefully clean and oil it. The loss of his favorite pistol was definitely worth the reward of saving the woman's life.

Although grateful that she had been spared, he was troubled over the outcome of the skirmish. They had killed many hunters tonight, but two had escaped, and more would come. Of course, Skeet Gallagher and Clyde Smedley had hardly honored legal niceties in killing bison on Comanche lands and in raping a woman; still, the massacre of their cohorts was bound to bring reprisals. Thank God the Comanche base camp had been moved. He and his brothers may have won the battle, but the war still raged on. The White Eyes would never stop coming until they stole all the lands and bison belonging to the People.

TWENTY-FOUR

At dawn, the raiding party headed home, after burying Big Bow in a sheltered canyon, where whites would be unlikely to see him and mutilate his spirit. White Wolf kept the woman they had rescued nearby, since she still seemed wary of the other Indians, with the exception of Bobcat, toward whom she appeared to be warming. White Wolf's brother continued to bring the girl food and water, and had saddled her horse this morning. Even now the boy rode directly behind them, his gaze riveted to the pretty girl dressed in buckskins, her pale hair spilling from beneath the brim of a large, plains-style feathered hat. White Wolf suspected that before they reached the tribe, the girl would be receiving a marriage proposal.

So far, White Wolf had learned that the girl was named Delilah Dinker and she was originally from Kentucky. Glancing at her, he noted the proud set of her chin and was reminded of Prairie Star. Despite her ordeal, the girl radiated a spirit, confidence, and matter-of-fact outlook on life that White Wolf found admirable. She would do well among his people if she chose to remain.

"Did you get any rest last night?" he asked.

She nodded. "I slept a heap sight better than I have since them varmints kidnapped me. Who'd a thought a passel of Injuns would have more kindness in 'um than a gang of white men?" Watching him frown, she hastily added, "Hey, I meant no offense."

White Wolf smiled faintly. "Tell me, Miss Dinker, how did you end up in Texas in the first place?"

"Please call me Delilah."

"Very well, Delilah, what brought you to our neck of the woods?"

She hesitated, sniffing at tears. "I come here from Kentucky three years ago with my folks and my older brother. We was camped south of the Red River, about to turn in for the night . . ." She paused to shudder. "Then a Kiowa raiding party come upon us like screaming demons in the night. Killed my ma and pa, and my brother, too. It was plain out a massacre."

White Wolf whistled. "How did you escape?"

"Guess I plum went loco," she confided. "When I seen what them Injuns done to my family, I snatched a half-burned log from the fire and waved it at 'um, and just screamed like worms was eating up my brain or somethin'. And the redskins just up and left."

White Wolf nodded; no doubt the Kiowa raiders had assumed the girl mad, and such potent medicine was feared among the Plains bands. "I'm sorry," he told her sincerely. "The conflict between the whites and the Indians here in Texas goes way back, but it was not the fault of you or your family. I doubt it's any comfort to you now, but many innocent lives have been lost on both sides."

Her gaze hardened slightly. "I know that, mister. Reckon I'm just grateful to be alive."

"How did you survive after you lost your family?"

She smiled ruefully. "Well, either that was a real stroke of fortune, or the devil jinxed me right good. After I lost my kin, I just wanted to lay me down and die beside 'um. But the next mornin' a passel of whores come along, bound for Fort Defiance. They helped me bury my clan and took me off with them. I've been working at the cathouse outside the fort ever since."

White Wolf shook his head. "How old are you?"

"Eighteen."

"And you've been stuck in that hellhole for three years?"

She shrugged. "It ain't so bad. The soldiers, when they get paid, can be right generous."

Generous if she delivered in equal measure, White Wolf thought cynically.

The girl regarded him curiously. "What about you, mister? You said you're part white. How come you're living with Injuns?"

"My mother was a white captive. She became the bride of my father, Chief Buffalo Thunder."

"You're the son of a chief?" she asked, clearly impressed.

White Wolf pointed to the north. "That's my father riding over there."

She craned her neck to see. "No offense, mister, but your pa looks plum whipped."

"He's quite advanced in years."

"And your ma? Is she waitin' at home with the rest of your squaws?"

"No. She died over ten years ago."

"Hey, I'm sorry, mister. Was she happy living with the Comanche?"

"No," White Wolf answered honestly. Watching the girl frown, he quickly added, "But other white women have fared well enough among us, and I still think you might be better off choosing our people over your own kind."

"Well, I'll think on it," the girl conceded noncommittally. She glanced behind them at Bobcat. "Why does that Injun keep staring at me? He was purely putting shivers up my spine before we broke camp this morning."

White Wolf chuckled. "I think my brother Bobcat is enamored of you. I doubt he's ever seen a woman with eyes or hair as pale as yours."

"Is he hankerin' for my scalp?" she asked in shrill horror, clutching her hat.

White Wolf shook his head. "Definitely not your scalp. You see, Bobcat doesn't have any wives yet."

"Wives?" the girl repeated, clearly amazed. "How many squaws do you Injuns have, anyhow?"

"Sometimes several—although I only have one. As I told you, she's a white woman like you."

"Ah," Delilah murmured. She glanced behind her at the boy again, fighting a smile when he grinned and waved. "You know, he's not a bad-looker for an Injun."

"And you might do worse than to become a Comanche bride."

She glanced at him sharply. "According to you, that ain't how your ma seen things. And what about your own white squaw?"

"She has not accepted her place, either," he conceded grumpily.

She snorted. "Well, for a fella trying to sell me on turning Injun, you shore ain't saying much to recommend the life, mister."

White Wolf sighed deeply. Doubtless Prairie Star would share Delilah Dinker's sentiments.

The group continued over the prairie, sending ahead two scouts to sniff out dangers and search for the relocated tribe. With the passing days, White Wolf became amused by the budding romance between Delilah and Bobcat, and his father remarked on this, too. The courtship began tenuously, with little courtesies: Bobcat giving the girl his comb to use, pointing out a stream where she could bathe, or offering her a cup of pemmican. Then, when Delilah began helping with the cooking at night, White Wolf noticed that she would always take Bobcat his food first. Their third night on the trail, he watched the two walk together toward the sunset, holding hands, obviously communicating in some universal language. The next night, he spied them kissing behind a tree—

Their fifth night out, he watched the white girl pick up her pallet and go make her bed beside Bobcat. The two cud-

dled together, and White Wolf knew that soon they would
become lovers.

White Wolf smiled in the darkness. The white woman
had adapted quickly to her circumstances. She was a survi-
vor. When they returned to the band, she would doubtless
be installed in Bobcat's tepee as his cherished bride.

He wondered at the differences between her and Prairie
Star. Obviously, having been used as a whore, then raped by
a gang of hunters, Delilah Dinker had no illusions left. Was
it such fanciful hopes that made Prairie Star so determined
to return to the white world? If he continued to insist that
they fulfill their destiny, would he crush her spirit in the
process, or would she, like Delilah, adapt?

These troubling questions left him at war with himself
and unable to sleep.

When the party departed again shortly after sunrise,
White Wolf noticed that Bobcat and Delilah now shared the
same pony. Looking supremely happy, the girl rode behind
the brave, her arms coiled tightly around his naked waist,
her thighs molded to his, her chin on his shoulder, their long
manes of hair—his midnight black, hers pale as the sun—
rippling together in the wind. The sight of the blissful couple made White Wolf remember the day he had given
Prairie Star riding lessons, and made him yearn for her with
a painful intensity.

They found the new Comanche village early the following afternoon. As soon as the scouts alerted the camp that
the war party had returned, the children of the tribe raced
out to exuberantly greet the triumphant warriors. White
Wolf hoisted one of his small nephews onto the horse with
him, and the boy laughed in delight as they cantered into
the village.

Near the center of camp, the women, a number with babies on their backs, converged on the band. With happy reunions going on all around him, White Wolf slipped off
Blue Wind, helped his nephew down, then searched the sea
of heads for Prairie Star. At first he could not see her. He

did observe Big Bow's wife, Fast Fox, searching through the ranks of the warriors, frantically trying to find him, and saw Buffalo Thunder painfully dismount and go to give the squaw the tragic news.

He heard Fast Fox's loud wail of grief and watched her fall prostrate to her knees. A split second later, he spotted Prairie Star standing apart from the others on a nearby rise, staring at him intently. In her pale deerskin dress, with her long red braids resting on her shoulders, she looked even more beautiful than he had remembered. Gladness and intense relief filled him that she was still here, that she hadn't tried to escape.

White Wolf strode toward her. She took a tentative step, and then, as if their hearts and minds had touched, both broke into a run. Within seconds, she thrust herself into his arms, raggedly whispering his name. He clutched her tightly, absorbing her softness and the sweet scent of her. She gazed up at him with a stark joy that warmed his heart, and he quickly, passionately, kissed her. They clung together, trembling, for a long moment.

At last she smiled up at him shyly. "You are all right?"

He caressed her soft cheek. "Yes."

"It's good to see you back."

"It's good to be home."

As they moved apart awkwardly, uncertainty and poignant longing seemed to hang in the air between them. Prairie Star glanced worriedly at Fast Fox, who was rocking and wailing beyond them. "Did Big Bow—"

"He was killed when we attacked the buffalo hunters," White Wolf related somberly. "But many of the villains died for their treachery on our lands."

"Then your raid was successful?"

"Yes." He forced a smile. "And how was your journey with the women and children?"

She drew a heavy breath. "I'm afraid we lost two young ones—Running Deer's adopted baby, and Morning Sun's little boy."

"I'm very sorry to hear that," he murmured sincerely.

All at once, Prairie Star's eyes grew huge as she spotted Delilah striding past, holding hands with Bobcat. The couple, who had eyes only for each other, were headed straight toward the young man's lodge. "Who is that white woman?"

"She's a girl-of-the-line by the name of Delilah Dinker. She was kidnapped by the hunters we tracked. On the night we attacked them, we found her being raped by the bastards."

"How horrible! And you saved her?"

"Yes, and convinced her to come here to live among the People."

Bitterness clouded her gaze. "You will not take her back to her own kind?"

"No."

He watched her ball her fists at her sides. "Then you're treating her as a captive—just like me?"

A muscle worked in his jaw. "Not exactly. You see, Delilah has adapted to her circumstances. She and my youngest brother appear to have fallen in love during our return journey, so I'm sure she now has no desire to leave the People."

Her expression resolute, she stared after the couple. "Well, I think I should speak with Miss Dinker myself to assess her feelings."

"By all means. I'm sure she would welcome your friendship."

Frowning in bemusement, she watched other couples pairing off and going to their tepees. Uneasily she asked, "Why are so many retiring to their lodges?"

He chuckled. "The warriors have been gone many days on the trail and they have missed their women. They wish to be welcomed home properly." Raising an eyebrow at her meaningfully, he added, "It is a tradition among our band."

She glanced away, her face hot.

White Wolf sighed, realizing Prairie Star would hardly invite him to their tepee for a private homecoming, since it was clear she still felt many of the same resentments toward him. Being this close to his bride—yet unable to demonstrate his feelings—was torture.

Determined not to let her see his disappointment, he said calmly, "Now that I know you are all right, I will go speak with my father and offer my condolences to Fast Fox."

Maggie watched her husband stride off proudly, and almost called after him. Somehow she managed to stop herself. In truth, she had missed him terribly over the past week and a half, and had felt overjoyed to see him. Never had she seen a more blessed sight than her magnificent warrior riding back into camp on his war pony, especially with the young child sitting before him on his horse. She still felt very tempted to welcome him back with all the passion his splendid image had stirred. And being in his arms just now had been paradise.

After all, he could have been killed. The very thought chilled her blood, and made her realize how precious and fragile both their lives were, how short might be their time together. And yet she still could not bring herself to surrender, for if she did, her entire future and identity could be lost . . .

Watching his son approach with a tense face and discouraged gait, Buffalo Thunder coughed raggedly. "Your bride does not welcome you as the other squaws greet their returned warriors?"

Shaking his head grimly, White Wolf noted how haggard his father appeared, with dark, sunken circles beneath his eyes. Buffalo Thunder never should have gone along on the raiding party.

The old man drew a raspy breath and continued solemnly. "A brave and his squaw who do not see each other for many days should have a powerful thirst, and should drink deeply of each other, like desert wolves on first spotting a stream."

"A thirst cannot be forced," muttered White Wolf.

"Perhaps not—but sometimes a squaw's obedience must be coerced."

Anxious to change the subject, White Wolf nodded toward Fast Fox, who was on her knees weeping and wailing several feet beyond them. "Fast Fox grieves badly for Big Bow."

"Yes, I fear she will soon immolate herself," the chief fretted. "She is too young to risk death that way. She has not bred yet, and needs a baby to distract and comfort her. She must have a new husband at once, I think."

White Wolf felt a prickle of alarm, for his father was staring at him meaningfully. "Give her to Black Hawk. I know he wants her. I have watched him summon her to his tepee on several occasions."

But Buffalo Thunder only shook his head. "Your brother already has more squaws than he can handle, and he also mates like a rabbit with the wives of his brothers. He takes the vows of marriage too lightly, I feel. I think Fast Fox would prefer a warrior such as you as her next mate."

White Wolf was astounded. "Me? But I already have a bride!"

"You have a squaw in name only, a wife who shows you nothing but contempt," Buffalo Thunder contradicted soberly. "You need a bride who respects and reveres you, and joyfully attends to your needs. Even though Fast Fox loved Big Bow, I have oft observed her serving you, and staring at you with the eyes of a doe on watching her stag approach."

White Wolf's sense of uneasiness deepened. "Exactly what are you proposing, my father?"

"As Big Bow's brother, you must accept responsibility for his widow. I give the woman to you as your second bride."

White Wolf groaned. "Prairie Star will not be pleased."

"Prairie Star's misery is of her own making," answered his father sternly. "It is time for your first bride to stop thinking of her own selfish needs and start seeing to yours. Perhaps the news of your second marriage will encourage your white squaw to assume her rightful place and attend to her duties."

White Wolf ground his jaw, fearing just the opposite might occur. Nonetheless, being asked by his chief to take on his brother's widow was a sacred obligation he was duty-bound to assume, unless his father was willing to release him from the responsibility.

Solemnly he said, "My father, I would prefer this honor be bestowed upon another. But if it is truly your wish that I care for my brother's widow, then I will take Fast Fox as my second bride."

"It is my wish."

White Wolf sighed deeply. "Then I will accept your dictate."

"I am pleased."

With faltering gait, Buffalo Thunder walked to the widow, Fast Fox, crouched low, and spoke with her. A moment later, she gazed up at White Wolf, her tear-streaked face brightened by a tremulous smile.

White Wolf nodded back to the girl, but felt deeply distressed. He knew Buffalo Thunder was giving Fast Fox to him to teach Prairie Star a lesson, to goad her into performing her wifely duties. But he also knew Prairie Star much better than his father did. He understood her pride, her stubbornness, and he sensed disaster in the offing. He very much feared that, far from disciplining Prairie Star, his father's ploy would only backfire in all their faces.

Maggie waited across from Bobcat's lodge, determined to speak with the white woman as soon as she emerged. Obviously the girl was well occupied at the moment, judging from the mating moans spilling out through the tepee walls. Those wanton, sensual sounds left Maggie feeling like a voyeur, and awash in her own potent longings for White Wolf.

At last Delilah Dinker emerged with Bobcat. Maggie gasped at the sight of the two of them together—the bronzed, slender, handsome boy-man, and the pale, beautiful white woman who so obviously was now his squaw. Delilah Dinker had changed into a lovely beaded deerskin dress; her long hair was braided. As for Bobcat, he wore only a breechclout, and was grinning brazenly at the girl, obviously well satisfied from their moments in bed. As Maggie watched in fascination, he placed his hands squarely on her behind, snuggled her close to his loins, and kissed her ardently. She curled her arms around his neck and kissed him back.

A moment later, watching Bobcat strut off still wearing a cocky grin, Maggie felt her hopes sinking. Delilah Dinker had found herself a Comanche husband, and would likely not be interested in joining Maggie in her crusade to leave the People.

Nonetheless, Maggie bucked up her courage and approached the girl with a smile. "Are you Delilah Dinker?"

The young woman grinned back. "Sure am—and I can't recall a time when being Delilah Dinker felt no better. You must be Prairie Star."

Puzzled that the girl knew her name, Maggie extended her hand. "Please, call me Maggie."

Delilah nodded and accepted the handshake. "Your husband told me all about you, Maggie, and I'm right happy to make your acquaintance."

"And I can't tell you how relieved I am to see another white face." Maggie touched the girl's arm. "Please go with me for a stroll. We must talk."

"Sure, whatever you say."

The two women proceeded down toward the creek, walking beneath the shade of large cypress and willow trees. They spoke at length, Delilah sharing her tragic background and telling of how the Indians had rescued her, Maggie relating her own dramatic tale of unwittingly marrying a half-Indian and later being kidnapped by him.

After hearing the details of Maggie's reluctant adventure, Delilah mused aloud, "You know, we've both been through hell, honey, but it's turned out for the best, ain't it?"

"What do you mean?" Maggie asked.

The girl smiled dreamily. "Bobcat has asked me to stay as his squaw, and I told him yes."

"You'd willingly stay with the Comanche?"

"And you would leave that handsome stud you're married to?" the girl countered, amazed. "White Wolf ain't just the purtiest man I ever seen—he's right smart and kind, to boot. Why would you want to leave him, honey?"

"Because he brought me here against my will!"

"You're his wife, ain't you?" the girl asked, nudging Maggie with her elbow. "Hell, that rascal wouldn't have to ask me twice to share his tepee—no offense intended, of course."

Maggie glowered. "I still don't understand why you would choose life with the Indians over the life you left behind."

"Working in a cathouse?" the girl scoffed. "Not to mention, gettin' hauled off and raped by buffalo hunters? You think all that was somethin' special?"

"No, but in the white world there are opportunities for a much better life—for us both. And I need your help to get out of here. I'm convinced that if both of us insist on being taken back to civilization, my husband may relent."

The girl's mouth dropped open. "Honey, have you gone plum loco?"

"What do you mean?"

"Where in blazes do you think you'll go—and what'll you do?"

"Why, I'll go back to Austin," Maggie asserted briskly. "I've a friend there, the landlady at a boardinghouse, who has promised to help me. And if you came along, I'm sure there are women in the community who would be willing to assist you, as well."

Delilah hooted a laugh. "Do you think them holier-than-thou queen bees will go anywhere near a whore like me? Hell, do you think they'll accept either of us back now that we've been sullied by redskins?"

Maggie paled. "I—I haven't been—that is, White Wolf and I haven't—"

Delilah waved her off. "It don't matter, honey, as long as they think you're tainted goods." She grabbed Maggie's arm and pulled her to a halt. "Let me tell you a story, honey. I been working near Fort Defiance for nigh onto three years now. Two summers back, an officer's sixteen-year-old daughter was kidnapped by Apaches. Missing for over a year, she was, till a cavalry patrol spotted her with the redskins. They chased off the Injuns and brought the girl back, still in right good shape. Weren't mutilated or nothin', like Injuns usually do."

"What happened?" Maggie asked anxiously.

"Why, she was plum ruined. Looked on with pity by all the ladies at the fort, and no man would go near her. The poor thing was brokenhearted. Within weeks, she run off to be with the Apaches again—and she died of exposure out on the prairie."

"Oh, my God!" cried Maggie.

"So you'd best accept what life has dished out to you, honey, 'cause it ain't gonna get no better than this," Delilah continued sternly. "Hell, I've received more respect from these Injuns since they rescued me than I ever got in the white world. I'm proud to be Bobcat's bride, and if I were you, honey, I'd be countin' my blessings and thankin' the good Lord for my handsome husband." Delilah nodded decisively. "Now I said my peace and I ain't sayin' no more."

The girl released Maggie's arm, turned, and started back for camp. Maggie numbly followed her. Delilah, with her earthy, no-nonsense wisdom, had raised points Maggie had hardly considered before. Was she ruined in the white world now that she had become an Indian captive? If this was the sober truth, then why wouldn't she accept her own lot, like this resilient girl who had lost her parents to Kiowa slaughter, and yet still was happy to become a Comanche bride?

Delilah might be a true realist, Maggie mused, but did that mean she must abandon her own dreams? She was still determined not to, and yet her feelings kept getting in the way. Intellectually, she was determined to return to her own kind; emotionally, she hungered to be in White Wolf's arms, in his bed . . .

She entered camp to spot an alarming sight—Big Bow's

widow, Fast Fox, was heading into her and White Wolf's tepee with a stack of belongings! Maggie rushed over to
Creek Flower, and knelt by the girl as she ground corn.

"What is going on?" she demanded. "Why is Fast Fox
going into my tepee?"

Creek Flower gazed at Maggie sadly. "Fast Fox new wife
of White Wolf."

"What?" Maggie cried, wild-eyed.

"Buffalo Thunder give Fast Fox to White Wolf as second
bride. Tonight the People have great feast to celebrate victory over buffalo hunters, and to honor new marriages—
Bobcat and Pale Eyes, White Wolf and Fast Fox."

Maggie was outraged. "Not if I have anything to say
about it!" She shot to her feet and was off in a flash.

TWENTY-FIVE

Fuming, Maggie rushed over to White Wolf, who was nearby, whittling lances with several of his brothers. "I must speak with you at once!" she declared.

White Wolf set aside his shaft of wood, shoved his knife in its sheath, and stood. He followed his bride to a secluded spot a short distance from the other men. "What do you want, Prairie Star?"

She whirled to face him, eyes blazing. "Why did I spot Fast Fox going into our tepee? Creek Flower said you have a second wife now."

White Wolf gazed at her narrowly, annoyed by her show of temper. "If I have a second bride now, then it appears you've just answered your own question, haven't you, Prairie Star?"

She gestured angrily. "You scoundrel—you mean it's true?"

"Yes. And why the tantrum? According to you, I don't even have a first wife—yet."

She seethed at his gibe. "Well, you certainly won't win me over by taking a second squaw."

"I thought there was no real chance of my winning you over."

She glared at him.

"I repeat, why are you so stirred up?"

Maggie felt hot color staining her cheeks. "Because— because it's the principle of the matter—"

"Ah, so now you're a woman of principle—and I presume that means you're a woman who lives up to the vows she makes?"

Floundering, she demanded, "How can you let that—that woman—share our tepee?"

"It is the way my people live, Prairie Star. Besides which, you're not afraid Fast Fox will see something, are you?"

She made a sound of strangled rage.

He heaved an exasperated breath. "Look, Maggie, my brother Big Bow was killed, and my father has decided that I must take responsibility for his widow—"

"And you have no say in the matter? Or do you *want* a second wife?"

His voice took on a hard edge. "According to the traditions of my people, caring for Fast Fox is both an honor and an obligation. To refuse my father's request would result in a great loss of face for him."

"Well, heaven forbid that Buffalo Thunder should lose face!" she flared, and stalked off.

White Wolf ground his jaw and watched his feisty bride storm away, not sure whether he wanted to grab her and kiss her, or turn her over his knee. He saw her approach their tepee, just as Fast Fox was emerging. He stood tensely as the two women exchanged words and gestures. Fearing an imminent catfight, he almost went over to separate the two, however inappropriate it might be for him to intervene. Then he breathed a sigh of relief when Fast Fox tilted her head high and walked off.

But White Wolf's sense of relief proved short-lived. Moments later, he watched in outrage as various belongings came hurtling out of the tepee opening—his war shield and lance, his bow and beaded quiver with arrows, as well as all of his and Fast Fox's clothing. This the other warriors quickly took note of; they gathered near the tepee to watch Prairie Star's shenanigans and laugh, only deepening her husband's sense of embarrassment and anger. Women and children assembled as well, observing the drama with amazement.

Wearing an expression of contempt, Black Hawk stalked up to confront White Wolf, communicating through passionate words and angry signs. "Your wife makes a fool of you. And now I hear our father has insulted all the warriors of this tribe by giving you Fast Fox. Why should you be rewarded with a second beautiful bride when you cannot even tame your first? Why will you not face up to your own lack of manhood and give both of your squaws to a warrior who is capable of mastering them?"

"Meaning you?" sneered White Wolf.

"Yes."

As White Wolf glowered back at Black Hawk, Silver Knife strode up, carrying a quirt. "Your wife throws you out of your own lodge," he said incredulously. "Shall I discipline her for you?"

Taking in the faces of all the warriors who regarded him with scorn, and at his father in the distance, who stared at him with pity, White Wolf quickly decided that Prairie Star had pushed him too far this time.

He grabbed the quirt from his brother's hand. "I will discipline my own bride!" he roared, and stormed off.

Looks of amusement were replaced by expressions of keen curiosity as White Wolf strode up to the tepee, yelling Prairie Star's name.

She emerged, faced him with defiance, and hurled his rolled sleeping pallet at his feet. A collective gasp flitted over those gathered as White Wolf stared murder at his bride and she held her ground with unflinching pride.

"What in hell do you think you are doing?"

"I refuse to share the tepee with you—or your second bride."

"That is not your choice to make!" he snapped back.

Waving his quirt, he gestured toward the possessions strewn
everywhere. "You have stepped over the bounds, woman.
Now you will replace all of my and Fast Fox's belongings
in the tepee."

"I will not!"

He grabbed her arm, and his voice rang with fury. "You
will, or I will thrash some sense into you—right now, in
front of the entire tribe!"

Maggie gulped as she spotted the rage glittering in White
Wolf's eyes, and viewed all the curious eyes focused on
them. "You would not!"

"I will, by damn—if you do not obey me this instant!"

Maggie gazed at her husband's murderous visage and realized he was serious. She hated him at that moment, even
as she still reeled with hurt and jealousy over his taking a
second bride. But she was also wise enough to realize that
he couldn't back down now, not with the entire tribe watching them.

"So you would resort to violence just to get your way?"
she demanded.

"You have driven me to it, woman!"

She shook free of his grip and faced him haughtily.
"Since you are determined to overwhelm me by physical
force, it appears I have no choice but to obey."

But as she started away, he seized her arm again. "I'm
not finished!"

She pivoted to face him. "What do you want now?"

"You will also help the other women prepare supper, and
then you will serve me—and my new bride—at the feast tonight."

"I will not!"

The rest happened so quickly, it made Maggie's head
spin. White Wolf dragged her to a nearby tree stump, sat
down, and hurled her across his lap, bracing a large hand at
the small of her back to hold down her squirming body. She
heard the quirt whiz through the air and felt as if her stomach had been punched; her buttocks tensed in anticipation of
the pain.

"All right!" she screamed.

He shoved her away and she landed, none too gently, on her knees. She glared up at him.

He stood and glowered down at her, his features implacable as he pointed the quirt at her. "Heed my warning, Prairie Star. Defy me again and you will be thoroughly disciplined—before everyone."

He walked off to the cheers of the other braves, and Maggie trembled in helpless rage.

Maggie savagely ground the pemmican she would serve tonight. Around her, several of the older squaws were tending buffalo stew, chopping roots or cactus fruit, or pounding grain.

To avoid the promised beating from White Wolf, Maggie had already replaced his and Fast Fox's belongings in their tepee; now she was unwillingly bowing to the second of his dictates, and helping with the meal.

Across from her at the center of the camp were crouched a huge number of Indians in a circle. Tonight both husbands and wives were being entertained by the medicine man, Spirit Talker, who danced about, singing and shaking his feathered charm, to the beat of drums and tambourines. The mood was festive—among the gathered couples were Creek Flower and Silver Knife, Delilah and Bobcat, and White Wolf and Fast Fox.

The sight of her husband with his second bride still made Maggie see red, although she had to admit that White Wolf had spoken the truth earlier; she had little right to criticize him for taking another squaw when she still refused to become a true wife to him. She recognized this reality on an intellectual level; emotionally, however, she was being torn apart. Part of her wanted to rush over, shove Fast Fox aside, and throw herself at White Wolf's mercy, and into his arms; part of her wanted to strangle them both. She felt furious, jealous, yet also hellishly vulnerable and hurt. She recalled the haunting night when she and White Wolf had become so intimate by the creek. How could he do this to her now?

Whatever his reasons, White Wolf was really rubbing her nose in her own defeat by forcing her to serve him and his second bride. But she knew with a sobering certainty that if she defied him, he would indeed beat her in front of everyone—and this humiliation, she could never endure.

One of the old squaws nodded at Maggie, then jerked her head toward the gathered couples. Maggie dutifully got up and began making her rounds, offering her bowl of pemmican to each Indian in turn. Black Hawk leered at her contemptuously as he grabbed a handful of the meal, and several other warriors hooted jeers. Her pride bristled and her sense of humiliation deepened. When she paused by White Wolf and his "bride" and bent over to serve them, Fast Fox took a handful of the meal and smiled at Maggie poisonously. Grinding her teeth, Maggie offered the bowl to White Wolf, and he smirked—

A split second later, all the remaining contents of the bowl were flung in White Wolf's face. Maggie gasped and jerked back, regarding her husband in horror, unable to believe what she'd just done—

The savage look on his face as he wiped away the mixture made her go sick with terror. With a roar of rage, he was up, and like a scared rabbit, she was off. She screamed as he chased her, the two of them overturning dishes and stumbling about, amidst the laughter of the entire tribe. Then Maggie was grabbed about the waist with a violence that all but took her breath away, and heaved over a powerful shoulder. She struggled, shrieked, and pummeled White Wolf's back with her fists, but he only strode purposefully toward their tepee. Oh, God, she thought in panic, this time she truly had gone too far and he would kill her—

He carried her inside, dumped her down, and made a dive for her. She crawled away frantically, but he seized her ankle, hauling her toward him, grabbing her about the waist, and hurling her facedown across his lap. He grasped a handful of her skirt and yanked it high over her hips. Mortified, she realized he intended to beat her bare bottom, and she squirmed wildly. He subdued her easily again by pinning a large hand at the small of her back; she felt the hardness of his loins against her bare lower belly, and shivers of mingled desire and fear coursed over her.

She struggled and screamed, "Let me go!"

For a moment he did nothing but continue to hold her powerless. Then the hand that would have punished her stroked her instead. Maggie gasped in outrage and renewed her mutiny, to no avail; White Wolf easily subdued her with one hand, while roving the other intimately over her bare backside, raising gooseflesh, shocking her to her Puritan soul.

A split second later, he tumbled her onto her back and came down on top of her, his massive, aroused body crushing hers. He tugged up his breechclout, all that separated their naked loins, and she gasped, her eyes growing huge as she felt his rigid erection.

One of his hands pinned both her wrists high over her head. She looked up to see that his eyes had gone near-black with passion and determination. A cry of fear escaped her right before his savage mouth descended on hers, his tongue drowning her, ravaging her mouth. Her incoherent protests were smothered in her throat. Maggie tried to resist him, but it was useless, for their struggles had unwittingly aroused her as much as they had stirred him. Within seconds, she was moaning softly; he released her hands and she curled her arms around his neck and kissed him back with complete abandonment.

She felt his stiff manhood probing her wetness, hurting her. He pulled back, stared into her eyes, and pressed harder. She winced and he smothered her sob with his lips. Still, he could not achieve more than the smallest penetration—

Suddenly both flinched as they felt objects battering the tepee, and heard the Indians hooting, whistling, and yodeling outside. White Wolf blinked rapidly for a moment and glared down at Maggie's bewildered face. Then he

withdrew from her, straightened his breechclout, stood, and
stalked out of the tepee.

Maggie felt utterly confused and bereft. She curled up in
a tight ball of pain and wept. She hurt not because of what
White Wolf had done, but because of what he *hadn't* done.

She did not leave their tepee again that night, so raw
were her emotions following the devastating encounter. As
the hours trickled by and White Wolf did not return, she felt
more miserable than ever. Where was her husband now that
darkness had fallen?

Obviously he was bedding his second bride, she thought,
heartbroken. She felt stunned by the depth of her own rage,
jealousy, and hurt over the fact that another woman was
now giving White Wolf what she still refused to give. If
only the other Indians hadn't interrupted! She would have
eagerly surrendered to White Wolf—and to hell with her
own fears and misgivings. Now it was too late. Desperate
sobs shook her at the realization that the man she loved lay
in the arms of another woman . . .

Actually, White Wolf was nowhere near Fast Fox. Indeed,
he had advised his second bride to remain away from their
communal lodge for her own safety. The girl slept tonight in
the lodge of Creek Flower and Silver Knife.

White Wolf sat by the fire, his spirit tortured, his body
burning with sexual frustration. Hours earlier, he'd come
closer than ever before to making Prairie Star his own. Now
his body craved her tight virginal flesh, but his spirit still
demanded the total emotional surrender necessary to make
her truly his. Anything less would be a rape of her spirit,
even if her flesh was willing.

He gazed up at the heavens and agonized, wondering if
there truly was a meeting ground for him and his Prairie
Star. Again he wondered if his vision was doomed.

Perhaps the white wolf was simply too far away from the
bright star, he mused sadly, and the vast gulf between them
could never be bridged; perhaps the wolf was only howling

at that very emptiness looming between them. He had come
to care for Prairie Star, with her pride, beauty, and spirit.
But had he taken this lovely star and turned her own dreams
into ashes? Should he at last relent and take her back to her
own kind?

He glanced up to watch his father lumber over to join
him. Sitting down painfully, Buffalo Thunder hacked out a
cough and asked, "Things are still not well between you and
your white bride?"

The look on White Wolf's face was ample answer.

The old man sighed. "I have a confession to make, my
son. I gave Fast Fox to you as your second bride in the hope
that my action would humble your first bride into assuming
her rightful duties toward you. But now it appears I have
miscalculated."

"I agree," muttered White Wolf. Then, feeling guilt at his
father's pained expression, he hastily added, "But Fast Fox
is far from the only problem between me and Prairie Star.
I do not mean to offend you, my father, but I must know,
how can I keep from following the same destructive path
you took with my mother?"

Buffalo Thunder long pondered the question, gazing up at
the heavens. "I will tell you a story, my son, of a wolf who
tried to take a mate among his pack. Both had proud spirits
and were meant for each other. But every time the wolf tried
to become one with his mate, she would hide behind the
others, or the others would run between them. Soon they
were split asunder."

"And what is the point of this parable?"

Buffalo Thunder stared solemnly at his son. "You brought
your white bride here, to be shaped by the Nerm to our way
of life. But I think you have followed this path as far as it
can take you. False pride between a warrior and his squaw
is a very private matter. Tonight, when you were in your
lodge with your woman, the entire village watched the walls
heave to and fro, and then the entire village watched the
shaking stop. It was then that your brother Black Hawk be-

gan throwing pebbles at your lodge, and goaded the other warriors into doing the same."

White Wolf nodded. "Black Hawk is still angry because you gave Fast Fox to me. He wants quite badly to bed both my wives."

The old man stared into the fire. "Were it not for his interference, I think your wife would have been shown her proper place by now."

White Wolf smiled. His father was very wise—and probably right. "What are you advising?"

Buffalo Thunder turned to White Wolf. "Only you can decide how best to mold and discipline your bride. But to speed you along that path, I have a suggestion, my son . . ."

TWENTY-SIX

Maggie JERKED AWAKE TO SEE HER HUSBAND LOOMING OVER her, standing just inside the tepee flap. He was bare-chested, wearing only a breechclout and long leggings attached to his moccasins. With his black hair down about his shoulders, his hard, taut body backlit by the sunrise, he appeared the totally ferocious savage. His words came harshly. "Get up and get out of here."

She was bewildered. "Why—"

"Do it, now!" he snapped murderously.

Eyeing his implacable visage and clenched fists, Maggie knew better than to cross him. She bolted to her feet and dashed out of the tepee. Then, to her stupefaction, she watched a repeat performance of her own rash actions of last night—White Wolf began throwing all of their belongings out through the entry flap.

"What do you think you are doing?" she yelled.

In answer, one of her moccasins sailed out through the opening and hit her in the belly. She gasped.

"What's wrong with you?" she shouted furiously.

This time she had to dodge White Wolf's *bois d'arc* bow as it flew out.

"Are you crazy?" she screamed.

His war shield and bear-claw necklace burst through the opening. Maggie shrieked epithets. But White Wolf ignored her ravings and finished hurling all their belongings outside. Then he emerged, breathing hard and glaring at her.

"Pack up your things," he ordered tersely. "We're leaving."

"You're taking me back to Austin?" she asked with a surge of hope.

"No. I'm taking you off to a secluded area, there to discipline you and teach you to become a proper squaw to me."

Maggie saw red. "The hell you are."

"The hell I'm not!"

"You've lost your mind!" she raved. "After all that has happened, you still think you can make me become a wife to you?"

His smile was cruel. "Yes."

"How dare you presume such a thing after you slept with another woman last night!"

Without commenting, he began taking down the lodge, yanking up the pegs holding down the tepee cover.

Maggie stamped her foot. "You have got to be the most stubborn and exasperating man I have ever met in my life!"

He was heedless, still tugging at the stakes. "And you're not the most stubborn woman?"

"I'm not going anywhere with you!"

"You are—or watch me finish what I started last night when I threw you across my knees!"

"You bastard! You're offering me no choice!"

He stormed over and seized her by the arms. His eyes blazed down into hers. "That's exactly right, Prairie Star. Maybe you spoke the truth the other day. Perhaps you did give up all your choices when you married me. Now, pack your things or I'm blistering your defiant little butt."

He turned and walked off, leaving her livid.

Maggie packed up her few meager belongings, downed some corn mush for breakfast, and seethed. Creek Flower joined her by the fire. The girl glanced askance at White Wolf, who was loading the rolled-up lodge cover and poles onto a travois.

"Why is your husband packing up your tepee?" the girl asked in Comanche.

"He says he is taking me off to properly tame me," Maggie replied in English.

Creek Flower frowned a moment, then brightened. "Perhaps it best the two of you work out your problems away from the others."

"Hah!" Maggie retorted. "He probably wants to take me off alone so no one will hear my screams when he beats me!"

The girl chuckled, then shook her head. "A warrior would never hesitate to thrash his wife in front of witnesses. White Wolf must have another goal in mind."

Maggie could guess precisely what that "goal" was. Her voice trembled with hurt and defiance. "If he thinks I will lie with him, after he bedded Fast Fox last night, then he is crazy."

"*Loco?*" the girl repeated, using the Spanish word. "But White Wolf did not lie with Fast Fox last night. Fast Fox slept in our tepee."

Maggie's jaw dropped. "Are you sure?"

Creek Flower nodded. "White Wolf slept alone, outside by fire."

Feeling as if the wind had just been knocked out of her sails, Maggie stared at her husband and gulped. The knowledge that White Wolf had ultimately not betrayed their wedding vows defused her outrage and made her feel very shaken and vulnerable.

What barrier did she have left against her husband, if not her anger?

Half an hour later, the couple started out of camp on separate mounts, White Wolf on Blue Wind, Maggie on the white pony Black Hawk had given her. White Wolf also led a mule laden with supplies and pulling the travois with their lodge.

The entire village assembled to observe their departure. Maggie's mortification and fury surged again as, all around them, men cheered and women snickered. The fact that her husband rode ahead of her, and did not even speak with her, only increased her righteous wrath.

On the outskirts of the village, Chico emerged from some trees and tried to trail along behind them, but White Wolf scolded him away. With a pathetic yelp, the dog retreated.

Observing her husband's action, Maggie felt uneasy; he must have some heavy disciplining in mind for her, or else he wouldn't have forbidden his pet to come along ...

White Wolf led his bride at a brisk pace for several hours, allowing them to stop only for a brief lunch of pemmican. Late that afternoon, he knew he'd found the perfect setting for their retreat when they eased over a rise to view a lush, rolling meadow afire with wildflowers—bluebonnets, Indian paintbrushes, and sunflowers. A deep creek offered water, and giant cypress trees provided ample shade.

Prairie Star gasped. "Oh, how lovely!"

He pivoted to stare at her, and watched color flood her cheeks. "Careful, Prairie Star, you're dropping your guard."

She glared.

He glanced back at the vibrant meadow, at a well-shaded clearing next to the stream. Pointing, he said, "We'll make our camp over there."

They cantered their ponies over to the open area. White Wolf dismounted and watched his wife slip from her mount.

She eyed him warily. "What now?"

"Now you are going to assemble our lodge, like a good little squaw."

She uttered a cry of outrage. "How dare you call me a squaw! Furthermore, you *must* be joking. I have no experience whatsoever in raising tepees!"

"But that is the purpose of this entire expedition, Prairie Star ... to give you some much-needed experience."

Fighting a new blush at his double meaning, she balled her hands on her hips. "Why should I oblige you?"

"Because if you don't, you'll find yourself sleeping on the bare ground tonight."

"Oooh! I'll sleep there with pleasure."

With a shrug, he turned to his horse and untied his quirt from the saddle. Pivoting to face her, he practiced slicing the whip through the air, an expression of fierce concentration gripping his handsome features.

The sound made Maggie nauseous.

"Are you certain you wish to defy me, Prairie Star?" he asked mildly, continuing his exercise.

Her eyes shot sparks at him as she stormed off to the travois.

Laying aside the quirt, White Wolf went over to lounge against a tree. Fighting a grin, he observed his feisty bride stalking about, studying the travois from various angles, her expression perplexed. Then she kicked the apparatus a couple of times, presumably to make sure it was dead, he decided with amusement. He took delight in the indignant movements of her shapely body, especially when she leaned over to untie the tepee from its moorings. He watched her skirt pull at her rounded buttocks, and barely restrained an urge to stride over and grab a tempting handful.

Her attempts to drag the rolled-up lodge with its stakes toward the middle of the clearing were downright comical. She could manage only to inch along the awkward contraption, huffing and puffing all the while, and soon she was red-faced and muttering curses. He almost relented and went to help her, then stopped himself. She had to be taught obedience—even if the lesson was arduous and bitter.

Finally she managed to haul the huge parcel into the center of the clearing. Hurling him a mutinous glance, she untied the lodge cover and rolled out the bundle of stakes. Dragging the heavy tenting off to one side, she frowned at the pack of twenty or so stakes that were bound together toward one end. She grabbed the stakes by the lashed ends and tried to raise the poles. The stakes skidded about crazily, and the entire structure began to collapse upon her. Horrified, White Wolf made a dive to save her. He heaved a huge sigh of relief when she managed to lunge out of range of the crashing poles in the nick of time.

They faced each other over the cloud of dust rising from the heap of stakes. "I hope you're satisfied now!" she snapped.

He laughed shortly. "Ask me that later. I told you to raise the lodge—not to commit suicide."

"Well, you should have known better. You should have brought along your second wife instead of me."

He grinned. "Jealous, Prairie Star?"

"Go to the devil."

He leaned over and began straightening the poles. "All right, let's try this again."

"You mean you're going to help me?" she mocked.

He stood to face her. "It seems I'm either going to help you, or I'm going to bury you."

"Then you'd have to console yourself with Fast Fox, wouldn't you?"

He glowered. "Prairie Star, I haven't slept with her."

She flipped her braids. "Did I say I cared?"

"You're acting as if you do. And actually, thanks to your defiance, I haven't *consoled* myself with any woman since our marriage."

"Hah!" she scoffed. "A man with two wives will never convince me he is as pure as a monk."

Now his temper was rising, and he waved a fist for emphasis. *"This* man takes his marriage vows seriously—"

"Both sets?"

"And if you don't curb that sassy tongue, woman, in a moment I'm going to call your bluff!" he roared.

They stared each other down for another charged moment. Prairie Star appeared baffled, as if uncertain how to take his comment, but evidently sobered enough not to provoke him further. White Wolf leaned over and, with angry, economical movements, finished straightening the stakes into an orderly line. He strode to his horse and fetched a length of rawhide and a bundle of pegs.

"What are you doing?" she asked.

Dropping the items on the ground, he hunkered down next to the stakes. "Attaching the anchoring peg."

She watched him attach one end of the rawhide rope to the knot holding the stakes together. "Then what?"

He stood and put a peg in her hand. "First we will raise the stakes together. Then while I hold up the frame, you'll tie the other end of the leather rope to the peg and anchor it in the ground at the center. Understood?"

She nodded curtly.

He leaned over and raised the bundle of poles with a strength that amazed her. "All right, Prairie Star, spread the stakes about evenly."

She obeyed his instructions, extending the stakes outward in a starburst fashion, while he braced the structure at its center, using his large body to keep the poles from collapsing. Although the afternoon was mild, their strenuous efforts soon raised sweat, and the intimate positioning of their bodies proved torture for Maggie. Even as angry and frustrated as she felt, it was difficult not to stare at her husband as he stood squarely in the middle of their work area, his arms raised, flesh gleaming, and muscles rippling. The scent of him drugged her senses, and the heat of him made her feverish. To make matters worse, in completing her duties, she brushed against his solid body several times, her cheek colliding with the flesh of his warm, damp back as she pushed at a recalcitrant stake, her bottom bumping against his muscled thigh when one of the poles skidded. By the time the entire structure was positioned, she was panting from more than her labors.

"Good," he told her. "Now anchor the poles."

Following White Wolf's instructions, Maggie attached the rawhide tie to the anchoring peg, then used a rock to pound the peg into the ground. With the structure reasonably secure, she helped White Wolf attach and raise the buffalo-hide tepee cover; once again, their bodies rubbed and bounced together scandalously. She felt grateful when they moved apart and began anchoring the cover to the ground with additional pegs. White Wolf then attended to the intricacies of attaching the front flap and properly positioning the smoke hole.

Maggie stared at the lodge, unable to believe she and White Wolf had erected it so quickly. "It really is a clever and practical device."

He pinned her with a burning look. "My father once said the supports of a tepee spread like the petals of a woman ready to receive her mate."

Not expecting this raw and provocative simile, Maggie gasped, her cheeks burning. So the sensual contact had stirred him, as well! "Count on you to make some crude comment."

He stepped closer, his expression solemn and intense. "The Comanche do not consider crude what happens between a man and his wife."

"Which wife?" she sneered.

"This wife!" He grabbed her arm and hauled her against his bare, gleaming chest. He looked her over in a heated, possessive manner that made her burn. "Will you spread for me like the branches of the tepee, and envelop me like its cover?"

Sucking in an unsteady breath, she jerked away. "Do you intend to force yourself on me like you tried last night?"

"There was no force last night and you know it," he retorted. "But neither was there a surrender. That's something you and I will settle between us here."

"Just what do you mean by that?" she demanded, her voice rising.

Again his gaze flicked over her with that heart-stopping ardor. "I am saying you arrived here still a virgin—at least, technically so."

Her face went crimson.

"But that is not how you will leave," he finished huskily.

"Then I won't leave," she asserted with bravado.

He laughed. "Shall we stay here until we are both old and

gray? That would be quite a sight—the two of us ancient and decrepit, and me still chasing you through the meadow."

She almost giggled, for despite her resentments, his humor was charming.

He reached out and touched the tip of her nose. "I think I will hunt up our supper now. Then you will cook it—or you will starve."

TWENTY-SEVEN

Maggie quickly caught on to White Wolf's strategy. Except for the one instance when he had cracked his whip, he clearly intended to conquer her through determination rather than by brute force. He preferred a power struggle to outright coercion. What's more, he had the upper hand and he knew it—and was thoroughly enjoying it, damn his eyes!

Unfortunately, as he was also aware, Maggie was at his mercy, dependent on him for everything: food, freedom, the bed she slept on, and whatever chance she might have for ever returning to civilization. White Wolf had already forced her to help raise the lodge or forgo her bed tonight; now he had issued a second ultimatum, that she cook his supper or go hungry.

What else would he demand before the night was out? Could she bear to continue to resist him, fully knowing she might be pushing him into the all-too-eager arms of Fast Fox?

Maggie shoved aside those unsettling questions. Determined not to starve, she walked along the creek and gathered wild berries, roots, and onions to augment their meal. Although she hated to admit it, she enjoyed being out in the brisk evening air, with the shimmering light cavorting through the foliage and the sweet breeze rustling the leaves. She watched squirrels race up tree trunks, listened to mourning doves calling, and smelled the grass and flowers.

She returned to camp to find White Wolf skinning a rabbit he had just killed. She gulped at the sight, since she had just observed several rabbits hopping about in the meadow beyond the trees. However, having lived among the Comanche for some weeks now, she had long ago conceded the necessity of slaughtering game for food.

At her husband's instruction, she built a fire, staked the animal, and roasted it over the flames. Soon the tantalizing aroma of barbecuing meat filled the air.

Over dinner, White Wolf and Maggie sat far apart, facing each other warily across the fire. Although the evening had turned cool, White Wolf remained shirtless, and Maggie was acutely aware of his bare, muscular chest, especially with the golden light of the flames dancing over his deeply tanned, satiny skin. Even with the blaze providing some heat, she wondered if he was cold, and was shocked by her own yearning to warm him. She watched his white teeth sink into a rabbit's leg, and imagined his savage mouth devouring her own flesh.

He glanced at her sharply, as if he had read her thoughts. She hastily averted her gaze and nibbled at her meal, thinking of the night to come with anticipation and dread. She and White Wolf had not shared a tepee together since before he had left on the hunting expedition; indeed, he had told her then that he wasn't sure he could share a lodge with her and leave her alone.

Could she keep her hands off him? He was continuing to watch her intently, unnerving her all the more. In the distance, a coyote howled, and she shivered.

After a moment, he asked, "What are you thinking, Prairie Star?"

Taken aback, she half choked on a morsel of meat. Watching him tense and move to help her, she held up a hand and took a gulp of water to force down the scrap and cover her own chagrin.

"Are you all right?" he asked.

"Yes," she said hoarsely, blinking at tears.

He chuckled. "My God, woman, what *were* you thinking?"

Feeling her face burn, Maggie set her food aside and frantically searched her mind for a suitable explanation. With effort, she forced a casual tone. "Oh, I suppose I was thinking about Aunt Prudence and Aunt Lydia."

"Oh, were you, now?" he teased.

"Yes." She shot him a self-righteous look. "I haven't written either of them since my arrival in Texas, and I'm sure they're worried. I meant to write them while I was still in Austin, but as you're aware, I was carried off by a wild Indian."

He shrugged. "They know you're a newlywed, don't they?"

"Newlywed," she scoffed. "So that's what I am?"

"Aren't you?"

She felt that same stubborn blush creeping up her face again. "I'll have you know Aunt Lydia and Aunt Prudence are two Boston spinsters who know nothing whatsoever about the life of a newlywed."

"Well, maybe you should enlighten them, eh, Prairie Star?"

Embarrassed, she cleared her throat. "I am hardly an authority on the subject."

"True." He chuckled, leaned back, and crossed his hands behind his neck. "But we can rectify that, can't we?"

Fighting the titillating effect of his words, and half-mesmerized by the play of his muscles as he lounged back, she drew herself up in outrage. "Must you turn every discussion we have into something lewd? My point is, it is quite unlike me not to write!"

He grinned. "I'm sure your aunts will make allowances. I'd imagine they're a lot more congenial and accommodating than you are."

"Hah!" she scoffed. "Just how do you define 'congenial' and 'accommodating'? I know of few Boston ladies who would react favorably to being kidnapped by ..."

"A half-breed and a heathen?" he provided helpfully.

"Yes!"

He sat up and leaned toward her, folding his arms over his raised knees. "Prairie Star, why are we indulging in this babble regarding your spinster aunts, when we should be talking about you and me?"

"Speak for yourself," she replied.

"You'd still rather be back in Boston, wouldn't you?" he demanded.

She rolled her eyes. "I'm surprised you even have to ask that. Any civilized setting would be preferable to this."

"What are you missing that's so all-fired special?" He gestured toward the meadow beyond them, gilded by the splendor of the setting sun. "Can springtime in Boston compare with the beauties of our prairies? Are your libraries there full of truths more sacred than those provided by the natural world surrounding us here?"

"Not according to you."

His tone turned belligerent. "Are you still wishing you'd married some pampered dandy you could order about?"

She smoothed down her skirt primly. "A man who believed in monogamy would have been nice."

He struggled against a grin, finally managing to maintain a stern facade. "Right now it's just you and me, and we were talking about the real issue here—how *you'd* prefer a man you can control."

Her green eyes burned with anger. "And you don't want to control me, sir?"

"That's different. You're my wife."

She made a strangled sound. "Oh, of all the ... ! First of all, I'm *one* of your wives! Second of all, you're arrogant! Third, kindly get it through your thick head, once and for all, that you will *never* control me!"

"Won't I?" He opened the small medicine bag at his waist. "Care to play dice, Prairie Star?"

She blinked at him, totally caught off guard by his unexpected ploy. "Dice? You're suggesting we play dice at a time like this?"

Mischief twinkled in his eyes. "I thought a game might prove diverting."

She studied his expression of unholy devilment and harrumphed. "Well, I for one do not approve of games of chance. But then you Indians love gambling, don't you?"

He shook the dice in his hand. "That's right, proper Bostonian Christian ladies don't indulge in such iniquities, do they? What would Aunt Lydia and Aunt Prudence say?"

She didn't reply, but a guilty smile pulled at her lips.

His gaze hardened. "What makes you think you and your kind are so much better than the rest of us?"

Taken aback, she replied, "I'm not saying I'm better—"

"Oh, yes, you are! From the very night we got married, you've made clear your contempt for Indians."

Guilt assailed her. "I didn't mean to imply that I hated—"

"Spare me such a feeble lie."

"We're . . . just different, I guess," she conceded miserably, avoiding his eye.

"Are we so different?" he pressed. "You believe in God—my people believe in the Great Spirit. You believe in heaven—my people believe in the Happy Hunting Ground. Don't we all ultimately want the same things—homes, happiness, a mate to love, children?"

"I thought you wanted *two* mates to love," she provided sweetly.

He beat a fist on the ground. "Damn it, my second marriage was not my idea."

She slapped her forehead and feigned an incredulous expression. "Oh. I totally forgot there was a gun at your back."

"And will you stop trying to divert me from the point I'm making?"

"Which is?"

"Are we really that different? Does it matter whether we

find our destiny here in the wilderness, or back in stuffy old Boston?"

She mulled over that a moment. "Your people want to kill my people," she accused.

"Oh, so now all the fault lies with my people?"

"Not all, but—"

"Prairie Star, warfare between our peoples was inescapable, considering the differences in our cultures—differences the white man has never understood or even recognized."

"And you're trying to use these differences to bring us together?" she scoffed.

"Yes," he replied passionately. "Because the only hope for us is that we stop thinking about your people and my people, that we forget how far apart our worlds are and become one as man and wife."

She lowered her gaze. His words had moved her to treacherous desire, but she could not afford to let him see this. Her voice trembled as she murmured, "I just don't think that is possible."

He was silent for a long moment, again rolling the dice in his hand. "Then why won't you play dice with me? Afraid I'll win? Or just afraid of me?"

She glanced at him warily. "I have nothing to bet."

His words came very husky. "Oh, yes, you do."

Her eyes grew huge. "I'd never bet that!"

He grinned. "Then bet a kiss ... a kiss if my number comes up."

"And what if mine does?" she challenged.

His wicked eyes tempted her brazenly. "I'll grant you one wish."

Maggie's heartbeat quickened. "*Any* one wish?"

"Any."

"You know what my wish will be!"

"Yes, I know."

She crawled over beside him and nodded decisively. "Throw the dice."

"What number?"

"Nine. What's yours?"

"Seven." He rattled the dice in his hand.

She caught his wrist. "Wait! What if neither number comes up?"

"We'll throw again."

She released his wrist, sat back on her haunches, and smoothed down her skirts. "Very well."

He chuckled at her demure response and tossed the dice.

Maggie could have died when she watched seven crop up. "You cheated!" she accused.

He hooked his elbow around her neck and hauled her close. "No, I'm lucky. Kiss me, Prairie Star."

She gazed up at his dark, amused, sexy face. He was so close that she could feel his warm breath on her lips, and she feared she might melt beneath the intense gleam of passion in his eyes.

"Kiss me," he repeated.

Before she could lose her nerve, she jerked forward quickly and pecked his cheek.

His scowl was murderous. "You can do better than that. Come sit on my lap and kiss me like my wife, like my woman—"

"Like your squaw?"

"If you prefer."

Even as Maggie squirmed, White Wolf pulled her onto his lap. She tried to struggle away, but was unable to budge in his strong arms.

She stared up at him mutinously. "What do you think you are doing?"

He ran his fingertips tantalizingly over her underlip. "Instructing you."

"Oh! Like you instructed me in raising the lodge and cooking dinner?"

He winked at her. "Yes. I can be a teacher too, you know."

"You can be a depraved lecher!"

"That, too. But I do promise you'll enjoy this instruction a lot more."

She bucked against him again, only prompting his laughter and a tightening of his arms. "You are brazen! Is this how you 'instruct' all your wives?"

"I am only interested in instructing *this* wife at the moment. And this wife still owes her husband a kiss."

Maggie made a growling sound.

"Wrap your arms around my neck, Prairie Star."

She glowered.

"I'm not letting you go until you comply."

Seething, she coiled her arms around his neck.

He appeared to be close to bursting with restrained mirth. "Now kiss me like a dutiful wife kisses her husband."

She edged closer, just brushing her warm lips against his—and immediately found herself pulled into a deep, drugging, captivating kiss. Simultaneously, both moaned with pleasure. Maggie realized the sensual teasing had aroused them both. His arms tightened around her, his tongue mated with hers, and Maggie was spinning away into the night with him—

"That's much better," he murmured after a moment, stroking her back. "Care to toss the dice again?"

She could barely hear him over her fiercely pounding heart. "I . . . no."

He tickled her ear with his lips, raising shivers. "You can throw them this time," he coaxed, "and you might just win and get your wish."

Maggie wasn't entirely sure what her wish *was* anymore.

He pressed the dice into her warm palm. "Toss the dice, Prairie Star. Nine for freedom—seven for paradise."

Breathlessly she tossed another perfect seven, then groaned.

"You cheated," he accused.

"What do you mean, I cheated?"

His fingers kneaded the nape of her neck, drawing her closer. His eyes were smoky with desire, his voice hypnotic. "You're just dying for another kiss, aren't you?"

"Oh, you beast! I am not—"

The rest was drowned by White Wolf's lips as he impa-

tiently claimed his second prize. Totally transported by the
reckless game they were playing, Maggie threw her arms
around his neck and gave herself over to his strength and
passion.

"Shall I toss the dice this time?" he asked an eternity
later.

Maggie could not catch her breath. "No—I don't think I
can bear another—"

"Another what?"

This time she kissed him, thrusting her tongue into his
warm mouth, running it over his smooth teeth. She heard
the rumbled sound of his response and felt herself falling. A
moment later, she landed softly on her back, his crushing
weight on top of her, his manhood bruising her sweetly, his
mouth grinding into hers. She dug her fingers into the
smooth muscles of his shoulders and arched against him
provocatively. He rocked in response, and hot currents of
desire shot straight through her. Maggie knew she should
not be doing this. He was a savage, a polygamist no less.
Yet she gloried in his untamed splendor. Being so near to
him all day, yet so far away, had been agony. Now she
could not seem to kiss him deeply enough . . . She was devouring him, yet she was starved . . .

He pulled back abruptly and took her breasts in his large
hands; she arched in pleasure. His gaze, black with yearning, held her captivated.

"Come with me to the tepee," he whispered. "Open yourself to me, as a rosebud opens its petals to the warmth of
the dawn. Take me into yourself and make our souls one.
Be my woman, Prairie Star."

His words at last wrenched Maggie from her sensual leth-
argy, as his saying her Comanche name made her remember
what her surrender would truly mean . . . that she would become his Indian bride forever, share his bed and bear his
children amid the tribulations of Comanche life. After all,
wasn't the object of this entire "lesson" to subjugate her, to
teach her to become his squaw? If she surrendered, she
would only start living a fool's dream with him. Besides,

how could she give herself to him when he had a second bride waiting for him back at the village? She felt heartsick, but no less certain in her conviction that this would not work.

"No—I can't!" she gasped.

He stared at her in disbelief, heaving huge, frustrated breaths. "Why? Why won't you listen to your heart this time?"

"Because my heart knows the truth," she replied in anguish. "I can never become your obedient squaw, your Indian bride."

He groaned, clenching his hands into fists. "Then you are indulging your pride to an extent I will no longer allow."

"Then don't allow it!" she burst out in despair. "Take me by force if you will! It's what you've wanted from the beginning, isn't it?"

She regarded him in torment, half hoping he would overwhelm her, that he'd let her keep her pride, and would end this agony for them both.

Instead he cursed vividly and rolled off her. His voice came charged as thunder. "You have made your choice. And I will make mine. If you refuse to lie with me as my bride, you will sleep on the bare ground tonight."

Maggie was outraged. "Why, you cad! Denying me my very bed unless I share it with you! That's a low-down Indian trick!"

Although she regretted her harsh words the instant they left her mouth, her insults had already met their mark. White Wolf bolted to his feet and stood above her with fist raised.

"The truth is, woman, you *have* no heart. Why I ever wanted to marry such a vindictive shrew is beyond me. It should not shock me at all that your marriage vows mean nothing to you, after you desecrated the only symbol I ever had of the love between my mother and father."

Maggie gasped and sat up. "What symbol? What are you saying?"

"Have you so soon forgotten that you broke my mother's necklace on our wedding night?" he demanded.

"No," she whispered in shame. "I haven't forgotten."

His eyes burned with passion. "Those beads were the only tangible object I had left of my parents' love—and you destroyed them!"

Maggie sucked in her breath, horrified to realize she had wounded him so badly. How could he have been so patient with her for so long, while carrying around this wrenching hurt? She started to utter an apology, but feared her words would sound cruelly inadequate.

All at once, he stunned her by leaning over and scooping her up into his arms. She froze, not certain what he intended as he quickly bore her inside the tepee and placed her none too gently on her pallet.

"White Wolf?" she questioned, her voice almost swallowed up by her roaring heartbeat.

He grabbed his own bedroll, then loomed just inside the entry flap. "You are welcome to this tepee—and your pride," he uttered, and stalked out.

TWENTY-EIGHT

W<small>ATCHING HIM GO</small>, M<small>AGGIE COULD HAVE DIED ON THE SPOT</small>.
Not until this moment had she known how terribly she must
have hurt White Wolf on their wedding night. And in this
moment she also realized how much she loved this proud,
brave, complex man. Why else would knowing she had hurt
him wound her even more? She still feared their relationship was doomed in the long run, but she knew in her heart
that denying their love and living in this purgatory was far
worse torture, for them both. Eventually she would probably
lose White Wolf to Fast Fox, or to some other squaw who
would better serve his needs. Eventually she would have to
return to her own kind. But she would not leave without
first knowing the glory of loving him, whatever her surrender might mean. She had to go to him and beg his forgiveness, bridge the distance between them. She had to, or she
would die . . .

White Wolf felt every bit as tortured as he sat outside on
his pallet. He gazed up at her star, so bright and alluring, so
cold and distant. He wondered at the depth of his anger and
hurt toward her. Was he angry because she wouldn't love
him, because she wanted to leave him? Yes, but couldn't he

understand her own desire to be free, her yearning to live among her own kind?

White Wolf realized he had kept Prairie Star with him for all the wrong reasons—mostly anger and wounded pride. Yes, he held in his heart love for her; but that love would surely be doomed unless Prairie Star came to him of her own free will. And at this point, he was convinced she never would. He had fought the good fight, but he had lost.

Then, as if his tortured thoughts had summoned her, he saw her standing beyond him, her visage outlined by moonlight, her face stark with tears.

"I'm sorry," she whispered.

He stared at her and didn't answer.

She came to kneel beside him, her plaintive features beseeching him. "I had no idea I had hurt you so . . . on the night of our wedding, and afterward."

He glanced away, certain that if he looked at her, he would haul her into his arms and devour her alive. No doubt she spoke out of her own innate sense of decency, and guilt over her own careless words and actions. She was a good Christian woman, after all. But she did not really care for him.

His words came bitterly. "I should have known that, like my mother and father, we were doomed from the start. But I guess I could not resist you. When I saw you, standing there at the station in your pretty green dress, with your hair of fire and your eyes like emeralds . . . I had to have you."

She made a strangled sound, like a sob, and for once he felt no remorse at her suffering.

"But I should have known better," he repeated. "My mother was white, my father of the People. They lived together in rancor for almost twenty years. I should have learned my lesson from them."

She spoke hoarsely. "But you say your mother loved your father—or so you thought, because of the necklace."

At last he met her tumultuous gaze. "My father gave the beads to my mother on their wedding night. For almost two decades, she refused to wear them, and later gave them to me to save for my own future bride. Then, as she lay dying, she called my father's name and begged me for the necklace. She clutched the beads in her hands as she passed away."

As he said the words, he watched a tear trickle down her cheek; he clenched his hands into fists to keep from touching her.

She leaned toward him, her face anguished. "So your mother did care for your father, after all. And I destroyed the token of that love. How can I ever make it up to you?"

He was silent for a long moment, struggling within himself. She reached out to touch his bare thigh with her warm hand, and he flinched as if in pain. Appearing bewildered, she withdrew her fingers. He felt bereft, but could not bring himself to take her hand and place it where he *really* ached for her.

"I have to make it up to you," she repeated, sniffing.

"Why?"

"Because it's unlike me to be so cruel."

"And how would you make amends, Prairie Star?" he asked softly.

She blinked away another tear. "By loving you—if you still want me."

He swallowed the painful lump in his throat. "I do not want you to give yourself to me out of guilt."

"It wouldn't be just guilt." With her heart in her eyes, she whispered, "I think you know I want you, too. Very much. Don't you know that when I first saw you—so tall and dark and handsome—I felt the same pull? I know I've fought it—this magic, this spiritual bond between us—but I can no longer deny that it's there. My feelings keep growing stronger."

He could not trust himself to speak.

"And I think you also know I'm a much better woman than the shrew who just behaved so dishonorably."

At the pain and yearning in her voice, White Wolf relented and reached out to caress her tear-streaked cheek.

"You *are* a good woman, Prairie Star, but something is haunting you, something you refuse to own up to."

Maggie gasped, stunned by her husband's perception. "What do you mean?"

"You know."

She was silent, her head bowed.

He stroked her jawline with his fingertips, then titled her chin until she faced him. It was then that Maggie spotted the tears in White Wolf's eyes, too. For a moment, she could have sworn she was looking at Bronson again as he whispered, "Tell me why you so hate Indians, Maggie, and I will let you go."

She wasn't sure how it happened, but a dam of emotion burst inside her, feelings she had tried to restrain for so long. Suddenly she was in his arms, and he was pulling her down beside him on the pallet, comforting her as she shook with sobs. The sensuous sounds of the night surrounded them like a cocoon, and for once, there was only the two of them in the whole world.

"I'm so sorry," she whispered brokenly. "I've been terrible to you."

"I've hardly been an angel myself."

"But you were hurt and you didn't know—"

"Know what, Prairie Star?" He stared solemnly into her eyes. "Why do you hate my kind?"

She smiled sadly. "I—I don't think I hate Indians. At least, not anymore. That would mean hating you, and—"

"And?"

She clung to him with a sweetness that made his chest ache. "I don't hate you. I think I understand you now."

His fingers caressed her back. "Tell me why you were so afraid of me and my people."

She drew a convulsive breath. "It was because of my fiancé."

"The one who died?"

"Yes." Stifling a shudder, she explained, "I met James a few years after the Civil War. He was an officer in the cavalry, and we were going to get married as soon as he completed his tour of duty in the West. He was stationed in Minnesota, and he was captured by the Santee Sioux during a massacre there. Later, a friend of his came back to Boston and told me about his death." Her voice caught on a low sob. "I think the man meant well, that he intended to comfort me, and especially to spare me the terrible details of James's death. But . . . then he broke down and sobbed and told me all about it, how both of them were captured, dragged back to the Indian village, and tortured horribly for days on end. James died, but his friend was rescued by the cavalry before he succumbed. I think he felt guilty that in the end, he was saved, but my fiancé wasn't."

White Wolf groaned, his heart aching for her, especially as the reasons for her behavior became clear to him. He kissed her forehead. "Oh, Maggie. No wonder you so feared and hated my people."

"The way James was killed devastated me," she admitted raggedly. "For a time, all I could think of was how unfair it was . . . He was so young, and such a fine man. For a time, I despised all Indians, and felt as if my life had ended. Then one day I woke up and decided I had to go on . . . So I poured myself into my teaching, my activities with the church, and helping out my aunts where I could."

"Then you met me and all those bitter memories came rushing back again, didn't they?" He groaned. "My God, when I think of how I came for you dressed as an Indian on the warpath—how I must have terrified you—"

"Don't," she interrupted gently, pressing her fingers to his lips. "You didn't know." Vehemently she continued, "And it wasn't fair that I blamed you. You had nothing to do with what happened to James. Knowing you and your people has made me understand that there are always two sides to every story. Even in the case of my fiancé, now I can look back and remember things his friend told me . . ."

"Such as?"

"He told me the Indians were on the warpath in Minnesota because the federal authorities had failed to live up to their treaty obligations. As a result, the Indians were often left to starve." She sighed. "At the time, I was in such a state of shock that the words floated past me, but now I remember—and knowing you and your people, I understand, because you are facing the same conflicts with the whites. The Indians owned this country first, and the whites have largely stolen it from them."

He clutched her tightly. "Thank you for sharing your heart with me, Prairie Star. For now I can understand you, too. And I'm so sorry for all you've had to suffer—"

She interrupted, her voice thick with tears. "I'm sorry, too, for all the hateful things I've ever said to you, and especially for destroying your mother's necklace. Now you'll never again have that symbol of your parents' love."

White Wolf, feeling bedeviled by guilt, murmured, "A moment ago, I did not admit the full truth."

"What do you mean?"

He smiled into her eyes. "After you left the hotel room on our wedding night, I patiently gathered up all the beads, as well as your wedding ring. I took these items with me when I returned to the tribe, and one of the Indian women restrung the necklace for me."

Her face lit with new hope. "So you have the necklace, after all!"

He touched the medicine pouch at his waist. "I still carry the ring and the necklace for the bride of my heart. For you, Prairie Star."

Maggie felt unbearably touched, yet a small doubt still nagged. "You will not want these items for your second bride?"

He sighed. "I must explain something to you. My second marriage is a duty, an honor, an obligation, and will forever be in name only. The necklace can only be worn by the true bride of my spirit. You have always been and will always be that bride."

"Oh, White Wolf!"

She threw her arms around his neck, and for an emotional moment, they clung together, glorying in their new feelings of communication and understanding.

Then Maggie became very conscious of how aroused they both were. Plaintively she whispered, "I want the necklace . . . and the ring . . . and you."

He pulled back, regarding her solemnly. "You are sure?"

"Oh, yes."

"Will you wear the necklace and the ring and nothing else?"

"Eagerly."

White Wolf watched, mesmerized, as Prairie Star knelt above him, drawing off her dress and then straddling him, naked and glorious, totally without shame. He solemnly took the necklace from his medicine pouch and placed it around her neck, watching the moonlight gleam on the beads that rested against her proud breasts. Then he lovingly slipped his ring back on her finger. He slid his hands over her, touching her soft face, her slender neck. She gasped as he drew the cool beads provocatively across her tautened nipples, then cupped her breasts with his hands. His fingers caressed her slim waist and long, creamy legs. He stroked that lovely, downy place where she lay open to him, rubbing the bud of her desire with his thumb, and watching her eyes dilate with passion.

"Never have you looked more beautiful," he whispered.

She leaned toward him, caressing the muscles of his chest. "Never have I wanted you more. It's been torture for me, too, you know."

He grunted with pleasure and undid the ties on her braids. He pulled her down onto the pallet beside him and ran his fingers through her coiled tresses, sniffing their heady fragrance. "That is because we are meant to be. This is meant to be. I saw us together long ago when I was eighteen, in my first vision quest."

Maggie felt awed. "What is a vision quest?"

He resumed caressing her and whispered, "When a young Indian man comes to the age of manhood, he goes out to the wilderness alone, to fast and meditate, and seek his spiritual shaman."

"And you found yours?"

He nodded. "I saw myself as the white wolf—a very powerful symbol to the Comanche. The wolf was alone out on the prairie, howling at a single bright star up in the black heavens."

An ecstatic sigh escaped her. "That was me?"

He nodded.

"That is why you call me Prairie Star?"

"Yes. And that is why you have saved yourself for me, for this moment." He rolled her beneath him. "You're my Prairie Star, my Stella-Sanna. You will always be my only love."

Maggie exulted at his words and the solid pressure of his male flesh against her. At last she understood why he had insisted they must fulfill their destiny together, and the sweetness of his utter faith in his vision filled her heart with love. She kissed him tenderly and ran her fingers over his muscled shoulders and arms. She heard his sound of impatience as he leaned over and tugged at her nipples gently with his teeth. She whimpered with delight as his ravenous mouth took her nipple, his tongue flicking to and fro, tormenting and delighting her. He roved his tongue and lips all over her breasts. When he thrust a finger inside her, while sucking deeply at her breast, she reeled in ecstasy and moved against him, deepening her own bliss.

"I must know something else, Prairie Star," he murmured against her throat.

"Yes?"

"Do you want my Indian baby? Will you love it? If not—"

She cut his words short with a fevered kiss. "I will love any child of yours."

"And the child's Indian blood?"

"I will be honored to carry that heritage inside me."

She felt a shudder course over his powerful body as he clutched her tightly. His fingers left her and his lips claimed hers in fiery need. He reached down and shucked his breechclout, drawing her fingers to his rigid manhood. She eagerly caressed him, driving his desires to an incredible frenzy. She quivered as he aligned their naked bodies. Gently but insistently, he pressed into her. She squirmed and gasped.

He drew back, and brushed a wisp of hair from her eyes. "Easy, my love. This will hurt at first, but I promise the pleasure we'll find together will be much greater."

She smiled and arched against him eagerly.

Thrilled by her willingness, he trailed kisses along her jaw, over her cheeks, and pressed harder. She cried out, and he smothered her moans with his lips.

"Oh, God, you feel wonderful," he whispered into her mouth.

And she did. Never had White Wolf tasted any woman who felt so right for him as his Prairie Star. The intense, bittersweet moments of their sharing had stirred him to a passion that was all-consuming, and the reality that they would soon be one in every way moved him to his soul. Still, he hated having to hurt her. Best not to prolong the torment. He slipped his hands beneath her, tilting her hips upward. His mouth came down hard on hers, and his manhood moved forcefully. He felt a tremor shake her as her virginal membrane gave way to his unyielding penetration. He comforted her with his lips while pressing deeper. Velvety warmth swamped him, squeezing him so pleasurably, tugging him into a vortex of wet heat until he buried himself in paradise . . .

Maggie reeled at White Wolf's vigorous thrust. She felt the solid heat of him splitting her apart and filling her exquisitely. Her soft sobs were melted by his kisses. Even the pain made her feel somehow connected with him. The discomfort soon faded, and she was swept away by the wondrous sensations of having him inside her, the searing heat, the explosive pressure that made her insides taut and throbbing.

Just when she was certain she could feel nothing more intense, more dazzling, he withdrew from her and surged deep again, wrenching a groan from her. She whimpered at the exquisite sensation and dug her fingers into his buttocks, pulling him into herself, wanting to feel him in her very core. Then he was thrusting powerfully, again and again, drowning her with more devastating kisses . . .

White Wolf fought to contain his wildly escalating desires. But after having wanted Prairie Star for what seemed an eternity, his thirst for her was uncontrollable. She was so perfect for him, her tiny vessel a hot, sweet vise about him, her mouth so trusting on his. As much as he wanted to make their passion last, he found himself devouring her, hurled toward a blinding orgasm. He plunged convulsively, coming to rest inside her . . .

Maggie gazed up at White Wolf, feeling deeply moved by what they had just shared, but also bemused and somewhat cheated. The coupling had been intense, shattering, hurtful . . . yet she still wanted more.

"Why did you stop?" she whispered.

He caught a ragged breath and arched against her. "Because I spilled my seed inside you. Can you feel it?"

She nodded. She was slightly raw, but also felt a spreading warmth that she recognized as his essence, that she knew could create his child . . . The very thought made her dizzy.

"Mainly, I stopped because I was hurting you."

"Not that much."

"No?" He withdrew from her flesh, and she winced.

She sought his lips, kissing him desperately.

"No?" he teased again.

Maggie felt confused again when he abruptly stood and scooped her up into his arms. "What are you doing?"

He was already walking toward the trees. "Taking you to the stream, to cleanse away the blood."

It was sheer heaven, being held in his strong, warm arms as he descended into the cool waters, and let the currents sluice over her sore flesh. He stood there holding her, kissing her, and her joy was unbearable. She felt in every way his mate, and she even felt fiercely protective of what they had just shared—

So much so, she spoke before she thought. "Won't the water . . ."

"Yes?" he asked tenderly.

Acutely embarrassed, she stammered, "Won't it wash away . . ."

He stared at her with stark joy. "You want my baby."

A little sob burst from her. "I know it's impossible, but yes, I want you so, I want—"

"Shhh," he whispered. "Quit worrying about what's impossible, and let yourself have what you want. As for what the stream may have washed away . . ." A sensual chuckle escaped him. "I have more than you'll ever need. I'll be happy to demonstrate tomorrow."

"Demonstrate tonight," she whispered recklessly.

White Wolf was so stunned and aroused that he released her. She slid sensually down his body, bracing her toes on top of his feet. She clung to him and rubbed her breasts provocatively against him, roving her mouth over his wet flesh. She stroked his arousal with eager fingers.

White Wolf's manhood throbbed to tortured readiness again. He hungered once again to invade the narrow passage where he had just found such heaven. Her mouth felt divine on his skin and soon her hands were roaming everywhere— over his back, his buttocks, then back to his agonized arousal.

"Please, I'm not a saint," he implored.

She stretched on tiptoe to kiss his chin. "Don't be a saint tonight. Give yourself what *you* want, too. Be my husband, and my lover."

He heaved a raspy breath. "Prairie Star, it may hurt."

"Please. I don't care."

He could endure no more. He grabbed his wife's bottom, then he lifted her and penetrated her greedily. She cried out with a tormented rapture that made his soul ring with delight. She wrapped her legs around his waist, and he clenched his teeth in ecstasy and felt himself sink deeper inside her. She was so delicious, so warm, her tight womanhood holding him in an exquisite embrace. Both of them moaned as their sensitized flesh abraded. His features gripped in agony, White Wolf tried to control himself, possessing her slowly and thoroughly, determined to drive his wife to a full climax.

When she began to sob and toss her head, he made the moment last, stretching out the sensation to an unbearable tautness. She grew frustrated, frantic, and when she unwittingly scored his arms with her fingernails, he clenched his forearms about her waist and pumped himself into her until he brought them both to a pounding release . . .

Maggie clung to her husband, understanding at last the full meaning of ecstasy, of how it felt to be utterly desperate, transported, and then utterly replete. In the arms of the man she loved, she felt a peace and rightness such as she'd never before felt in her life . . .

For a long moment, White Wolf held her there, comforting her, allowing their wild heartbeats, their labored breathing, to subside. Then he tenderly carried her back to the pallet. Damp and satiated, they slept together naked, their bodies tightly coiled beneath the stars.

TWENTY-NINE

Maggie awakened to a distinctly pleasurable throbbing between her thighs. She became conscious of her husband's firm, crushing weight on top of her, and especially of his manhood surging to life inside her again. She opened her eyes to see White Wolf staring down at her with an intensity that left her gasping. Beyond his passion-clenched features and black hair, the blue morning sky loomed. They were both stark naked outside on the pallet, as they had lain together all night. The sweetness of the morning, the scents of dew and nectar, the sounds of birds calling and tree leaves rustling, only added to the aura of sensuality surrounding them.

Memories of the torrid hours they had shared flooded her mind, heightening the deep, ecstatic thrill she felt. White Wolf had been inside her throughout much of the night, several more times awakening her, soothing her moans with his mouth and thrusting into her slowly, taking them both from one wrenching climax to another. Maggie's breasts felt tender, her mouth half-bruised. She was sore all over—especially where her husband now so sweetly abraded her—yet never had she felt so good.

Somehow, she managed to speak over her pounding heart. "White Wolf . . . you're going to kill me."

"Forgive me, Prairie Star," he replied huskily. "Ever since I've tasted you, I just can't get enough."

She moaned as his next plunge more than demonstrated the point.

Hearing his bride's cry and fearing he might indeed be hurting her, White Wolf reined in his control, rocking against her gently, kissing and cuddling her for long moments. His withdrawal from her flesh prompted a squeak of misery.

Ruffling her hair, he rolled off her and smiled. "I need to leave you alone for a while, don't I?" he asked, sitting up and reaching for his breechclout. "You're very tender, aren't you?"

Clutching the blanket about her and gazing at his still-aroused manhood, she nodded.

He pulled on his leggings. "We'll make breakfast, then I'll go hunt up our lunch. Perhaps later, we can go for a ride together on Blue Wind?"

Maggie again nodded, wrapped herself in a blanket, grabbed her garment, and went inside the tepee to dress and comb her hair. She sighed ecstatically. Her body felt like a new body—part White Wolf's now. Her heart felt like a new heart—all his. She was awed by how much her life had changed in just one magical night. She was now hopelessly in love with White Wolf, and her body craved him again this very moment . . . no matter what the consequences. The depth of her newfound feelings was staggering to her.

They were almost shy as they sat together eating breakfast, exchanging longing looks and secret smiles. Maggie wondered what White Wolf was thinking. Did he realize how alive he had made her feel? Did he know she doubted she could ever resist him again?

White Wolf wondered if Prairie Star felt any regret concerning her surrender last night. Even as passionate and loving as she had been, the issue of their future still loomed unresolved between them. Would she ask him to return her to her own kind as he had promised last night? He was beginning to regret having given his word, for now that he had known the sweetness of loving her, he wasn't sure he ever could let her go. Last night he had known the glory of seeing his vision fulfilled. Now at last, the white wolf and the prairie star were one. Surely he would not lose the other half of his soul.

Indeed, he kissed his bride with special fervor before he rode off to hunt their next meal . . .

After he left, Maggie felt at loose ends. She tidied up the camp and bathed herself in the stream. Toward midday, she was shocked to hear the sound of barking, and looked up to see a familiar small dog bounding into the clearing.

"Chico!" she cried, kneeling and snapping her fingers.

The little brown and white dog raced across the open area and leaped onto Maggie's lap. Laughing, she petted Chico affectionately as he licked her face and wagged his tail.

"Just can't live without White Wolf, can you?" she asked.

Could she? Absolutely not!

"So we have a visitor, Prairie Star?"

The sound of her husband's voice seized her attention, and her heart quickened as she watched White Wolf ride back into camp. A pheasant was tied to his saddle horn.

"Guess Chico missed you," she called.

Did you? White Wolf wondered. He slipped off his pony and hunkered down, whistling to the dog. "Come here, boy."

The dog vaulted over to his master, and White Wolf happily petted him.

Maggie walked over to join them. "That's a nice fat pheasant."

"We'll have it for our lunch."

They worked together in companionable silence, White Wolf plucking and cleaning the bird, Maggie roasting it. They sat together beneath a tree eating their lunch. They laughed at the antics of some squirrels, and made a game of throwing scraps to Chico.

Afterward, White Wolf stood, extending his hand toward

his bride. "Think I'll go bathe in the stream. Want to join me?"

Maggie laughed, knowing precisely what would happen if she did. "I think I'll be safer here."

He grinned at her, then strode off. Maggie went insane as she watched him shed his clothing as he walked. He bathed himself while Chico languished on the bank, chewing on the pheasant carcass. With erotic memories of their moments in the water last night bombarding her, Maggie felt strongly tempted to join her husband. He had been so gorgeous in the moonlight as he'd made love to her, and now he appeared even more spectacular with the sunlight pouring over his huge, bronzed, naked body and drenched black hair.

After he bathed, he only magnified Maggie's discomfort level as he strode about wearing nothing but his breechclout, which clung to his damp loins in a most provocative manner. The rest of his body, including his long hair, was wet, dripping, gleaming, and utterly splendid. Maggie found herself powerfully tempted to offer to lick all the moisture off his shiny, irresistible flesh. Fearing she would soon attack him—and render herself incapacitated—she strolled off to gather some berries.

But only about fifty yards from camp, she found a fallen bird's nest, with four tiny baby birds chirping piteously inside. Leaning over, she carefully retrieved the nest and took it back to White Wolf.

"Look!"

He scowled at the tiny birds. "Why did you take that nest down from the tree? Can't you see there are live birds in it?"

"Of course I can see there are live birds, and I didn't take it down!" she protested. "It fell." Suddenly she smiled. "Will you put it back, please?"

"Do I look like a tree squirrel?" he teased.

She laughed and looked him over, still barefoot and in his breechclout. "You look like a wild Indian perfectly capable of climbing a tree."

He chuckled. "Very well. Which tree?"

"Follow me," she replied primly.

Maggie led White Wolf to the large oak, and shamelessly watched him climb it. From her vantage point, his breechclout hid nothing. She could see all the muscles of his thighs and buttocks as he climbed . . . and she could see much more. Her breathing quickened and her mouth went dry.

He reached down. "Give me the nest."

With trembling fingers, she placed it in his hand.

He carefully placed the nest on a limb, then slipped to the ground, dusting off his hands. "May I do anything else to please my bride?" he inquired suggestively.

"Er . . . no, thank you, sir." She panted the words with her hand on her heart.

He raised an eyebrow at her. "Why are you so breathless? I did all the work."

Embarrassed, she blurted, "Well, I was . . . er . . . very busy, too, you see . . . er . . . watching the baby birds."

He regarded her skeptically and started back for camp.

Back in the clearing, he lounged in the grass playing with Chico, while she squirmed nearby and continued to ogle his magnificent body. She felt the need to reach out to him, to communicate in more than just a physical way, to demonstrate what he meant to her . . . but she wasn't sure just how to proceed.

After a moment, Chico bounded off after a rabbit, and White Wolf turned to watch him. Maggie giggled as she spotted several leaves and a few twigs stuck in the back of her husband's hair.

"What is so funny?" he asked.

"You're wearing souvenirs from the tree."

Although he merely shrugged, Maggie went to the tepee and soon emerged with a buffalo horn comb. She went to kneel beside White Wolf and extended the comb. He eyed her in bemusement.

She backed away slightly. "What is wrong?"

"I guess I am not accustomed to your serving me, Prairie Star."

She smiled tenderly. "Then grow accustomed, White Wolf. Right now, I wish to serve your hair."

His gaze raked over her. "My hair and what else?"

"Behave yourself." She wrinkled her nose at him impishly.

He did not protest further as she gently plucked leaves and twigs from his hair, then began disentangling the thick locks. The smell and heat of his vibrant body once again excited her. Much as she knew she should be resisting temptation, Maggie found herself deliberately inching closer to him, even grazing his chest with her breasts.

At last he caught her wrist and slanted her a chiding glance. "Prairie Star, do you think I have the self-control of a Boston puritan?" he rasped.

Her expression guilty, she sat back on her haunches. "I know you don't. Unfortunately, neither do I."

"Why are you teasing me?"

Now she shrugged. "Perhaps I like to live dangerously."

He regarded her curiously. "Tell me what you're thinking."

"Why do you assume I'm thinking something?"

"Oh, I know that look. Come closer and tell me."

She sat down next to him, flashing him a tentative smile.

He took her hand, kissed the fingers, then chuckled. "You know, we are as shy as two newborn colts together."

She felt entranced by the image. "You're right. We are just born in a sense, aren't we?"

He nodded solemnly. "What is so difficult for you to say, Prairie Star?" As she glanced away, he grasped her chin in his fingers, forcing her to meet his suddenly scowling visage. "Are you going to ask me to take you back to your own kind now?"

Taken aback, she asked, "What brought on that question?"

"What I promised last night. Remember?"

"Yes." Biting her underlip, she asked, "Would you take me back if I asked you to?"

He glowered, then melted as he watched her eyes fill with tears. "Now what's wrong?"

She was crestfallen. "Don't tell me you *want* to take me back?"

Tempted to laugh aloud, White Wolf grabbed her and crushed her close, cradling her on his lap. "My God, woman, what do you think?" Nudging her ear with his lips, he whispered fervently, "Perhaps I should let you go, but I'm not sure I can."

She quickly kissed him, then regarded him with utter sincerity. "White Wolf, I'm not asking you to take me back. Not now, anyway."

He grinned, his relief obvious. "Then tell me what is on your mind."

She curled her arms around his neck and kissed his strong chin. "I'm thinking it's time to give your way a chance."

Hope lit his eyes. "Really?"

She nodded.

"Are you certain you mean that?"

"I'm certain."

He studied her closely, noting again the telltale brightness of her eyes. "Then why more tears?"

"Because I'm wondering . . ." Helplessly she regarded him. "I'm wondering if you hate me for resisting you for so long."

Now he did shout with laughter. "Hate you? Hardly, Prairie Star."

Even as he ducked his head down, she stretched upward to kiss him again. A moment later, she slid off his lap and boldly clutched his aroused manhood with her fingers.

"My God, Prairie Star!"

Heedless of his protest, she caressed him wickedly, and gazed into his eyes with luminous emotion. "When I think of all I've missed by being so stubborn . . ."

He groaned in torment. "Careful, Prairie Star, you're getting yourself in trouble—"

"I want to be in trouble," she panted recklessly, her mouth on his again. "In *big* trouble. If you want, you can make me suffer for every minute I've resisted you. Because every second I'm not close to you has become torture—"

White Wolf hauled his bride close and kissed her with devastating passion. She clung to him and sobbed her joy.

"Are you my wife?" he asked huskily.

"I'm your wife."

"Are we one when I'm inside you? One body?"

"Yes!" she cried. "One body."

"One heart, one spirit?"

"Yes!"

She saw the naked joy blazing in his eyes, then he squeezed her close again and his mouth ravaged hers. She kissed him back with desperate need.

Simultaneously he was hauling off her dress and she was untying his breechclout. She pushed him to the ground and straddled him. He gripped her bottom and brought her tightly into position.

"Oh, God, I *am* going to kill you—kill us both," he groaned.

"Kill me," she urged recklessly.

"Unbind your hair," he demanded hoarsely.

She pulled loose her braids and shook her bright locks free. He surged deeply inside her, wrenching a soft scream from her. He braced a hand at the nape of her neck and hauled her down to him, kissing her rapaciously. A moment later, he rolled her beneath him. Maggie felt him delve deep into her tender flesh, and she tossed her head. His hands slipped beneath her and held her against his ravenous strokes. The pleasure was agonizing. Maggie mused that she did feel as if she were dying—dying of sheer, raw ecstasy.

White Wolf gloried to his bride's response as he jolted her with each powerful plunge of his manhood. Thus they had been all night ... Thus he wanted them to be forever. Never would he let her hold herself apart from him again. *Never*. And he would always remember her this way, his beautiful spirit mate—

Prairie Star's head was tossed back, her fire red hair spilling out onto the grass. Her nipples were red and tight, her back arched in rapture. The bright beads of their wedding necklace rubbed sensually against her breasts and his chest as they moved together, flesh devouring flesh, bodies becoming one. Her low cries and the provocative squirming of her bottom only increased his ardor. He held her immobile against him until she softened, melting into each powerful penetration. He pressed her into her climax and watched the wanton pleasure flood her cheeks and fill her eyes. Her frantic gasps hurled him toward his own intense orgasm. He spiraled into her and felt himself explode in a last, stabbing stroke. She quivered and cried out, and he seized her lips in an ardent kiss.

They clung together for a long moment, kissing and caressing.

THIRTY

THE IDYLLIC DAYS BEGAN.

From the very moment when they made love so passionately outside their tepee, White Wolf and Prairie Star forgot their troubles and succumbed to the age-old magic of being newlyweds.

They began by rushing to the stream, naked, laughing and splashing each other. They returned to camp and made love again, licking the moisture from each other's bodies. Afterward, they went riding together bareback on Blue Wind. Sitting in front of her husband, Maggie squirmed as already tender parts of her were further chafed. White Wolf settled her closer onto his lap, only increasing her torment.

They paused at the top of a mesa to watch bison graze in the valley below. The dynamic panorama of the plains, the vast ocean of waving buffalo grass, seemed to stretch into infinity. The air about them was thick and dew-scented, the clouds above slightly overcast, with occasional bursts of thunder and streaks of lightning.

"Look, Prairie Star," White Wolf whispered.

"What?" she asked.

He pointed to the sky. "Golden eagle. Powerful medicine to Comanche."

Shielding her eyes with her hand, Maggie gazed upward and watched the powerful bird glide about, then dive—

"He's going after the rabbit, yonder," White Wolf explained.

Maggie watched, captivated, as the eagle dipped into the canyon, grabbed the hapless rabbit in its talons and soared off, the magnificent bird backlit by a dramatic flash of lightning.

She shuddered as thunder boomed. "Oh, how sad! That poor rabbit!"

"It's nature's way. Only the strongest can survive."

"It reminds me of when you came and carried me off," she teased.

He chuckled, tightening his arms about her waist. "Are you glad now?" he asked, grazing her cheek with his lips.

"Oh, yes," she replied breathlessly. "I wouldn't have missed this for the world."

They continued to watch the bison move about lazily and chew the grass. They laughed at the antics of a mockingbird scolding a snake near a tree.

"Why is the bird attacking the snake?" Maggie asked.

"She is protecting her young in the tree, I would think."

Watching the snake slither off, the bird fly back to its nest, Maggie was amazed. "How did you learn all this?"

"By growing up among the People."

"Your childhood must have been wonderful."

He nodded. "I was as wild and carefree as the boys in our village."

"No wonder you love this existence so much. One thing I have come to admire about your people is the way you don't punish your children, but shape and mold them."

"As I have shaped and molded you?" he teased.

She wrinkled her nose at him. "Brute."

He chuckled. "In all matters, my people honor natural laws as old as time. We revere the world surrounding us, instead of looking at Mother Earth as a resource to be exploited, like the White Eyes do."

"But your people kill the buffalo," she pointed out.

"For food, clothing, and shelter. We don't simply skin off the hides and leave the meat to rot like the hunters do."

She grew pensive. "What will your people do when all the buffalo are gone? Didn't you tell me the government is now encouraging the hunters to kill off all the great herds?"

He sighed. "Yes. I don't know how my people will survive when their food supply vanishes. They may be forced to go to the reservations."

They fell silent, neither willing to address these troubling realities nor the possible implications to their own relationship and future. White Wolf cupped Maggie's breasts with his large hands; she moaned as he nibbled at her ear.

Suddenly the clouds opened up and fat raindrops pelted them. Laughing exuberantly, the newlyweds galloped back to camp and took refuge, drenched, in the tepee.

White Wolf hauled Maggie close and kissed her. "You're shivering. Take off your dress and I'll make you warm."

As much as his words thrilled her, she pressed her palms against his chest and grimaced. "Please, I just can't again—not now."

He laughed. "Don't worry, I noticed you squirming against me during our ride. I take it you are temporarily incapacitated?"

"Yes," she replied ruefully. "And I fear that with you, my impairment may soon become permanent."

He hugged her tightly to him and groaned with satisfaction. "As my bride, you will never be allowed to become too frisky or footloose. That way, I won't have to worry about you sleeping with my brothers—"

"Oh!" Outraged, she shoved him away. "Beast!"

He hauled her back into his arms. "That's one Indian tradition I intend to abandon now that I'm married."

She froze. "What do you mean, now that you're married?"

He yawned, then confided arrogantly, "When I was younger, I slept with my older brothers' wives."

Her mouth dropped open. "You did what?"

"It is traditional."

"Oh! No wonder Black Hawk now expects—"

"He can expect all he wants to," White Wolf cut in with a passionate glower. "I'll never share you, Prairie Star."

To reinforce his words, he began tugging off her dress, while she giggled and squirmed. He ignored her token protests, stripping her naked, then shucking his own wet leggings and breechclout. He pulled her close on their bed of pelts. They lay side by side, kissing and touching, listening to the sounds of the thunder and the spring rain pelting the tepee.

"I never thought . . ." Maggie murmured.

"What?" he asked.

She looked at him through sudden tears. "That I could feel this happy with you."

His face too was lit with joy. "I always knew it was our destiny."

"Because of your vision?"

"Yes."

She wrapped her arms around his neck. "I want to know all about you."

Feeling her lush breasts stroking his chest, he slanted her a stern look. "Continue to tease me like this, Prairie Star, and you won't be getting much talk out of me."

"Oh." She jerked away.

He touched the tip of her nose. "What do you want to know?"

"Well, I already know a lot about your parents, your life with the tribe . . . Tell me more of your time in the white world."

He appeared hesitant. "Like what?"

"Your time with your uncle, and at Harvard. You went to college during the War Between the States, didn't you?"

"Yes . . ." A scowl furrowed his brow. "Although I did want to enlist."

"To fight for the Confederacy?"

He nodded. "A year after my mother died, Uncle Sam and I had a big fight about it. He had hired special tutors to prepare me for the university, and was able through some contacts back east to arrange to get me admitted to Harvard. War broke out just as I was preparing to leave, and I insisted on joining the cause."

"Why?" she asked.

"I suppose because I was just coming into my identity as a white man, and felt the elemental urge to defend my new homeland. And doubtless the young Comanche brave in me thrilled to the prospect of battle. Anyway, Uncle Sam was horrified. As I've told you before, he felt that because we owned no slaves, it wasn't our fight. I think he was also scared he might lose me, since he still hadn't recovered from the death of my mother."

"What happened?"

Bitterness gleamed in his eyes. "I didn't listen, of course. I stormed off to Austin and tried to join Hood's brigade. But as soon as the sergeant inducting me saw on my enlistment papers that my father was Buffalo Thunder, chief of the Penatekas, I was coldly informed that the Confederate States of America could win the war quite nicely without the help of any filthy, thieving half-breeds."

Maggie flinched. "My God. I'm so sorry."

He kissed her forehead and forced a smile. "I went back to Uncle Sam with my tail tucked between my legs, and he shipped me off to Harvard."

"Were you ostracized at college, too?"

"Somewhat. I was snubbed by most of the fraternal organizations, although I did gain respect as captain of the rowing team. My professors seemed to find me an interesting anomaly—a civilized red man. Social occasions were often the most difficult—I didn't exactly attract the best lady companions from Beacon Hill. I stayed away from many of those events, or went alone."

"We were alike in a lot of ways," she murmured. "I was not much of a social butterfly, either."

"You had a fiancé."

"James was an old friend of my family's. I saw him mostly at family functions, or at church."

"You were a good Irish Catholic."

"Yes—and I still am."

He grinned.

"My faith sustained me when I lost my parents as a teenager—and later, when I lost James."

He stroked her bare thigh. "I'm almost jealous of him, though I know it's unfair to resent a dead man. At least he did not take your innocence. That I would have found unbearable."

"Would you?"

He clutched her possessively. "I never would have gone off to soldier and left you a virgin. But I'm glad he did."

She slanted him a look of reproach. "You say that—but you had a woman in Rio Concho."

"I've had many women," he admitted unabashedly. "In Rio Concho and elsewhere."

She punched his arm playfully. "So you're saying it's fine for you to have come to the marriage sexually experienced, but not for me?"

He smiled at her tenderly. "I'm saying, Prairie Star, that I love you so much that it makes me wild to even think that someone else may have touched you."

Maggie felt staggered by his words. She stared up into his dark, handsome face, and found his vibrant gaze intently focused on her. "You love me?"

He nodded, then rolled her beneath him on the pallet. Roving a hand over her body, he whispered, "How else could I feel about a woman so fiery, so beautiful, with such a tempting body . . . and so much damn trouble?"

"Hah!" she cried. "I'm trouble? How do you think I felt when you married Fast Fox? Here, you say just knowing I had a fiancé makes you wild. How do you think I felt when I saw you with that squaw? Don't you know it made me—" Realizing she had gone too far, she clamped her lips shut.

"Made you what, Prairie Star?" he teased.

She hesitated.

He pinched her behind. "What?"

"Insane," she whispered hoarsely.

"Jealous?" he suggested, his expression delighted.

"Yes," she admitted grudgingly.

"So that's why you threw everything I owned out of the tepee."

She smirked.

"Why did you go on such a tirade, Prairie Star?"

Too afraid to speak her heart, she impulsively kissed him. They clung together, until his manhood instinctively burrowed into her, and she winced.

With a groan, he withdrew, resting his forehead against hers and breathing raggedly. After a moment spent reining in his desires, he drew back slightly and stroked his finger across her wet mouth. "There's something that still confuses me about you."

"What?"

"Why did you leave Boston? Was it because of your fiancé?"

"Oh, that," she muttered. Maggie briefly explained to him about The Incident, how she had been humiliated and discharged from her post, due to no fault of her own.

Afterward, he glowered. "I'd like to call out the scoundrel who did that to you."

She smiled at him radiantly. "It no longer matters. I'm very glad I'm here."

He kissed the tip of her nose. "You're right. Whatever either of us may have suffered in our pasts, what matters now is that we're together, that there will never again be anyone else for either of us."

"Not even Fast Fox?"

"Especially not her. We will be totally faithful to our vows—even if we are parted."

His words brought sudden tears to her eyes. "You say that as if you think we will be."

He gazed at her sadly. "What our future holds will largely be in your hands, Prairie Star."

"Are you giving me the freedom to decide my own future?" she asked, puzzled.

"In time, I may have no choice."

Considering his words, she swallowed the aching lump in her throat. "I think you are right about something."

"And what is that?"

Her arms tightened about his neck, and she spoke in a breaking voice. "No matter what happens in our future, I don't think there will ever be anyone for me but you. I think you are my destiny, too, White Wolf."

"Oh, Prairie Star."

They kissed, for once in total agreement.

THIRTY-ONE

THE LOVELY TIME STRETCHED ON . . .

White Wolf and Prairie Star roamed the meadows with
Chico, playing with the dog and picking wildflowers. They
gathered berries, and White Wolf taught Maggie how to
shoot game with a bow and arrow. They talked for hours on
end. They took long, lazy rides on Blue Wind together.
They played naked in the stream.

They enjoyed each other's bodies . . . After the day when
Maggie became so sore from the marathon lovemaking,
White Wolf did not make love to her again for two days. He
kept saying he wanted their next time to be very special,
and soon the tension became excruciating for them both as
they continued kissing, teasing, and touching.

They spent long hours doing just this on the third day after their idyll began. They lay on the pallet in the tepee,
both naked, the fire glowing nearby.

White Wolf stared down at his woman, so lush and vibrant beside him. He craved her now in every way. He felt
as insatiably curious about her as she had been about him.
He wanted to probe into her deepest, most secret thoughts

before they made love again, and to explore those hidden yearnings to bring them closer together.

He leaned over and kissed one of her fiery tresses. "Years ago, Prairie Star, did you ever see yourself like this?"

She laughed and ran her fingertips over his chest. "You mean did I see myself naked, married to a savage? Living in a tepee out on the prairie? No, I never saw myself like this."

He chuckled and nuzzled his lips against her neck. "I've told you about me and my vision, when I first became a man. What about you when you were younger? Did you have dreams?"

"Every young woman has dreams."

"Such as?"

She smiled wistfully. "I dreamed of getting a college education, and becoming a teacher—both of which I later did."

"What else did you dream about?"

"I suppose I imagined the usual—that one day I'd have a pretty home somewhere near King's Chapel, children playing in the yard—"

He brushed his lips over her breast. "Did you ever dream of this?"

She laughed, running her fingers through his hair. "Who could have imagined this?"

"And your husband? What would he have been like?"

She bit her lower lip. "You mean . . . before James?"

He nodded. "When you first imagined yourself with a lover."

"Oh!" she gasped, mortified. "I certainly never imagined a lover!"

He chuckled. "But of course you did. Otherwise, where did those imaginary children come from? Did they spring up from a cabbage patch?"

She shoved him playfully. "The stork brought them, of course!"

"Come on now," he teased. "Tell me about their father . . . and the husband of your dreams."

She sighed. "I don't know—he would have been some-one from my world, I suppose, a professional man, a banker, lawyer, perhaps a Harvard professor—"

"Ah, a sedate, sober, responsible, dull individual? That's who you saw lying with you in that big featherbed up-stairs?"

She grinned. "What big featherbed?"

"Doesn't every young woman's fantasy include a big featherbed?"

"It was carved rosewood," she admitted guiltily.

"Ah, carved rosewood. And what would you two do when you were alone upstairs in that lovely bed? Would he lift your gown, fumble over you for a few moments, and give you those children?"

She blushed. "I'm not sure. Probably."

"But you imagined that part, too, didn't you?"

Her eyes wide, she nodded.

"But you never allowed your dreams to go wild, did you?"

She shook her head.

"You never saw yourself with a savage like me?"

"No."

"You never saw yourself with an Indian baby?"

"No." She curled her arms around his neck and smirked seductively. "But I'm liking the idea more every day."

He appeared pleased, shutting his eyes as her taut nipples tortured his own flesh. "That fine man of yours . . . did you ever see the two of you naked, with you in his lap, and him making you scream with pleasure?"

"N-No."

"Did you ever see him doing this to you?"

Prairie Star tensed as White Wolf leaned down, parted her thighs, and kissed between her downy curls. A sizzling cur-rent of desire shot straight through her. Appalled and elec-trified, she tried to close against him, but his strong hands held her open to him.

"What are you doing?" she gasped.

He glanced up at her. "I want to give you pleasure this way—pleasure like you never before imagined."

"Why?"

He gazed up at her tenderly. "So all your new dreams will be about me."

"But they already are," she protested, and then she could no longer speak.

"I want to release all your inhibitions," he went on, parting and kissing the folds of her flesh. "I want us to be joined not just physically, but spiritually, and for our child to be the manifestation of our shared souls."

Maggie groaned. Who could argue with that?

Still, it was difficult not to struggle when she felt his hot tongue thrust out to probe her scandalously. All her Bostonian, Puritanical instincts railed out against the brazen contact, even as her body reveled in it.

White Wolf was not daunted. He hooked his elbows through her knees and easily held her immobile against him. She sobbed and pleaded and clenched her fists, but he was heedless. Then, as he began to delight her, as his lips and tongue delved deeper, she ceased fighting and at last surrendered to the powerful tide of feeling tugging her away. Pleasure swamped her in frighteningly intense, incredible waves that built relentlessly until she was desperate, frantic, unwittingly crying out his name in Comanche and arching rigidly against him, then going utterly limp, gasping softly in the aftermath of her climax.

She was only distantly aware of him moving away to throw several more logs on the fire. After a moment, he returned to her and pressed his mouth tenderly to hers.

"Oh, White Wolf," she half sobbed, holding him tightly. "You are right—I've never felt anything like that before."

He trembled against her. "You said my name in Comanche for the first time."

"Yes, I know I did. Please, look at me."

He drew back and stared into her eyes, his own gaze bright with tears.

She smiled with all the love she felt. "A few days ago,

you said it didn't matter what happened in our pasts. But I think it does matter to you. I think you're still afraid the memory of a white man may take me from you." She cupped his magnificent face in her hands and sweetly kissed his lips. "Know this, my love. After knowing you, no man can ever compare . . . ever!"

He groaned then, and captured her lips in a long, deep, ardent kiss. Afterward, he drew away, sat back on his heels, and extended his hand toward her. His gaze was hot with desire.

"Come. It is time for us to be one again."

Maggie needed no coaxing. Her mouth had already gone dry at the look in his eyes, the size of his erection, which her body was throbbing to receive. She eagerly took his hand, but was bemused when he pulled her closer to the fire. "It's growing so warm in here."

"Yes. The heat will make our bodies sweat and help our souls mingle."

Maggie stared at him, her heart hammering.

"Come mount me," he whispered. "I want us to meditate together while our bodies are joined. I want our spirits to touch."

She felt suddenly shy. "I'm not sure I know how to do that."

"I do not expect you to know, for I will teach you. It is a great honor for a woman to meditate with her mate. Usually only the *puhakut* are allowed to connect with the spirit world."

He stretched out his hands to her, and she eagerly linked her fingers with his. She moaned in ecstasy as he pulled her on top of him, then gasped as he clamped his hands to her waist and pressed her home.

"Is it too soon?" he asked.

"No . . . no," she moaned, and felt herself sliding deeper.

His voice hypnotized her. "Close your eyes, Prairie Star. Link your mind with mine. See us together, alone, in our night meadow. I am the White Wolf—you are the Prairie

Star. We were far apart, but now we are drawing closer together, so close. It is our destiny to be one."

"Yes! Yes!" she cried as he rocked her gently.

White Wolf held his woman and whispered to her words
of love and joy and communion. With almost imperceptible
movements, he wrenched low sounds of pleasure from his
bride. He plied her flesh with exquisite restraint, making her
breathless and frantic, then pulling back short of their climax so that they could drift together in a euphoric state.
Soon their bodies were wet with sweat and slid together
sensually, and both craved release with an intensity that was
unbearable. The torment of their bodies became the bliss of
their spirits as White Wolf felt their souls joining . . .

When at last neither could endure more, when they were
propelled to the unavoidable pinnacle, he lowered her to
the bed and pounded into her, until both felt the melding to
the depths of their beings . . .

THIRTY-TWO

THEY SEEMED TO COME TO THE REALIZATION AT THE SAME time . . . It was time to return to the tribe.

To White Wolf it made sense, for he and Prairie Star seemed of one mind and heart now. They were lovers and friends, totally in harmony with the natural world. They would face many challenges when they left their idyllic retreat, but with the strong underpinnings of their love, surely there was hope for their future. He knew he could not keep her among the People forever—as much as he would love to—that sooner or later, their love must be tested.

They reached the turning point on a balmy late spring morning. They had just finished breakfast and were lounging outside the tepee, Prairie Star braiding her hair, White Wolf petting Chico. He soon became conscious of the fact that his wife was staring at him.

"You look as if there is something on your mind," he murmured.

She laughed. "I was just going to say the same thing about you."

"And what do you think is on my mind?" he asked with a wicked grin. "Besides ravishing you again, that is."

She appeared pleased by his remark, yet there was a hint of sadness in her smile. "I think you are concerned about your people, and worried about your father. I think you want to return to the tribe."

"You know my mind now," he murmured tenderly.

"Your mind and a lot more. Am I right?"

He nodded. "Considering the tension between the tribe and the buffalo hunters, and possible complications with the Indian agent and the cavalry, yes, I am worried, and anxious to get back."

She tossed her braids. "Perhaps you miss your squaw?"

Abruptly he moved to her side, caught her in his arms, and rolled her to the ground beneath him. "Which squaw is that?"

She regarded him impudently. "Fast Fox."

His lips twitched with amusement. "I have a feeling Fast Fox has kept herself well occupied. She has always been an industrious little vixen. And, as you're aware, I've been more than fascinated by my first bride—my *only* bride."

She lazily curled her arms around his neck. "Ah, yes. Do you think you've tamed me now?"

"You're about as tamed as I want you," he teased back. "A little wildness in bed will always be fine with me."

"So I've noticed."

His expression turned wistful as he ran a tormenting finger down her throat. "I'll miss this. Terribly."

"So will I." Tentatively she asked, "But when we get back . . . what then? You know that sooner or later, you must make a choice between the white and Indian worlds—"

"And the choice I make will affect you?" he cut in with regret.

She nodded. "We can't avoid it forever, White Wolf. I wish we could . . . but we just can't."

"I realize this." He fell silent for a long moment. "But we're together now, Prairie Star, together in every way. Let's take the rest one step at a time."

"And what's the first step?" she asked.

"You should know that by now," he replied huskily, lowering his head to kiss her.

They made love with bittersweet intensity, each privately feeling threatened by their planned return to the Indian community. Despite the great progress they had made, White Wolf feared his bride would soon ask him to take her back to civilization. Yet given the terrible conflicts now facing his tribe, the possibility that he might need to become chief, he wasn't certain he could disregard the needs of his people and live with her permanently among the White Eyes. But living without her, after having known the heaven of her love, seemed impossible, as well . . .

Maggie too feared that their love could not withstand all the obstacles they would soon face. White Wolf had recently told her that their future relationship would largely be decided by her, and she trusted him now not to hold her captive indefinitely, to release her if she asked for her freedom—

At this point, she was afraid to ask. She loved White Wolf, but could never live the rest of her life among roving Indians. If she chose to return to the white world, would he be willing to abandon his obligations to the tribe, and to his heritage? Would he place their love first?

Would she? Could she stay with her husband if he refused to leave his people?

The sun was sinking low in the afternoon sky by the time White Wolf, Maggie, and Chico approached the tribe. Even before they reached the outskirts of the village, they were spotted by the scouts, who alerted the People of their coming. Small children rushed out to greet the couple with sunny smiles, several of the youngsters petting Chico. White Wolf leaned over and scooped up Little Bear Claw, handing the boy to his wife. Prairie Star hugged the precious cherub and he chortled back. She rode into camp with the child sitting before her on the saddle.

At the center of camp, the adults came forward, amid smiles and curious looks. Prairie Star spotted Delilah emerging from a tepee with Bobcat. Both were flushed and disheveled—and it was obvious what they had been doing over the past weeks!

Did they ever do anything else? Now that she was a new-lywed herself in the truest sense, Maggie found she could certainly understand Delilah and Bobcat's passion.

White Wolf dismounted his horse and helped Prairie Star and the child down. They watched Buffalo Thunder approach with a faltering gait, coughing badly. White Wolf felt deep sadness at the sight of his father. He had hoped the old man's health might improve while they were away; instead, Buffalo Thunder appeared as emaciated as before, his color ashen and his breathing very labored.

"Welcome home, my son," he said hoarsely. Glancing at Maggie, he added, "The time you spent with your bride was good?"

White Wolf wrapped an arm about Prairie Star's shoulders and grinned. "Yes, it was very good."

Others stepped forward to greet them, Creek Flower hugging Prairie Star, Meadow Lark coming to take Little Bear Claw. A tense moment ensued when Black Hawk strode up proudly, scowling fearsomely at the newcomers, a guilt-faced Fast Fox trailing behind him.

Arrogantly he announced to White Wolf, "Brother, you went away with your white squaw and deserted your Comanche bride. She sleeps in my tepee now."

At his brother's unsurprising announcement, White Wolf glanced at Fast Fox, who averted her own eyes in shame. Actually, he was tempted to laugh out loud at this particular turn of events, which could solve for him the troubling matter of Fast Fox.

To Black Hawk, he feigned a deeply disappointed expression. "You are right, brother, as much as it grieves my heart to admit it. A wife should not be ignored. I failed my second bride, and I deserve to lose her. If it is agreeable to our father, let Fast Fox sleep in your tepee now."

Black Hawk at once turned to Buffalo Thunder, who fought a smile and nodded gravely. Black Hawk grinned broadly, and even Fast Fox appeared relieved. The arrogant warrior turned and announced his good fortune to the entire tribe, and the Indians loudly cheered.

"What has happened?" Prairie Star asked White Wolf.

"My brother has claimed my second bride—with our father's blessing," he said smugly.

"Good for Black Hawk," she replied with a satisfied nod.

White Wolf and Prairie Star were ushered toward the central fire, where food was brought. Pipes were passed, flutes and drums drawn out. Several braves performed a dance to honor the return of the couple. Squatting next to White Wolf, Buffalo Thunder rocked and sang while the drums and flutes were played. Nearer to the fire, his warriors stomped about, shaking rattles and tambourines.

Sitting with her husband, Maggie felt amazed by how at home she felt. She realized the People had sensed the change in her and White Wolf's relationship, and had welcomed them accordingly. She glanced around at happy faces—Delilah and Bobcat, Creek Flower and Silver Knife, Black Hawk with his several wives, including Fast Fox. She watched mothers nurse babies, while older children dozed next to their fathers, lulled by the rhythm of the drums and music, the warmth of the fire.

She could understand now why White Wolf felt drawn to this simple, pastoral existence. Were it not for the threat from the whites, these people had no pressing troubles beyond the inevitable toll nature took on them, the need to gather food. It was truly not their fault that their ancient ranges had been violated, and treaties broken. They responded the only way they could. And they accepted her, even though she was not one of them. In the reverse situation, the whites would never be so generous.

The feast lasted well past sundown, and soon Prairie Star was yawning.

"Go on to bed," White Wolf urged. "I'll be in soon."

"Good night," she murmured, kissing him, then heading off for the tepee.

White Wolf watched her leave, then announced proudly
to his father, "She is my woman now."

"I know," murmured Buffalo Thunder wisely. "The two
of you are as one spirit. It is apparent in your faces, in your
eyes."

"Your advice was excellent, my father."

"But what of your future now?"

White Wolf sighed. "We are deciding that slowly."

"You will have to make a choice," Buffalo Thunder said.
"A choice about where the white wolf will roam with his
mate, and rear his young."

"I know—and it won't be easy." He glanced somberly at
his father. "Ultimately I can't hold Prairie Star here against
her will. If she does not choose to stay . . ."

"You will leave with her?"

"I don't know yet. I'm still very concerned about the
tribe. What occurred while we were away?"

Buffalo Thunder sighed. "Stone Arrow and his brothers
stopped here for a powwow. He and Black Hawk had another skirmish with the buffalo hunters. The White Eyes Indian agent came again—"

"They found the tribe, even after we moved our camp?"
White Wolf interjected with alarm.

Buffalo Thunder nodded. "Their Tonk scouts found us."

"And what did the agent say?"

"Again the Quaker prevailed upon us to leave for the reservation. He warned that soon more white soldiers will
come, that the commander at Fort Defiance intends to send
them to gather wild mustangs on our hunting grounds."

"This is an ominous turn," White Wolf muttered, knowing full well how his brothers would respond to the intrusion.

Buffalo Thunder confirmed his son's thoughts. "Black
Hawk was enraged by the arrogance of the *tahbay-boh*. He
told the Quaker that if the soldiers plunder our hunting
grounds, they will be killed. The White Eyes warned Black
Hawk that any such action will likely mean total annihilation for our people."

White Wolf groaned. "So matters have not improved at all?"

"They have worsened."

He glanced out at his happy brothers and sisters, wondering how much longer tragedy could be avoided. "I suppose we'll need to move the tribe again."

Buffalo Thunder made a gesture of resignation. "Where, my son? The White Eyes lie in all directions now."

Where, indeed? White Wolf wondered, feeling the gravest concern for his people.

It was very late when White Wolf returned to the tepee, and his heart was heavily laden. The parting of the tepee flap sent a shaft of silvery light spilling over Prairie Star. His bride lay as she so often slept, on her belly with one knee hiked. Tonight her position seemed so unconsciously provocative that his breathing quickened and his mouth went dry. He grinned. She was still enough of a Boston lady to sleep in her dress— but she would not for long.

She was his mate, his woman. But how long would she be his? They were at harmony now with his people, but how soon before the White Eyes tore them asunder?

Tortured by these possibilities, he lay down beside her, and wrapped his arms possessively about her. He moved aside her braids and kissed the nape of her neck. Her heard her sleepy moan. He raised her skirt and stroked her soft bottom. She squirmed, sighed, and moved against his hand. He slipped his free hand beneath her at her front, stroking and parting her. She panted in her sleep. Growing impatient and torturously aroused, he tugged her dress off over her head and ran his lips over her bare back. He felt the gooseflesh rise on her skin and heard her little sighs of arousal. He reached around her to take her breasts in his hands. Her flesh was soft, her nipples as tight as she would be when he buried himself inside her—

Aroused past sanity by the prospect, he raised her to her knees. She gasped, as if startled, and he soothed her, pressing his mouth to her ear and whispering Comanche love words.

"Mate with me, Prairie Star," he whispered intensely. "Let me take you as the wild wolf claims his mate out on the midnight prairie."

His impassioned words raised a fevered moan from her, all the encouragement White Wolf needed. He clamped his forearms tightly around her waist and plunged into her from behind, delighting to her raw cry, and the way she held him, unflinching, despite the intense pressure and friction of their joining—

He claimed his bride with powerful thrusts, melding his body with hers, longing as never before to give her his child, to create a bond that went beyond themselves and their mortality. He heard her desperately calling his name, while writhing greedily to take him deeper—

He held her to him and spent himself with soul-searing ecstasy. Her primitive wail was hoarse with her own rapture. For a moment, they rocked as a single being. He drew her down on the pallet beside him, caressing her and murmuring to her soothingly. He felt so shaken, so humbled by their love—and the prospect of losing her—that tears filled his eyes.

When Prairie Star awakened the following morning, White Wolf was already gone, but the memory of him was real and overpowering. Her belly ached pleasurably and her face flamed with memories of the torrid passion they had shared. Never had he taken her quite so brazenly, so thoroughly. He must feel as threatened by their return to life with the tribe as she did.

In the days that followed, their passion remained strong. But Prairie Star noted increasingly that her husband seemed preoccupied and remote since their return. He had frequent arguments with his half brother Black Hawk, and spent long hours in council with Buffalo Thunder and other braves. But whenever she asked him what was wrong, he shrugged off her concerns and refused to share.

Reality intruded quickly enough. A couple of weeks after they returned to the tribe, Black Hawk and several warriors left on a hunting party. Three days later, the braves returned, whooping and hollering as they rode about camp. Emerging from her tepee, Prairie Star spotted Black Hawk on his prancing pinto pony, with fearsome black war paint streaking his face and a scalp pole in his hand. As he galloped past her, screaming exultantly, she caught sight of several grisly war trophies on his bloody lance. Horrified and sickened by the sight, she rushed into the woods to vomit . . .

White Wolf was away from camp, chopping firewood, when the war party returned. Hearing their loud hollering, he set aside his ax and rushed back to the village. Spotting Black Hawk riding about with the scalp pole, he quickly scanned the area for Prairie Star, praying his bride had not witnessed the terrible sight. She was nowhere in sight—hardly a comfort under the circumstances.

Black Hawk galloped up to his brother and arrogantly hurled the lance with its many scalps into the ground near White Wolf's feet. He reined in his pony, which pranced and reared in protest, and grinned at White Wolf.

"What have you done?" White Wolf demanded in Comanche.

"We caught the White Eyes soldiers stealing our mustangs," Black Hawk replied triumphantly. "We slaughtered all of them."

White Wolf stared at the pole in revulsion. "Why did you have to murder the soldiers? There are plenty of mustangs on the plains, enough for all of us—"

"No!" Black Hawk interrupted, reinforcing his words with angry signs. "The White Eyes violated our hunting grounds!"

"Perhaps they did, but now they will hunt us! The tribe will have to be constantly on the move, chased by the *tahbay-boh!*"

"We will not be chased like women!" Black Hawk declared vehemently, waving his fist. "We will make a stand like men! We will pursue the soldiers and the hunters, and kill them all!"

Before White Wolf could protest, Black Hawk galloped off, whooping with his brothers.

White Wolf cursed his frustration, and resumed his search for Prairie Star. How he hoped she had not witnessed the return of the war party. Finding her absent from their tepee only increased his distress, although he felt relieved when he spotted her pony grazing with the other mustangs. At least she had not run away in her horror.

At last he found her lying in the grasses near the stream. Alarmed, he knelt beside her and felt her forehead. "Darling, are you ill?"

She twisted about to face him, her features stark, her cheeks wet with tears. "The scalp pole . . ."

He groaned and pulled her up into his arms. "I'm sorry you had to see that."

"What happened?"

"Black Hawk and the others massacred a detachment of soldiers who were hunting mustangs on our land."

"Oh, no!"

He nodded soberly. "I fear my brothers behaved most foolishly. Now the soldiers will track us. The band will be forced to go on the run, and the freedom of my people may well be in jeopardy."

She shuddered against him. "I cannot live this way."

Alarmed, he drew back to regard the conflicted emotion on her face. "What are you saying?"

"I no longer hate your people, I understand them," she told him, wiping away a tear. "But I cannot stay in this world, not with the violence, the savagery, and the uncertainty. I suppose I am just too civilized. I came to Texas to put down roots—not for myself and possibly our children to become nomads."

White Wolf sadly recognized that Prairie Star had spoken the truth. They had been living on borrowed time, and sooner or later, reality was bound to intrude.

He pulled her close again and stroked her back. "I know, darling. You are right. I will take you back to my ranch."

"Will you stay with me there?" she asked plaintively.

He groaned. "I'm sorry, Prairie Star. Right now I can't make any promises. The threat to the tribe has become so much more real and immediate."

"I know. Will you at least stay for a time?"

"Of course."

They clung together, the warriors' wild whoops of blood vengeance still ringing in their ears.

THIRTY-THREE

SEVERAL DAYS LATER, MAGGIE AND BRONSON RODE ONTO THE Kane Ranch, both still dressed in their Indian buckskins. In order to expedite their journey, Bronson had left Chico behind at the Indian village.

He felt grateful that their trek had been largely uneventful, since he had routed them away from civilized areas as much as possible. A couple of tense moments had ensued, once when they had spotted a detachment of cavalry, and later when they had happened upon a group of buffalo hunters. Both times Bronson had safely hidden himself and Maggie before they could be detected. He had explained to her that, since they were both dressed like Indians, the whites might well shoot first and ask questions later. She had agreed, while scolding him for burning up her white clothing weeks ago.

Their days had been filled with hard riding, their nights with fevered, almost desperate lovemaking. Bronson had sensed that his bride felt as anxious as he did concerning what their return to civilization might mean to their relationship.

Already he and his wife had slipped back into calling

each other by their white names, and had dropped the scattered Indian words and signs they had used previously. Maggie seemed content to leave their time with the tribe behind her, and this troubled Bronson, since he knew his Indian heritage was something he could never completely abandon. Indeed, it worried him to be leaving the People at this critical juncture, with his father's health failing and the threat from the whites increasing. However, for now, he had to place Maggie's needs first; she had given his world a fair chance, and it was time for him to take her back to be with her own kind. Where they went from there, only the Great Spirit knew.

Near the ranch house, Bronson spotted two wranglers about a hundred yards to the north of them, gathering stray cows. He whistled and waved a greeting, and the men waved back, by now accustomed to seeing him returning from Indian country. Both men did stare in open curiosity at the young woman with red braids riding beside Bronson.

Maggie was taking no note as she gazed at the sprawling ranch house in the gentle valley beyond them. She was entranced by the one-and-a-half-story whitewashed structure with its high tin roof, and its inviting gray porch with cozy rockers and hanging baskets spilling out greenery and bright flowers. The house was shaded by large pecan trees and surrounded by neat outbuildings and sturdy corrals. It struck her that this could be a beautiful place to put down roots and raise a child—the child she already suspected she and Bronson may have conceived on the night they returned to his tribe.

"What a lovely home," she murmured to Bronson.

"I'm glad you're pleased," he replied. "Our little adventure kind of sidetracked me from showing you my ranch, didn't it?"

She smiled. "How many acres do you have?"

"Almost ten thousand, and at least that many head of longhorns."

She gasped. "And you would be willing to abandon all of this for your people?"

"I'm half-white, Maggie," he replied. "I can never completely turn my back on that side of my heritage, either."

His words brought her some sense of relief. "It feels odd to have you calling me 'Maggie' again."

He shrugged. "We're back in the white world. Besides, you always preferred 'Maggie,' didn't you?"

She frowned, for suddenly she was not entirely sure. In truth, no name had ever sounded more beautiful to her ears than "Prairie Star," when White Wolf had whispered it to her while they were both in the throes of passion.

"You're probably eager to get back into civilized clothing," he remarked. "I guess we'll have to go into town to buy you some new duds."

She laughed. "Actually, these Indians dresses have spoiled me. They are so comfortable, and it's such a relief not to have to wear a corset, or . . ." Her voice trailed off and she blushed.

"Believe me, it's even more of a convenience to me," he agreed with a devilish grin.

She wrinkled her nose at him. "I may give your uncle quite a start in my current costume—not that I'm ashamed of it."

"Believe me, Uncle Sam won't be shocked. He's even seen me return from Comanche territory still wearing war paint."

"Are you anxious to see him?"

He nodded. "Sam's a good friend, and I enjoy my time with him here on the ranch."

After crossing the shallow stream, they halted their horses in the swept yard in front of the ranch house. Bronson slipped to the ground and helped Maggie dismount. They went up the steps and were stunned when the door flew open and a woman neither had expected to see stepped out to greet them. Short, plump, and middle-aged, she had a pretty rounded face graced by dimples and lively green eyes. She wore a striped and bustled broadcloth frock with high neck and long sleeves. Her brownish gray hair was pinned up in a bun topped by a ruffled white house cap. She was staring at the newcomers, particularly Maggie, with utter astonishment.

"Margaret Prudence Donovan!" she exclaimed in a slight Irish brogue. "By the saints, child, what has happened to you? Why, you've turned into a wild Indian, by the looks of you!"

"Aunt Lydia!" Maggie cried. "What on earth are you doing here?"

The woman held out her arms. "First, come greet your old aunt properly, you wayward girl!"

Laughing, Maggie rushed forward to hug her aunt, feeling soothed by Lydia's loving, familiar presence and the well-remembered scent of her rosewater. Moving back, she wiped away a tear. "It's so good to see you! Now tell me why you're here."

Lydia balled her hands on her hips. "Why, Pru and I about had apoplexy over you, child, when weeks passed and we never heard a word. Finally I got in touch with Mr. Bryce, and since he'd heard nothing, as well, he and I decided to embark for Texas to investigate. Mr. Bryce notified Mr. Samuel Kane of our plans, and then we started west."

"Calvin is here?" asked a flabbergasted Bronson.

Lydia turned to him. "Yes, sir, he is." She raised an eyebrow to Maggie. "This is your husband, child?"

"He is, indeed. Lydia Donovan, meet Bronson Kane."

Lydia shook Bronson's hand, but regarded him with a dubious frown. "Pleased to meet you, Mr. Kane, although I'll be having a word or two with you regarding your outlandish behavior toward my niece. Now, come inside, you two. You have a lot of explaining to do."

Exchanging amused glances, Maggie and Bronson followed Lydia inside to the parlor, where Lydia parked her girth in a rocker near the flagstone fireplace, and Maggie and Bronson sat down together on the leather settee. Maggie glanced around at the large room, taking in its scarred wooden floors, dusty braided rugs, and worn leather furniture. A collection of sad-looking greenish gray dimity curtains hung at the windows, and yellowed newspapers and

cigar butts were scattered about. She decided this room—
and likely the entire house—could definitely use a woman's
touch.

She smiled at Lydia. "How's Aunt Pru?"

"As crotchety as ever," Lydia replied. "Are you folks
hungry or thirsty?"

Bronson glanced at Maggie, and she shook her head.
"Where are Calvin and Uncle Sam?" he asked Lydia.

"Out riding the range."

Bronson laughed incredulously. "Calvin Bryce is riding a
cutting horse?"

Lydia heaved a great sigh. "Given the fact that we've had
so much time on our hands waiting for you folks to reappear, Mr. Bryce decided to make himself useful by gathering information on life in the Wild West for his readers back
in Boston." She slanted a reproachful glance toward them
both. "So, while Mr. Bryce has been pleasantly amusing
himself, I've had plenty of time to wring my hands over you
two."

Maggie grimaced. "Aunt Lydia, Bronson and I are deeply
sorry if we've caused you to fret."

Lydia harrumphed. "When Mr. Bryce and I first arrived
in Austin and Mr. Kane wasn't sure of your whereabouts, I
wanted to call out the cavalry." She shifted her stern gaze to
Bronson. "But your uncle convinced us to hold off for a
while, since he had a notion you had probably taken your
bride off to meet your father. Is that what happened, Mr.
Kane?"

Bronson grinned wryly. "In a manner of speaking, yes."

Lydia drew herself up irately. "Then why, in the name of
all that's holy, did you steal my niece out of her bed in the
middle of the night and carry her off, without notifying a
soul?"

Maggie and Bronson exchanged amazed glances. "How
did you figure out all of this, Aunt Lydia?" she asked.

"Why, by putting our heads together, of course," came
the indignant response. "As I've already explained, Mr. Sam
Kane met Mr. Bryce and myself at the train station in Aus-

tin. He apologized that the two of you were missing, and explained that you'd had something of a falling out. He said that you"—she nodded to Bronson—"had gone off to see your father, and you"—she inclined her head to Maggie—"had likely remained behind in Austin. Accordingly, the three of us went from house to house in the capital city making inquiries about you, Margaret, and that's how we met your kindly landlady, Minnie Walker. She told us how you had vanished in the middle of the night and left all your belongings." Lydia paused to catch her breath, gazing narrowly at Bronson. "After all of us discussed the matter at length, your uncle concluded that you had probably taken Margaret off. He mentioned some nonsense about your father having done the same thing almost thirty years ago."

Bronson grinned sheepishly. "Sometimes Uncle Sam knows me better than I know myself."

Lydia stared at Bronson sharply. "You neglected to tell my niece you were half-Indian, didn't you, sir?"

"Aunt Lydia, please!" protested Maggie.

"It's all right, dear," Bronson told his wife. To Lydia he replied adamantly, "Calvin didn't tell her. It was his idea to choose me a bride in the first place, and I only went along with his scheme with the understanding that he would inform my future bride of my Indian heritage. So that part, at least, wasn't my fault."

"Now, don't go getting on your high horse, young man," Lydia admonished. "I certainly don't hold your Indian blood against you. Why, when our family first settled in this country almost a century ago, it was a Delaware brave who saved Margaret's great-grandfather from drowning in the well at the family homestead. Do you remember that, Margaret?"

She frowned. "I seem to recall hearing the story during my childhood."

"Considering what happened to Margaret's fiancé, I can understand why she may have been somewhat leery of your heritage, Mr. Kane." Lydia raised an eyebrow and stared meaningfully at Maggie's squaw outfit. "Though it appears she's overcome her skepticism."

Both newlyweds laughed.

"So what happened to you two?" Lydia demanded.

Maggie glanced at Bronson, who explained, "As you already know, Maggie and I began our marriage under something of a cloud. We parted company for over a week, then I came back to get her and took her off to live with my tribe for a while."

Lydia was rolling her eyes. "A rather innocuous-sounding explanation, considering your nefarious behavior, young man." She turned to Maggie. "What's it like living with wild Indians?"

Maggie burst out laughing, prompting a new glower from Lydia. "I can't begin to tell you right now, Aunt Lydia. It's a totally new world. And for me, it was quite an education."

Bronson squeezed his wife's hand. "Maggie's been an eager pupil, just as she's a good teacher. She has enriched my people as much as I hope they have enriched her."

Watching Maggie smile at Bronson, Lydia leveled a suspicious glance at him. "You're not expecting this refined young lady to live with your tribe permanently, are you?"

Bronson shook his head. "No, I don't expect that of her."

"Good. Now, as for this ranch . . ." Lydia glanced about the room, and nodded. "Lord knows the house could use some spit and polish, but it has possibilities. On the other hand, the town is a disgrace. Your uncle has been showing me around—a very nice man, he is."

"Thank you."

"Are you going to settle down here and make a home for my niece?"

Bronson hesitated, throwing Maggie a pleading look. She implored, "Aunt Lydia, please, not right now."

Lydia waved off her niece. "Oh, I know. I'm a nosy old windbag, and you two look worn-out. Why don't you go get settled in? Calvin and Sam should be back by suppertime."

Bronson nodded to Maggie. "Yes, I would imagine Maggie would like to wash and change."

Lydia smiled at her niece. "We brought your trunk back from Austin, dear. I believe Sam had it put upstairs in your husband's room."

"Thanks, Aunt Lydia," said Maggie.

Bronson and Maggie headed upstairs together. He ushered her into a large, sunny room with a braided rug and a four-poster bed.

"This is your room?" she asked, spotting her trunk over near the window.

"It's our room now," he replied, pulling her close for a kiss.

They clung to each other for a long, intense moment. Maggie pulled back slightly and studied her husband's distracted face, noting the worry lines. She mused that they were both already feeling the strain of their return to civilization.

Especially Bronson. She frowned as she watched him stride off to gaze out the window.

THIRTY-FOUR

THEY BOTH WASHED OFF THE TRAIL DUST, THEN CUDDLED UP on his bed and napped together.

Bronson stared down at Maggie, dozing beside him on the mattress, and mused that this was the first time they had shared a real bed together . . .

Later, she gazed up at him, asleep with his head on the feather pillow, and wondered if they would ever again make love naked out on the prairie beneath the stars . . .

They awakened late in the afternoon, got up, and put on their "civilized" clothing. They faced each other awkwardly, Bronson in denim trousers, a white shirt, and boots, Maggie in a bustled, long-sleeved dress of polished yellow cotton.

Both started slightly at the loud sound of hoofbeats outside. Bronson went to glance out the window. "I see Uncle Sam and Calvin riding up. Guess we'd best head on downstairs."

"Guess so."

He took her hand and they proceeded downstairs just as the two men burst in the front door, sweeping the odors of the cattle trail in with them. Maggie recognized Calvin Bryce—a tall, brown-haired, handsome gentleman with a thin mustache. Behind him stood a pleasant-looking, deeply tanned middle-aged man Maggie assumed was Samuel Kane.

The older man rushed forward to greet them with a warm smile. "Bronson! Good to see you back, son! And this must be your bride! Get on down here, you two!"

Bronson led Maggie down to join the others. "Maggie, this is Sam Kane." Raising an eyebrow, he finished, "You already know my friend, Calvin Bryce."

"Yes, I do. How do you do, Mr. Kane?" Maggie shook the hand of each man in turn, and each murmured back a greeting.

"Hello, Bronson," Calvin added with a rueful grin, extending his hand.

Bronson hesitated, then grudgingly accepted the handshake. "Calvin. This is some surprise."

"And you've sprung a few surprises on us, too, haven't you, son?" Sam put in with wry humor. He turned to smile at Maggie. "Welcome to the Kane Ranch, honey. We're all mighty relieved to see you safe and sound. My, but you're the prettiest thing I've ever laid eyes on—" He paused to wink at Lydia, who had just stepped out to join them from the parlor. "Besides your aunt, of course."

Everyone laughed, and Lydia winked at Bronson. "Your uncle is a real charmer, son. Some of it must have rubbed off on you, or else you never would have won Margaret over."

"Agreed," Bronson replied, wrapping an arm around Maggie's waist.

Calvin stepped closer to Bronson and said sheepishly, "Glad to see you two seem so pleased with each other."

"No thanks to you," muttered Bronson.

Clearing his throat, Calvin continued, "Where have you two been, anyway? We've all been worried sick."

Bronson glowered at his old friend. "I'm surprised you have the nerve to ask that, Calvin. As a matter of fact, I've a big bone to pick with you concerning Maggie."

"Now, no fussing, young men," Lydia scolded, wagging a finger at them. "You'll ruin dinner."

"That's right," said Sam. "Smells like Stovepipe has our grub almost ready." Sniffing the air, redolent with the aromas of biscuits and beef stew, he grinned at Lydia. "Did you make another of your wonderful sweet potato pies, Miss Donovan?"

She preened back at him. "I did, indeed, Mr. Kane."

Sam offered Lydia his arm. Observing the two, Bronson raised an eyebrow at Maggie, and she stifled a smile. The small group headed into the dining room. The aging trail cook, whom Sam introduced to Maggie as Stovepipe Tipton, ambled in with a huge bowl of stew. Eyeing the tall, thin man, Maggie decided his nickname was quite appropriate.

During the meal, Maggie and Bronson gave Sam and Calvin a laundered account of their adventure, leaving out the more personal aspects of their relationship, as well as omitting the grisly details of the Comanche band's skirmishes with buffalo hunters and the cavalry. Lydia then filled in Maggie on events in Boston, including a hilarious account of how Aunt Prudence had developed a disastrous home remedy for Father Joseph's gout. Calvin spoke excitedly about the articles on life in the West that he was writing for the *Beacon*.

Over Lydia's excellent sweet potato pie, Sam asked Bronson, "How is your father?"

Bronson set down his coffee with a sigh. "He's declining, I'm afraid."

"Sorry to hear that, son," said Sam sincerely. "When I went to Austin to meet Lydia and Calvin, I heard some troubling talk about Indians."

"Yes?" inquired Bronson.

As everyone at the table listened intently, Sam explained, "Seems folks are really stirred up ever since the massacre in Crockett County last month. They're saying it's as bad as the Wagon Train massacre last year. And there have been a lot of other Indian raids all along the Brazos frontier this spring. Rumor is Ranald McKenzie may soon be heading down this way with his buffalo soldiers. As you know, he's the one who's been chasing Quanah Parker all over the Llano Estacado."

"Ah, my old friend Peta Nacona," murmured Bronson with a faint smile.

"Of course, Quanah has really given McKenzie a run for his money up in the Panhandle," Sam continued with a rueful grin. "I hear tell one of Quanah's warriors even put an arrow through McKenzie, and wily Quanah has managed to escape after every raid. I reckon McKenzie is mad enough to spit up brimstone by now, and I hear Sherman and Sheridan are getting mighty frustrated over the entire Indian situation here in Texas." Sam sighed. "That doesn't bode well for your tribe, son."

Bronson nodded grimly. He was well aware that Ranald McKenzie had a reputation as a ruthless and effective Indian fighter. And although Quanah Parker had been very successful in evading the skilled horse soldier up in the Texas Panhandle, McKenzie was now heading toward less desolate parts of the Staked Plain, where not every Comanche band would be able to escape him and flee high up into the wilderness.

"I am saddened but not surprised to hear of the spring raids along the frontier," Bronson told Sam. "I've known for some time that Comanche and other Indian bands roving to the north of us are just as incensed over the intrusion of the settlers and the buffalo hunters as are many of the warriors of my own tribe. And the whites are now equally riled because we all won't simply retreat to the reservations. I'm afraid my people may be forced to be on the move from now on."

"Well, young man, I sincerely hope you'll never expect my niece to take up such a hair-raising life," put in Lydia with a look of horror.

"I've already told you I don't expect her to," Bronson replied firmly.

Calvin spoke up, coughing. "I . . . Bronson, I just wanted

to say that I hope my withholding of some pertinent information from Maggie didn't cause undue trouble between you two."

Bronson scowled at his friend. "I'm glad you've raised the issue, Calvin, because I think we've been avoiding this subject long enough. So tell me ... why didn't you tell Maggie that I was half-Indian, as we agreed?"

Calvin hesitated, as all eyes became focused on him. "I started out following your instructions to the letter," he confessed quietly. "I ran your ad, and interviewed all the young ladies that answered it. Several suitable prospects emerged, but the problem was, every time I told one of the young ladies that you were half-Indian, she all but ran away screaming. Then, when I met Maggie and realized at once that she was perfect for you ..." He smiled at Maggie, then offered Bronson a gesture of entreaty. "The truth is, I just didn't have the heart to tell her and spoil everything. I thought that if only the two of you could meet first, you might have a chance." He brightened. "And I was right, wasn't I?"

Bronson stared hard at his friend for another moment, then turned to Maggie. "Was he?"

She startled everyone when, instead of replying, she burst into tears and rushed from the room.

"Darling, what is it?"

Upstairs, Bronson joined Maggie on the bed and pulled her into his arms. She sniffled against him for long moments before she could speak.

At last she raised her tear-streaked face to his. "Oh, Bronson. I'm so glad Calvin spoke out as he did."

"Are you?" Bronson gently caressed her cheek. "I'm sorry his actions caused you so much pain."

"Perhaps that is true, but now I know my suffering was necessary."

"Necessary. But why, darling?"

She drew a shuddering breath, her expression stark. "Because not until this moment have I completely understood the unjust prejudice you have had to face in your life. And not until this moment have I completely believed you had no part in the deception that made me your wife."

He clutched her closer. "Oh, Maggie."

She continued in a breaking voice. "The sad part is, if Calvin had told me the truth, I would have run away, just like the others did. And I would have been so wrong. I would have denied myself all the joys of loving you."

He kissed her hair, and groaned.

Her next words were barely audible. "And I do love you, Bronson. No matter what happens, I want you to know that I do . . ."

"I love you, too."

Bronson kissed his bride with deep tenderness. Tightly embraced, the lovers soon succumbed to all the bittersweet joys their love had brought them . . .

Maggie awakened sometime later to see her husband standing by the window, naked, looking out at the night sky. At once she sensed what was troubling him.

"You are worried about the tribe?"

He turned back toward her, and she spotted the turmoil in his eyes. "Yes. Especially after what Uncle Sam told us tonight. Maggie, my father's health is rapidly failing, and I fear my brother Black Hawk will continue to take the tribe down the wrong path, one of violence, death, and destruction. How can I help my tribe if I let Black Hawk become chief?"

Although Maggie understood her husband's dilemma, her heart ached with the knowledge that the tribe could ultimately prove more important to him than she was, or their marriage. In a small voice she asked, "You know I can't go back with you to live among the tribe, don't you?"

"I know," he replied tightly.

"Would you leave me to lead your people?"

He started toward her. "I wouldn't want to." A shaft of moonlight outlined his stark features. "But, Maggie, if you stay with me, I can't promise I'll choose to remain in the white world."

Anguish assailed her. "It's not just your father and the tribe, is it?"

"What do you mean?"

"It's you, Bronson. I've seen that faraway, restless look in your eyes ever since we arrived back here. There are two men living inside you—the untamed savage and the civilized white man. I still don't know which man will win. But I do know the spirit of the Nerm is in your blood—and I'm afraid you won't be able to resist the lure of the wild tribe."

"You think I would turn my back on you for that?" he asked in torment.

"To live free among your brothers? I'm afraid you might."

"Oh, Maggie. Don't you know me better than that?"

He slipped into bed beside her, but when he reached for her, she turned away, her throat raw with sorrow.

THIRTY-FIVE

By the time Maggie awakened late the next morning, Bronson was gone. She dressed, went down to the kitchen, and found Lydia there washing dishes at the sink. The room was cozy and rustic, with its pie safe, pine cupboards, chintz-covered table, and huge cast-iron stove that emanated much heat at the moment. The air was thick with the smell of bacon grease, ham, eggs, and hot, strong coffee. A sweet morning breeze wafted through the gingham curtains at the windows.

"Good, morning, Aunt Lydia. Have you seen my husband?"

Lydia turned and wiped her hands on her apron. "Oh, good morning, child. I was just tidying up after Stovepipe." She stepped forward and hugged Maggie. "As for your husband, he and Calvin were off at dawn for a ride together. I think those two must have a lot of catching up to do. Anyway, since I was already up, Bronson asked me to tell you they'd be back by noon. Take a seat, dear, and I'll bring you some coffee."

"Thanks, Aunt Lydia."

Maggie sat down at the kitchen table. Lydia brought her coffee in a blue and white pottery cup, then took pot holders and picked up a filled plate that sat warming at the back of the stove. "I saved you some breakfast, too."

Maggie eyed the generous servings of eggs, grits, ham, and toast. "Oh, this looks—and smells—divine. But really, I should be serving you, Aunt Lydia."

"Nonsense. After all you've been through, you need to recover your strength."

Maggie patted her aunt's hand. "I'm fine. Please, Aunt Lydia, get some coffee and join me."

Lydia beamed. "Just what I was thinking."

The spinster fetched a cup of coffee and sat down across from her niece. She offered a sympathetic smile. "You have been through quite an ordeal, haven't you, dear?"

"It was an education, to say the least."

Lydia sipped her coffee. "You know, at this point, I'm more curious about what you haven't told me than about what you have."

Maggie laughed. "Such as?"

"Well, I'm dying to learn more details of your little adventure. Did your husband really snatch you out of your bed in the middle of the night, with no warning?"

Maggie rolled her eyes. "You have no idea. Bronson kidnapped me dressed as a Comanche warrior, complete with war paint."

"My kingdom, child! You must be jesting."

"No. He scared me halfway out of my wits. And I must admit I deserved it."

Lydia gasped. "How could you possibly deserve such horrible treatment?"

Maggie told Lydia about the initial misunderstandings of her marriage, and how she had broken the sacred beads Bronson gave her. "My conduct was pretty callous, too," she finished.

"But very understandable, under the circumstances," Lydia put in wisely.

"Perhaps, but it wasn't Bronson's fault that Calvin broke his word. When I learned the truth about Bronson's background, I reacted out of fear and ignorance—something I keenly regret now. And I've also come to realize that I was wrong to condemn all Indians because of what happened to James."

Lydia smiled gently. "Then something very good has come of this, dear, if you've been able to lay those old demons to rest. Have you and Bronson gotten things worked out?"

Maggie regarded her aunt with anguished eyes. "Not everything. But I love him, Aunt Lydia."

"Of course you do, dear. He seems a fine man, much like his uncle. I'm sure he'll make a fine husband and father."

"If he'll stay with me," she muttered.

"You're afraid he'll go back to live with the tribe?"

Maggie explained Bronson's dilemma regarding the Penateka band. "I wish I could live permanently with my husband among his people, but I'm afraid the Indian life is just too nomadic and uncivilized for me."

Lydia nodded. "I know that in the Bible, Ruth says, 'Whither thou goest, I will go,' but I don't think the good Lord ever intended for a civilized woman to have to live with a band of Indians on the warpath. And what about your children?"

That question prompted a troubling and equally awesome prospect in Maggie's mind, making her again remember that night when she and Bronson had made love so splendidly, and how her woman's time was overdue.

"Maggie?" Lydia prompted.

Maggie flashed her aunt an apologetic smile. "You're right. I could never raise my children among Indians."

"Amen," concurred Lydia.

Maggie touched her aunt's sleeve. "Enough about me. Tell me about you and Sam Kane."

Lydia actually blushed. "Why, whatever do you mean, child?"

Maggie wagged a finger. "You can't fool me, Aunt Lydia. You may have claimed for years that you're an avowed spinster, but I can tell you have eyes for that man—and vice versa."

Lydia appeared eminently pleased. "Is it that obvious?"

Maggie feigned an irate expression. "You never used to make your sweet potato pie for me more than once a year."

Lydia chuckled. "I suppose my guilty secret is out."

"So tell me, how did this little romance start developing?"

Lydia sighed dreamily. "Well, dear, I suppose there's just something so charming about these southern men. Sam has been a perfect gentleman, and so attentive, from the moment he helped me step down off the train in Austin. And one evening, as we sat on the porch together, he told me how, for all these years, he has loved Bronson's mother—you know, dear, the one who was taken off by Indians, and later came home to die."

"Yes, I know. Bronson told me all about his mother, Agnes, and how Sam loved her."

Lydia nodded. "There's something so endearing about a man who would be true to the memory of a dead woman for so long, especially when he was never even married to her."

Maggie winked at her aunt. "Sounds to me like he needs a fine living woman to take his mind off things."

"I'm working on it, my dear," Lydia replied brightly. "Believe me, I am."

"Looks like you and Maggie are getting along famously," said Calvin Bryce.

"I still wish you had told her the truth about my heritage," replied Bronson.

The two men had been for a brisk ride around the ranch. During the course of the morning, Bronson had confided in his friend much about the past weeks he'd spent with his bride—including the details of his kidnapping Maggie and taking her to live among his people, and his later taking her off alone.

Now they had paused their horses at the edge of a mesa. As the animals snorted and puffed, Bronson and Calvin watched the wranglers work the herd in the valley below. The shouts of ranch hands, neighing of cutting horses, lowing of cattle, and barking of dogs filled the air. The odors of dust and manure hung over the canyon, mingling with the sweet scents of dew and nectar on this mild early summer morning.

"I suppose I was negligent in not adhering to our bargain," Calvin admitted. "But if I had told Maggie the truth, she never would have come here."

"Damn right," said Bronson. "Were you aware that her first fiancé was a cavalry officer who was tortured and killed by the Sioux in Minnesota?"

Calvin whistled. "I had no idea—although she did seem somewhat leery about coming to Texas, having heard tales about Indian troubles here."

Bronson snorted a laugh. "And you reassured her, I presume?"

"As best I could," Calvin admitted guiltily. "Like I said, I could tell as soon as I met Maggie that she was the one for you." He flashed Bronson a sheepish smile. "Knowing I had only the best of intentions at heart, will you forgive me, old friend?"

Bronson mulled over this for a moment. "I guess under the circumstances, I should," came the reluctant reply.

"Thanks," said Calvin with a relieved grin.

The two men fell silent, watching the drovers pushing the herd toward the north. "What's the sentiment on the Indian situation back east these days, Calvin?" Bronson asked.

"It's shifting," he admitted. "For some decades, Congress has been sympathetic toward the plight of the Plains tribes. But their sympathy wears thin with each new report of a massacre out west."

Bronson nodded grimly. "According to Sam, the wind's blowing pretty much the same way here in Texas."

"And as you're probably aware, Grant has essentially given his generals, Sherman and Sheridan, free rein to seek out and destroy the Comanche in Texas."

Bronson stared off toward the horizon. "I'm afraid my brothers will soon be forced onto the reservations—more due to the loss of their food supply than because of harassment by the cavalry. And I fear this is a fate they will never adjust to."

"Where does all this leave you and Maggie?"

Bronson sighed. "I'm not sure . . . a major reason I wanted my bride to know of my mixed blood in the first place."

"That did not stop you from abducting her," Calvin pointed out.

Bronson glared back. "By then we were married."

"And from what you've told me, you're far beyond the point of no return now."

Bronson spoke with hoarse emotion. "I love her desperately, Calvin, and the thought of losing her scares me to death."

"But if you do decide to return to the tribe, won't you be giving her up? It's pretty clear to me that Maggie won't live with your tribe permanently."

"I know," Bronson conceded unhappily. "But how can I completely turn my back on my Comanche brothers, especially with my father so old and frail?"

Calvin sighed. "I wish I had the answer, my friend."

The two men conversed a bit longer, then rode back toward the ranch house. They were crossing a county road when they spotted a woman approaching in a buckboard.

Watching Bronson rein in his horse, Calvin followed suit. "Who's that to the south of us?"

Bronson was peering down the road with a hand shading his eyes. "One of our neighbors, Judy Lynn Blake. Let's wait here and have a word with her."

The two paused until the woman halted her buckboard near them. Bronson smiled at Judy Lynn, who looked quite comely this morning in a gold and brown calico dress and matching slat bonnet. He noticed that her stomach had burgeoned noticeably since he had last seen her.

"Good morning, Judy Lynn," he said.

"Hello, Bronson," she replied brightly, glancing from him to Calvin. "This must be your guest from Boston."

Bronson frowned in puzzlement. "Yes, it is. Mrs. Blake, please meet my friend Mr. Calvin Bryce."

"Welcome to Texas, Mr. Bryce," Judy Lynn said.

Calvin removed his hat and smiled. "Thank you, Mrs. Blake."

"How did you know Calvin was staying with us?" Bronson asked.

"We just saw your uncle in town at the store. He told me about your guests from Boston, and that you're married now. Is that true, Bronson?"

Bronson grinned. "Sure is."

She smiled warmly. "Congratulations, then. I'm very happy for you."

"Thank you."

"Your bride's from Boston, too?"

"Yes."

"George and I will hope to have the pleasure of meeting her soon."

"Thanks." Frowning, Bronson glanced about them. "Judy Lynn, not to pry, but why are you driving your buckboard alone?"

She chuckled. "I'm not alone." She lifted a shotgun, holding it barrel-down for the men to see. "I'd like to see some no-good son of a gun try to stop me."

Bronson shook his head. "You always were a spunky girl, but it could still be dangerous, you out here all by yourself."

"Don't worry, I'm keeping my eyes peeled," she replied, "especially since someone's been stealing our cattle." Carefully she added, "You wouldn't happen to know anything about that, would you, Bronson? I mean, George keeps finding signs that Comanches have been around—arrows near the barn and such."

He shook his head. "I can tell you one thing—it wasn't the band of my brothers. I would have known."

She nodded. "I believe you, then."

"I wouldn't be shocked if Skeet Gallagher is in on the rustling," Bronson mused soberly. "He and his gang of ruffians have certainly stolen cattle around here before, and tried to blame it on the Comanche."

"Well, if I catch the thievin' varmints on our land, they're dead," Judy Lynn asserted.

"You still shouldn't be traveling to your ranch alone," Bronson scolded.

She wiped her brow with the sleeve of her dress. "I have no choice. Two of our best workhorses are down with the colic, and I've got to get on back and doctor them. George couldn't leave the store to escort me home."

Bronson shook his head and frowned at Calvin.

"Why don't we do the honors, old friend?" Calvin asked.

"I was just going to say the same thing myself."

"Don't be ridiculous," Judy Lynn protested. "I'll be fine."

"No more arguing," Bronson said. "I was showing Calvin around the area, anyway. You head on home, and we'll follow you till you get to the house."

Bronson was heartened to watch a relieved smile spring to her face. "Very well, fellas. Thanks."

Judy Lynn worked the reins and clucked to her team, and the buckboard rattled off. Bronson and Calvin followed, staying just behind the cloud of dust raised by the wagon wheels.

"George Blake is a fool," muttered Bronson. "I'd never let Maggie travel from town to the ranch alone, especially not if she was pregnant."

Calvin nodded. "These are dangerous parts in which you live, aren't they? Who is this Skeet Gallagher the two of you were discussing?"

"He's the head of a nest of bad hombres, buffalo hunters who often hole up in Rio Concho," Bronson explained. "When Maggie and I were with the tribe, my brothers and I had a run-in with Skeet and his cronies. They had killed many bison on Comanche lands, and we also caught them raping a white woman."

"How despicable. Was the woman—"

"We rescued her, and she chose to remain with the People."

Calvin removed his hat and scratched his head. "But if this Skeet Gallagher is so nefarious, why haven't you notified the authorities?"

Bronson laughed bitterly. "Lefty McBride, sheriff of Rio Concho, is Skeet's number one compadre."

Calvin whistled. "You've got some really dirty dealings going on here, don't you?"

"Something to write home about, my friend," quipped Bronson.

They were now approaching the Blake ranch house, and Calvin flashed Bronson a quizzical smile. "This Judy Lynn . . . Is she the one you told me about, when you first arrived at Harvard?"

"She is."

"She can't hold a candle to Maggie, you know."

"No woman can compare to Maggie," Bronson replied vehemently, as the two men waved to Judy Lynn, then turned their horses back toward the Kane Ranch.

Toward sundown, everyone gathered in the dining room for a supper of chili and beans. Sam Kane was excited, after having returned from Rio Concho with the mail.

"My friend Jim Wilson has invited us all to a barbecue at his ranch outside Waco. He's launching the campaign of Richard Coke for governor."

"How exciting," said Lydia.

"Coke should have good prospects of election next year, with Davis being so universally disliked by Texans," Sam went on. He nodded to Bronson. "Jim mentioned that he hoped to see you at his barbecue, son. Why don't we all make it an excursion?"

Bronson glanced at Maggie. "What do you think?"

"Sounds like fun," she said. She glanced at her aunt. "What about you and Mr. Bryce?"

"I'm game," said Lydia eagerly.

Calvin was frowning. "Actually, I had hoped we'd be starting back for Boston before then, Miss Donovan."

Watching Lydia's happy expression fade to dismay, Bronson spoke up to his friend. "Why don't you cover the event for your paper, Calvin? Davis is one of the few radical Reconstructionists still in power in the South." He glanced at Lydia. "No offense, ma'am."

"None taken," she replied feelingly. "I never did condone Congress's desire to punish the South for the war. If dear

Abe Lincoln hadn't been assassinated, I know things would
have turned out far differently."

"So shall we all go, then?" asked Sam, smiling at Lydia.

"I wouldn't miss it for the world," she replied. "Maggie
and I will start planning what we'll wear this very afternoon, won't we, dear?"

"Yes," she said, feeling warmed that Bronson was joining
them on this outing into civilization.

Sam was frowning. "By the way, Bronson, I ran across
Sheriff Lefty on my way out of the post office."

"Did you?"

"He was with that scoundrel Skeet Gallagher. They said
they were expecting a detachment of cavalry to come here
out of Fort Defiance, and they asked about you."

Bronson's fingers tightened on his coffee mug. "I hope
you told them that if they have any business with me, they
can discuss it with me to my face."

"Of course I did, son."

Maggie glanced anxiously at her husband, and he smiled
back at her, but she could spot the underlying tension in his
expression.

"Well, folks, who would like dessert?" asked Lydia.

"Lydia has made us bread pudding tonight," announced
Sam, patting his stomach.

For the remainder of the meal, they all discussed additional details of the outing to Waco, but Maggie noticed that
the mention of Sheriff Lefty had definitely cast a pall over
the gathering.

At sunset, Maggie and Bronson sat on the front porch
swing together. Beyond them, Lydia and Sam stood at the
corral, watching newly gathered mustangs prance about.
Calvin was upstairs writing a letter to one of his associates
at the newspaper in Boston.

Bronson nodded toward the corral. "I think romance is in
the air."

"You've noticed, too? I think it could be the best thing
that ever happened to my aunt."

"And my uncle. I know Sam never married before due to his devotion to my mother . . . but what about your aunt?"

"She cared for my grandfather until he died a few years back," Maggie explained. "By then she was in her mid-thirties, and an avowed spinster. But I guess the right man can change all that."

He wrapped an arm around her. "Can it, Mrs. Kane?"

She smiled. "It can, indeed."

He leaned over and kissed her.

She gazed out at the pink-gold sunset and sighed. "I really love it here, Bronson. I could live here . . . with you, I hope."

"I do love this country," he admitted.

"And you're comfortable about the outing to Waco?"

He nodded. "You gave my world a chance, Maggie. Now I must do the same with you."

She gestured toward the sweeping horizon. "This is your world, too."

"I know it is. And it wouldn't hurt me to see if I can't become more involved in Texas politics. Uncle Sam has always been very active, and has often hinted that I could use his contacts to help my people."

"Oh, Bronson, that would be wonderful," she put in excitedly. "Then you wouldn't have to return to the tribe."

His gaze darkened as he reached out to caress the curve of her cheek. "You know I can't promise you that, Maggie."

Both fell silent for a moment, watching Sam and Lydia. "Why do you suppose Sheriff Lefty asked Sam about you?" Maggie asked.

Bronson shrugged. "He's probably just out to harass me, as always."

Maggie nodded, but she suspected Bronson was making light of his anxieties, and this increased her own.

The next morning, Bronson and Sam were finishing an early breakfast when they heard a loud rap at the front door. Both men strode into the entry hallway. Sam opened the door to see Sheriff Lefty standing on the porch, along with a cavalry officer. In the yard were a dozen or so blue-uniformed soldiers on horseback.

"Good morning, Sheriff," Sam greeted the man coolly. "What can I do for you?"

Lefty jerked a thumb toward Bronson. "We're looking for the breed there."

While Bronson stared at Lefty in cold silence, Sam retorted, "If you're referring to my nephew, you can damn well address him properly!"

"You mean the boy don't care to own up to his Injun blood?" Lefty sneered.

Even as Sam would have answered, Bronson held up a hand to his uncle. "It's all right, Uncle Sam. I can handle this." He swung his contemptuous gaze to Lefty. "What do you want, McBride?"

Lefty nodded toward the cavalry officer, who was young and blond, with a thick mustache. "Colonel Morgan here is investigating the massacre of one of his patrols by Comanches. You wouldn't happen to know anything about that, would you, breed?"

"No, I wouldn't," Bronson snapped.

The colonel addressed Bronson in an eastern accent. "Sir, the sheriff has told me that you frequently live among the Comanches. Is this true?"

"Yes."

"Just over a week ago, one of our patrols was captured, scalped, and killed by a Comanche war party. Are you saying you know nothing about this?"

Bronson did not flinch. "That is correct."

Morgan shot Bronson a steely look. "Sir, if you are withholding information about the unlawful activities of your tribe, let me assure you that you will be prosecuted for obstruction of justice."

"I've studied the law—you don't have to explain legal terms to me."

"Where were you ten days ago, sir?"

"I was with my Comanche brothers—and as I've already told you, I saw no soldiers harmed."

Morgan glanced at Lefty, who drawled, "I think we should take Kane in for questioning, don't you, Colonel? According to one of my deputies, Skeet Gallagher, this breed's band of Penateka is also responsible for massacring a party of buffalo hunters several weeks ago."

"Is this true, Mr. Kane?" Morgan asked.

Bronson feigned amazement. "Why, Sheriff McBride. You don't mean to say one of your *deputies* and his cronies have been killing bison on Comanche lands?" Shaking his head, he glanced at Morgan. "That would be illegal, wouldn't it, Colonel? Especially if the scoundrels were also raping a white woman."

While Morgan appeared perplexed, Lefty roared, "Hush up, breed, before I shet you up!"

"Mr. Kane, do you know something about the massacre the sheriff is referring to?" Morgan asked with a scowl.

"No, I do not," Bronson answered.

"Let's take the breed in and loosen up his no-good lyin' tongue!" Lefty jeered.

"You men have no cause to take my nephew anywhere!" exclaimed an angry Sam.

The two camps were regarding each other tensely when Maggie endorsed Sam's words from the staircase. "Mr. Kane is right. There will be no need to take my husband in for questioning, Sheriff. For the past several weeks, I have been with Bronson Kane and his Comanche brothers—and I assure you that I, too, saw no cavalrymen harmed."

The group of men turned to watch Maggie descend the stairs. Sheriff Lefty ogled her rudely, then glanced at Bronson. "That your squaw, breed?"

This time Lefty's insult brought much more than its desired effect. His expression livid, Bronson slammed his fist into McBride's jaw and knocked him to the floor.

As Maggie gasped in horror, Colonel Morgan grasped the hilt of his sword, and Lefty clambered up in a flash. He waved a fist at Bronson, his features enraged. "Why, you low-down bastard! You're going to jail for this!"

Lefty was charging toward Bronson when Colonel Morgan stepped between the two men. "That will do, Sheriff."

Lefty glared at the man. "Get out of my way, Morgan! This half-breed assaulted an officer of the law. I'm taking him off to jail . . . after I beat the livin' shit outa him!"

Yet Morgan held his ground, facing McBride with unflinching determination. "Sheriff, you came to this man's home and insulted his wife. Furthermore, you are continuing to use the most foul, reprehensible language in the presence of a lady. Under the circumstances, I cannot blame Mr. Kane for reacting as he did."

"Well, I'll blame him, and a helluva lot more!" retorted Lefty.

"Nor will I sanction your arresting Mr. Kane, under the circumstances," Morgan continued sternly. "At the moment, we have no real cause to hold him. Now, I would suggest that you let me finish interrogating Mr. Kane alone, or do you need some assistance in leaving his porch?"

Glancing at the mounted and armed soldiers waiting in the yard, Lefty spat tobacco juice on the porch, then stalked off belligerently.

Bronson wrapped an arm about his wife's waist. "Thank you, Colonel Morgan."

Morgan glanced coldly at Bronson. "Don't thank me too soon, Mr. Kane. I only reacted as I did to defend the virtue of a lady, as any honorable gentleman would have done under the circumstances." He nodded to Maggie, then turned his attention back to Bronson. "I ask you again, sir, do you have any information regarding the massacre of a cavalry brigade out of Fort Defiance a week ago?"

"I repeat, sir, that I do not," replied Bronson.

Morgan addressed Maggie. "Will you vouch for your husband's word on this, ma'am?"

"I certainly will," answered Maggie forthrightly.

Tipping his hat to Maggie, the officer said, "Very well, Mr. Kane, I'll accept your word for now. But if I discover any reason to believe you've withheld the truth from me, I'll be back. And next time I'll arrest you."

THIRTY-SIX

"You're lucky you're not in jail, you know," said Maggie to Bronson.

"Lefty McBride is lucky he's not dead," he replied.

Soon after the cavalry and sheriff departed, Bronson asked Maggie to go with him for a walk. They paused only for Maggie to eat breakfast, and to explain the situation to Lydia and Calvin, who came downstairs right after the men had left.

Maggie sensed that Bronson had much on his mind following the tense confrontation with Lefty and Colonel Morgan. "Now you're even more anxious about the tribe, aren't you?" she asked.

He kicked a small rock out of their path. "Yes. I warned Black Hawk that something like this was bound to happen, especially after he massacred that detachment of soldiers. The federal authorities may not become too riled over the deaths of a few thieving buffalo hunters, but when it comes to the slaughter of their own cavalrymen, they sit up and take notice."

"And you lied about everything to the colonel," she added.

"So did you," he reminded her. "I wish you had let me handle things, Maggie."

She flung a hand outward in frustration. "What was I supposed to do? Let Lefty McBride haul you off to jail? I'm sorry it was necessary for both of us to be deceptive—but once you told the colonel you knew nothing, of course I had to support you."

"Should I have just turned my back on my people and given them over to slaughter by the cavalry?" he asked.

"No, of course not," she quickly reassured him. "It's just an impossible situation, any way you look at it."

He nodded. "The tribe is in great peril. Morgan will likely be on their trail soon, with Ranald McKenzie to follow shortly, according to Uncle Sam."

"Will you go back to the tribe now?" she asked quietly.

Just beyond the corral, he pulled her to a halt and stared down at her, his features mirroring his torn emotions. "I'm not sure I have a choice, Maggie. How can I not warn them about the threat from the cavalry?"

"What will they do?"

"What they've always done—stay on the run. Only, soon there won't be any hiding places."

She stared at him intently. "If you go . . ."

"I know. You won't come with me."

"But you'll go anyway?" she asked in anguish.

"I think I have to, Maggie."

"You don't *have* to do anything, Bronson."

He regarded her with pained resignation. "That's not true. When a man lives by a certain code, his actions are limited."

"Is that why you punched Sheriff Lefty for calling me a squaw? I had assumed that all along you wanted nothing more than for me to become your squaw."

"I hit him because he saw the term as an insult to you—as I'm sure you did, too."

"I did not," she replied vehemently. "I'll admit that at one time, I considered the term derogatory. But since I have lived among the People, I have found there is much honor and dignity in being a squaw, even in performing the most menial tasks."

"But you won't go back with me."

"I can't," she said quietly.

With irony, he paraphrased her own words. "You can do anything you want, Maggie."

"Not that. I can't condemn myself and possibly our future children to the doomed existence of your people. I have a code, too. And have you thought of what might happen to me if I lost you in the coming conflict, of how vulnerable that would leave me?"

He regarded her with grave concern, then pulled her close. "You're right. You mustn't go."

"When will you leave?" she asked.

"I'm not sure. Soon." He touched her cheek. "Will you be here when I return?"

Even as she struggled to face him bravely, her lower lip trembled. "Will you return, Bronson?"

His eyes gleamed with pain and regret. "Of course I will. If you'll stay."

Could she stay? Maggie wondered. Could she bear to remain here long enough to find out whether he would come back to her? Could she linger not knowing whether he would ultimately choose her or the tribe? And what if he was killed due to the choices he was making? How would she bear it?

"Maggie?" he prodded. "Will you wait for me?"

At last pride answered where her heart couldn't. She raised her chin and met his gaze. "Sheriff Lefty may be back again, causing more trouble. I—I'll stick around at least until the danger dies down."

Hurt seared Bronson at his wife's words. She was saying she would stay only to protect him against the law? Wasn't there much more between them than that? At once, the proud Comanche brave inside him rose up in defiance at this assault on his manhood.

"I don't need a woman to protect me," he told her harshly. "You can leave any damn time you want."

He turned and strode off for the house.

* * *

Later that day, the decision about leaving was taken out of Bronson's hands. He was out riding the prairie, trying to sort out his mixed feelings regarding Maggie, their marriage, and the new threat to the tribe, when he heard a familiar bird call coming from a nearby stand of cypress tress. He recognized the whippoorwill song as a signal from one of his Comanche brothers.

"Bobcat?" he called. "Are you there?"

Bobcat rode his pinto pony out from behind the shelter of the trees. He appeared trail-worn and tired, his hair and clothing coated with dust. "I have been waiting for you all day, my brother," he greeted White Wolf anxiously. "I feared I would have to ride up to your White Eyes house."

"What are you doing here?" Bronson asked.

"Your father is calling for you," the brave replied. "He grows weak and will soon succumb to the death throes. His breathing grows labored and his lungs bleed. Spirit Talker has been unable to revive him."

Bronson's heart sank at this news, so long expected but still painful to hear. "I will ride with you at once for Comanche territory. But first you must wait for me here, while I go tell my wife good-bye."

The young man scowled. "She will not come with you? Pale Eyes and Creek Flower have both spoken of how much they miss Prairie Star."

"I will miss her too," Bronson replied heavily, "but she will not come with me this time."

Bobcat nodded. "Then, go, my brother. Hurry. I will wait here."

Moments later, Bronson walked into the parlor of the ranch house to see Maggie, Lydia, Sam, and Calvin all gathered there.

"Hello, son," Lydia called out. "Come join us. We were all just visiting before dinner."

"Thanks," Bronson said with a tight smile, "but I need to speak with my wife."

Maggie glanced at Bronson's drawn face, then murmured, "Excuse me."

They moved out onto the porch. He smiled at her sadly and took her hand. "Maggie, I've got to leave—now."

"To warn the tribe?"

"Not just that," he replied. "I just ran across Bobcat out on the range. He's waiting for me now." His voice shook. "Maggie, my father is dying."

She thrust herself into his arms. "Oh, Bronson. I'm so sorry."

"I must go to him," he whispered.

"Of course you must. But when he dies . . ."

"I know. Either Black Hawk or I must lead the tribe."

She pulled back, gazed at him with intense longing, and struggled not to cry. "And what if you are chosen?"

His expression was equally tortured. "Maggie, can I just turn my back on my people, and let Black Hawk lead them to ruin?"

She was silent, blinking at tears.

"Will you wait for me? I mean, after my father is laid to rest, I'll come back and let you know what I've decided—"

"If you aren't killed!"

He caught her in his arms. "I won't be killed, honey. Just tell me you'll wait for me. I need to hear that now."

"I know you do." She stared up at him with brimming eyes. "I'll wait for you. At least until you decide. After that . . ."

He smiled down at her, brushing a tear from her cheek. "I know. Just be here this time. All right?"

She nodded bravely.

He glanced toward the house. "Will you explain things to the others? I really don't have time to do more than—"

"Change into your Indian buckskins?"

"Yes."

"I'll explain to the others," she said, sniffing. "Now hurry. Your father needs you."

"Not yet." He caught her hand.

She made a sound of desperation. "Bronson, please, I don't think I can bear—"

"Not yet."

He hauled her close for a deep, tender kiss. Only the sound of her broken sobs stopped him. He watched in torment as she fled for the house. Then he, too, headed inside to do what he must . . .

After three days of hard riding, White Wolf and Bobcat found the Comanche camp. They were greeted by Black Hawk on the outskirts of the village. The brave and several other warriors galloped up on their prancing war ponies. The braves' faces were painted black; they wore buffalo helmets, and carried the lances, bows, and rifles of a war party. White Wolf mused that they must be heading out for another raid.

"So you are back, my brother," Black Hawk sneered.

"How fares our father?"

"He lingers still, and calls for you."

"While I was in the white world, I was confronted by a cavalry officer named Morgan. He is hunting you and your war party for massacring the detachment of cavalry."

Black Hawk laughed with bravado. "Let the bluecoats come—we will cut out their tongues and stake them all out on ant beds on the prairie."

As several of Black Hawk's company cheered or howled war cries, White Wolf replied, "You cannot defeat them all. More will come—including the feared McKenzie with his buffalo soldiers."

"He will never find us," scoffed Black Hawk. "We will evade him as skillfully as has our brother Quanah in the Llano Estacado."

"Don't say I haven't warned you," said Bronson. "Now I will go see my father."

"And persuade him to choose you to lead our tribe?" Black Hawk scoffed.

"Perhaps I can keep our people alive."

Black Hawk waved his lance. "You are wrong. Yours is

the road of weakness and capitulation. The White Eyes only understand violence and death."

"And that is where you are bound now—to kill the *tahbay-boh?*" asked White Wolf.

"We will join our brother Stone Arrow and his company," Black Hawk announced proudly. "All of us have had our fill of the White Eyes. Together we will kill the hide hunters who have again been spotted on our lands."

"While our father is dying?"

Black Hawk's expression hardened. "Let the women comfort him . . . and his son who has lost the soul of a warrior."

At Black Hawk's whistle, he and the other warriors whooped their war cries, spurred their ponies, and galloped away. White Wolf's mood was grim as he and Bobcat rode into the camp. He proceeded at once to his father's tepee. Inside, he found his father lying near the fire, dozing on a bed of hides. The sight of the dying man jarred him deeply. Buffalo Thunder appeared a mere ghost of his former self, his frame emaciated, his features waxen, his breathing raspy. Fair Moon was wiping his fevered brow, her face lined and anguished. Stepping closer, White Wolf smiled at the old woman. She nodded back and slipped out of the tepee.

Bronson knelt by Buffalo Thunder. "Father, I am here."

Buffalo Thunder opened his eyes and smiled wanly up at his son. "White Wolf . . . I have prayed to the Great Spirit to allow me to see you one last time." He tried to say more, but fell into a fit of coughing.

The hacking sound, and the blood his father was coughing up, alarmed White Wolf. He took the rag Fair Moon had left and wiped his father's face and chin.

"I'm sorry you're so ill," he said gently. "I wish there were something I could do."

"There is nothing, my son," the old man said hoarsely. "I have completed my journey in this world. I am bound to the Happy Hunting Ground, where the fields are green and full of bison, where no White Eyes will come to track us and steal away the life we love."

"May the Great Spirit guide your passage," whispered White Wolf fervently.

The old man touched his son's arm. "But your journey, my son, is only beginning. Where is your bride?"

White Wolf sighed. "With the White Eyes. She will not live with me here."

"And you will not force her to return?"

"No. I will not live with her here, unless she comes to me of her own free will."

The old man nodded. "Perhaps it is for the best. I always dreamed I could change your mother's heart, but I could not."

"Maybe the two of you will meet again."

"So I will hope," said the old man wistfully. "As you know, I always felt the greatest warmth for your mother— but her destiny was never with the Nerm. I tried to force our way of life on her, and the result was tragedy for her."

"I know." White Wolf thought of the parallel to Maggie, and felt deeply saddened.

"Look at me, my son," Buffalo Thunder whispered.

White Wolf glanced into his father's face, and found that, even as Buffalo Thunder lay dying, his dark eyes radiated great fire and spirit. "Yes, my father?"

"You must help your people, my son," Buffalo Thunder announced ominously. "I have seen a vision . . . The bison will turn to bones on the plains, slaughtered by the hunters. The People will starve. The buffalo soldiers will come, and keep coming until all of the Comanche are forced behind fences on the reservations, their spirits crushed forever."

White Wolf nodded soberly, fearing his father's prophecy would soon prove true. "What must I do?"

"It must fall on you to decide whether you will help our people as their next chief, or in the white world."

White Wolf was astonished. "You will not choose the new chief for our tribe?"

Buffalo Thunder shook his head. "You must decide the

right path for our people . . . whether the eagle will lead, or the hawk."

"Does Black Hawk know this?" White Wolf asked.

"I have made my wishes known to your brother, and to Spirit Talker, who will perform the ceremony to honor the new chief."

White Wolf nodded grimly. No wonder Black Hawk had been so hostile, knowing his father had given over the selection of the new chief to him.

Buffalo Thunder began to cough again, interrupting White Wolf's musings. He fetched his father a cup of water and helped him sit up and take a few sips.

"Rest now, my father," he said, gently lowering Buffalo Thunder's frail shoulders back to the pallet.

Exhausted by his efforts, Buffalo Thunder drifted back to sleep. White Wolf sat with his father, his heart heavily burdened.

THIRTY-SEVEN

Maggie became convinced she was pregnant during the excursion to Waco.

At first she didn't want to leave the Kane Ranch with Sam, Lydia, and Calvin; she clung to the hope that Bronson would soon reappear to tell her he had chosen the white world permanently. Yet Lydia insisted that Maggie had to go, arguing that it would be improper for her to venture forth alone with two men. And besides, her aunt argued, Maggie would go insane waiting at the ranch, for who knew when Bronson might return?

Finally Maggie gave in and agreed to the outing. Taking along four ranch hands as guards, the four left in Sam's covered buckboard and proceeded west over the frontier until they connected with the well-traveled Chisolm Trail.

For Maggie, traveling on the trail was quite an education in itself, as they passed everything from peddlers in their bandwagons, to cattle drives, to settlers in their prairie schooners. The group spent their first night at the Shady Villa Hotel in Salado, then pressed on to Waco the following day, entering the city via the spectacular new suspension bridge, which Sam proudly explained was the longest in the world. They checked into an elegant downtown hotel, and Lydia and Maggie spent the balance of the day shopping, since they had been unable to find suitable dresses for the barbecue in Rio Concho.

The next morning, leaving the cowhands to enjoy a day off in town, the foursome left for the Wilson Ranch just south of Waco. Lydia and Maggie wore the new Texas-style calico dresses and bonnets they had just purchased, and Calvin and Sam were both attired in dark suits, hats, and black string cravats.

Maggie was impressed by the Wilson spread, with its vast ranges, its sprawling three-story Victorian ranch house, its neat corrals and outbuildings. Close to the house, she spotted two drovers turning a huge side of beef over an open pit. The tantalizing smell of barbecue was heavy in the air.

Since Jim Wilson had asked Sam to come early to discuss the annual joint cattle drive the men did each fall, Maggie and the others were among the first to arrive. Sam's knock at the front door was answered by a huge bear of a man sporting a red checked shirt and dark pants, and wearing a friendly smile.

"Sam Kane, if you ain't a sight for sore eyes," the man greeted, pumping Sam's hand. "And who are these fine-looking folks?"

Sam grinned. "Jim, I'd like you to meet your very special guests from Boston. This is Bronson's bride, Maggie, her aunt, Lydia Donovan, and Bronson's good friend Calvin Bryce, a newspaperman. Folks, meet my good friend Jim Wilson."

All three shook hands and exchanged greetings with Jim.

"Well, a Texas-sized howdy to you all," Jim drawled. He frowned at Sam. "Where's Bronson? I was hoping he would be here to discuss the fall drive with us."

"I'm afraid the boy's father took sick, Jim."

"Sorry to hear that."

"But he'll come along with us on the drive in the fall—you can count on it."

"Great," replied Jim jovially. "Heck, folks, where are my

manners?" he added, motioning them inside. "Y'all come on in and have some coffee. The other guests should be arriving before noon."

Jim ushered them back to the huge kitchen, which Maggie found to be a noisy, bustling hub of activity where the rest of the Wilson family sat eating their breakfast. Jim introduced the newcomers to his wife, Theta Jean, and his six children, who ranged in age from fifteen months to nine years.

"Won't you folks join us?" Theta Jean asked as she fed the baby oatmeal.

"Oh, no, don't trouble yourself," answered Lydia. "We already stuffed ourselves back at the hotel. Now, let me know what Maggie and I can do to help."

"Ladies, I'm going to steal Sam and Calvin and leave you to your duties," announced Jim. To Calvin he added, "Would you like to see my spread, Mr. Bryce?"

"I was counting on it," Calvin replied eagerly. "And some reminiscences of your past cattle drives would sure please my Boston readers."

"Son, you've come to the right place," Jim said, and the three men trooped out.

Maggie found the rest of the morning to be fun and lively. She and Lydia helped Theta Jean, her older daughters, and several servant women finish preparing the mountains of potato salad, coleslaw, beans, bread, and tea that would be served with the midday meal. Maggie spent much of the time holding the baby, Gladys Marie, so that her mother could attend to other duties. The fifteen-month-old child was adorable with her curly dark hair, rounded face, and plump little body. Maggie fed the child a couple of nursing bottles of milk and played with her. Watching the baby smile, hearing her gurgle and coo, Maggie could no longer ignore her own symptoms of past weeks—the occasional queasiness and the fact that she had skipped her last monthly, something she never did.

The reality that she was pregnant filled her with a strange combination of panic and wonder. Of course, she gloried in the fact that she and Bronson were to have a child; but she feared his response when he learned about the baby. What if he insisted she and the child live with him back at the tribe? How could she subject her child to the tribulations of life among a roving Comanche band?

She couldn't, of course, which meant she must proceed with caution as far as telling her husband was concerned. She recalled his telling her that if Judy Lynn had gotten pregnant from the night the two of them had spent together, he would have forced her to marry him. He had certainly made clear that he would never allow a woman to steal his child, and this made Maggie feel tempted to withhold her news. And yet, was it fair not to tell him she carried his baby?

Maggie was subdued for the balance of the day, even amid the revelry of the arriving guests. She met a number of prominent Texans, including Richard Coke, the Republican candidate for governor. Coke was a kindly, balding man with a long gray beard; he greeted Maggie most warmly out in the yard.

"Well, Mrs. Kane, Mr. Samuel Kane was telling me about your husband," Coke said to her. "Once I'm elected, I'd really like to meet Bronson and hear his views on the Indian situation here in Texas."

Pleasantly surprised by the request, Maggie smiled back. "I'll be sure to pass on your invitation to Bronson, sir. I know he'll be thrilled to hear of your interest. And best of luck with your campaign."

Coke gestured expansively at the dozens of couples and families gathered near the house. "With all this support, how can I fail?"

During the afternoon, Maggie met several other people who inquired about Bronson, and for the most part, she detected only warm feelings toward her husband, not dislike or even pity. And, despite her own warning from Delilah Dinker, she noted no attitude of ostracism toward herself for being Bronson's bride.

Of course, it was doubtful any of these people even knew

that she'd spent time living with her husband among the Comanche. Still, she realized that she and Bronson could have a good life among these people, if only he would give decent Texans a chance. He even had an invitation to give the future governor of Texas his opinions on the Indian situation!

While her husband seemed respected by his fellow Texans, Maggie soon surmised that the attitude of the citizens toward the Comanches was far less charitable. As she returned to the house to refill a pitcher of tea, she overheard a group of men chatting on the porch about the Indian situation.

One elderly rancher said, "I'm all for the cavalry exterminatin' them murderin' red varmints. I hear tell the Comanches slaughtered almost two dozen mule skinners in Crockett County last month."

Another answered, "The sooner them thievin' heathens are shoveled six feet under, the better."

"Hell, burying's too good for 'um," added a third. "We should just scalp 'um all and leave 'um on the prairies for the buzzards to eat."

Maggie shuddered as she heard several other men endorse the gruesome suggestion.

Later, another unpleasant moment ensued for Maggie when a middle-aged matron confronted her at one of the buffet tables outside.

"You Bronson Kane's wife?" she asked.

"Yes," Maggie answered, smiling at the plump woman, who wore a green gingham dress and matching slat bonnet.

"Where is he—off raiding with the Comanches?"

Maggie blanched. "My husband is with his dying father."

"I'm going to give you some advice, honey," the woman said sternly. "Texans are a generous lot. They accept Bronson Kane because his uncle is so well liked and respected. Besides, it ain't the boy's fault his ma was took off and Comanche blood runs in his veins. But if he up and turns Injun on us, he'll find the patience of his fellow Texans wearing thin."

Maggie felt her pride bristling. "Not all Indians are savage animals. My husband is one of the kindest, gentlest men I've ever known. And I'm proud of his Indian blood."

The woman shook a finger at her. "You listen to me, honey. It was that same Indian blood that took my husband. He was one of the teamsters slaughtered by the Comanches and Kiowas at Salt Creek Prairie last year."

"I—I'm sorry," Maggie replied. "My husband and his people had no part in that massacre."

"Every Injun had a part in it!" the woman retorted. "They're all scalpers and thieves! And you tell Bronson Kane he'd best decide where his loyalty lies, and not to push the rest of us too far."

The woman shoved past Maggie, leaving her feeling very unsettled.

Toward sunset, the "hoedown" began, and the Texans gathered on a wooden platform outside the barn to square-dance to "Camptown Races," "The Arkansas Traveler," and other favorites beneath the lights of Chinese lanterns. Maggie sat on the porch rocking little Gladys Marie, listening to the music of the fiddlers, the laughing, stomping, and cheering of the crowd. She had to smile as she observed Aunt Lydia dancing with Sam, the two laughing and obviously having a grand time together. Even Calvin had found himself a pretty partner, the daughter of one of Jim Wilson's neighbors. Maggie wished she could participate in the gaiety. But right now, she could only miss Bronson and ache with the wondrous knowledge she could not share with him.

During a lull, Aunt Lydia came over to the porch. Breathless and flushed, she sat down heavily in the rocker next to Maggie's, and fanned her face with a plump hand.

"Young lady, let me hold that baby for a while, and go join in on the fun. I realize Bronson isn't here, but you're not a widow yet."

Maggie smiled. "I just don't feel very frolicsome, Aunt Lydia."

"And why not?"

Maggie avoided the question. "You and Sam appear to be having a fine time."

Lydia beamed. "Can you keep a secret?"

"Of course."

"Sam has asked me to marry him."

Maggie felt overjoyed. "Oh, Aunt Lydia! I'm so happy for you! I do hope you said yes?"

"I did, indeed." Lydia glanced about them. "No doubt, Prudence will miss me, but I love this raw, new land. Don't you, dear?"

"Yes." Wistfully Maggie gazed out at the glorious pink and gold horizon. She did love this land, and despite all, she still hoped there could be a future for her and Bronson here.

Lydia touched her arm. "You look troubled. What's on your mind, honey?"

"You know me so well," Maggie replied ruefully. "Can *you* keep a secret?"

"Come on, Maggie, you know I always do." Lydia solemnly crossed herself.

"I'm pregnant."

Lydia's face lit with delight. "Oh, honey! I'm so thrilled for you."

Maggie stroked the sleeping baby's pink cheek and smiled. "Thanks, Aunt Lydia."

"Have you told Bronson you're in a family way?"

Maggie's features revealed her conflicted feelings. "Not yet. What if I tell him, and he insists that the child and I live with him among the tribe?"

"Oh, Maggie," Lydia muttered with intense sympathy. "I wish I had a simple answer for you there. Maybe when he returns, he'll tell you he's ready to stay in the white world permanently."

Maggie sighed heavily. "Maybe. But with the conflicts facing his people, I'm not sure he can. He may have to become chief following his father's death. I did promise Bronson I'll remain until he returns to let me know what he's decided—and I'll keep my word. After that . . . I just don't know what I'll do."

"But regardless of what he decides, you and the child can still make a good life for yourselves at the ranch with Sam and me," Lydia argued. "Furthermore, I can't believe Bronson would force either of you to go on the run with him and his tribe—not in the current hostile climate."

Maggie frowned, for Lydia had raised some valid points.

Lydia regarded her niece with keen compassion. "It's tearing you up inside, isn't it, honey?"

Maggie nodded as tears welled. "Yes. The baby, Bronson's dilemma, not knowing what is right, my fears that I may never see him again ... Sometimes it's almost more than I can bear."

Lydia squeezed Maggie's hand. "Well, you don't have to bear it alone, dear. You've got me and Sam—and if I'm any judge of character, you haven't seen the last of Bronson Kane, either."

Wails of grief filled the air of the Comanche camp. After lingering in the death throes for several days, Buffalo Thunder had passed away only moments earlier. Inside the dead chief's tepee, his two squaws, Fair Moon and Shy Dove, were washing and preparing his body for burial tomorrow.

White Wolf stood at the center of the village. Around him, squaws were wailing and slashing themselves, warriors were cutting their hair to symbolize their own mourning. White Wolf had already trimmed a lock of his own hair to mark Buffalo Thunder's passage.

Black Hawk now stormed up to him, tossing his own shorn hair at White Wolf's feet. "Our father is gone. Who will be chief?" he asked belligerently.

"I do not know yet," White Wolf replied patiently. "I will meditate on it tonight."

Black Hawk held up a fist. "Know this, my brother. If you choose yourself as chief, half our warriors will depart with me to form a new band. We will not be led by a brave with the heart of a woman."

White Wolf groaned; according to Comanche tradition, if warring factions developed within a tribe, the tribe split company. He had been half expecting this ultimatum from his half brother.

"Please, do not act hastily, Black Hawk," he implored.

"My mind is made up. The fate of the tribe is in your hands, brother."

With a heavy heart, White Wolf watched Black Hawk stalk off. He stared up at the dark heavens. "Oh, my father," he whispered. "Why did you leave it to me to make this choice? If I decide in error, the result will be a catastrophe for our people."

He hated to even consider what his decision might mean to him and Prairie Star. Now, with his father gone, he could count only on the Great Spirit to guide him.

Later, when all was quiet, White Wolf sat alone on a rise, next to a fire he had built. Eyes closed, he chanted softly and meditated in the darkness. Deep into the night, the visions came—first, of his father crossing over into the Happy Hunting Ground, his spirit young, wild, and free again at last. Tears filled White Wolf's eyes at the beauty of it.

Next, he saw the white wolf howling at the prairie star, the wolf forlornly chasing the star until it faded with the dawn. Anguish seared him and a terrible longing gripped his heart. Finally, with the blood red sunrise came the black hawk, talons bared, screeching for vengeance and ready to drive the white wolf from the land. At last, with the rising sun, the black hawk and the white wolf had their reckoning . . .

THIRTY-EIGHT

As soon as Maggie, Lydia, Calvin, and Sam arrived back at the Kane Ranch, Calvin prepared to leave for the East. On the sunny morning he was to depart, Sam was out riding the range with the drovers, and Lydia was at a quilting bee at a neighboring ranch. Although Maggie had been invited to accompany her aunt, she decided she wanted to go with Calvin to Rio Concho to have a look at the town, to find a last-minute present for Aunt Pru, and to see him off.

As a cowhand drove them away from the ranch in the buckboard, Calvin flashed Maggie a smile. "I'm really glad you've decided to stay around."

"I'm staying for now," she replied. "Once Bronson returns . . . I guess he and I will have to figure things out from there."

Calvin nodded soberly. "I'm praying the two of you will make it. I realize this hasn't been easy for you—finding out about Bronson's heritage, not to mention having him called away last week to his father's deathbed. I feel so responsible. Perhaps Bronson was right—I should have told you the truth from the outset."

Maggie offered him a look of encouragement. "I'm really glad you didn't. I don't regret having met Bronson." *Or having loved him,* she added to herself.

"Please don't give up hope, Maggie," Calvin added.

"Oh, I haven't," she assured him. "Right now I just want to see Bronson come home safely."

The two fell silent. Before long, they approached the outskirts of Rio Concho. Maggie was not particularly impressed by the small burg with its dusty main street flanked by a double line of weather-beaten frame storefronts, including several grog shops. The shabbiness was relieved only by two frame churches, a post office, a couple of presentable-looking shops, and a modest hotel with pots of geraniums on the windowsills.

The ranch hand stopped the buckboard in front of the general store, where a couple of old-timers sat on a bench beneath the eaves, ruminating over their newspapers. Calvin helped Maggie down and the wrangler unloaded Calvin's trunk and placed it on the boardwalk.

While the drover waited in the buckboard for Maggie, Calvin drew out his pocket watch. "The noon stage should be along in a few minutes. Why don't you go inside the store and look for your aunt's gift?"

Maggie was turning to do so when a friendly feminine voice called out, "Well, hello, folks."

Maggie and Calvin watched a pregnant woman emerge from the shop with a broom. Pretty, with her chestnut brown hair in a bun at the back of her head, she wore a gown of sprigged yellow calico covered by a large white apron.

The woman was smiling at Calvin. "Good to see you again, Mr. Bryce."

Calvin removed his beaver hat and bowed. "Mrs. Blake, what a pleasure to see you. Have you met Mrs. Maggie Kane, Bronson's wife?" He turned to her. "Maggie, this is a friend of Bronson's, Mrs. Judy Lynn Blake."

Maggie went pale at the realization that she was staring at her husband's former lover! For a moment, speech failed her.

But Judy Lynn was already warmly extending her hand. "I'm happy to meet you, Mrs. Kane. Welcome to Rio Concho."

"Thank you," Maggie murmured, recovering her composure and shaking the other woman's hand. "I'm pleased to meet you, as well."

Judy Lynn scowled. "You folks waiting for the noon stage? It's about as predictable as my aunt Minerva's laying hens. You're welcome to come inside out of the heat."

"Why don't we, Maggie?" Calvin asked.

She forced a smile. "That sounds nice, and I do need to look for a present for my aunt."

As Judy Lynn preceded them inside the homey, dark store, Maggie tugged Calvin aside just inside the doorway. "When did you meet that woman?" she asked in a tense whisper.

"Bronson and I encountered her one day when we were out riding the range," he explained. "The Blake ranch borders the Kane spread."

"Oh, I see," Maggie muttered.

From across the store at the counter, Judy called, "Come on in, folks. Don't be shy. I've got fresh coffee in the back if you'd like some."

Maggie and Calvin moved toward the counter, and she gazed around at the collection of supplies stacked everywhere—ranging from yard goods and ready-made garments, to bags of flour and sacks of grain, to hardware and riding tack. The smells of tobacco, coffee, leather, and new fabrics mingled with a slight odor of must.

"So where are you folks bound, if I'm not being too curious?" Judy Lynn asked.

Maggie and Calvin exchanged an awkward glance, then he explained, "I'm returning to Boston, Mrs. Blake. Mrs. Kane merely came into town to see me off and do some shopping."

Judy Lynn appeared perplexed, staring at Maggie. "Bronson didn't come with you?" When her question was met by cool silence, she quickly amended, "Hey, don't mind me, I'm being far too nosy, as usual. Won't you folks have something to drink? If it's too hot for coffee, I've some fine apple cider."

Calvin edged back toward the door and gazed into the distance with a hand shading his eyes. "Thanks, Mrs. Blake, but I'm afraid there won't be time, since I see the stage coming." He glanced at Maggie. "Maggie, if you want to buy a present, you'd best hurry."

She nodded. "Thanks, Calvin."

As he stepped outside, Maggie went to the counter and quickly examined some ladies' gifts laid out there—silver-plated hairbrushes, porcelain cachepots, hand-painted hair jars, and crystal bottles of perfume. Studying a collection of silk fans, she smiled at Judy Lynn, who was straightening bolts of fabric.

"When are you expecting your baby?" she asked.

The woman beamed. "Three more months. George and I can't wait."

"I'm so happy for you." Maggie held up a lovely silk fan with pearl sticks which was fashioned in the image of a brilliant turquoise peacock spreading its feathers. "And I think I'd like to buy this for my aunt."

"Sure." As Maggie dug for a coin in her reticule, Judy Lynn regarded her quizzically. "Look, please tell me if it's none of my business, but you went pretty pale when I mentioned Bronson. I hope he's all right."

Maggie glanced up into Judy Lynn's compassionate face and at once recognized the other woman's sincerity. "Bronson is with his dying father."

Judy Lynn's features sagged. "Good heavens, Mrs. Kane. Where does that leave Bronson, once he loses Buffalo Thunder?"

"I'm not sure," Maggie admitted honestly. "He may feel duty-bound to become the next chief of his people."

"Oh, honey. Bless your heart."

Without rancor, Maggie asked, "You know a little about the conflicts facing my husband, don't you, Mrs. Blake?"

Judy Lynn nodded soberly. "Is the situation with Bronson's tribe causing trouble between the two of you?"

Maggie lifted her chin. "I'm very hopeful my husband and I will overcome any difficulties we may face."

Judy Lynn glanced toward the door, as if to ensure that they would not be overheard. Then she leaned toward Maggie and spoke confidentially. "Like I said, Mrs. Kane, Bronson is my friend, and because of that friendship, I'm going to tell you something I've never shared with anyone else. Ten years ago, I listened to my daddy and walked away from that man, and I've regretted it to this very day."

Maggie stared at the woman, electrified. She felt as if Judy Lynn had read her mind, and the matron's revelations had also caused Maggie's own thoughts to congeal. Proudly she stated, "I'm not going to walk away from Bronson, Mrs. Blake."

Judy Lynn broke into a smile. "I'm relieved to hear it."

"And I really appreciate what you just shared."

"You're very welcome."

"Maggie! The stage is ready to leave."

The sound of Calvin's voice caused Maggie to jerk about to see him hovering in the doorway. "I'll be right there, Calvin."

He nodded and ducked back outside.

Maggie turned to give Judy Lynn a gold piece. "Guess I'd best hurry. Thanks again."

Judy Lynn smiled as she handed Maggie her change. "You just take good care of Bronson, and give him my best."

"I will."

Proceeding quickly outside, Maggie joined Calvin, who was waiting anxiously by the stagecoach. Smiling, she handed him the fan. "Please give this to Aunt Pru with my love. And don't worry about Bronson and me. I think we're going to be just fine."

"Do you really mean it?"

"You just take care. Don't worry, we'll write. And thanks again for bringing the two of us together."

He broke into a delighted grin. "I know a match made in heaven when I see one."

"Then why don't you go find one for yourself?" she teased.

Calvin laughed, quickly kissed her cheek, and was gone. After watching the stage disappear in a cloud of dust, Maggie happily strolled back to the buckboard.

On the way back to the ranch, Maggie found herself looking again at the Kane Ranch—the sweeping ranges dotted with cattle, the picturesque ponds surrounded by clumps of cedar and chaparral. She remembered Aunt Lydia's argument in Waco—that she could make a good life here for herself and her child, whatever choice Bronson might make.

The notion was making more and more sense to her. After all, this land was her child's white birthright. The atmosphere of the town was far from ideal, but there were good people around, such as Sam Kane and Judy Lynn Blake; perhaps, in time, changes could be effected for the better. In any event, here she could build a solid future for her child—with Bronson if he remained, near him if he chose to remain with the Comanche, and even without him, if he died in the coming conflict.

The thought of losing him brought sudden tears. Maggie realized that knowing and loving him had changed her profoundly, that she would never, ever be the same again. For this, she was deeply grateful. She wanted to be near him always—no matter what.

She also felt thankful to Judy Lynn Blake, for she knew now that she could *never* walk away from Bronson—for she *would* regret it for the rest of her life.

When Maggie arrived back at the ranch and entered the house, she was stunned when she all but collided with her husband just inside the front door.

"Bronson!" she cried.

"Maggie!" he exclaimed.

For a moment, they stared at each other. At first, Maggie blinked, not sure she could believe her own eyes. But yes, it was Bronson, dressed in denim trousers and a green and white checked shirt. Never had she seen a more blessed sight. And he was gazing back at her as if he expected her to disappear at any moment.

"What are you doing here?" she whispered.

"Looking for you," he replied, and hauled her close.

"Oh, I'm so glad to see you!" she cried, clutching him tightly, absorbing the comforting smells of him—leather, shaving soap, and man.

"Me, too." He leaned over and kissed her hungrily. "I just got back to the ranch and found everyone gone. Then I heard the buckboard driving up, and I prayed it was you. I'm so glad you're still here."

"I promised I'd wait for you, didn't I?"

"Of course you did." He clutched her to him, his arms trembling with emotion. "Let's go to the parlor and talk."

Inside the parlor, they fell into each other's arms again, kissing even more ardently. Bronson tugged off Maggie's bonnet and kissed her cheeks, her chin, her neck.

"Oh, Maggie, I've missed you so much," he said hoarsely.

"Me, too. And I have so much to tell you."

"Me, too."

He led her over to the settee, and they sat down together. She glanced at him anxiously. "Your father?"

Deep sadness shone in his eyes. "He's gone, Maggie."

She tightly hugged him. "I'm so sorry."

He sighed deeply and stroked her back. "His suffering is over now. I'm glad of that." Pulling away slightly, he regarded her tenderly. "Let me tell you what I've decided."

"No, let me tell you."

He raised an eyebrow quizzically.

"I'm going to remain permanently at the ranch."

"You are?" he asked, delighted.

"I'll live here and be here whenever you need me," she continued fervently. "Even if you must live with the tribe. I love you so much that I don't care."

"Oh, Maggie." He embraced her again, and his voice shook as he whispered, "I love you, too, darling."

"I just want us to be together as much as possible—all three of us."

He jerked away, eyeing her in astonishment and awe. "Three?"

She nodded back through tears of joy. "I'm going to have your baby."

"Oh, darling."

Maggie thrust herself eagerly into her husband's embrace. They kissed and shared their bliss for many long moments.

He pressed his lips to her cheek. "I'm so thrilled we're going to have a baby."

"Me, too."

"Are you ... feeling all right?"

"Never better."

"Thank God. Now let me tell you what I've decided."

She twisted about to gaze up at him intently. "Yes?"

His expression was utterly solemn. "We don't have to live apart, darling—not you, me, or the baby."

"But—"

He pressed his fingers to her mouth. "Hear me out. When my father lay dying, he placed the future of the tribe in my hands. He told me I must choose who was to lead—me or Black Hawk. This became the true defining moment for me. After my father's death, I meditated ... And at last I saw the truth."

"Yes?" she asked tensely.

Both the joy and the pain of his realization were reflected in his eyes, his wise smile. "Maggie, I've been trying to make the Comanche over into something they are not. My people were always meant to be warriors and rovers. I think the red man in me always recognized this, but the white man in me always wanted to change the basic nature of my brothers. It wasn't until I had my vision that I at last saw the truth clearly. In fact, I think my father may have sent me his wisdom from beyond the grave."

"Oh, Bronson! Please, tell me!"

"In my vision, I saw myself as the white wolf, confronting the black hawk, pitting my medicine against his. Only, my medicine was doomed, because I was trying to turn the hawk into a dove. The more I tried to civilize the hawk, the more ferocious it became."

She frowned. "I'm not sure I understand."

"I know now that my brother Black Hawk is the true Comanche, the true warrior, not me. My People may be doomed, but they must follow their destiny to roam and hunt. I cannot impose another fate on them. Instead, I must do my best to help them among the *tahbay-boh.*"

Her face lit up with joy. "Oh, Bronson—I'm so glad you feel that way. Not that I don't love your people, but for our children's sake—"

"Believe me, Maggie, I understand," he cut in gently. "Because I also did the same thing with you."

"What do you mean?"

"Didn't I try to turn you into something you were not?"

She smiled wistfully. "Perhaps in a way you did. But you also taught me so much, and I'll never regret the insights I gained from your people."

He squeezed her hand. "Then we can both use our knowledge to promote the People's cause in the white world."

"We will. But . . . are you sure you're happy with your decision?"

"Totally," he assured her. "I feel as if I have at last reconciled my Indian and white natures." He stroked her cheek and stared at her lovingly. "And it's you who has brought me that wondrous harmony, darling, who has made me a whole man at last."

"You've given me far more," she replied in a choked voice. "You've helped me to find peace of mind and overcome my own prejudice. For that I must always thank you and your people."

He nodded. "We'll still see the tribe from time to time. I want our children to understand their heritage."

"Oh, of course," she concurred.

"But I want us to live together and raise our family on the ranch."

"You're absolutely certain?"

"Yes."

"But what will the tribe do now—without your leadership?"

A resigned frown tugged at his lips. "I'm not sure. Black Hawk may well go on the warpath, despite my arguments to him that he needs to move the People further south, away from the cavalry. He may even attack the town, as he has longed to do for years, since he blames the citizens for shielding the buffalo hunters."

"Oh, how terrible."

He nodded. "But let's not worry about that now. I've got something else on my mind."

"Yes?"

He nudged her to her feet, took her hand, and led her out of the room toward the stairs. By the newel post, he paused to look at her, his eyes burning with his desire for her. "Is it all right to make love to you now, Mrs. Kane?"

"All right?" she asked with a laugh, throwing her arms around his neck. "I'd be very insulted if you didn't, Mr. Kane."

Bronson scooped Maggie up into his arms, carefully carrying her up the stairs and into his room. He lowered her onto the soft featherbed and lovingly undressed her. He roved his eyes and lips over every inch of her cherished flesh. There, in the mellow light, the Comanche and the white man inside him melded into a single being and finally became one with the woman he loved . . .

THIRTY-NINE

DURING THE NEXT FEW DAYS, BRONSON AND MAGGIE BASKED in a newfound bliss. Sam and Lydia were delighted to learn that the couple planned to live at the ranch permanently. While Lydia and Maggie dove into plans for Lydia and Sam's wedding, and to refurbish the ranch house and decorate a nursery, Bronson resumed his duties running the ranch with Sam. His only remaining anxiety was over the tribe, especially the possibility that Black Hawk might still attack the town. But as the days passed and no Comanches were spotted in the vicinity, his fears eased a bit. When Maggie and Lydia begged to be taken in to mass on Sunday, Bronson and Sam grabbed their shotguns and escorted the ladies to town.

A couple of days later, when a kick from a recalcitrant mustang aggravated Sam's old knee injury, Bronson insisted on going into town for the weekly supplies in his stead. Maggie begged to come along to look for yard goods at Blake's General Store. Yet when the couple arrived in Rio Concho on the warm early summer morning, they were surprised to find the store closed, the front curtains drawn.

Bronson suggested that they go for coffee at the hotel and come back in a few minutes.

Twenty minutes later, they were in the dining room of the Hobart Hotel finishing up coffee and pastries when they heard an unholy ruckus out in the street. Bronson excused himself and went over to the window, scowling at the scene outside. In the middle of the street, a crowd of townspeople were gathering around Sheriff Lefty and George Blake. The throng appeared very agitated, with fists being waved and several people scurrying about raising the alarm. Although Bronson couldn't make out specific words being said, the collective shouting had a clear ring of hysteria.

"What's wrong?"

At the sound of Maggie's voice, he turned to see her standing beside him wearing an expression of concern. "I'm not sure, honey. There's a crowd gathering outside. I'll go investigate."

"I'm coming with you," she said.

Bronson argued that Maggie should remain behind, but she proved adamant about accompanying him. Bronson paid their bill, and they hurried outside to the street. Bronson led Maggie through the horde and up to Sheriff Lefty; nearby stood George Blake holding a feathered arrow.

"What's going on?" Bronson asked Lefty.

The sheriff turned to regard him with an expression of sadistic pleasure. "Well, speak of the devil!" He jerked a thumb toward George Blake. "George's wife here has just been carried off by your redskin brothers—and her in the family way, to boot!"

In alarm, Bronson addressed George. "Is this true? Has Judy Lynn been kidnapped?"

George nodded anxiously. "Soon after my wife went downstairs this morning, I heard her screaming out on the back porch. By the time I got down there, she was gone . . . but I found this on the stoop." He extended the arrow toward Bronson. "You know anything about this, Kane?"

With a scowl, Bronson took the shaft and ran his fingers over it. "This is not a Comanche arrow. It's carelessly crafted and will not fly true. A Comanche would never whittle a shaft with a curvature like this, nor would he counterweight it with eagle feathers." He handed the arrow back to George. "This might have been made by Tonks or Lipans, but not by my Nerm brothers."

"And you're a no-good, lyin' breed who likely knows a lot more about this than you're letting on," retorted Lefty. He nodded decisively to one of his deputies. "Place this man under arrest."

At Lefty's order, a collective gasp rippled through the crowd. Maggie grabbed Bronson's arm protectively, and even George appeared taken aback. "Sheriff, I don't think Bronson Kane had anything to do with Judy Lynn being took off—"

"He's half-Injun, ain't he?" Lefty sneered. "That makes him responsible."

"What about Skeet Gallagher and Clyde Smedley?" Bronson interjected to Lefty. "I don't see them in town at the moment, and I've sure seen Skeet leering at Judy Lynn before." He turned to Blake. "Isn't that true, George?"

George hesitated, glancing from Bronson to the red-faced, fuming sheriff. Gulping, he replied, "I ain't sure I rightly recollect, Bronson."

As Bronson shot George a look of disbelief mingled with disgust, Lefty snarled, "And you ain't gonna dodge your own guilt, breed, by blaming one of my deputies!"

Maggie addressed Lefty with determination. "Sheriff, I insist you must not arrest my husband. He has been with me for days now and couldn't have possibly been involved in this incident."

Bronson leveled a stern glance at his bride. "Maggie, you'd best stay out of this."

"But, Bronson—"

"I'm telling you I don't want you involved," he reiterated, shaking a finger at her.

"That's right, honey, stay out of it," drawled Lefty. He jerked a thumb at one of his deputies. "Take the half-breed to jail, Travis."

The young deputy came forward, seizing Bronson's pistol and grasping him by the arm, jerking him away from Maggie. "Sorry, Bronson," he said awkwardly.

Even as Maggie uttered a cry of dismay, Bronson protested to the sheriff. "Lefty, you're being totally asinine. You know damn well you have no cause to hold me. If my wife weren't present and I didn't want to hurt Travis here, you and I would have it out right now."

With a snarl, Lefty drew out his Colt and pointed it toward Bronson. "You intend to resist arrest, breed?"

"Bronson, please!" beseeched a frantic Maggie. "Just go to the jail."

He ground his teeth and swore under his breath, but made no further move to resist.

A grinning Lefty holstered his Colt and turned to the crowd. "All right now, folks. You women head on home. I'll need all men present to ride with me for Fort Defiance. We'll alert the cavalry and then go find Mrs. Blake."

The throng sprang into action, the women dragging away children, the men, including George Blake, running for their horses to form the posse.

Watching the deputy pull Bronson away at gunpoint, Maggie called after them, "I'll tell Sam!"

"You just be careful!" Bronson retorted over his shoulder. "And don't you dare try to go back to the ranch alone!"

Maggie watched Bronson disappear with the deputy inside the stone jail, and a moment later, the men of the town rode off in a cloud of dust. Soon she was staring at the deserted street, wringing her hands and wondering how she could get word to the ranch that Bronson was in trouble, when all at once she watched Sam and Aunt Lydia appear at the end of the street in the buckboard. Intensely relieved, she hurried down the boardwalk and waved to them.

Near Maggie, Sam halted the conveyance, hobbled out, then helped Lydia down. Both rushed over to join her.

"Maggie, girl, thank goodness you're all right!" Lydia cried, hugging her. "I was so worried about you that I got poor Sam out of bed and made him bring me in to town."

As Maggie glanced confusedly from Lydia to Sam, he explained, "A neighbor came by and told us that Judy Lynn Blake has been carried off by Indians. Soon as we heard, we started out for town to check on you and Bronson and see if we can help." Sam glanced about them in puzzlement. "By the way, where is my nephew?"

"I'm afraid Bronson has just been arrested by that scoundrel Lefty McBride," Maggie informed him distraughtly. "The lying blackguard accused my husband of being in on the plot to kidnap Judy Lynn."

"What?" cried Sam. "Bronson is in jail? You must be pulling my bum leg!"

"I'm afraid I'm not, Sam."

"Well, we'll just see about that!" Sam replied with a menacing frown. "You ladies wait here, and I'll take care of this."

"Oh, no, you don't!" scolded Lydia, seizing his arm. "Maggie and I are coming along, too!"

He swung about to glower at her. "Lydia—"

"Don't you dare try to stop us!"

Sam grimaced at the two determined women. "Very well," he conceded grudgingly.

As the threesome started down the boardwalk toward the jail, Sam still limping badly, Lydia asked Maggie, "What's the news about Mrs. Blake?"

"Nothing so far, except that Bronson said Comanches didn't carry her off," she replied.

"How did he figure that?" asked Lydia.

"Whoever abducted her left an arrow on the porch. It had an eagle feather, and Bronson said Comanches never use eagle feathers for their shafts. In fact, Bronson thought Skeet Gallagher might be involved. He mentioned that Skeet had leered at Judy Lynn before." She snapped her fingers, a look of realization springing to her face. "You know, while Bronson and I were with the tribe, he and some other braves rescued a white woman the hunters had captured."

"I wouldn't doubt Skeet Gallagher and his kind would stoop to such dirty dealings," added Sam as he swung open the door to the jail and gestured impatiently for the women to precede him inside.

In the interior of the small building, Maggie at once spotted Bronson sitting on a decrepit cot in the single cell. She smiled at him in encouragement, and he waved back.

"What can I do for you folks?"

At the surly greeting, all three turned to regard the thin, freckle-faced young man who sat behind the scarred desk. Sam grinned at the deputy. "Well, if it ain't Travis Tipton." To the women he explained, "Travis is the son of Stovepipe, our cook out at the ranch."

"Ah," murmured Lydia, eyeing the boy with an assessing smile.

At once the deputy shot to his feet, his features tense with embarrassment. "Don't you dare try to use my pa as leverage to get Bronson out of jail, Mr. Kane. I'm just following orders."

"So you think Bronson helped kidnap Judy Lynn?" Sam demanded.

"Naw, I didn't say that." The young man appeared uncomfortable, shifting from boot to boot.

"You must know Bronson's been with us at the ranch for almost a week now," Sam pursued.

"I ain't doubting your word, sir," acknowledged the deputy miserably.

"Well, if you think my nephew is innocent, why in blue blazes don't you let him out?" Sam blustered. "You know damn well Lefty McBride has always had it in for Bronson."

The boy shoved his hands in his pockets and avoided Sam's eye. "I know, sir. It ain't nothin' personal. I'm just—"

"Look, son, I'll vouch that Bronson will appear in court if any charges are filed. Isn't the word of a Kane good enough for you?"

Scratching his head, the boy glanced with uncertainty at Bronson. "Will you give me your word, too, that you'll answer the charges, Bronson?"

"I certainly will," he said.

Wearing a sheepish expression, the young man picked up an iron key ring. "I'm sure going to get in a heap of trouble for this—"

"You'll be in a heap more if I tell your daddy you held my nephew without just cause," cut in Sam vehemently.

The boy trudged off to the cell, and seconds later, Bronson rushed out into Maggie's waiting arms. Bronson retrieved his pistol from Travis. After both men thanked the deputy, the foursome emerged from the jail onto the boardwalk.

"What do you want to do, son?" Sam asked.

With an arm around Maggie's waist, Bronson glanced grimly at the deserted street. "I think if I'm going to clear my name, we're going to have to find out who kidnapped Judy Lynn—and hopefully, rescue her." He turned to Maggie sternly. "And I want you to promise me you won't worry."

Although her expression mirrored great concern, Maggie nodded bravely. "I suppose you don't have a choice, do you?"

"No, honey, I don't."

Lydia appeared unconvinced. "Won't the posse find Mrs. Blake?"

"The posse?" Bronson laughed scornfully. "For obvious reasons, Lefty McBride has decided my Comanche brothers kidnapped Judy Lynn, and he couldn't be more wrong."

"Bronson is right," said Sam. "With Lefty off on the wrong trail and maybe even in cahoots with the perpetrators, we're this young woman's only hope."

Maggie squeezed Bronson's hand. "You two won't try to rescue her alone, will you?"

"No, we'll stop off at the ranch and gather as many of the hands as we can find," Bronson assured her. "Then we'll go to the Blake ranch and pick up the trail." He stroked his jaw and frowned at the women. "I'm trying to figure where you two will be safest—here, or at the ranch."

"Oh, don't worry about us," said Maggie. She winked at

Lydia. "Especially if we women aren't allowed to wring our hands over you."

"Of course we'll worry," retorted Bronson.

Sam gestured toward the jail, then addressed Maggie and Lydia. "I say you gals are better off staying here for now. Like Bronson said, the Comanches likely aren't behind this, but they may get stirred up before it's over. Even if Indians should raid the town, you can duck into the jail with Travis. With the stone walls and that heavy bar, it's practically impregnable."

"What do you think, Bronson?" Maggie asked.

He stared at the jail. "I think Sam may be right. Between the posse and the hunters roaming the vicinity, we likely shouldn't risk taking you two back to the ranch just yet. But we'll send back as many hands as we can spare to help guard you."

"Bronson, you'll need all the hands to help you rescue Mrs. Blake," protested Maggie.

"We're sending a guard back here, and that's final," came his adamant reply.

"I agree with Bronson," said Sam. "Guess we'd best head out, then." He glanced at Lydia.

She fell into his arms. "You take care, now," she scolded. "I'm in no mood to lose my bridegroom."

"Don't fret, honey," he replied, patting her back.

Next to the couple, Bronson and Maggie had also embraced. "Promise me you'll be careful," she whispered.

"Of course I will. Promise me you'll take no chances with yourself—or with our child."

"I promise." Maggie made her vow with a smile, yet her heart sank as she watched Bronson and Sam ride out of town.

An hour later, Sam and Bronson had gathered a contingent of ranch hands and had sent half a dozen others to Rio Concho to guard Maggie and Lydia. The group of almost two dozen men had quickly picked up the trail the kidnappers had left behind at the Blake Ranch. Proceeding due west from the ranch, they were now clipping along a trail long ago carved by western immigrants, passing stands of sagebrush and chaparral, and curving through fields of waving buffalo grass.

"Whoever kidnapped Judy Lynn, the idiots left a trail a child could follow," said Bronson as he scowled at the tracks along the pitted road.

"You hit the nail on the head there," agreed Sam. "What do you make of the shod horses and the wagon wheels? Sure don't look like Indians to me."

"Who else but buffalo hunters?" Bronson scoffed. "Probably some of the same bastards who carried off and raped Delilah Dinker. Skeet Gallagher is likely among them, too, since he sure wasn't in town today."

"Wonder why Lefty headed out for Fort Defiance instead of following this here trail," Sam remarked cynically.

Bronson laughed. "Lefty knows damn well Comanches didn't kidnap Judy Lynn. He's only leading everyone on a wild-goose chase, trying to pin the dastardly deed on my Nerm brothers to save his no-good hide hunter cronies."

The men galloped on while Bronson inwardly agonized over the fate of Judy Lynn and her child. Fortunately, the hunters had taken along two wagons—that would slow them down, and perhaps give Bronson and his rescue party the edge they needed.

At last, as they crested a butte, Bronson spotted the group plodding through a stark, rock-strew valley below—about twelve hunters, ten on horseback, two driving wagons. And Judy Lynn sat next to Skeet Gallagher in one of the wagons!

Sam spotted the hunters at the same moment, and held up a hand to halt the riders. "What you want to do now, Bronson? If we just attack, she'll likely be killed."

Reining in Blue Wind, Bronson nodded grimly. "I know. Let's approach slowly and see if we can talk them into releasing her." He turned to address the drovers. "Men, have your pistols handy, but don't shoot until I signal you."

The group rode at a cautious pace into the valley, and the hunters, spotting them, halted and drew out their weapons, several of them taking positions behind the wagons. Bronson, Sam, and the others also pulled out pistols or rifles as the group carefully approached.

"They don't look none too friendly," Sam mumbled next to Bronson.

He was studying the look on Judy Lynn's drawn face—a mixture of terror at her plight and forlorn hope at the approach of the riders.

"That's far enough, Kane!" Skeet Gallagher bellowed, pointing his Sharps rifle at Bronson. "Come any closer and I'll kill the female—and scalp the rest of you varmints."

Bronson reined in his horse and signaled to the drovers to halt, but he stood his ground with Skeet. "What do you want with Mrs. Blake, Gallagher?" he yelled. "Why don't you just let her go?"

Skeet snorted a laugh. "Well, maybe if you and your redskin pals didn't steal our women, we wouldn't have to swipe new ones."

Several of the hunters guffawed—but nervously, Bronson noted. "You're terrifying an innocent, pregnant woman who's done nothing to you," he argued.

"Nothin' ?" Skeet scoffed. "Well, maybe I'm sick of her and them other holier-than-thou females of Rio Concho putting on airs to me and my kind. Figured it's high time to start puttin' 'um in their place. Eh, boys?"

As the hunters erupted in raucous laughter, Bronson studied Judy Lynn's frantic face and decided to try another tack. "You're outnumbered, Skeet," he called. "Release Judy Lynn now and we'll let the rest of you hightail it, unmolested. Hurt her, and I'll personally kill you before you can recock your rifle."

Skeet blanched slightly at this, and another hunter called, "Skeet, maybe we should listen to him."

"Shet up!" Skeet hollered, then hurled a glare at Bronson. "I said move on, Kane, or you're a dead man."

"You'll be a dead man before I let you take that woman off!" Bronson retorted.

"Skeet, she ain't worth it!" another hunter whined from behind the wagon.

"I'll kill her before I give her up—and her brat too!" Skeet roared at the man.

While Skeet's head was turned away, Bronson was relieved to watch Judy Lynn use the hunters' brief argument among themselves to her advantage. Tossing Bronson a beseeching look, she quickly clambered down onto the floorboards of the conveyance, freeing his range of vision so he could make a clean shot. Bronson did not hesitate, at once firing his Colt and hitting Skeet in the temple. The buffalo hunter slumped, dead, across the seat, while the other hunters panicked and began shooting at Bronson's men.

The riders returned a fierce fuselage of fire, and the outnumbered hunters scrambled for their horses, a couple of them falling out of their saddles as they were hit by bullets from Bronson's men. It was all over in seconds, with only a lingering haze of acrid smoke left to attest to the brief, fierce battle. Bronson was pleased to note that Judy Lynn was still safely crouched on the floorboards of the wagon, that only a couple of his men had received minor wounds, and that Sam was unharmed beside him.

"Shall we chase 'um, boss?" yelled one of the drovers.

Continuing to peruse the immediate area, Bronson spotted Clyde Smedley dead on the ground beyond one of the wagons. "Naw, let them run like the rats they are. With their leaders dead, I doubt we'll be seeing those bastards in these parts again."

Bronson cantered his horse over to the wagon. He dismounted and reached out to touch Judy Lynn's quivering shoulder. She flinched and cried out.

"It's all right, Judy Lynn," he told her gently. "You're safe now. Let me help you out of there."

She gazed up at him, her face stark and her eyes bright. This time she didn't resist as he carefully assisted her down out of the conveyance. He noted she appeared unharmed though very shaken, still trembling badly with fright.

He smiled down at her. "You're going to be fine, honey."

With a broken cry, she fell into his arms. "Oh, Bronson! You saved my life—and my baby's."

He eyed her anxiously. "Did they mistreat you?"

She shivered. "Not yet, but they were going to. Ever since they grabbed me this morning, they've been bragging to each other about how they intended to take turns raping me tonight."

He patted her back. "It's over now."

"Thank God."

"What happened?"

"I—I heard a noise this morning as I was fixing breakfast. Thought it might be rustlers sniffing around the place again. I grabbed my shotgun and went outside, and the next thing I knew, Skeet got the drop on me, seized my gun, and hauled me off the porch."

"I'm so sorry," said Bronson.

She glanced at Gallagher's remains and shuddered. "I don't know why Skeet took me off. Course, he's been hanging around the store for ages, trying to flirt with me, and acting ugly whenever I wouldn't give him the time of day. The other day, he riled me so bad, I chased him out of there with a broom. Maybe that's what sent him over the edge."

"Well, he'll never hurt you again." Cupping a hand over his mouth, Bronson yelled, "Manuel and Jake, come hoist these corpses over a horse, and we'll take them back to town. Joe and Dan, see if you can't help those wounded hunters flailing about over near that stand of cactus. I imagine we'll be needing them for witnesses."

Judy Lynn frowned at Bronson. "Why witnesses?"

He shook his head ruefully. "I'm afraid Sheriff Lefty claimed that Comanches took you off. Instead of following the trail left by the hunters, he and the cavalry are off looking for you in Indian country, I imagine."

"Why, that low-down snake!" she cried. "Is George with them?"

"Yes. But don't worry, we'll head back to town and get everything straightened out as soon as the posse returns."

"You bet we will!" replied Judy Lynn. "I can't wait to

give that good-for-nothing sheriff a piece of my mind—and I'm going to box George's ears but good for believing his hokum. As for Lefty McBride, it's high time the decent folk of Rio Concho rode that varmint out of town on a rail!"

FORTY

Bronson and the others escorted Judy Lynn back toward town, Sam driving the young woman in one of the hunters' abandoned wagons.

Not far from Rio Concho, Bronson held up a hand as he heard gunfire erupting from an area due west of them. Reining in Blue Wind, he strained in the saddle, shading his eyes against the sun, and glimpsed a haze of gunsmoke gathering over a distant rise.

"Do you suppose it's the cavalry?" Sam called out from behind him.

"Could be," Bronson shouted back. "You stay here with Judy Lynn while we investigate." He cupped a hand over his mouth and yelled, "You boys leading horses with the dead and wounded hunters, stay behind with Sam. The rest of you, come with me."

Sam and the others hung back as Bronson and his company advanced toward the sound of the gunfire. The riders crested the escarpment, and Bronson groaned at the spectacle ahead of them. Sheriff Lefty and the detachment of cavalry were trapped, pinned down in a small wooded gulch, while Black Hawk and his huge war party swarmed all around them, whooping war yells, hurling lances, and discharging rifles.

Bronson was amazed at the numbers of warriors—at least three dozen, by his best estimate. The size of the war party confused him until he spotted Black Hawk's friend Stone Arrow, recognizing the chief's elaborate feathered headdress. He realized his brother had again joined up with the other Penateka band, which explained the sudden proliferation of braves.

Bronson turned to yell to his contingent. "Men, don't shoot anyone unless you have to—and that means Indians, too! Fire your guns into the air, and maybe we can scare my brothers away."

Bronson and the others charged, firing their pistols and rifles into the air. Bronson spotted Black Hawk reining in his mount and staring haughtily at the approaching riders. After a moment spent assessing the threat, Black Hawk turned to shout and gesture wildly at his company, and the Comanches wheeled their spirited horses into rapid retreat.

Watching the war party gallop away to the west, Bronson heaved a great sigh of relief and signaled to his men to stop firing. Thank goodness for the innate practicality of his brothers, he thought; to a Comanche warrior, there was no disgrace in fleeing when outnumbered.

As Bronson and his party closed the distance to the gulch, Lefty and his posse, as well as Colonel Morgan and his troops, were mounting their horses and riding out. Colonel Morgan was the first to emerge and halt his mount before Bronson.

"Sir, my men and I must thank you for your opportune arrival," he greeted.

"Opportune, my butt!" scoffed Lefty as he galloped up to join them. To Morgan he announced furiously, "This man is an escaped prisoner, a half-breed who is likely to blame for our being ambushed in the first place."

Morgan frowned at Bronson. "Is this true, sir?"

"No, sir, it is not," answered Bronson. Staring with contempt at Lefty, he explained, "This scoundrel arrested me for being part of the kidnapping of Judy Lynn Blake, and he claimed my Indian brothers were responsible. But in truth, Lefty McBride was only trying to shield his buffalo hunter cronies, who were the real culprits."

"That's a damned lie!" Lefty blustered.

"Is it, Sheriff?" Morgan asked.

All at once, the men fell silent, turning to watch Sam drive up in the wagon, with Judy Lynn beside him. Following the wagon were several more drovers leading horses bearing the wounded or dead buffalo hunters.

With a look of incredulous joy on his face, George Blake hopped off his horse and raced over to his wife. "Judy Lynn, honey! Thank God you're safe!"

George carefully helped his wife down and hugged her. Lefty, meanwhile, spotted the corpses of Skeet and Clyde and cursed violently. "Look at that, Colonel! Bronson Kane killed one of my deputies!"

Morgan turned to Bronson. "What do you have to say about this, Mr. Kane?"

Before he could answer, Judy Lynn rushed forward to confront Lefty, waving a fist. "You know damn well why Skeet and Clyde are dead, Lefty McBride! Those sorry sidewinders kidnapped me! If it weren't for Bronson Kane rescuing me, I'd be a dead woman! And you've been in on Skeet and Clyde's shenanigans from the start, you lying polecat!"

While Lefty gulped and went pale, Colonel Morgan removed his hat and stared in consternation at Judy Lynn. "Mrs. Blake, are you telling me that one of Sheriff McBride's deputies was a party to your abduction?"

"A party?" she scoffed. "Skeet Gallagher was the bastard who yanked me down off the porch this morning!"

As several of the men in Lefty's posse mumbled to one another in alarm and stared at the sheriff with burgeoning suspicion, Morgan turned to him. "Is this true, Sheriff?"

"I'll tell you what's true!" Lefty blustered, hauling out his Colt. "I'm taking Bronson Kane into custody for murder, and I'll kill any man who tries to stop me."

"Then you'll have to slaughter my entire brigade, Sheriff," Morgan said. He snapped his fingers at another soldier. "Lieutenant."

The lieutenant barked an order to the troops, and Lefty flinched as a dozen soldiers pointed their rifles at him. "Why—why, this is outrageous, Colonel! Tell them to put their guns away."

"Put *your* weapon away, McBride." Morgan glanced dispassionately at his lieutenant. "If Sheriff McBride shoots Mr. Kane, kill him."

"Yes, sir!" The lieutenant cocked his rifle and leveled it at Lefty.

Appearing frantic with fear, Lefty implored members of his posse. "Al, Bill, help me out here. You know I'm in the right!"

But the men only shook their heads in disgust. "We're standing with the colonel and Bronson Kane on this one, Lefty," one replied.

"Yeah—we in the town have had our fill of you, McBride," sneered another.

Lefty hesitated, still pointing his Colt at Bronson.

"Sheriff, if you want to live, put your gun away," Morgan warned in an emotionally-charged voice.

"Then what?" Lefty asked shrilly.

"Of course, there will have to be a thorough investigation into your activities, but I promise you I'll do my best to ensure that the authorities are fair."

With trembling fingers, Lefty holstered his gun. Then, stunning everyone, he spurred his horse and galloped off.

Morgan quickly shouted to his lieutenant. "Andrews, choose several men and ride after him."

"Yes, sir!"

The lieutenant sprang into action, and the small party he chose quickly rode off.

Morgan glanced speculatively at Bronson. "Well, Mr. Kane, what do you suggest we do about your brothers, the Comanches?"

"I imagine they'll leave you alone if you don't attack them again," Bronson replied ironically.

Morgan laughed. "Attack them? Mr. Kane, we were on our way out to their territory to hunt for Mrs. Blake when they attacked *us*."

"Damn," Bronson muttered under his breath. So Black Hawk had finally gone fully on the warpath. "Under the circumstances, Colonel, I hope you'll ride with us back to Rio Concho. The town may be in danger."

Maggie and Lydia were waiting in the lobby of the hotel, guarded by several drovers from the Kane Ranch, when they heard many riders thundering into town. Maggie glanced out the window, then turned to her aunt in joy. "It's Bronson, Sam, and the others!"

The two women rushed outside, followed by the ranch hands. Bronson and Sam soon joined the women on the boardwalk. As both couples hugged exuberantly, the ranch hands grinned and sauntered off to speak with the other returning men.

"We found Judy Lynn," Bronson told Maggie. "She's fine."

"Thank God!" exclaimed Maggie. "Who kidnapped her?"

"Skeet Gallagher and his gang of scoundrels." At her gasp, he added, "Don't worry, honey, Skeet's dead now. I had to kill him to save Judy Lynn."

"Oh, Bronson." Knowing how he hated bloodshed, she hugged him tightly.

"What about the others?" Lydia asked.

"Clyde Smedley was also killed, and a couple others were wounded," Bronson explained. "The rest of the hunters fled south—and Sheriff Lefty with them."

"Good riddance!" said Sam feelingly.

"Colonel Morgan sent a small detachment of soldiers after Lefty and his cronies, so they may not be out of the woods yet," Bronson added with a grin.

Maggie glanced in confusion at the soldiers positioning

themselves at various points along the street. "Why are all these cavalrymen here?"

He sighed. "I'm afraid Black Hawk has gone on the warpath, along with Stone Arrow and his warriors. They attacked the cavalry and the posse outside town, had them all pinned down in a gulch. Our group happened upon the scene after we rescued Judy Lynn. We fired our guns into the air, and my Comanche brothers fled."

"Oh, no. You really think Black Hawk will attack the town now?" Maggie asked.

"After what we just witnessed, we have to be prepared," Bronson replied grimly.

"And I think we'd best not head back to the ranch until the danger is over," Sam added.

The next half hour passed tensely. At the direction of Colonel Morgan, Bronson, Sam, and all other available men took positions guarding the town. Maggie and Lydia waited at the hotel.

Then Maggie heard one of the cavalrymen perched on top of the hotel yelling out the alarm. "Injuns! Women and children take cover!"

Maggie and Lydia were heading for the door when Bronson rushed inside. "I've come to escort you two over to the jail," he said tensely. "I've already assigned men to guard you there. Black Hawk and the others have been sighted approaching the town."

Glancing at her aunt, Maggie said to Bronson, "But can't we help? Aunt Lydia and I could reload rifles or something. And what if any of you are wounded?"

Bronson stared down into her eyes. "Maggie, I'm hoping there won't be a battle at all. I haven't discussed this with the colonel yet, but I intend to ride out and speak with Black Hawk alone."

"No!" she cried. "You can't face that many warriors alone! You'll be killed!"

Bronson shook his head. "No, Maggie. Black Hawk is my brother and he won't harm me."

"But I don't want to lose you!"

He pulled her close. "You're not going to lose me," he whispered intensely. "You're simply going to have to trust me one last time. Now, let's get you and Lydia over to the jail. I've got to hurry and speak with the colonel."

Both Maggie and Lydia tried to reason further with Bronson, but he proved adamant. He escorted them quickly to the jail, where at least a dozen armed ranch hands had already taken positions outside. He swung open the door for them, and leaned over to kiss his bride's lips.

"Bolt the door behind me," he ordered.

Maggie smiled back bravely, even though her heart felt lodged in her throat.

Bronson rushed toward the saloon, where Colonel Morgan had established a command station. An eerie quiet gripped the street. There was no sound at all save for the sign on Blake's Store, which squeaked on rusty hinges in the breeze. All around him were men crouched with rifles . . .

And then at the end of the street he watched Black Hawk and Stone Arrow's war party materialize like a ghostly nightmare! The band of three dozen or more warriors emerged at the edge of town, then paused, magnificent in their battle finery, their headdresses frightful, their faces black, their lances sharp, their ponies impatiently stamping the ground.

Bronson ducked inside the saloon and crouched near Morgan at a window. The colonel also had his eye on the war party.

"The brave leading the attack is my half brother Black Hawk," Bronson explained. "Let me ride out and speak with him."

Morgan regarded him skeptically. "Are you sure that's wise, Mr. Kane?"

Bronson nodded. "I think I may be able to forestall a lot of bloodshed—on both sides."

"I'm not sure, Mr. Kane."

"Look, my brothers wouldn't be on the warpath at all except that the White Eyes stirred them up. Skeet Gallagher and his cohorts stole food from their lands, and that's why they're so angry."

Morgan glanced sharply at Bronson. "I suspect this is the same war party that massacred the cavalry detachment out of Fort Defiance."

"And the soldiers did nothing to provoke the Indians . . . like stealing mustangs from Comanche lands?"

Morgan scowled.

"Colonel, I'm not trying to excuse everything my brothers have done. But if Black Hawk attacks, people will die on both sides. What will be resolved by more bloodshed? And what have you got to lose by giving my plan a chance?"

"Nothing except your life, Mr. Kane."

"That's right."

He nodded. "If you're willing to accept the risk, very well. I'll have one of the men fix you up a flag of truce."

Moments later, Bronson rode out of town with a white rag waving from the tip of a cavalry saber. Black Hawk, Stone Arrow, and the others watched warily as he approached. Absorbing the tension from so many dark eyes focused on him, Bronson mused that the colonel had been right that his life might well be in jeopardy. His heart ached that the conflict between him and Black Hawk had come to such a desperate pass.

"Black Hawk, I must speak with you," he called.

"Get out of my way, my brother," sneered Black Hawk. "And take your *tahbay-boh* wife with you. My argument is not with the two of you, but with the town."

"I am the town now," Bronson replied. He paused his mount next to Black Hawk's and spoke vehemently. "As you know, I have decided to remain in the white world and to try to help our people here. If you attack the town, you attack me." He gestured toward Black Hawk's company. "You will also lose many of our brothers to the bluecoats who have come to defend the town."

"You would shield the hunters with these others?" Black Hawk asked incredulously.

"The hunters are gone now, as is the corrupt sheriff. The hunters kidnapped a white woman and tried to blame their crime on the People. But I and some others rescued the woman from the hunters, and now the citizens of Rio Concho know the truth. They have no war with you, and you have no war with them."

Black Hawk was silent for a long time. "Where have the hunters gone?"

"My guess is they'll head south, to hide out in the *tierra despoblada* in northern Mexico."

Black Hawk raised his lance arrogantly. "Then we will pursue them, and stake their hides to the plains just as they have done with our buffalo." He stared hard at Bronson, and heaved a great sigh. "I will not kill the white wolf, for he is my brother."

Feeling intensely grateful that Black Hawk had yielded, White Wolf reached out to clasp hands with his brother. "May the Great Spirit guide and protect you."

"And you, my brother."

Black Hawk let out a whoop, and he and the others galloped off. Bronson watched his brother leave with mixed emotions, realizing that his path and Black Hawk's had come together fully at last in one sense, yet had diverged forever in another. For Black Hawk, the path ahead would be troubled; for White Wolf, the trail had ended and he was home at last.

He rode back into town to the cheers of everyone, and rushed into Maggie's waiting arms.

EPILOGUE

"Easy, honey," Bronson moaned in tortured tones. "Don't forget about the baby."

At daybreak, three months later, Bronson Kane's bride was doing wicked things to him. She had awakened him at first light, her mouth rooted to his manhood. She had tormented him with her lips and tongue until he was certain he would burst in her mouth. Frantic, he had pulled her astride him, and buried himself in her silken depths. Now she was riding him, so tight and hungry on top of him.

His hands were inside her lacy nightgown, cupping her warm breasts—and rubbing their marriage beads against the lovely mounds that had become so much fuller in the past three months. Maggie's belly was just beginning to curve outward with his child, and her body was more sensual and ripe than ever. With her fiery red curls tossed back, catching the rays of the dawn, her lovely features gripped with passion, she had never looked more gorgeous to him.

They were here in San Antonio on a delayed honeymoon, along with Lydia and Sam. Only three days ago, both couples had said their vows together at a Catholic church.

Drifting in the window of their room at the Menger Hotel

were the sounds of the plaza springing back to life this July morning—a wagon creaking past, a tamale vendor calling out, a woman singing a lilting Spanish melody. But the newlyweds were totally consumed with each other.

As Bronson thrust more vigorously, Maggie began to pant softly, gripped by the powerful waves of her climax. She braced her hands on his shoulders and dug in her fingernails. Her insides squeezed him, unbearably luscious and hot. He groaned, approaching the sweet agony of his own release. His hands gripped her waist and he plunged home, spending himself inside her and hauling her close for a ravenous kiss.

A moment later, she rolled gently off him, both of them gasping for breath. He wrapped an arm around her shoulders and kissed her tenderly.

"What brought on *that,* Mrs. Kane?" he teased.

She giggled and ran a hand possessively over his hard thigh. "Now that I've gotten you back, you don't think I'm going to let you go, do you?"

He feigned a scowl. "I've been hearing this for three months now."

She trailed a fingertip over his mouth. "You'll be hearing it for the rest of your life, Bronson Kane. Complaining, are you?"

"Never!" He kissed her again.

Maggie flipped her long hair away from her neck on the pillow. She fanned her flushed face with a hand. "Besides, I have to get in my claim on you early in the day, Mr. Kane, before it gets too hot."

He laughed. "You, Mrs. Kane, are always too hot."

"Amen," she agreed unabashedly.

They cuddled for a moment, then Bronson mused aloud, "Wonder what Lydia and Sam are doing right now."

She giggled. "What do you think?"

"They sure are spending a lot of time in their room."

"Well, what did you expect? They've only been married three days."

"So have we . . . according to the church."

Maggie nodded, remembering the beautiful double ceremony performed by a French priest at Mission Espada. She chuckled. "It was something having you and Sam study catechism for three whole months back in Rio Concho—especially as anxious as poor Sam was to marry my aunt."

His response was solemn. "You came to understand and accept the traditions of my people, so how could I argue about converting to Catholicism? Besides, I knew it was critical to you that our union be blessed by the church. Sam understood Lydia's feelings, as well—impatient though he was."

She stretched dreamily. "We're all going to be so happy living together on the ranch."

He flashed her a look of wry amusement. "Well, we won't exactly be living together . . ."

"What do you mean?"

"Sam is planning to build a separate house for himself and Lydia west of the main house."

"But that won't be necessary!" she protested.

Bronson pressed a hand to her lower belly. "Honey, you know we've decided we want a big family, and they'll be needing their privacy, too."

She sighed. "I suppose you're right. But we'll be seeing them plenty, especially with you and Sam running the ranch together."

He stroked his stubbled jaw. "Well, I'm not so sure about that, either. You'll certainly see Lydia a lot, but I may have to depend on Sam to run the ranch pretty much single-handedly."

"Why so?"

He grinned. "George Blake and several other prominent men from Rio Concho approached me last week about running for sheriff in next month's election."

"Oh, Bronson, what an honor!"

Ruefully he replied, "Well, I'm not so sure it's an honor, but I'm happy to see the town accepting me at last."

"High time—after you saved all of their hides." She paused to scowl. "Do you want to run for sheriff?"

"Actually, I'll be the only candidate—if I accept. Well, what do you think? The salary sure won't make us rich."

"We're already rich, aren't we?"

"True."

She mulled it over, then smiled. "If it makes you happy, I'm for it. I know you'll make a very fair—and very handsome—lawman. Only . . ."

"Yes?"

She pouted. "Every lady in town will fall in love with you!"

He hauled her close and spoke vehemently. "Honey, they can fall all they like . . . but this half-breed is taken." He demonstrated with a searing kiss.

She purred back. "Well, I guess it would be a good idea, then—much better than waiting for the next scoundrel like Lefty McBride to come along." She frowned. "Although I do think it's a shame that Lefty evidently escaped justice, with the cavalry never finding him and all."

"Oh, I have a notion he didn't escape," replied Bronson wisely. *Not if I know my Comanche brother,* he added to himself. To Maggie he said, "Anyway, my becoming sheriff is a beginning . . . a first step in my becoming involved in Texas politics and helping my people."

"Our people," she corrected.

"Our people," he acknowledged happily. "And who knows—maybe down the road, I'll run for the state legislature, and eventually even for Congress."

"Oh, Bronson! That would be wonderful. Then you can really advance the Indian cause at the federal level." She turned pensive. "Do you think you'll ever see Black Hawk again?"

He drew a heavy breath. "Not a word from him since he and the tribe headed south. But I have a strong feeling my brother and I will meet again." He nuzzled her forehead with his lips. "Just so you know, it will always be you first, darling—you and our children."

She curled her arms around his neck. "Maybe I'd like just a little more convincing on that score, Mr. Kane."

"With pleasure, Mrs. Kane," he murmured, and rolled his bride beneath him.